BENEATH THE MAIZE

A Novel

STEPHEN GOLDHAHN

Rigel Publishing

BENEATH THE MAIZE

Paperback ISBN: 978-0-9965551-2-8

E-book ISBN: 978-0-9965551-3-5

Cover Design by Ivan Zanchetta (Bookcoversart.com)

Map Illustrations by Hal Taylor (haltaylorillustration.com)

Beneath the Maize is a work of fiction, a mixed-genre crime mystery that combines elements of magical realism, science fiction, fantasy, and Native American folklore. While places and historical events are borrowed from the real world—with the exception of the "Underworld," of course—all names, characters, and incidents are products of the author's imagination. Any resemblance to persons, living or dead, is entirely coincidental.

Rigel Publishing is the author's DBA registered with Camden County, NJ, and the state of New Jersey.

❀ Created with Vellum

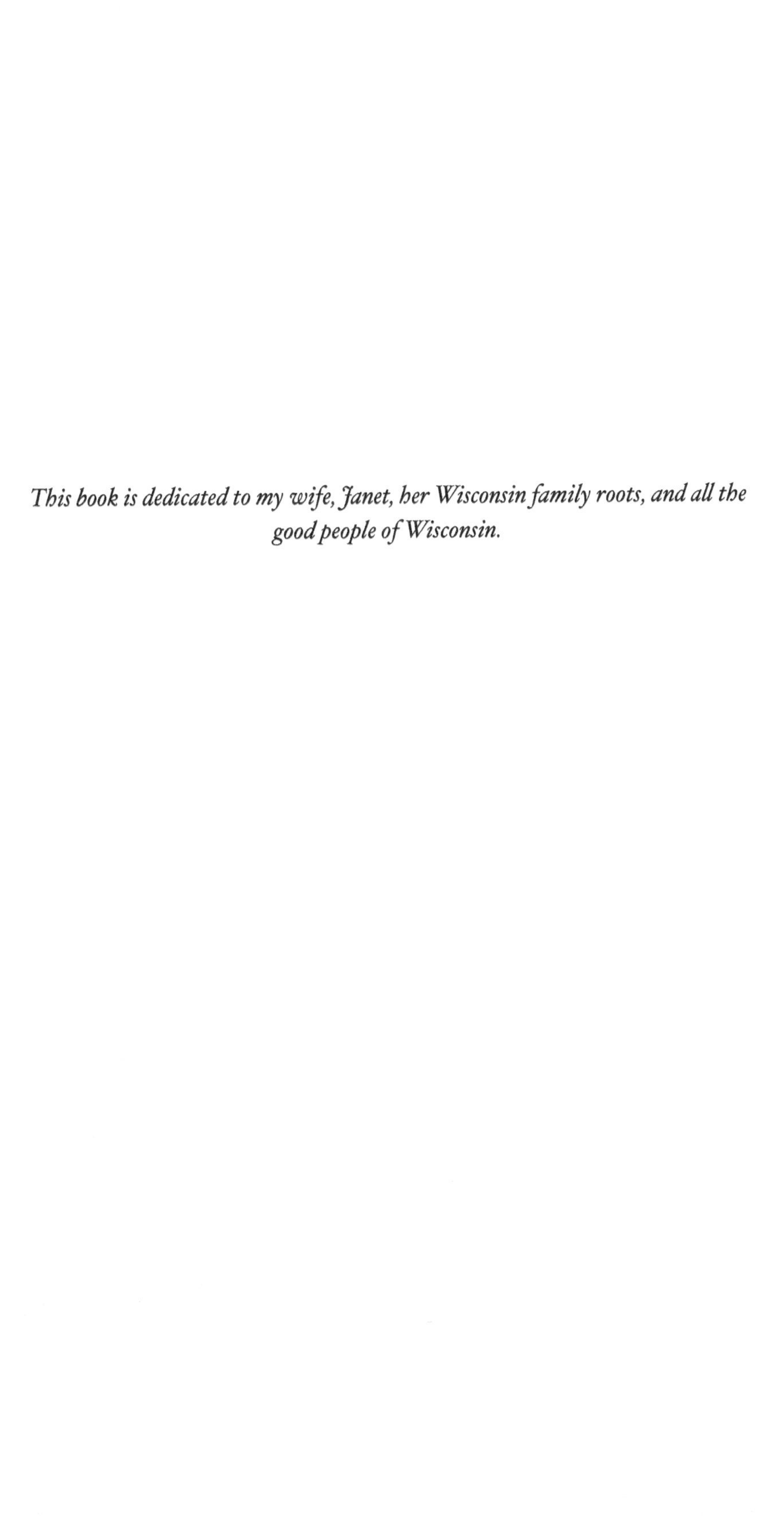

Wisconsin State Map

Sheboygan County and Environs

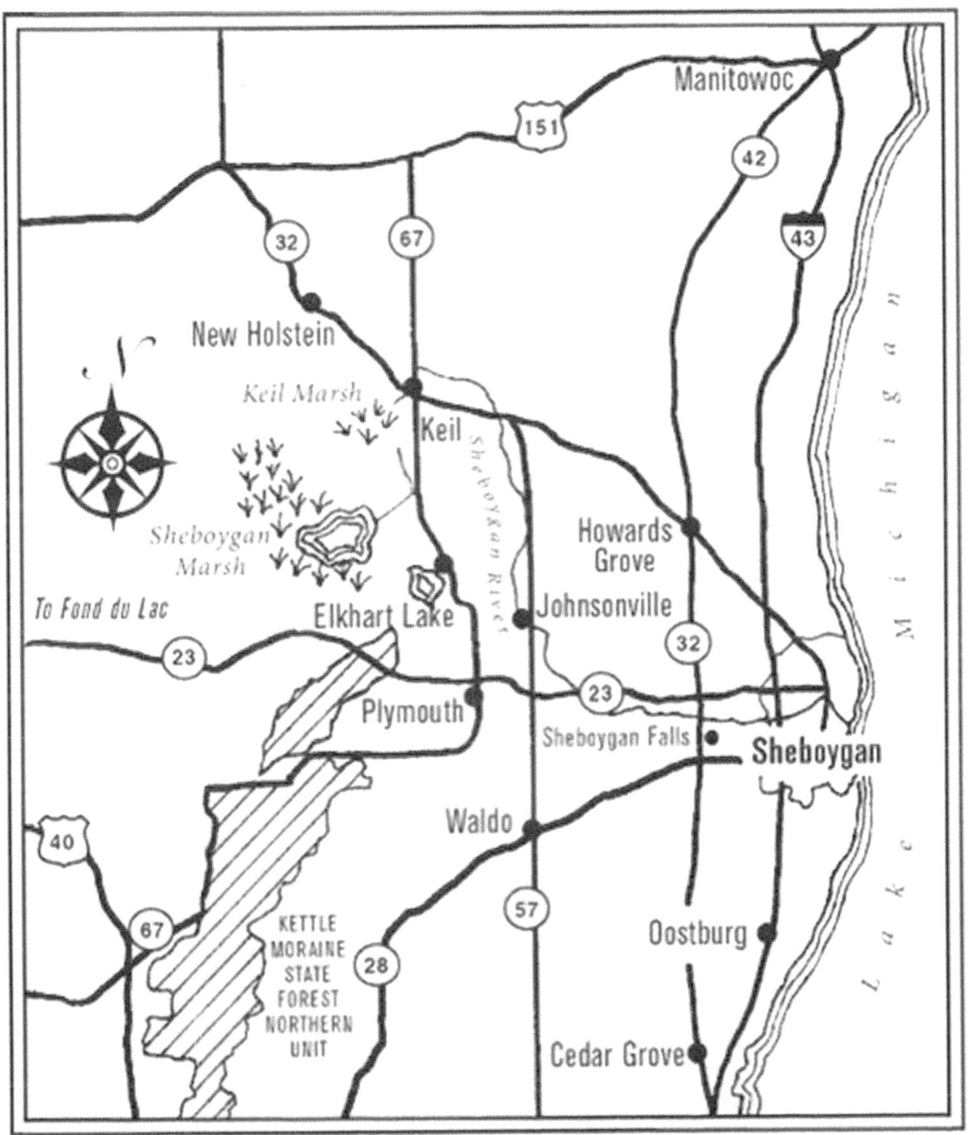

CONTENTS

Part Three

THE UNDERWORLD

Part One

SHEBOYGAN

Chapter One

NACITS

Sheboygan County, Wisconsin

Under a clear August sky, the little girl with the pigtails and calico dress and apron ran skipping toward the cornfield. Clenching something tightly in one fist and concealing a small leather pouch in her apron pocket, she giggled as she went, with three older boys on bicycles in hot pursuit, trailing some fifty yards behind on the long, single-lane country road. Dead Man's Road—that's what the locals around Elkhart Lake called it. There were many stories of how the road got its name, but no one could vouch for the real truth of the matter.

"Hey, wait up, yous guys! No fair! The cornfield is off limits," shouted the smallest of the boys pulling up the rear, his chunky, prepubescent frame huffing and puffing as he tried his best to keep up.

The little girl disappeared from view as she slipped into the dense field of corn and was quickly swallowed up amid its towering stalks, their ripening ears all plump and nearly ready for what promised to be a bumper crop harvest.

In a burst of dust, the first two boys came to a pivoting stop at the field's edge where they'd last seen the girl. The chunky one soon joined them as he brought his bike to a slow, sure stop.

"I don't see her," the first boy said as he dismounted his prized Schwinn, brushing aside a shock of red hair that partially covered his eyes and freckled face. He wore a red flannel shirt and faded jeans threadbare in the knees.

"But I can still hear her," the second boy said. He was shorter, stockier than the first. His jeans were even more worn, marking him as the obvious leader of the pack.

The girl's giggling voice mixed with the rustle of a gentle breeze from across the field. "Betcha can't find me!" she taunted. "You gotta find me if you want them back!"

The stocky leader turned to the chunky one. "It's your fault, Pudge!" he scolded. "If you hadn't let her in the tree house to begin with, she wouldn't have taken them. I don't care if she *is* your sister!"

Pudge looked down, nervously fingering the streamers on his handlebars. "Aw, it's okay, Chuck. We'll get them back. She's just teasing. That's how she is. Always teasing, 'n so."

The tall, freckle-faced boy in front perked up. "Shush! I think I see her. Over there." He pointed. "See? Where the tassels are moving."

The boy darted off in the direction of the moving tassels, but his progress was hampered as he entered an especially dense stand of corn. His two companions trudged close behind, trying their best to keep up.

"I can't see anything," Pudge shouted out. "The corn is way too high and thick."

True. The corn towered over even the tallest of the three boys, though he seemed loath to admit it. "Nah! Just keep up with me," he said. "She can't be that far ahead of—"

The space just ahead of them erupted in a flurry of feathers and flapping wings as a flock of nesting pheasants bolted into flight, coursing past the startled boys in a frenzied rush.

"Ah! What the—!"

Like a three-car pileup, the boys collided, falling to the ground in a single heap.

"Hey, get off me!" Chuck protested, disentangling himself from the scrum. "C'mon, yous guys! It's just a bunch of crazy birds."

Sprawled out on the ground, they all sat up, laughing and tossing broken ears of corn at one another.

"Okay, let's get serious," Chuck said, trying to take control of the situation. "We gotta find her." He looked up. Pudge followed his gaze. The sky directly overhead was sunny and blue.

"Nacits!" Pudge said.

"Not really," Chuck replied. "See over there?"

Indeed, angry-looking clouds were approaching from the west not far away.

"Yeah. Looks like a storm headin' our way, fer sure," said the freckle-faced boy. "I can feel it in my ears. Pressure droppin'. Sure sign of a storm."

The other boys looked at him quizzically.

Chuck laughed. "What? You can *feel* it in your ears?"

"You betcha!" Freckles answered. "I can always feel a storm comin'. The hair on my head starts tingling from the electric charge. And the pressure drops, ya know. And this one's droppin' fast. Might even be a twister, eh?"

"Cool!" Chuck said. "Never seen a real twister before."

But Pudge wasn't liking the thought of it one bit. He gave a big holler across the cornfield. "Hey, sis! Better come out, okay? There's a big storm brewin', ya know."

The boys quickened their pace through the cornfield as Chuck led the way this time. Pudge was sure they had lost her trail but didn't want to be the first to admit it. At last, Chuck stopped in his tracks and turned to the others.

"Look," he said. "I think we should split up. Better chance of at least one of us finding her."

His two friends paused. But before either could respond, there was a loud scream and a commotion to their left, far and away from the path they had been following.

"What the—!"

The boys reacted together, momentarily freezing in their tracks.

The girl's screams continued as clouds of dust mixed with torn shards of cornstalks flung high above the distant tassels.

"Oh my God!" Chuck said. "Something's wrong. Let's go!"

The boys darted in the direction of the screams and dust. Pushing their way through the field of corn, the tall stalks appeared to stiffen, taking on an almost sentient nature, seemingly bent on impeding their progress. The screams were becoming fainter, even muffled, now.

"Hang on, sis!" Pudge cried.

"We're comin', Allie!" Chuck shouted.

When they finally got to where they thought she should be, they found themselves in a patch of open ground surrounded by a veritable wall of corn, twisted and skewed in a generally counterclockwise, spiral pattern. The earth beneath them was all churned up and littered with uprooted, broken stalks, like someone had taken a plow to it. But there was no sign of Pudge's sister, Alice.

The boys stood there, dumbfounded.

"So, where is she?" Pudge exclaimed.

"Uh, maybe... a *twister*?" Chuck offered.

Freckles shook his head. "No way. Twisters just don't, well, just don't act this way, ya know?"

Pudge reached down and picked up something from the ground.

"Well, here's the rabbit's foot she took from the treehouse," he said. He looked around. "But I don't see the pouch anywhere."

The leather pouch contained treasured items from their tree-borne clubhouse: an assortment of genuine Indian artifacts unearthed from neighboring fields, arrowheads, small fishhooks carved from bone, copper trinkets, a few kernels of corn, and a small wad of tobacco they had added for authenticity's sake.

"Okay. Fine," Chuck said. "So, where is Allie, for Pete's sake? She must still have the pouch."

The boys shouted out her name, but there was no reply. No sound at all, except for the cawing of crows and the rustle of corn as a stiff breeze started up out of the northwest.

Two hours later young Deputy Dan Meyers and Sheriff Ben Hodges arrived on the scene in response to a frantic call from Pudge's mom reporting "our little Alice" missing. By now the fast-moving storm had passed, leaving behind a rainbow calling card and a dank, soggy field of corn. Ben and Dan had quizzed the boys over and over on what had happened, trying to trip them up, but their stories always remained the same.

Ben was in the cruiser filling out the initial police report as Dan stood at the edge of the cornfield some ten feet away sketching a map of the crime scene. He wrote down the letters N-A-C-I-T-S, then read them aloud—"Nacits"—in a barely audible tone.

"Huh? Whatcha say?" Ben responded.

Dan turned to see Ben adjusting his hearing aid. He smiled and spoke up clearly. "Nacits! 'Not a cloud in the sky.' Remember, that's what that little pudgy kid said."

"Mm-hmm," Ben mumbled.

Dan repeated the word to himself, over and over, as he pictured that little kid, the girl's older brother, the one his friends called Pudge, and the utter sadness in his eyes. "Sure is a puzzlement." He scratched his head. "How she could have just vanished into thin air, 'n so?"

"A puzzlement indeed," Ben replied with a grunt. "But puzzles were meant to be solved, Dan. All it takes is good police work."

Dan chuckled. "And a little luck, eh?"

Ben harrumphed. "Serendipity, young man. I call it serendipity."

Dan was fresh out of the academy, eager to serve, eager to please. Ben was eager too, as Dan knew—eagerly awaiting retirement once his term of office expired. "Getting too old for this kind of work," Ben was often heard to say of late.

"Ya know, Dan, I have a young granddaughter," Ben said. "Six years old. Same age as Alice." He gave a wistful sigh. "And this case tears at my heart. Sure rings of child abduction. And I swear, before I retire, I'm gonna hunt down and find the sick bastard who took her! Luck or no luck, mark my words."

Dan nodded. "Yes, sir." He peered back into the cornfield, the words of the young boys and their story reverberating through his head. He turned to face Ben.

"Well, so far, all I've been able to come up with is this here arrowhead." Dan held up the plastic specimen bag for Ben to see. "I don't think it has any bearing on the case. Unless we got some renegade Indians hiding out in the cornfield, eh." He chuckled at the thought as he studied the arrowhead and looked up. "I'd like to go back in there, Ben. Take another shot at it."

There was dogged determination in his voice.

"Okay," Ben said. "See what you can find. Footprints, articles of clothing, any signs of foul play." He reached into the back seat. "Here, you may need these." He handed Dan a pair of latex gloves and some more plastic specimen bags.

Dan put down the map, took the bags, and went back into the cornfield, intent on scouring the area one last time for clues.

"You know, it's really strange," he called out after a few minutes. "I can't get over the way the ground is all stirred up, like a bomb went off or something." A little while later he shouted back over his shoulder in a sullen tone. "Well, nothing here, Ben. Just... Hey! Wait a minute!" He perked up.

There on the ground not ten feet away, the glint of something trapped in the tangled mass of stalks and husks had caught his eye. He approached the object and knelt down. The earth all around was churned up and had a strange gauzy look to it, like cotton mixed in with the soil. Picking up the object with his gloved hand, Dan brushed it clean and gave it a once-over before placing it in a specimen bag. As an afterthought, he scooped up some of the strange-looking white soil, filled several specimen bags, and returned to the cruiser, holding up his shiny-object find to Ben.

Ben squinted. "Ah, looks like a gold band wedding ring." He took the bag for a closer look. "Woman's ring by the size of it. Stone's missing. Hmm, appears to be something engraved on the inside. Can't quite make it out." He handed the bag back to Dan. "If we can find the owner of this, it just might lead us to the girl. We'll have the boys in forensics see what they can make of it. Good work, Dan." He did a quick double take. "So, what's in the other bags?"

"Oh, just some soil samples." Dan held up a bag so Ben could see. "Looks kinda strange, dontcha think?"

Ben grunted. "If you say so. Tag them for forensics."

Dan labelled and dated the specimen bags—August 20, 1999—while Ben put the finishing touches on his report.

"Not much more we can do now," Ben said. "Go ahead and mark off the area with yellow crime tape. I'd like to come back with a shovel and cadaver dog and see what else we can find. If the boys' stories are true, though, I doubt we'll find anything. Simply no time to bury a body."

Dan nodded in agreement as he glanced down at the group of specimens.

"So, really Ben. What should I do with this arrowhead?"

Ben harrumphed. "Add it to your collection of Indian artifacts."

Dan's brow furrowed as he studied the arrowhead. "Don't have a collection," he called out.

"Then start one!" Ben shouted back.

Chapter Two

AKECHETA

Wisconsin Wilderness

The small band of braves, six in number, emerged from the forest tree line into the open, snow-covered meadow. Laden with the bounty of a successful hunt—carcasses of deer, raccoon, rabbits, and wild turkey piled high on pulled sleds or wrapped around the men's shoulders —no man returned unburdened. Their leader, Akecheta, paused and looked up, squinting into the midafternoon sun. The days were getting longer now, with the promise of spring less than a full moon away. He smiled. The good-hunt medicines concocted by the shaman had proven effective.

Akecheta and his brothers were members of the Ho-Chunk, or Winnebago, tribe, a Siouan-speaking people who occupied a large portion of present-day Wisconsin, extending from Green Bay in the north, westward to the Wisconsin River and beyond, and as far south as the Rock River in present-day northern Illinois. This area was also occupied at various times by other Indigenous peoples, predominantly the Algonquin-speaking Menominee and Potawatomi tribes with whom the Ho-Chunk shared many of their cultural traditions.

Akecheta was of the Bear clan, one of twelve family clans that comprised Ho-Chunk society. Each clan was associated with a particular animal and strength and had certain, well-defined roles within the village. Men of the Bear clan were responsible for policing and maintaining tribal discipline. Whatever the situation, whether on the hunt, in times of war, or when the tribe was on the move, Bear clansmen would assume the vital role of leaders.

As the six men approached the village, packs of gnarling dogs ran to meet them, drawn by the scent of the fresh kill. Close behind came the young boys of the village, their toy weapons waving in the air, eager to see and greet their elder champions.

Akecheta smiled as one of the older boys approached him.

"Here, Enapay, take these rabbits to your mother. Tell her there is much more to come."

For a hunting party of this size, Akecheta, being the eldest, held claim to the hides and was granted the right to apportion the meat and other animal remains. Other customs of apportionment often applied, depending on the number of individuals involved in the hunt, their status within the tribe, and the particular animal killed. In almost every case, the individual who made the actual kill had little say over apportionment. In the end, however, food distribution within the tribe was largely a matter of courtesy between individuals, and equity prevailed.

Approaching the village from the north, Akecheta and his hunting party came upon the first clusters of family dwellings, or wigwams— dome-shaped timber structures covered in bark and straw matting. There was nothing haphazard about village organization and the placement of these dwellings. In fact, everything about Ho-Chunk society was executed in an orderly fashion, with all clans having their assigned roles and responsibilities, established by long-standing traditions.

This first grouping of dwellings were the lodges of the Bear clan. The lodges of the other seven *manegi* ("people of the earth") clans lay in various clusters throughout the northeast half of the village. These were the Wolf, Water Spirit, Deer, Elk, Buffalo, Fish, and Snake clans.

The four remaining clans—Thunderbird, Pigeon, Eagle, and People-of-War—comprised the *wangeregi* ("people of the sky") clans. Their lodges occupied the southwest portion of the village, with the Thunderbird clan, home of the tribal chief, located in the farthest southern reaches. And so it was, a division of clans, both a geographical and familial partitioning within the village. Tribal norms and marriage customs allowed only the pairing of men and women of clans from opposite "sky" and "earth" divisions. In Akecheta's case, he had married a woman from the Thunderbird clan, a permissible pairing.

The Thunderbird and Bear clans were, arguably, the most important clans in the tribe. In times of peace, the village chief was chosen from the Thunderbird clan. But in times of war, a leader from the Bear clan would assume this important role. Akecheta himself had served in this capacity more than once, when warring tribes of the Illinois Confederation—the Illiniwek or Illini—from the south had challenged their hold on these hunting grounds.

ANGPETU WAS busy preparing the evening meal with her two daughters when she spied Enapay approaching in the distance with a broad smile and two rabbits draped around his neck. Her eyes lit up. "Good!" she said. "There will be fresh meat for tonight's meal!"

She then turned to her younger daughter. "Ehawee, please mind the corn chowder while I help your brother prepare the rabbit." Her older daughter continued tending the fire and sunflower-seed cakes baking on the stone griddle.

Women who were especially gifted at food preparation were highly valued within the tribal community. Akecheta's wife, Angpetu, was one such woman.

Corn, or *maize*, was a major staple of the Ho-Chunk diet, grown in many varieties—yellow, red, sweet, white flint, and blue flint—and prepared in more than fifty ways. Along with other preserved food items —beans, seeds, squash, dried berries, wild rice, dried meats, and fish— maize carried them through the harsh winter months until their stores could be replenished.

Another crop of major importance was tobacco. Far beyond the recreational use it was to enjoy among the Europeans who would later arrive, tobacco assumed a significant, even spiritual, role in tribal affairs. As a sacred offering, it possessed the power to protect against and ward off evil spirits. It was no wonder, then, that corn and tobacco were believed to be the direct gifts of Mother Earth: one to sustain the body, the other to fortify and protect the spirit. It was said that from one breast of Mother Earth grew corn; from the other breast grew the tobacco plant.

⁓

THROUGHOUT THE REMAINDER of the afternoon, Akecheta and his fellow braves worked diligently to dress and apportion their kill, with Akecheta retaining the deer and raccoon hides according to custom. After the evening meal, Akecheta took two of the deer hides and headed south through the village toward his wife's clan of origin, where he made a gift of one of the hides to the village chief and the other to his wife's father, along with a portion of the deer meat. The gifts were well received.

From this southernmost vantage point situated high on a bluff, Akecheta had a clear view of the expansive marshlands that lay below and marked this area as a choice place to live for all the tribes of the region. Besides the Ho-Chunk, this included the Potawatomie and Menominee at various times. It was a veritable garden of Eden of hunting, trapping, fishing, and farming, with vast marshlands below and meadows and forests behind. As far as the eye could see, the bluffs were lined with wigwams and ribbons of smoke rising from distant evening campfires.

With a full moon rising in the early night sky, a cold wind began to blow from the north. As the wind grew in intensity, an unspoken urgency and uneasiness took hold as the people set about gathering up and securing loose items before adjourning to the warmth and safety of their lodges, safe from the cold winter wind and the terrors that, legend says, came with a night such as this. Gathered about the family fires, the village storytellers recited tales of the Ice Giants, a beastly race of beings that swept down from the north upon the north wind to work their evil mischief. Woe to the lone soul who fell victim to these giants and ended up boiled, skewered, or stewed in their large food kettles!

According to oral tradition, these Ice Giants once roamed the land devouring whole villages. To restore balance to his creation, Ma-ona the Creator, also called Earthmaker, sent Rabbit and Turtle, two principal deities, down to Earth to destroy these two-legged giants, leaving only remnants in the far north country to provide a check on human overpopulation.

To confer some measure of protection to his family, Akecheta had taken tobacco, turkey feathers, and food and arranged them some distance from their lodge on the perimeter of the village as offerings to the Ice Giants. Other families had done the same, encircling the village in a ring of protection. Now, safe within their lodges, the storytellers did their work, reciting myths and legends well into the night as the lodge fires burned and the cold winds howled. Surely, the Ice Giants had come! Not as assuredly, the offerings and storytellers' tales would keep them safe through the night.

Chapter Three

MISSING PERSONS

Monday, September 29, 2014

The Sheboygan County Sheriff's Office was open for business. It was a new day, a new week, and the county had yet another missing persons case on its hands.

Dan Meyers—now Detective Dan Meyers following his recent promotion—was on the case. Upon entering the interrogation room, Dan nodded to his fellow officer, Jimmy Collins, already seated at the interrogation table. The room was a sparsely appointed, confining, and intimidating space. Seated with his back to a large two-way surveillance mirror—the only major architectural room feature other than the door—Dan adjusted the remote table mic for optimum pickup and opened his notebook to a bookmarked page. Taking a deep breath, he motioned to Jimmy to start the video camera.

Dan leaned into the microphone. "10:00 a.m., Monday, September 29, 2014. Detective Dan Meyers interrogating Mr. Jacob Emery of Plymouth, Sheboygan County, Wisconsin." His voice was deep and gravelly but unwavering.

Dan sat back and studied the person seated across from him: a larger-than-average, middle-aged man with piercing blue eyes and thinning gray hair crowning a mildly ruddy complexion. A wrinkled pair of denim bib overalls mostly covered a red plaid flannel shirt rolled up above the elbows, exposing two hairy arms decorated with an odd assortment of faded tattoos.

"So, Mr. Emery. Do I need to remind you of your Miranda rights?"

Mr. Emery shook his head *no*.

Dan was patient. "Mr. Emery, would you please respond *verbally* if you are able to do so."

The man let out a deep sigh. "I do know my rights," he said, in a sulky, baritone voice. "You 'splained them to me before. You needn't 'splain them again."

That was true. This was Mr. Emery's second visit to the sheriff's office since his wife went missing three weeks earlier on Labor Day weekend.

"Mr. Emery, just for the record, can you please state your full name, age, and occupation?"

Obviously annoyed, the man took a deep raspy breath. "Jake Emery. Sixty-two last time I checked. Own and operate a refuse removal and septic tank servicing company, along with my three sons and"—he paused—"my wife, up to her disappearance three weeks ago."

The video camera recorded a glint of moisture in his eyes.

Dan looked down at his notes.

"So, Mr. Emery, you previously stated that your wife—Gloria, that's her name, correct?" Jake nodded. "Yes, so your wife, Gloria, went missing on Saturday, the fifth of September. Can you please explain why it took you two days to report her missing?" Checking his notes, Dan said, "In fact, it was your son, Scott, was it not, who actually first reported her missing to the Plymouth Police Department?"

Jake repositioned himself in his seat. "Yeah. If you say so."

Dan looked puzzled. "Can you please explain to me again, Mr. Emery, how it was that your son, and not yourself, reported her missing?"

Jake slumped and began fingering one of the buttons on his overall vest. "Well, Scott, my youngest son, had gone fishing with his brother, Seth, that weekend. Chartered a boat on Lake Michigan outta Sheboygan. Didn't get back till"—he massaged his whiskered chin—"late Sunday afternoon."

Dan nodded. "Yes, that was Scott's account as well. And we have the charter boat captain's testimony corroborating Seth's and Scott's whereabouts that weekend." Dan flipped a page in his notebook. "Scott said they came home Sunday afternoon with a good catch and asked about his stepmom's whereabouts. Said you seemed 'distant and confused.' They were his words, I believe. The next day Scott reported Gloria missing."

Jake stared blankly across the table, like he was somewhere else. His left eye twitched once. Then twice.

"Mr. Emery, can you please tell us again what happened that Saturday? When you last saw your wife?"

"Well, like I told ya before." The man was visibly agitated. "Me and Gloria went into town for groceries. And the bank. On the way home we stopped at a farmers' market once to pick up some apples, peaches, corn. But Gloria didn't like the corn. Said the ears were too... *shriveled.*" He swallowed hard. "So, I went back out to a different farmers' market, off by the side of the road up toward Johnsonville, to pick up some more corn." He paused. "Took longer than 'spected, dontcha know."

The beads of sweat forming on the man's brow did not go unnoticed by Dan.

"Well, ya see, when I returned back home, Gloria was, uh, nowhere to be found, 'n so."

Dan nodded calmly. "Hmm, I see. So, Mr. Emery, what do *you* figure happened to your wife?"

The man squirmed in his seat, tight-lipped. Eventually he spoke. "Well, she had been talking earlier about getting together with her good friend Mabel for the weekend. So, I figured Mabel came by and picked her up. Maybe went off to the shopping mall or something and decided to stay over."

Dan checked his notes. "Well, Mr. Emery. We questioned Gloria's friend, Mabel Snyder. And she had no recollection of such a rendezvous as you mention."

Jake shook his head. "Then I don't know where she went!" he blurted out. "Sometimes, well, she'd just head out on her own. Had a willful spirit, dontcha know!" His voice trembled.

Dan sat back, let out a deep sigh, and closed his notebook with a snap.

"Mr. Emery," he said, "we *will* get to the bottom of your wife's disappearance. With or without your help. We are gathering *forensic* evidence as to her whereabouts. But it would go much better for you if you would be more honest and forthcoming."

In reality, though, there was no forensic evidence. Not yet anyway. A preliminary examination of the Emery property and vehicles presented no usable evidence—no witnesses to foul play, no bloodstains, no DNA —except for some hair samples that could be reasonably explained. An empty burlap bag and shovel recovered from the bed of Mr. Emery's pickup both proved negative for human blood and DNA. Soil samples from the shovel were taken for testing, but the results would prove inconclusive.

But for Detective Dan, the most troubling thing about this case was its uncanny familiarity to a previous cold case from sixteen years ago that also involved Jake Emery. It happened in 1998, the year before he joined the force, when Jake's *first* wife, Laura, went missing under similarly suspicious circumstances. Her body was never recovered and there was virtually no evidence directly linking Jake Emery to her disappearance. Laura was the biological mother of Jake's three sons.

"Like I said," Jake continued. "Don't know nothing about Gloria's whereabouts. And that's the God's honest truth!"

The detective played one more card.

"Mr. Emery, would you be willing to submit to a polygraph?"

Jake massaged his chin. "Ya mean one of them lie detector tests?"

Dan nodded.

"Well, yeah. I suppose that could be arranged," Jake said. "But I'll need my lawyer present for that, 'n so."

Dan anticipated his response. "Certainly. I understand."

Dan sat back and motioned Jimmy to shut down the video camera.

Jake Emery was free to go.

At least for now.

Chapter Four

SHEBOYGAN DISPATCH NEWSROOM

Monday, May 4, 2015

Luke was in the break room waiting for the sputtering Keurig to spit out a cup of coffee when Anita found him.

"I thought I'd find you here," she said with a conquering smile. "Sorry to interrupt, but Mr. Holtz would like to see you in his office right away."

Ted Holtz was editor in chief of the *Sheboygan Dispatch*. Anita was his special assistant.

But it would take two brewing cycles to fill Luke's bucket-sized Wisconsin Badgers mug. Ted would have to wait.

Luke gulped. "Sure thing, Anita. Is there anything wrong?"

She laughed. "No, I'm sure there's not. With Ted, everything has a sense of urgency."

Luke Kramer was the paper's newest hire—a trim, fit young man of medium height, hazel-blue eyes, and short-cropped, sandy-blond hair. He'd liked Anita from the start. With her girlish figure and cute brunette pixie cut, he couldn't help but find her attractive. So he was surprised—and disappointed—when he first learned how old she was: forty and married with three children! He thought she could easily pass for a millennial like himself. It was Anita who treated him to a birthday cake and impromptu office party when he turned twenty-six on April 19, the same birthday as her youngest child. As the office newbie, Luke appreciated the gesture and the instant notoriety it afforded him with his coworkers.

"Listen, Anita," Luke said as he retrieved his filled mug from the machine. "I was wondering if you wouldn't mind having my desk nameplate replaced."

She looked puzzled. "Why is that, Luke?"

"Well, you just called me Luke. That's what I like to be called. But the nameplate says 'Lukas.'"

"Hmm, but 'Lukas' is your legal name, is it not? Lukas Kramer?"

Luke squirmed. "Sure. But I really prefer 'Luke.' I mean, Lukas is still okay. It's better than what they used to call me when I was a kid."

"Oh? And what would that be?"

"Uh, I'd rather not say," he replied, his head bowed sheepishly.

Anita smiled. "I understand. My name is Anita, but I'm sometimes forced to respond to 'Annie,' which I hate. Even the boss calls me Annie," she said with grudging resignation. "Ted is notorious for getting names crossed. You'd think after thirty years in the newspaper business he'd have gotten that part of the job right." Sighing, she quickly returned to the subject at hand. "Well, you don't want to keep Ted waiting... Luke." She smiled. "I'll see what I can do about your nameplate."

"Thank you. Do you think Mr. Holtz would mind if I took my coffee along?"

"No, I don't think so." She chuckled. "How can any self-respecting reporter function in the morning without a hot cup of java?"

He gave her a nervous smile as she turned to leave.

Mug in hand, he passed by his desk to retrieve his notepad, then headed toward Ted's office at the far end of the newsroom floor. Picking up his pace, he turned his head just enough to smile and nod at a pretty young woman standing by the bubbler with a glass of water, chatting with two friends. He failed to notice a minor fold in the carpet and lost his footing, spilling his coffee, with some splashing on his shirt front. Blushing, he quickly excused himself and headed back to the break area for a napkin. He could hear the women snickering behind him.

Recovered, Luke pulled himself together and tried it again.

Ted's office was set off from the open newsroom floor with glass wall partitions. As an added perk, he enjoyed a window view overlooking the downtown neighborhood rooftops toward Lake Michigan. The name-plate on the door read TED HOLTZ, EDITOR IN CHIEF.

Luke knocked softly.

"Come in, come in!" a gruff voice commanded in from the other side.

Luke entered.

"You wished to... see me, sir?" he offered timidly.

"Close the door and have a seat!" Ted replied, pointing to a small metal-framed chair to his right.

Luke obeyed.

"So, Lukas—"

"Uh, you can call me Luke, sir," Luke said. "If you don't mind, I much prefer *Luke*."

Ted took a quick, raspy breath, remaining silent for a moment. Like someone straight from a crime noir novel. The only thing missing from his classic newsprint editor persona was the Havana cigar—but that was only because smoking was not permitted in the workplace. Luke would often see him taking his stogie-chomping habits to the streets during lunchtime and afternoon breaks.

He quickly amended his request. "I mean, if that's okay, sir."

Ted nodded his approval. "Luke," he said, drawing out the word like he was testing the sound of it. "Okay. Luke it is." Ted stared at the coffee stains on the young man's shirt. "Had an accident, Luke?"

"Uh, oh, yeah. Just a minor spill, sir." He squirmed in his seat to get more comfortable.

"You needn't 'sir' me, young man. This isn't the army. And if it were, I'd more likely be your drill sergeant, not a sir. Understand?"

"Uh, yes, sir... er, I mean, Sergeant... er, Mr. Holtz."

Ted laughed. "Just call me Ted."

He then asked Luke to look around the room and tell him what he saw.

Luke studied the room. "Well, you've got some really nice pictures hanging there on the wall behind you. If I'm not mistaken, you like to fish."

There were several large, framed photos of men, obviously fishermen, in various group shots, and Ted was in all of them. The largest one showed Ted posing next to two large Chinook salmon hanging from a gantry and hoist in front of a docked charter fishing boat.

"That's right. Came close to winning the prize two years ago for largest catch of the season. Right here on Lake Michigan. Some of the best sport fishing in the country." Ted got up and walked over to the picture. "That shot was taken right here, dockside in the Sheboygan River Harbor." He turned to Luke. "Ever been fishing on Lake Michigan, son?"

Luke shook his head. "No. Can't say that I have. I grew up on a farm farther inland, close to Elkhart Lake. Did some fishing there as a boy, but never caught anything *that* big."

Ted returned to his desk. "Tell me, Luke, what else do you see in those pictures... besides the fish and the boats?"

Luke stood up, eyes narrowing as he took a closer look.

"Well, there are quite a few birds hanging about. Seabirds, I'd say."

Ted's face lit up. "Bingo! Seagulls, my boy. Pesky seagulls!" He leaned on the desk and looked straight at Luke. "Damn nuisance bird if there ever was one."

Luke was taken aback.

"If you've ever been down to the harbor and riverwalk you'd know," Ted continued. "Especially since the condos, restaurants, and resorts moved in along the riverfront. The gulls have always been there," Ted explained, "but since the riverfront and harbor area have been built up in recent years, it's become a real problem for visitors and locals alike. Bird droppings everywhere, dontcha know. A real health hazard. And what's bad for visitors is bad for business."

Luke was a bit bewildered. "So... what do you want *me* to do?"

Ted reached into his desk drawer, took out a notepad, and jotted something down.

"There's this Randy fellow," he said, tearing off the note and handing it to Luke. "He's got an invention that keeps the gulls away. A mechanical contraption that simulates a hawk in flight. Even sends out the sound of the hawk. Said to be quite effective at chasing the gulls away. Gets mounted high up on a poll."

"Like a scarecrow, huh?" Luke said. He knew about scarecrows, having grown up on a farm.

Ted laughed. "Yeah, you could say that." He sat back down behind his desk. "I want you to do a story on this Randy and his invention. Stress the human-interest side, you know? How he came up with the idea. And how it will help restore a clean riverfront for visitors and the rest of us."

Luke took the piece of paper and studied it briefly before putting it in his shirt pocket.

"Sure thing, Ted. I can certainly do that. When do you want the story?"

Ted sat back in his chair. "I'd like to publish this in installments. Just like the GMO feature series you and Pam are working on. Do you think you can have something for me by next Sunday's supplement?"

Luke swallowed hard. "Uh, yeah, sure. I can do that. But... I may have to make some adjustments on the GMO story schedule with Pam."

Ted smiled. "Good!"

Luke continued to stand there.

"Okay, Luke. You can go now. You're, uh, dismissed, son. As they say in the army."

"Uh, yes sir... I mean, Mr. Holtz—Ted."

Luke turned, took a deep breath, and left the room.

Chapter Five

PRIZE IN A BOX

Saturday, May 16, 2015

The sun was breaking over the horizon as John Henkel of Plymouth, Sheboygan County, emerged from his barn, milking chores complete for the time being.

"C'mon, hon!" he shouted over his shoulder. "And don't forget about Molly!"

A little girl in blond pigtails and blue overalls appeared from the barn, jealously guarding the contents of a bucket she held close to her chest. Close behind her followed their four-year-old mixed-breed terrier, yapping in restless anticipation of her usual morning treat.

"Here, Molly. Come get your breakfast."

The little girl giggled as she tossed Molly the wads of cheesecloth soaked with the rich, warm, filtered residue of raw milk.

Her dad smiled.

"Okay. Now it's time for Papa's breakfast," he said as he took the bucket and gently patted his daughter on the head.

Leaving Molly to her treat, father and daughter headed across the barnyard, past the vegetable garden toward the back door of their modest but well-maintained, white clapboard, two-story farmhouse, coolly nestled in a healthy stand of ash and beech. John, in his mid-thirties, walked with a slight limp, the result of a tractor accident when he was twenty. The oldest of three sons, he had taken over the family's eighty-acre dairy farm two years earlier when his father passed away.

The early-morning sun now shone brightly though the back kitchen window, highlighting the golden bangs and pigtails of young Jennifer Henkel. Her mom, Lori, was there to greet them as they came through the door.

"Hi, Mom! Guess what? Dad let me help him milk the cows and let me feed Molly," she said giggling. "You should see him with the"—she turned to her father—"what was that, Dad?"

"The milk filters," he said.

"Oh, yeah. The milk fitters," Jennifer said.

"*Filters*, sis! The word is *filters*." Jennifer's big brother, James, the eldest of three children, never missed an opportunity to correct his sister. Matthew, the youngest child, typically remained silent on such matters.

Lori frowned. "That's enough, James! Don't make fun of your sister's speech impediment. You know she is doing so much better now that she's being coached at school, 'n so."

John grunted as he turned the page of his morning paper. "The Emery family is in the news again," he said. "Looks like another missing persons case. A young college student, Emma Hauptmann. One of the Emery boys is being held for questioning."

"Tsk, tsk. I think it's a crying shame," Lori said. "My word, did they ever find the body from the first case?"

"Hmm. Don't think so, m'love. When was that? About eight months ago?"

"Yes. Wasn't that old man Emery's wife, Gloria?" she asked.

"Hmm. Yup. Think so," John replied. "And then there was his first wife's disappearance seventeen years ago. Never did recover her body, either. No body, no murder case, dontcha know."

Lori simply shook her head with another "tsk, tsk" and returned to the question at hand. "So, how do we want our eggs this morning?" She posed the question at large, though primarily intended for their three children in various states of preparedness seated about the kitchen table.

The two boys responded almost in unison. "Scrambled!"

John paused from his morning paper as he poured himself a cup of coffee. "You know how I like mine, babe. Over easy."

Lori nodded.

"I just want corn flakes, Mom," Jennifer said.

"Corn flakes?" her mother replied. "That's not enough for a growing girl like you."

"That's because she's a wimp! 'Wimpy Flakes' is what they should call them," James taunted.

Jennifer picked up the box of unopened corn flakes and continued undeterred. "But look! See, there's a coupon inside. If I collect a bunch I can send for a prize."

"But that's not enough, dear. How 'bout I make you one scrambled egg to go with your cereal?"

Jennifer pouted. "No, I'm not hungry for eggs. I just want cereal."

John put down his paper. "Oh, for cripes sake, Lori! Let her have the corn flakes. If she gets hungry later, well, that's on her."

Lori caved in with a sigh.

Jennifer beamed as she ripped open the new box of corn flakes from the bottom end, knowing that's where the coupons were. She reached into the box, sending flakes crunching to the floor, grappled for the coupon, and held it up with pride.

Her mother smiled. "Yes, dear. Now don't forget to pour yourself a bowl."

Jennifer poured the crispy flakes into her bowl. As she did, there was a *clinking* sound. It even caught John's attention. Brushing the flakes aside, she carefully retrieved a pearly white object from the bottom of the bowl. Her eyes lit up as she raised it in the air for all to see.

"Hey, look! There's another prize in my cereal!"

Her mother and father looked on, dumbfounded. Even James was rendered momentarily speechless, but he was the first to speak up.

"It must be plastic," he said. "Can't be real, can it?"

Her father took the object from her hand and examined it closely, fondling it carefully between his thumb and forefinger. His expression turned to wonder and disbelief.

"It seems real enough," he said.

Lori reached out and took the object from John's hand.

"Oh my God, John! Why... it's a human *tooth*! A perfectly formed molar!"

Chapter Six

NEW DRINKING BUDDIES

Friday, May 22, 2015

"So, how's by you, Luke?" asked the pretty barmaid from across the bar.

"Not bad. Thanks for asking, Lil."

Lil swooped in, picking up the cash tip with one hand and an empty glass with the other. "So, watcha havin' tonight?"

Luke pointed to the lineup of taps. "A pint of Leinenkugel. Summer Shandy."

"Sure thing. With lime?"

Luke considered. "Nah, not this time, Lil. Just the beer, eh?"

"You got it!"

Duke's Tavern was Luke's favorite after-work watering hole, mere minutes from the *Dispatch* and an easy walk to his apartment, a rented condo overlooking the Sheboygan City harbor. The tavern was just one of many popular eating and drinking establishments that had sprung up along the Sheboygan riverfront in recent years, contributing to a welcome rebirth of the downtown business district and harbor areas of this quiet, Midwestern town whose commercial interests now centered largely on the recreational, restaurant, tourism, and sport fishing industries. The harbor, located at the mouth of the Sheboygan River where it empties into Lake Michigan, was once a major port for Great Lakes tanker ships and coal trafficking, and a site for other industries, like furniture and toy manufacturing. Now, through major revitalization and cleanup efforts, dormant former industrial properties, like the C. Reiss Coal Company's expansive coal and coke storage and distribution site, had been replaced with waterfront condominiums, shops, restaurants, a convention center, and a full-fledged family resort, all within easy view from the dockside deck of Duke's Tavern. Even at its widest point at the Rotary Riverfront Park, the river wasn't much more than 500 feet across.

On the large-screen TV mounted high on the wall behind the bar—one of many screens scattered throughout the tavern affording everyone a view of the action—the sportscaster was reviewing the results of the recent NFL draft and offering his assessment of the Green Bay Packers' chances for next season's Super Bowl, showing captioned highlights from prior seasons and featuring an interview with quarterback Aaron Rodgers. Above the barroom din and chatter, the televised replays were met with the occasional cheer and approving nods from the 'Scansin faithful in the room. To be from Wisconsin was to be a Packers fan—a cheesehead! No question! It was, after all, the only publicly owned team in the NFL, so every Wisconsinite could literally take stock in the game.

Luke was nursing his Leinenkugel and momentarily lost in a fog when a male voice broke through his reverie.

"'Scuse me, is this barstool taken?"

A startled Luke turned. "Uh, what? Sure. I mean, no, it's not taken."

Somewhere in his mid- to late thirties and taller than average, the well-groomed, chestnut-haired man maneuvered himself onto the seat next to Luke. He had that kind of resonating, baritone voice that commanded confidence, entirely suited to the role of TV doctor or documentary film narrator.

"So, how do you think the Packers are going to do this season?" he asked.

Luke took a closer look at his new drinking companion before responding. His strong angular features, crew cut, and general deportment suggested a person of authority. "I think they've got a real good chance," he said at last. "If they can get past the Seahawks."

"I hear you," the gentleman replied. He tapped the counter to get the barmaid's attention. It worked.

"So, what'll it be, Dan?" she asked.

"I'm gonna go with an Omissions. Trying to go gluten free, ya know."

"You got it!" she responded.

Before she could get away, Luke spoke up. "Lil. You can put that on my tab."

Dan smiled. "Well, much obliged, my friend. And you are…?"

"Luke. Luke Kramer."

Dan reached out his hand. "Dan Meyers."

Luke took his hand. *Dan Meyers? Where have I heard that name before?*

"So, Dan. Are you from around here?"

Dan laughed. "All my life," he said. "No place better suited to a law-abiding fan of football, hunting, and fishing like me!" He turned to Lil. "Why, thank you, my dearest Lil."

Smiling, she popped the cap and placed the open bottle before him. "You're quite welcome, Dan."

He gave her a wink, then turned back to Luke.

"The question is," he said, "where are *you* from? I don't believe I've seen you in here before."

"Well, I've been coming here pretty regular for a few months, now. But you're right actually. I'm originally from the Elkhart Lake area."

Luke proceeded to give Dan a thumbnail version of his life history, such as it was at the tender age of twenty-six. Brushing over the first fifteen years of his life spent growing up on a dairy farm outside Elkhart Lake, he picked things up during his college years at Northwestern University, where he majored in journalism with a minor in English literature. After graduating cum laude in June of 2011, he took a job on the East Coast at a weekly rag in Philly where he interned. That was where he spent the first three and a half years of his professional life until being laid off five months earlier, the result of a takeover by a larger syndicate. His mom, who still lived in Elkhart Lake, emailed him that there was an opening with the *Sheboygan Dispatch*.

"So I applied, and voilà! Here I am. Back in the land of dairy and cheeseheads!"

"So, how'd you like life on the East Coast?" Dan asked.

Luke smirked. "Well, it was something of a culture shock. The cheesesteak sandwiches and hoagies were great. But the first time I asked where the 'bubbler' was, they looked at me like I had two heads, 'n so!"

Dan chuckled. "Yeah. I can believe that."

Pausing, Dan took a swig and looked askance at Luke. "You said the Elkhart Lake area?"

"That's right," Luke replied. "Just a few miles out of town, on a farm overlooking the Sheboygan River. You know, up near its source."

Dan nodded. "Sure. I know the area well. Sheboygan Marsh. Great wildlife area." Dan assumed a serious tone and continued. "Sheboygan. Do you know where that name comes from?"

Luke thought a moment, rubbed his chin, and shook his head. "Dunno," he said. "Sounds like it could be an old Indian name."

"Well, you are actually correct," Dan said. "It *is* an old Indian name. Comes from an old Indian legion."

"Really?" Luke said. "So, what is this... *legion?*"

"Well, you see, in the beginning times, there was this Indian chief," Dan began. He took another sip and drew closer to Luke. "Brave and victorious in battle. A mighty chief of all the tribes to the north. The chief had four sons."

Dan paused.

"So, that's good, right?" Luke replied.

"Yes, very good. But not good enough. What he was longing for was a *daughter*. A daughter whose hand he could offer in marriage to the chief of all the tribes to the south, thereby uniting the tribes in one mighty alliance. One mighty nation."

Luke nodded.

Dan continued. "So, the chief of the north approached his medicine man and asked for a potion that would ensure that his next born was a girl. When the time came for his wife to deliver, he went to the river to chant and immerse himself in the cool, flowing river waters, just as the medicine man had instructed him to do. As he was emerging from the river, his wife's midwife ran toward him to deliver the news he was anxiously awaiting."

Dan repositioned himself in his seat as he took another sip of beer, taking his time.

Luke was taken in by the story and eager for the outcome. "Okay. So what happened?"

"Well, like I said, the chief was getting out of the river when he saw the midwife approaching. He shouted out to the woman, 'So please tell me. Is it a girl? Do I now have a daughter at last?' The woman replied solemnly, with downcast eyes, 'No, Chief. *She-boy-again!*'"

Utter silence.

Dan turned away, straight-faced, and took a long swig.

"What!" Luke sat back. "*She-boy-again?* You gotta be kidding! No way!"

"It's true," Dan replied matter-of-factly. "At least, that's the story my mom told me growing up."

Luke just laughed and shook his head. "Okay, for that, you gotta pick up the next round."

Dan smiled and motioned Lil for another round.

"She-boy-again. Jeez," Luke mumbled.

Lil delivered, and the two raised their glasses in a toast.

"To Sheboygan!" Dan offered.

Luke gave a little chuckle. "Yes. Here's to 'She-boy-again'!"

As Dan leaned back, Luke noticed what looked like a police photo identification badge attached to Dan's belt.

"Okay, Dan. I told you a little bit about myself. So tell me"—he eyed Dan's badge again—"what is it exactly that you do? I mean, when you're not fishing or following the Packers or making up Indian legends."

Dan followed Luke's gaze. "Oh, not much. Just chasing down speeders and other violators of the law. That's all."

Luke took a closer look at the badge. "So, you work for the sheriff's office. You're a deputy?"

"Used to be. It's *Detective* Dan, now."

Luke pursed his lips. "Oh, nice. So, working on any interesting cases, Detective?"

Dan smiled. "Not that I'm free to divulge. Except for what you can already read in the papers. But then, you should already know about that, right, Luke?" he said with a wink.

Luke grinned and shook his head. "Except I don't work in the news department. My area of reporting is... let's see, how did my editor put it... 'Special Interest Stories and Public Events.'"

"Ah, I see. So, what 'special interests' are you pursuing now?"

Luke sat back. "I'll divulge my stories... if you divulge yours. Quid pro quo."

Dan paused and smiled. "Okay. But you go first."

"Sure. Well, right now I'm working on two projects. One is a human-interest story about a local inventor who came up with an interesting device to keep seagulls away from the harbor."

"Hmm. Sounds like a useful invention. Does it work?"

Luke gave a twisted smile. "Can't say for sure. That's what I need to find out. Gotta reach out and talk to this guy. Name is Randy. I just got the assignment today."

Dan took a swig. "Okay. So what's the other story?"

Luke adopted a more serious tone. "Well, it's a series of articles, actually. I'm collaborating with another reporter. It's about GMOs."

Dan looked puzzled. "You mean... UFOs?"

Luke laughed. "No, it's GMOs, short for 'genetically modified organisms.' Or more specifically in our case, GMO food crops. You know, like corn and soy that have been genetically modified to increase their productivity or resistance to pests and herbicides."

"Well, that actually sounds pretty good to me. So, where's the story in that?"

That was all Luke needed. He launched into a treatise on the subject, in particular the pros and cons of genetically modified corn—or maize; the reported controversaries concerning possible health risks; and the impact on other, useful, insects and plants via something called *gene flow*, the inadvertent transfer of modified genes from one plant species to another.

Dan listened attentively, nodding or interjecting a confirming "Uh-huh" or "I see" at the appropriate times.

"Well, sure sounds like you have your hands full with that story," he said when Luke had finished.

Luke smiled, quite pleased with himself and delighted to have found a willing—or perhaps merely captive—audience for his story.

"But, if you don't mind a suggestion, I know a certain young scientist, a biologist friend of mine, at the university down in Madison. She might be able to help you with your project. Don't know how much she knows about this GMO stuff, but she might be another resource, a subject matter expert, we like to say in the law enforcement business. Or she might know someone who does. A foot in the door, so to speak."

Luke perked up. "Sure. Any lead helps. What's her name?" He pulled a notepad and pen from his shirt pocket.

"Her name is"—Dan paused for a moment—"*Aiyanna*."

"Aiyanna," Luke repeated and pursed his lips. "Pretty name."

"Hmm, yes," Dan replied, almost wistfully. "It's a Native American name. Means 'Eternal Blossom.'"

"So how do you spell it?" Luke asked, barely hearing what Dan said.

"Here, let me." Dan took the pen and notepad and wrote down her name—AIYANNA-NEZ—then handed it back to Luke.

Luke read the name. "Aiyanna... is that *Nezz* or the French *Nay?*"

"It's pronounced *Nezz*," he said. "The anglicized version."

Luke returned the notebook and pen to his shirt pocket. "Thanks, Dan. I owe you one."

Dan just waved it off.

"Okay. Your turn," Luke said.

Dan appeared confused.

"Your story." Luke raised a brow. "The case you're working on. Quid pro quo, remember?"

"Oh, yeah, sure. Okay." Dan cleared his throat. "Well, you should be aware of the latest missing persons case. It's been all over the news."

Luke nodded.

"Actually," Dan continued, "we've been investigating a series of missing persons cases that haven't even made the evening news. Goes back over seventeen years when I was starting out as a young deputy fresh out of the police academy. Most of these cases have gone cold. Except those possibly involving old man Emery and his clan."

Luke had heard of this. The Emerys operated a trash pickup and septic tank cleaning service outside of Plymouth. An odd bunch. Seemed every time something went wrong that no one could explain, they'd blame it on the Emerys. Not that "old man Emery"—Jake—didn't have a checkered past. He had served time for burglary and statutory rape as a young man growing up in Milwaukee. When his first wife, Laura, disappeared under suspicious circumstances seventeen years earlier, everyone was sure Jake was involved. But the body was never recovered. Jake had since remarried, and now his second wife, Gloria, had disappeared under similarly suspicious circumstances only eight months ago.

The newest disappearance, however, involved a young woman, Emma Hauptmann, a college student from UW Oshkosh, who worked as a part-time clerk for the Emerys. She was reportedly last seen the night of Friday, May 8, when Jake's eldest son, Adam, dropped her off in downtown Plymouth after work. Emma's mother said she never made it home. According to Adam's sworn statement, "she was 'spectin' to meet someone at the Pony Bar and Grill," only a few blocks from her parents' home. But the folks at the Pony said they never saw her.

"Corpus delicti. No body, no murder," Dan explained. "A crime must be proven to have occurred before a person can be convicted of committing that crime. There have been exceptions, to be sure. Overwhelming circumstantial or forensic evidence can sometimes convict. But, without a body or even the slightest human remains, it's damn near impossible."

"Yeah, I know. I watch *Forensic Files*," Luke replied.

Dan smirked and wagged his head. "Damn good show."

"But it sure is a puzzlement," Luke continued in the most somber of tones. "People just vanishing into thin air."

Dan leaned back, cocked his head, and studied Luke like he was looking at him for the first time. The words Luke spoke seemed to spring loose a memory.

"*Nacits!*" Dan said finally, slowly drawing out the word.

The blood drained from Luke's face. He hadn't heard that expression since his childhood. Something he and his friends had come up with. Like a secret club password. He stared back at Dan. Could it be?

Reaching down slowly, Dan pulled a wallet from his back pants pocket. From the wallet he produced a crumpled piece of paper, unfolded it, and handed it to Luke without saying a word.

Luke's eyes filled. There, staring back at him from the yellow, aging newspaper clipping was the faded image of his younger sister, Alice, gone missing in a cornfield on that carefree summer afternoon sixteen years ago. One of those cold cases Dan had referred to.

"I'm so sorry, Pudge... I mean, Luke... that we weren't able to do more," Dan said. His voice seemed on the verge of cracking.

Luke stared at the clipping. "I know," he said at last. "Tell me. They say they found a ring. A gold wedding band with the diamond missing. Did anything ever come of that?"

Dan shook his head. "There was an inscription on the inside of the ring. It read, 'Laura and Jake—Love Forever.' We were able to trace the ring to a jeweler in Plymouth, who sold it to Jake Emery ten years earlier, the year he and Laura were married. Well, Laura disappeared a year before your sister went missing. So, we thought we had a slam-dunk case against Jake, placing him in the cornfield the day of your sister's disappearance. Jake even made a positive identification of the ring, saying it was indeed his wife's wedding ring. But he denied any wrongdoing. Had no idea how the ring got there. And he had a perfect alibi. Turns out he was fishing on Lake Michigan with friends the whole weekend that Alice disappeared, and they vouched for him. Then again, as you might recall, there was no other forensic evidence placing him—or anyone else for that matter—at the scene of the crime. No tire tracks. No nothing."

Luke lowered his head. "Scene of the crime," he repeated. "Corpus delicti. Isn't that what you said? No body, no crime. You can't even prove a crime was committed, right?"

"Well, uh, I mean..." Dan stammered.

"Yeah," Luke said. "So I guess disappearing into thin air ain't a crime, eh?"

Chapter Seven

JAKE'S NIGHTMARE

Late May 2015

Jake Emery awoke with a start. He turned and looked at his clock radio: 3:00 a.m. The bedroom was awash in a dull green glow. He thought that odd. The curtains hanging over one of two windows in the room, the one facing the backyard, began to sway ever so slightly in the breeze.

"Coulda swore I closed that window," he mumbled.

He tossed back the covers and sat up on the side of the bed, annoyed at being awakened from a perfectly sound sleep. That's when he first heard it: the distant cawing of a crow. Or rather, crows. "Must be a whole flock," he said. "What's got them so riled at this hour of the night?"

As he stood up and started toward the window, he heard another, even more disturbing sound. It was the cry of a woman, a plaintive cry. Mixed in with the sound of the crows, it carried on a cold, stiff breeze coming through the open window, playing havoc with the curtains, now strangely frayed and flailing in the wind.

Jake went to the window and looked outside. Below him lay a field of corn, ears ripened to the point of bursting, as far as the naked eye could see. The field was bathed in a pulsating green glow, though the moonless sky above remained stark and starless. A flock of crows hovered over the corn, like hawks above carrion or some soon-to-die creature of nature. The woman's cries for help grew more intense.

"I'm coming!" Jake shouted out. "Hold on! I'm coming!"

He hastily donned his robe and slippers and took to the stairs. Dashing to the kitchen back door, he found it unlocked and ajar.

"Damn it! Boys must've left it open. Gotta remind them about that in the morning."

Passing into the backyard, Jake headed straight toward the field of corn and the sounds of the crows and the crying. There was a path in the corn, like you'd find in a Halloween corn maze. Funny. He hadn't remembered seeing that before from his bedroom window.

Jake ventured down the path and into the field of corn. The farther he went, the taller the stalks became, towering over him, higher than he ever remembered seeing corn grow. The crying and cawing grew more intense, and the sound of one woman crying now became the sounds of two women crying. When the path suddenly split in two, he had to decide which way to go: toward the one crying sound or the other. He chose one. Yet before long, he encountered another split and had to make the same choice, followed by another, and another. He soon lost track of all the twists and turns and realized he was lost. Lost in a maze and immersed in the cries of distress from two women whose voices he had now come to recognize.

"Hold on!" he shouted. "I'm coming!"

Penetrating ever deeper into the field of corn, Jake had the eerie sensation of being watched. Like the corn had eyes! The stalks took on personality, sentience, as the green glow grew more intense, even ghoulish. The source of the glow was clear now: it emanated from the ground itself! Like the phosphorescent glow of sea creatures on a moonless night, the soil rippled in waves of bioluminescence, illuminating the roots just beneath the ground's surface. The stalks seemed to draw energy from the green glow.

Pausing to reassess his increasingly desperate situation, Jake turned and gasped. Like good soldiers closing ranks, the stalks had converged to seal the path behind him! He was left with no choice but to go forward. Soon, though, even the path before him narrowed as the stalks crowded in on him, conspiring, reaching out with their leaves and tassels to enfold and ensnare. Jake struggled to remain free, all the while calling out to the women whose cries he heard.

"I'm coming, Laura! Hold on! I'm coming, Gloria!"

～

JAKE SPRANG up in his bed, terrified and confused, soaked in a cold sweat. He turned and looked at the clock radio: 3:00 a.m. Placing his head in the palms of his hands, he began to sob.

"Oh my God! Another bad dream."

Regaining his composure, he slowly got out of bed and went to the window. It was closed, just as it should be.

He parted the curtains and looked outside. The moon was full. The stars shone brightly in a cloudless sky. The yard below him was filled with the familiar clutter of vehicle parts, stripped-down truck chassis, a dilapidated shed, and patio furniture.

But there was no field of corn.

He shook his head and wiped his sweaty brow with his pajama shirtsleeve.

"Gotta get a hold of myself. Gotta... get help," he said.

Chapter Eight

RIVERS, LAKES, AND CAVES

Wisconsin Wilderness

The small band of women emerged from the forest tree line into the open meadow, a carpet of tall grasses and wildflowers buzzing with new life, effusing aromas of a world reborn under springtime skies.

Angpetu, wife of Akecheta, led the way with her two daughters by her side. The women bore baskets of freshly harvested berries and mushrooms that grew in abundance in the forests and marshlands surrounding the village. There were tender morels picked from decaying elm and white ash and the fleshy, shelflike formations of oyster mushrooms retrieved from stumps and fallen trees. Later in the season would come the hen-of-the-woods found growing in clusters at the base of oaks; chicken-of-the-woods, with their unmistakable golden-yellow fruit bodies; and the delectable honey mushrooms of the genus *Armillaria*.

On entering the village, they encountered the hustle and bustle of fellow villagers making apparent preparations for a journey of some kind. Some were busy packing baskets with dried foods and tobacco or bundling utensils, blankets, clothing, trinkets for trade, and other provisions. Teams of men set about building or repairing birchbark canoes or fashioning new hollow log canoes from the trunks of fallen trees, an arduous and painstaking process.

The Ho-Chunk were preparing to join other friendly tribes of the region, like the Menomonee and Potawatomi, for their yearly migration —a several-day journey—to the shores of Te-ŝiŝik ("Bad Lake"), present-day Lake Michigan, to join in the great annual whitefish harvest. Springtime was when the whitefish returned in vast numbers to the shallows of the broad sandy shores of that Great Lake to spawn. Area tribes used this opportunity to replenish their food reserves of fish for the coming year. Whole villages migrated from as far away as the present-day Mississippi River to partake in the great bounty of the whitefish harvest.

ON THE EVE of their seasonal adventure, the elders gathered in the chief's wigwam to smoke tobacco and receive the blessings of the village shaman. It was also a time for storytelling, the last telling of the winter season. Tonight, it was the Bear clan's privilege to deliver the parting tale. This was one of Akecheta's favorites: the Legend of the Big Eagle Cave Mystery.

The storyteller began his tale:

"One day, long, long ago, three young boys left their village to hunt deer in the hills. Several days passed and they failed to return. So, the village chief, Caxcepxetega ('Great Eagle'), fearing they may have been captured by a hostile tribe, sent a band of warriors to find them. The boys' trail led through a deep ravine to the mouth of a cave that had but one entrance. With the aid of pine-tar torches, two of the men braved the darkness to enter the mouth of the cave. The day passed into evening and still the men did not return. The others called out to them, but there was no response. Then they heard a sound—a strange, haunting, but beautiful sound, more beautiful than they had ever experienced, echoing from the depths of the cavern. It was an Indian death song."

With the words *death song*, a chill ran up Akecheta's spine.

"The warriors drew back in astonishment," the storyteller continued, "but several of the remaining braves grabbed their weapons and, with renewed purpose, ran into the cave, determined to rescue their lost companions. They, too, did not return. With the sun setting low, the haunting refrains of the 'Song of Death' resumed, striking terror in the hearts of the remaining warriors as they hurried back to their village.

"The next day, Great Eagle himself led a larger band of warriors to the cave. Yet as many men entered the cave, the same number did not return. Only the majestic and haunting 'Song of Death' remained.

"The chief considered what to do next. He decided to tether a volunteer with a rope tied securely about his waist. As his companions held firmly to the free end of the rope, the man entered the cave and disappeared from view. Suddenly, the rope went slack. The men looked at one another and, with a single thought and purpose, pulled hard to retrieve their brave companion. But there was no man, only an empty loop, unbroken, same as it had been tied around the waist of the lost man. Terror again gripped the men as the 'Song of Death' echoed its haunting refrain.

"From this day forward, Great Eagle forbade anyone from going near the cave, which, except for the foolhardy few"—he chuckled—"needed no enforcing."

The storyteller paused to take a puff on the pipe they were passing around. His listeners smiled and nodded approvingly as the storyteller continued his tale.

"Many moons passed. One day there came from the forest a young boy of ten summers leading a blind old man, a stranger, with white flowing hair and fair skin who knew not the tongue of the Ho-Chunk people. His young companion served as his interpreter. The old man soon gained a reputation as a great healer, with abilities far surpassing those of any known medicine man.

"One day the chief told the old man the story of the cave of the 'Song of Death.' At the old man's request, the chief led him and the young boy to the cave, accompanied by a great throng of tribespeople. As the old man and his boy companion walked down into the darkness, the 'Song of Death' rose to a deafening pitch, reverberating throughout the forest, casting great fear upon the people. Suddenly, there came an alarming silence as the 'Song of Death' ceased. Minutes later the old man emerged, alone, with a serene countenance. He stopped, lifted up his hands to the heavens, and in an unknown tongue sang the 'Song of Death' as he walked toward the river, carrying the song with him. At the river's edge he stepped into a waiting canoe, and without so much as a paddle, the canoe carried him away to parts unknown, never to be seen again.

"Several days later, three of the braves returned, and one even dared to venture into the cave. To the amazement of his companions, there was no 'Song of Death' and he emerged unharmed, saying he had explored the cave to its farthest limits to where it narrowed to the width of a man. Gaining courage, he and his two friends reentered the cavern and passed through the far narrow passage on their bellies, reemerging in a large chamber. Upon lighting their torches, they were astonished to find a huge stone throne carved into the far wall. Lying before it face-down in a large semicircle, as if worshipping the throne, were the skeletal remains of the hundreds who had perished.

"Terrified, the men quickly returned to the village to tell their tale. Great Eagle and his medicine man surmised the cave was the sacred abode of some great spirit. He ordered the cave sealed with dirt and rocks, never to be entered again."

The gathering had listened attentively throughout the telling of this tale, mesmerized by the words and tone of the storyteller's voice. Now, there were quiet murmurings as the men discussed what the meaning of this legend could be.

Akecheta was the first to speak up. "So, please tell us. Where is this place? This 'Song of Death' cave you speak of?"

The storyteller smiled. "No one knows. After a few generations, knowledge of its location was lost. The legend itself would have perished if not for the story-loving warriors of the forest keeping its memory alive." The storyteller paused to take a puff on the pipe offered to him before continuing. "But I can tell you what I think."

Everyone, to a man, became still and silent.

"There is a place, perhaps a two days' journey in the direction of the setting sun, a place my father told me about, where he spent his youth. A place where the waters of a great river flow past high, red sandstone cliffs, great sentinels of stone carved by the Creator. Like honeycombs are the many caves that penetrate these cliff walls. It is a place that holds much mystery. You ask me, so I tell you. I believe this is where the cave of this legend can be found."

Akecheta nodded, pensively stroking the pendant that hung about his neck. It was an amulet carved from bone in the shape of a bear's head, inlaid with copper nuggets for eyes, something his father had given him as a young boy. Something he treasured and would someday pass on to his own son.

~

THE NEXT DAY, Akecheta sensed excitement in the air as the tribe made final preparations to depart for Bad Lake. While a remnant would remain behind to tend the crops and care for the elderly and infirm too weak to travel, the major portion of the tribe would be making the journey. Backpacks and sleds were loaded with provisions and the poles and coverings of disassembled wigwams that would later be used to reconstruct their summer village. Families assembled by clan, papooses strapped to their mothers' backs as the women shared the burden of drawing the sleds with the men.

With Akecheta and the other men of the Bear clan leading the way, the tribe set out on its journey. Walking single file in a long procession, the people made their way along the well-trodden trails that interconnected the diverse tribes of the region with their popular fishing and hunting grounds. At every major stop, Akecheta and his fellow clansmen planted poles firmly in the ground to identify the furthest limits of travel. Woe to any individual who dared to venture beyond these bounds, so powerful were the policing powers of the Bear clan.

A small contingent of braves, however, led by Matoskah, a trusted friend of Akecheta, was making this journey by canoe. Traveling downriver, they planned to link up with their overland brothers at the lakeshore. The canoes would serve them well and provide a marked advantage when fishing.

The locals had a name for the river that carried them to the Great Lake. It was Sheub-wau-wau-gum, today's Sheboygan River, variously spelled and translated as "rumbling water" or "water that runs underground." Navigable by canoe for most of its eighty-mile course, the river snaked its way from the marshlands surrounding their base village through woods and meadows before emptying into the Great Lake. Nearing its end, a small portion of the river required portage where the falling land created a series of rapids not far from where it picked up two other major tributaries, today's Onion and Mullet rivers.

The tribe completed its overland journey in less than four days. There to greet Akecheta were Matoskah and his canoe-paddling braves.

"What took you so long?" Matoskah chided.

Akecheta simply smiled. "Have you secured a campsite, my friend?"

Matoskah led the way to a choice site on a bluff overlooking the lake. It didn't take long for their village to spring to life, as wigwams sprouted up as quick as mushrooms from a damp forest floor. Before long, with the arrival of other tribes, the shores and bluffs became an enterprising patchwork of migrant settlements and fisheries.

The usual method of lake fishing was to wade in the shallow waters and spear the fish or shoot them with bows and arrows. Matoskah's canoes, however, provided the added advantage of taking the fishermen farther offshore. And at night, flaming bark torches mounted to the bows of the canoes lit the way and attracted the prey.

While the men fished, the women processed and preserved their catch by drying it over open fires or, weather permitting, under the heat of an afternoon sun. The dried fish was stored in baskets of cedar and basswood bark for transportation back to their inland villages. Many took the added step of pounding the dried fish into powder for easier storage and transportation.

When not fishing, Akecheta took every opportunity to explore the area with his son, Enapay. On one occasion, they traveled upriver by canoe until they reached the falls. Akecheta instructed his son to kneel and put his ear to the ground.

"Do you hear the sound of the underground waters, my son?"

Enapay smiled and peered upward, meeting his father's eyes. "Yes, Father! I hear it!"

Akecheta smiled. "That is how the river gets its name."

He paused before adding, with a touch of prescient mystery to his voice, "There is much about the underground world that we do not know, my son."

Chapter Nine

MECHANICAL GULLS AND A TOOTH IN A BOX

Friday, June 5, 2015

"There! I think that does it," Luke concluded with a self-congratulatory slap on the knee.

The newsroom bustled with the usual activity and phone chatter preceding a Sunday deadline. Luke leaned far back in his chair, his hands interlaced behind his head for a good back stretch, as he stared at the glowing computer screen before him, admiring his most recent—and hopefully final—version of the last installment of his series on the harbor seagull crisis and the invention that promised to rid the harbor once and for all of those pesky gulls: a "mechanical flying, squawking hawk" mounted high on a pole. His final article installment stressed the human-interest aspects—as Ted Holtz had insisted—and recounted the story of Randy, the local man responsible for its invention.

Luke smiled as he reflected on it. *The great thing about the invention is that it actually works!*

His self-indulgent reverie was interrupted by a familiar voice from behind.

"Ted asked me to remind you that your story's deadline is tonight."

"Sure thing, Anita," Luke replied, regaining his composure. "Not a problem. Got it all"—tapping his laptop—"right here."

Smiling, she gave him a thumbs-up, then continued on her way.

Luke turned back to the keyboard and hit the Print key for a final check. Technology be damned, he always had trouble relying on screen edits and preferred making final edits on a hard copy.

Just then his desk phone rang. He didn't recognize the caller. It was a Milwaukee number. He picked up. "Luke Kramer, *Sheboygan Dispatch*."

There was a slight pause.

"Well, hello stranger! Welcome back to Wisconsin," came the voice at the other end. It was a man's voice, oddly familiar, but difficult to place.

"Yes... well... it's good to be back," Luke replied, trying his best to pin down the speaker's identity. An awkward moment of silence followed, with a muted chuckle from the caller.

"Uh, I know that voice," Luke continued. "But you're gonna have to help me out here."

The caller laughed. "So, how's the weather by you?"

Luke's face brightened with the sudden recollection of an old childhood friend. A mixed reaction at best, as not all his childhood memories were pleasant.

"Freckles! *Freckles* Hollander!"

"You got it," came the response.

Luke let out a "Whoa!" that caught everyone's attention in the newsroom. Embarrassed, he cupped the receiver and turned to face the room. "An old friend," he explained, then returned to the phone.

"So, where are you calling from?" he asked in a more muted tone.

"Milwaukee."

"Yeah, I can see that. From the number. But what are you doing in Milwaukee?"

"Well, you remember how I always dug the weather?"

Luke remembered. As a kid, Freckles—his real name was Albert— had a penchant for predicting the weather. He said it had to do with the pressure in his ears. He could always tell a storm was coming as the pressure dropped. A regular human barometer!

"Well, I'm doing the weather here on the local TV station."

Luke laughed. "No way!"

"Yes way!" Albert countered.

"Wow, nice gig."

"Yeah, well, I gotta do something to put food on the table. Got a wife and a kid, now, with one more on the way."

"Hey, that's great. Congratulations," Luke said in a slightly wistful tone. Luke was thinking about the day his sister disappeared. Freckles was there. It was Freckles who predicted the coming storm. It was all a kind of blur in Luke's memory now, and he was never sure if it was a storm, a twister, or something else entirely that took his sister away.

"So, how long has it been?" Albert asked, interrupting Luke's drifting thoughts.

"Uh, what?" Luke stammered. "Uh, how long since when?"

Al laughed. "Since when? Since we last saw each other. Just as scatter-brained as ever, eh?"

Closing his eyes, he sighed. "Nah, I've got it together now, Al."

"Glad to hear," Albert said, and paused for a moment. "Say!" he continued in a perkier tone, "did you ever keep in touch with Chuck Evert? The leader of the pack. I remember he always envied my prized Schwinn."

Luke let out a deep sigh. "You don't know?"

"Know what?"

"Chuck joined the Marines right out of high school. Shipped off to Afghanistan. He came home six months later in a body bag."

"Oh my God!" Albert replied. "Damn! I didn't know."

"Yeah, well. You know. That's life," Luke said stoically. "I always liked Chuck."

Silence.

"Hey, listen," Albert said after a bit. "Maybe we can get together once. Over a beer. Catch up on old times."

"Sure, that'd be great!" Luke said, forcing a smile. "There's a great sports bar down by the harbor here in Sheboygan. I don't live far from it. Within crawling distance, actually."

Albert laughed. "Sounds good. Maybe catch the next Packers home game, eh?"

They concluded their conversation by exchanging contact information and promising to link up soon. Still, Luke was not so sure about reviving old childhood memories.

After hanging up, he sat there for a moment, getting his thoughts together.

A young woman in a plaid shirt and blue jeans suddenly appeared, plopping down a small pile of papers on Luke's desk.

"Hey, like, I'm not your personal assistant, Luke, but I didn't know when you'd get around to picking this up from the printer."

"Huh? Oh, yeah. Thanks, Pam. I was going to pick it up. Got distracted by a phone call from... an old friend."

Pam smiled. "Not a problem. So when are we getting together to talk about our GMO series? Did you ever get in touch with that scientist in Madison? What's her name? Aiyanna or something? You think she can help us tie a bow on this GMO thing?"

A pert blond, short, stocky, and attractive in a quirky way, Pam was a quick talker. Desultory and importunate at times, her questions always came in rapid succession, leaving no time to respond. A challenge for most people, but especially so for Luke. A holdover from childhood ADHD, which he had largely overcome. Not much younger than Luke, Pam had joined the *Dispatch* a year earlier, right out of college, and was not shy about discussing her ambitions to be a nationally syndicated columnist someday soon.

"Uh, yeah, sure," Luke stammered. "I, uh, gave her a call. And we plan to get together... sometime soon. She promised to get back to me."

Pam pulled up a chair. "Cool!"

She quickly changed the subject, holding out a printout of an article she had found on the internet.

"You see this story about the kid in Plymouth who found a human tooth in her cereal box? I mean, whoa! An intact bicuspid molar! So how the hell did a tooth find its way into a box of corn flakes? I think we can do something with this, Luke. I mean, *corn* flakes. GMO *corn*. Missing teeth."

Again, Pam was light-years ahead of Luke. Tortoise and the hare. What a team. He finally caught up.

"Uh, so, you think there's a connection between GMO corn and, uh, this unusual find?" he asked.

Chuckling, she sat upright. "Hey, maybe. Or maybe we can *make* the connection. Get people's attention, right?"

"Sure." Luke nodded. "I guess."

Pam stood and handed the article to Luke.

"Here. Give it a read. I'm gonna contact this young lady in Plymouth and get the whole scoop. You wanna come?"

He mulled it over. "No, don't think so. Got this deadline to make on the mechanical seagull story. Why don't you go. We can get together later and talk about it."

"Okay. Suit yourself."

And Pam was off.

Chapter Ten

WALL PIN MAPS

Monday, June 15, 2015

At 9:30 a.m., Detective Dan Meyers stood back a few feet to take in the entirety of the wall map before him, his butt leaning against the desk as he braced himself with one hand and polished his chin with the other.

"Hmm, very interesting," he mused, peering through narrowed eyes.

The map was of Sheboygan County. Decorating the map were push-pins of different colors. A handwritten legend on the side of the map identified the red pins as "Missing Persons–Recent," blue pins as "Missing Persons–Found," and yellow pins as "Missing Persons–Cold Case." While the blue pins were scattered in a mainly random fashion, there was a definite pattern to the red and yellow pins, which was what Dan found interesting. The yellow occurred mostly in a cluster in the vicinity of Plymouth and Elkhart Lake. As that area expanded outward, mainly to the south and east, the pins turned predominantly red.

"So, what are we doing, sir? Playing pin-the-tail?" came a voice from behind.

Dan grimaced and replied without turning. "That's right, Sam. It's called 'pin the tail on the bad guy.'"

Sam Riley was a new deputy hire at the sheriff's office, straight out of the police academy. Young, confident, and always ready with a wisecrack, he'd been assigned to Dan to assist with his investigations.

"These are all the reported missing persons cases for the past twenty years, Sam. I'm trying to see if there is a pattern."

Sam put his coffee cup down on Dan's desk and studied the map for a moment. "Like maybe a serial killer or something?" he asked with growing interest in his voice.

Dan grunted. "Yeah. Like maybe a serial killer... or something."

With a look of annoyance, Dan reached out, lifted Sam's cup, and placed it on a coaster. Pulling a tissue from his pocket, he wiped away the coffee ring. Sam didn't even seem to notice.

"Well, so far," Dan continued, "all we have are missing persons. No bodies. So, technically, no crime. The other thing is that all the unsolved missing persons—the yellow and red pins you see there—run the gamut from young to old, male and female. They don't seem to fit any particular profile. *Except* for this geographical pattern." He pointed to the map.

"But you do have suspects, right?" Sam said. "Like that Emery guy? Didn't you bring him in for questioning for the latest missing persons case?"

"You mean Emma, the missing coed who worked for the Emerys? Sure." Dan paused. "And the one before that. Last fall. You must have heard about that one. Jake's second wife, Gloria?"

"Sure, I remember reading about it in the papers."

"The strange thing is," Dan continued, "it was Jake's youngest son, twenty-year-old Scott Emery, who first reported his stepmom missing two days later. When we questioned Jake, all he could say was he went to the farmers' market and when he came back home, she was gone."

"Hmm, sure sounds fishy," Sam said. "Has anything turned up since then?"

Dan sighed. "Well, Jake did agree to a polygraph. But that was inconclusive. When questioned about his whereabouts and the last time he saw Gloria, the needle showed he was lying or equivocating at best. But when asked directly whether he killed his wife, he passed with flying colors. And anyway, they must've taught you at the academy that polygraph evidence is not admissible in criminal court in the State of Wisconsin."

"Uh-huh," Sam said, slurping his coffee.

"I think it may all come down to this geographic profiling." Dan gestured to the wall map.

Opening his top desk drawer, he removed a package and plopped it down with a thud on the desk. "Did they teach you anything about forensic geographic profiling at the academy?"

"Sure!" Sam might have been a little too cocky and quick with his answer, though. He looked askance at the package and added, "Well, a little bit." His eyes remained on the package. There were two book-sized boxes wrapped in cellophane with colorful graphics and large, bold lettering. "Looks like computer software of some kind."

"Very good!" Dan replied. "Rigel Analyst, the latest in forensic geographical profiling software." Dan removed the cellophane from the boxes as he spoke. "It utilizes a sophisticated software algorithm to create a two-dimensional probability map overlaying a conventional street map to show the most probable areas for a suspect's base of operation. Especially useful for serial crimes to narrow down and help identify the perp."

Sam gulped. "So, what do you want me to do?"

Dan put his right hand on Sam's shoulder and spoke softly, like father to son. "I want you, my dear boy, to learn how to use this darn software so we can get a handle on these cold missing persons cases going back almost twenty years, 'n so." He indicated the pins on the wall. "That wall map can only take us so far. I need a better mousetrap to catch this rat!"

Sam fingered the loose cellophane on the desk. "And you think this Emery fella might be the rat? A serial killer maybe?"

"Well, ol' Jake would be top on my list, but there may be others. We need to keep an open mind. Expand our list of suspects. And our area of investigation." Dan moved toward the wall map. "You see those yellow pins grouped above the Elkhart Lake area?" He took a loose pin from the box of pins and placed it high on the map, above the county line into neighboring Manitowoc County in the city of Kiel. "I need to talk to Sheriff Bradley up in Manitowoc. Expand our database of missing persons to include this area. I have a feeling our perp, or perps, may be no respecter of county lines."

Sam nodded.

Dan turned to Sam and pointed to the package on the desk. "So, you know what you have to do. Right, Sam?"

"Uh, oh yeah, sure thing." Sam gathered up the boxes and proceeded to his desk in the next room. "I'll get right on it, sir."

Chapter Eleven

JAKE'S PLACE

Wednesday, June 17, 2015

A weathered sign hung above the ramshackle barn:

EMERY REFUSE REMOVAL

AND

SEPTIC TANK SERVICING

PLYMOUTH, SHEBOYGAN COUNTY

Parked at random angles in the large open space between the barn and a construction trailer that served as an office was an odd assortment of tanker trucks, garbage trucks, and pickups in various states of repair.

One of the pickups had its hood raised, reluctantly propped open by a two-by-four. A young man in greasy T-shirt, worn jeans, and motorcycle boots lay bent over, half-swallowed up by the engine compartment.

"Okay! Giv'er some gas, once!" he commanded.

A large, shadowy figure seated behind the wheel responded. The engine sputtered to life in fits and puffs of brown exhaust and eventually assumed a low, steady rumble as the truck awakened from its long-dormant state.

The young man emerged from beneath the hood, removed the piece of timber, and let the lid slam shut as it seemed so eager to do. He grabbed a greasy rag from his pants pocket and wiped his hands, unsure where the balance of grease actually wound up: on the rag or on his hand. He smiled and squinted into the afternoon sun.

"Yeah, I think that should take care of this old bear," he said. "Give her another lease on life, 'n so."

The shadow behind the wheel emerged into the daylight.

"Good work, son," the man replied in classic Wisconsin twang. His gait was slow, almost staggering, his voice weak, not befitting a man of his size.

Scott smiled, but he was worried about his dad's health. Ever since Gloria had gone missing nine months earlier, Jake would often wake up in the middle of the night, screaming, in a cold sweat. "Bad dream," he would say, after he finally got it together. "Just a bad dream."

The police hounded him for months following her disappearance. But his story always remained the same: "I told you. I went out to the farmers' market, and when I came back, she was gone. I figured she went to visit a friend and decided to stay for the weekend."

Scott believed his dad. But he also knew that his dad and stepmom argued a lot. As far as he could tell, it had something to do with her not being able to have children. After two difficult pregnancies and miscarriages she was advised by her doctor not to try again. Following that, well, the flame of passion kind of died, replaced by the tedium of life's daily routine.

Scott placed his hand on his dad's shoulder. "So, how 'bout we go in the house for a beer, Dad. I think the Brewers are playin' this afternoon."

Jake simply nodded.

Born and raised in Milwaukee, Jake Emery loved the Brewers almost as much as he loved the Packers. He'd started the family business soon after moving to Plymouth some thirty-plus years earlier with his first wife, Laura, to escape the big city and its ne'er-do-well influences. They had three sons together: Adam, Seth, and Scott, with fourteen years separating the oldest, Adam, from the youngest, Scott.

No doubt about it, though, twenty-two-year-old Scott was his favorite. A born mechanic, fixing things was something that came easy to him. A "natural bent," Jake would say. Scott kept Jake's fleet of trucks running well past their rightful lifetime and was arguably the single most important person in his life right now. But not only because of his mechanical prowess. Scott had his mother's eyes.

Scott was just five years old when his birth mother, Laura, went missing. Jake had taken two of his sons, Seth and Scott, to Green Bay to see a Packers game one Saturday afternoon in late September 1998. When they returned home, Laura's car was gone and she was nowhere to be found. Adam was living alone in a trailer at the time—having had a temporary falling out with his dad—so he claimed to know nothing of his mom's whereabouts. At first, Jake figured she had gone to one of her yoga classes, or maybe visited her sister in Elkhart Lake who was recovering from cancer surgery. But he waited three days before reporting her missing after finally calling his sister-in-law to inquire after Laura. Her sister said she had been expecting Laura that Saturday afternoon, but she never showed up. And when the sheriff's deputy knocked on Jake's front door a week later to say they had found her car abandoned off the side of a road up near Elkhart Lake, Jake became a person of interest.

"So, why did you wait three days before reporting her missing?" they had asked.

Jake repeated what he'd already told them. That he had gone to Green Bay with two of his sons to see a Packers game, and when he returned home, she was gone. "She had been talking about visiting her sister, so I assumed that's where she went."

Seth corroborated his dad's story and vouched for his whereabouts since returning home after the game. Finally, casting an angry stare at the questioning officers, Jake erupted. "So, why aren't ya out there looking for her? Or for whoever may have done her harm, 'n so?"

In the end, the sheriff's office eliminated Jake as a suspect thanks to his solid Green Bay Packers game alibi. But Laura's remains were never found and her whereabouts never known. This became the first of many cold cases that remained on the books of the Sheboygan County Sheriff's Office. And it wouldn't be the last one to involve Jake or members of his family.

Chapter Twelve

ADAM'S PLACE

Later That Night, June 17, 2015

"Where the hell have you been?" Milly demanded, clutching her infant daughter to her chest. "It's almost ten o'clock!"

Her husband, Adam Emery, staggered into the kitchen of their mobile home stinking drunk, slamming the door behind him. He, Milly, and the baby lived a few miles from Jake's family-run business. Adam, Jake's eldest son, along with his middle brother, Seth, supervised the teams of haulers and septic tank workers responsible for doing the actual fieldwork.

"That no-good son-of-a-bitch brother o' mine... accusing me of slouchin' off!" Adam stammered, slurring his words as he navigated his tall frame to the refrigerator and grappled with a bottle of beer.

Milly spoke up. "Well, maybe if you would just—"

"The opener! Where's the goddamn opener!" he exploded, spewing a shower of spit into his wife's face.

Milly backed off and held her daughter firmly to her breast.

Adam managed to find the opener, where it always was, hanging on a string from the kitchen wall cabinet. Staggering to the kitchen table, he plopped himself down and gulped a healthy swig of brew.

"Damn police! Won't let me be!" He let out a long belch and mumbled something unintelligible.

Adam had always had a drinking problem. But ever since Emma, their company's young clerk, went missing last month, things had gotten out of hand. Milly was forced to fill in for Emma at the office until they could find a replacement, which made things even more stressful, what with the baby and all.

"Why won't they believe me?" he muttered. "I told 'em everything I know!" He took another swig. "Damn police!"

By now the baby was crying. Wailing, actually. Milly took her into the bedroom and tried rocking her to comfort her. She'd always suspected Adam had a thing for Emma. When he offered to drive Emma home to Plymouth the evening of May 8, he never bothered to call home to tell her that he'd be late. It was past midnight when he showed up back home. Even then, he didn't say where he'd been. But the booze on his breath gave him away.

"The Pony!" he confessed at long last. "Okay? I stopped at the Pony Bar and Grill with some old friends."

But that part of the story never ended up in the police report.

"He was home by seven, right after dropping Emma off in Plymouth," was Milly's official sworn statement concerning the events of the evening of May 8, the night Emma went missing.

It was now getting late. With Adam passed out on the couch, Milly rocked her baby to sleep humming a lullaby tune.

Alibi baby, on the treetop…

Chapter Thirteen

THE VINTAGE CAFÉ

Saturday, June 20, 2015

Luke checked the clock on the wall: 12:00 p.m. He stretched his neck to get a better view of the café's entrance over the field of intervening heads, then doodled a few anxious strokes in his notebook as he asked the server for another cup of coffee. First-time encounters always made him nervous. Especially with members of the other sex.

The Vintage Café, located on Washington Avenue in the heart of Cedarburg's historic downtown district, was as good a spot as any, and cozier than most, for first-time meetings. It was Aiyanna who'd suggested it when they spoke on the phone five days earlier.

"Well, I plan to be in Cedarburg this weekend for the Strawberry Festival," she had said. "How about we meet there? The Vintage Café at noon. Ever been to Cedarburg?"

Luke had to admit he had not. Growing up in Wisconsin, how could he have let that happen? Cedarburg was, after all, a celebrated small-town champion of local festivals. You name it, they had a festival for it: CedarBrew Fest, Strawberry Festival, Oktoberfest, Christmas Fest, Winter Festival, Wine & Harvest Festival, and more. And located where it was, more or less midway between Sheboygan and Madison, it offered a more or less logical place for them to rendezvous.

Busy fussing with his cell phone, Luke felt the sudden presence of another.

"Please excuse me, but you wouldn't be Lukas Kramer, the journalist from the *Sheboygan Dispatch?*"

He jumped. Though he recognized the voice from the phone call, he was startled for having missed her approach.

"Y-yes. Of course. Miss Aiyanna, I presume," he replied, nervously pocketing his cell phone and standing. "I'm sorry. Please, have a seat."

The young woman smiled and took a seat across from him, setting her leather satchel on the floor by her side. She wore blue jeans and a buckskin vest. An amulet carved from bone in the shape of a bear's head, inlaid with copper nuggets for eyes, hung about her neck.

Luke was taken slightly aback by her appearance. In a good way, actually. He knew from his friend Dan that she was of Native American descent. He'd been expecting, perhaps, an older, more heavyset woman with wizened features. Not so. She was young and lithe, smooth skin almost radiant. Luke scolded himself for succumbing to stereotypical imaging.

Reaching across the table, she presented her business card:

Aiyanna-Nez Black Bear, PhD
Associate Professor
University of Wisconsin Madison
College of Agriculture and Life Sciences

"Just want to make this official," she said.

Luke read aloud the name on the card.

"Aiyanna-Nez Black Bear." He looked up. "I thought your name was just Aiyanna Nez. That's what Dan told me."

Aiyanna frowned and cocked her head. "Dan? Dan Meyers?"

"Uh-huh."

"Yes, well, I'm not surprised." She paused with a sigh. "That's a long story. Not something we need to get into here. But you can call me Aiyanna. Everyone else does." She seemed eager to change the subject. "So, Lukas, tell me—"

"Please," he interrupted. "Please, call me Luke."

Aiyanna sat back, taking a moment.

"Why, yes, certainly," she said, adjusting her tone. "So, Luke, you mentioned over the phone that you're doing a piece on GMO crops. Corn in particular. I'm sure I can help you with that."

Luke nodded with a smile. "Yes, I was hoping you might."

"But you must know my specialty is mycology. The study of fungi, with a special interest in mushrooms."

He returned a blank stare. "Mushrooms?"

Laughing, she reached down and pulled an article from her leather satchel and handed it to him. It was a reprint of an article from *Scientific American*.

Luke took the article and read the title. "'Strange but True, the Largest Organism on Earth Is a Fungus.'"

He looked up. "Really?"

Aiyanna smiled. "Yes, of course," she said matter-of-factly. "The giant *Armillaria ostoyae* mushroom, discovered in 1998 growing in Oregon's Blue Mountains."

"Wait a minute," Luke replied. "You say there's a giant mushroom growing in the Oregon mountains?"

"That's right. Bigger than a blue whale."

Luke's eyes widened. He sat back and shook his head. "That's ridiculous! A mushroom that's bigger than a blue whale?"

Aiyanna let him chew on this for a few moments before explaining.

"You must first realize that what you see growing aboveground are just the fruiting bodies of mushrooms. The major portion of the organism grows underground, or inside rotting vegetation, and consists of the mycelium, a white, cottony living web of filamentous fibers, or hyphae. This mycelial mass typically extends for a wide area surrounding the fruiting bodies."

She shifted in her seat and drew closer to the table.

"Now, certain species of the genus *Armillaria*, commonly known as honey mushrooms, have a special ability to extend their range, which can be quite large given the right genetic makeup and environment."

Luke's interest was piqued. "Really? How large?"

"Would you believe up to four square miles?"

His jaw dropped. "That's big!"

Aiyanna chuckled. "Yes. And not only that. Based on its current growth rate, the fungus is estimated to be at least 2,400 years old! So, that makes it not only the biggest living organism, but the oldest as well!"

She went on to explain that the initial scientific interest in *Armillaria ostoyae* was due to its pathogenic nature. The fungus caused Armillaria root disease, which attacked conifers in many parts of the United States and Canada. A fungus would typically attack a tree by extending its hyphal growth along the root system and secreting digestive enzymes that destroyed plant tissue. But Armillaria had a special ability to bridge food sources and expand its range by creating rhizomorphs, a special aggregate growth of hyphae.

"Hmm. Well, this is all quite interesting," he said. "But what has it to do with GMO corn?"

Her mouth puckered. "Perhaps nothing, but you must admit it's an interesting phenomenon. And it's not isolated to the far northwest," she added. "In fact, the first giant fungus was discovered in Crystal Falls, Michigan, in 1992. About a four-hour drive north of here. Right in our own backyard!"

Luke leaned forward and jotted down a few notes. "So, I guess you guys are on the hunt for a giant Wisconsin mushroom, eh?"

Aiyanna smiled. "You got it. In fact, my research is taking me right into your neighborhood—the marshy lake regions around Elkhart Lake."

"The Sheboygan Marsh Wildlife Area?"

"Precisely!"

"My old neighborhood," Luke said with a smile. "I grew up on a farm not far from Elkhart Lake."

He jotted down a few more notes. "Just for future reference," he said, and turned the page. "But what I'd really like to do now is talk about GMO corn."

With a nod, Aiyanna opened her satchel. They spent the next hour talking about GMO corn: crop reports, recalls, areas impacted. She had all the agricultural data and produced maps showing the areas in Wisconsin where GMO corn and other crops had grown over the past twenty years since genetically modified corn varieties resistant to glyphosate herbicides were first introduced by Monsanto in 1996.

"Other major companies quickly followed suit," she explained. "Companies like Santoma, a large overseas-based conglomerate that quickly became a major competitor in the States."

Luke was delighted. This was much more information than he could absorb in one sitting, but Aiyanna was happy to leave the data and maps with him.

He looked up only to realize he'd become so absorbed, he hadn't noticed they'd taken over two adjoining tables and were being met with glares from the restaurant staff and other customers. Suddenly aware of their transgressions, Luke quickly gathered up the documents into a neat pile and placed them in his briefcase.

"I guess that about does it for the time being," he said with a satisfied sigh.

Aiyanna smiled. "Yes, but don't hesitate to call me. And I promise to reach out to you the next time I'm in your neighborhood..."

"Looking for giant mushrooms." He completed the sentence for her.

"Yes. Doing my field research," she said in a professorial tone.

Luke put up his hands. "Sorry. I stand corrected. I'll tell you what," he continued as he eyed the menu. "My stomach's starting to growl. How 'bout some lunch? Compliments of the *Dispatch*, of course."

"Sounds good. But we'll have to make it quick." She looked at her watch. "I want to make the wine-tasting event at three o'clock."

"No problem," he replied. Her pretty smile produced an afterthought. "Mind if I join you? I'm more into beer than wine, but I could do with a little cultural refinement."

"No, I don't mind at all."

He grabbed two menus from the side of the table and handed one to Aiyanna. "So, do you think they have any mushroom wine at this wine tasting?" he asked.

She laughed. "That would be strange, now, wouldn't it? No, I don't think so. Maybe we can put it in the suggestion box."

In the course of the afternoon, Luke learned much about Wisconsin wine and even more of Aiyanna's Native American heritage and lineage.

She was a member of the Ho-Chunk Nation of Wisconsin, a branch of the Winnebago tribe that remained in Wisconsin following a series of westward relocations of its peoples to Minnesota and Nebraska in the mid-1800s under various treaty arrangements with the federal government.

"You see, many of our people refused to go, or returned to Wisconsin, our ancestral home," she explained, "where they would be routinely rounded up and sent back to Nebraska, only to return a month later!" She laughed. "Eventually, the US government got tired of sending us back and allowed the Wisconsin Winnebago to settle here. Today, the Winnebago Tribe of Nebraska and the Ho-Chunk Nation of Wisconsin are recognized by the federal government as two separate tribes, each with its own tribal government."

"So, do they... I mean, do *you*, live on a... reservation?" Luke asked with some hesitation.

Aiyanna sighed. "Well, that's the interesting thing. The Wisconsin Winnebago, or Ho-Chunk Nation, is the only federally recognized Native American tribe *without* a reservation!"

Luke raised an eyebrow. "So where do you live? How do you govern yourselves?"

Aiyanna explained that the tribe was headquartered in Black River Falls, Wisconsin, and owned about five thousand acres scattered across parts of twelve counties in Wisconsin. "And one county in Minnesota, I believe," she added. "By last census, we number over eight thousand members and operate a number of casinos to generate revenue." She paused. "We are also pursuing the acquisition of surplus federal land in Sauk County, the site of the old Badger Army Ammunition Plant. But that is still under litigation."

Luke nodded. "I see. Very interesting."

As she took a sip of wine, his attention was drawn to the amulet pendant dangling from her neck.

"That's a very interesting pendant," he said. "Tell me, what's the significance of the bear's head?"

Aiyanna turned pensive as she took the amulet in her right hand and gently rubbed it. "This is very special to me," she said slowly, continuing to study the pendant. "It was handed down to me from my ancestors.

The Bear clan." She looked up. "You see, I am a member of the Bear clan."

Nodding, he pretended to understand.

"Let me explain," she said.

Luke sat back and listened.

Chapter Fourteen

MUSHROOMS AND CORN

Wednesday, June 24, 2015

When Aiyanna drove up to the Pony Bar and Grill in Plymouth, Luke was there waiting for her. She had wasted no time. The day after their meeting in Cedarburg, she'd called to invite Luke on a field trip to the marshy regions around Elkhart Lake to hunt for the giant *Armillaria ostoyae* mushroom, or a suitably related species. This was her first venture into this area, having come up empty in previous searches in nearby regions to the north and west. Maybe he would bring her good luck this time.

Luke was seated at a booth just inside the front door, sipping coffee, studying his notes, when she arrived.

"Good morning! How's the coffee?" Aiyanna asked.

She had apparently taken him by surprise. He looked up. "Uh, yeah, sure. Coffee's great. Colombian."

Luke quickly cleared some space at the table and motioned to the waiter. After setting down her knapsack, she took the seat across from him. Dressed in army fatigues, she wore her hair in a ponytail, which passed through a Brewers baseball cap in the back.

"Like the hat," he said with a smile. He couldn't seem to keep his eyes off her ponytail. "Brewers fan, eh?"

"All my life," she said.

"Have you had breakfast? The omelets are to die for."

"That's okay," she replied. "I ate before leaving Madison. Coffee is just fine." She looked up at the waiter. "Coffee, please. To go."

Luke began gathering up the maps and notes, putting them back in his briefcase. "I was just going over the GMO crop maps you gave me last week. Thinking maybe we could drop by a few fields and talk to the farmers. Get their take on GMO. Corn in particular. That is, if you think we have the time."

Aiyanna smiled. "Not a problem. Kill two birds at once, so to speak."

He beamed. "That's great. I know the area pretty well as it is. But with the maps, I've been able to pinpoint some *particular* fields I'd like to, well... explore." His voice faded almost to inaudible, as if he was distracted by a distant thought or memory.

The subtle change in tone was not lost on her. She smiled weakly as the waiter returned with her coffee.

After a moment, Luke glanced out the window and seemed to perk up. "Well, it certainly looks like a good sunny day for mushroom hunting, eh?"

"*Any* day is a good day for mushroom hunting," she replied. His sudden mood shifts caught her a little off guard. "Actually, though," she added, "I prefer a drizzling rain. Makes the digging easier."

"Huh, yeah, well I guess. Didn't think of that."

She took a sip of coffee and smiled. Luke was right about the coffee. After another sip, she looked over at him. "Okay, so, what d'ya say we get to work?"

"Ready when you are." He motioned to the waiter. "Check, please!"

Outside, Aiyanna placed her knapsack in the back seat of her red Blazer SUV and climbed in behind the wheel, coffee cup in hand. Luke joined her on the passenger side. He opened his notepad and began making more notes.

"So, you're planning to document this field trip?" she asked.

"Right. Strictly from a journalistic point of view, naturally, subject to your editorial on-the-record approval, of course."

She laughed. "I don't think I'll have anything to hide. Except I do reserve first publication rights on any major find of a scientific nature."

"Not a problem," he said as he jotted down a few more notes. "So, what's the plan? You have a route mapped out for this expedition?"

She motioned with a twist of her head. "Check the visor."

When he pulled down the visor, a folded map fell onto his lap.

"Okay. So I am the designated navigator?"

"You got it!" She pulled onto the main street heading west out of downtown Plymouth. Not far down the road, she made a right onto Route 67 north toward Elkhart Lake.

"Know how Elkhart Lake got its name?" she asked.

He gave her a crooked smile. "You mean, for real?"

Aiyanna squinched her face. "What do you mean 'for real'?"

Luke snickered. "Well, the last time someone asked me a question like that, I bit hook, line, and sinker."

She smiled. "Well, I assure you, this is no joke. Just an old Native American legend. A story of jilted love, actually."

"Hmm. Guess nothing ever changes," he replied with a wry grin.

Aiyanna huffed. "Do you want to hear it, or don't you?"

"I'm sorry. Please proceed."

Clearing her throat, she adjusted in her seat.

"So, there once was this handsome young warrior named Elkheart who was well known among his people for his bravery and hunting skills, which he demonstrated on one occasion by slaying an elk and devouring its heart. Hence his name, Elkheart. Much sought after by all the young maidens, he began courting one named Silver Birch. However, not totally satisfied, his attention was soon drawn to another, called Singing Bird. This left Silver Birch brokenhearted.

"One evening, as the two new lovers paddled out on the lake under a full moon, an arrow from the bow of the dejected Silver Birch found its mark. *Kersplash!* Elkheart fell into the water. Horrified, Singing Bird dove in after him, followed by the sorrowful Silver Birch, who had nothing left to live for. All three met the same fate, drowning in the clear waters of the lake under the light of the full moon." She paused for dramatic effect. "Now, it is said that whenever the moon is full, you can hear the spirit of Silver Birch crying out Elkheart's name as she passes over the lake."

"Star-crossed lovers," Luke said. "I like that. A classic love triangle, like *The Great Gatsby*."

Aiyanna snorted. "Or you could say *The Great Gatsby* is kind of like the Legend of Elkheart."

Luke pursed his lips. "Touché! Guess it's all a matter of cultural perspective. It's like... Hey, wait!" he shouted. "Slow down and pull over!"

"Wha...?"

"Right there! Pull over!" He pointed.

Reacting to the urgency in his voice, she braced herself and brought the Blazer to a screeching halt on the side of the road. Turning her head, she followed his gaze up a gravel driveway toward a well-maintained white clapboard, two-story farmhouse, neatly nestled in a healthy stand of sprawling ash and beech. Nothing seemed amiss.

"Nice farm" was all she could think to say, somewhat perplexed.

"This is it! This is the Henkel farm!" he said.

She remained puzzled. "The Henkel farm?"

He turned to her. "Sorry. But you must've heard of it. The human molar found in the box of corn flakes! Pam, my associate, ran a series of articles on it. Ended up in the hands of the Wisconsin Department of Agriculture."

She strained to look. "Oooh, yes! I do recall something about that. So... you wanna stop and talk to the Henkels?" she asked hesitantly.

Luke tilted his head. "Well, maybe on the way back. If there's time."

Aiyanna sighed. "Yes. If there's time."

LUKE AND AIYANNA spent the remainder of the day taking soil and mushroom samples in the woodlands and marshlands in and around the Sheboygan Marsh State Wildlife Area, an area through which the Sheboygan River flowed on its meandering eighty-mile journey to Lake Michigan. Their search also took them into the farm country south of the marsh toward Elkhart Lake, a region Luke knew particularly well. This was where he grew up—an area that harbored many memories, both good and bad. Some very bad. It was an area that, even as an adult, he chose to avoid.

But today was different. Today he had the support of someone he trusted. Today he would venture into territory he hadn't set foot in since that terrible day in August 1999—the remote farm country that stretched east of County Road J to the Sheboygan River.

"Are you okay?" Aiyanna asked.

Luke squirmed in his seat. "Sure." He paused briefly. "I'm fine."

And he was... for most of the day. It was late afternoon when, driving down a narrow country road bordered on both sides by tall stands of corn, he broke out in a cold sweat. *Dead Man's Road!* He turned to Aiyanna. "Can you please pull over here? There, just up ahead by that signpost," he said, pointing.

Aiyanna complied. "Anything you say."

She pulled over and cut the engine, keeping the windows open.

An eerie silence lay over the field. Nothing but the sway and rustle of corn leaves in the gentle summer breeze, the buzzing of dragonflies, the harsh *caw-caw* of distant crows seemingly undeterred by scarecrow sentries dotting the field. A sign had been posted in front of the cornfield: Tenderbrooke Farms Co-op GMO Corn and Soy.

They sat there, silent and still for a moment. Luke spoke first. His tone was somber.

"I grew up on a farm not far from here."

Slowly, he opened the door and stepped out. Planting his feet firmly on the ground, he remained standing there, looking out over the vast fields of sweet corn, stalks topping seven feet, ears plump and bulging, just days away from harvest in time for Fourth of July cookouts. His mind began to drift, and his thoughts took him back to that terrible August day in 1999. He swore he could hear the giggling, innocent voice of a young girl mixed in with the sounds of a summer breeze from across the field. *"Betcha can't find me!... You gotta find me if you want them back!"*

The voice was as clear as the day was bright.

Finally, he turned to Aiyanna and murmured, "Can you please take some soil samples... from this field?"

Aiyanna paused. "Sure. I can do that." Slowly she climbed out of the vehicle and went to Luke's side. "But can I ask you why?"

Hesitating, he looked at the GMO corn sign. "I don't know. Just a feeling."

He began recounting the events of that awful day in August 1999. The day his sister, Alice, disappeared without a trace. Right there, in that cornfield! He then opened up about the days, the weeks, the months that followed. How he was somehow blamed, not by his mother but by his father. Guilt by association is how he figured it in his later adult years. The loss drove his dad to drink—or rather, back to the bottle, which he had successfully avoided since joining Alcoholics Anonymous.

"So, what happened to your mom and dad?" Aiyanna asked.

Luke let out a wistful sigh. "Well, my dad died of lung cancer in my junior year of college."

"Oh, I'm sorry," she said.

"No. That's okay. The docs said it was probably due to all the fertilizers and chemicals he handled on the farm. Never smoked. He was only forty-five, though."

"Damn. That's nasty business," she said. "And your mom?"

"Well, the summer I graduated, in 2011, she sold the farm and bought a place in town, in Elkhart Lake. Runs an antique barn, now. Does quite well, actually."

"Really? Well, maybe we can, you know, drop by to see her on the way back."

Aiyanna stopped short. Luke shifted his gaze to see her biting her lip.

"Uh. Nah. Not today," he said with a wan smile. He thought about the last time he brought a girl home to meet the family. It didn't end well. "But I tell you what." He perked up a bit. "My mom is having some people over for a brat fry on the Fourth." He turned and faced her full on. "I'd like you to come. I've invited an old friend from Milwaukee who I haven't seen since high school, now married with a kid. And," he added, thinking this would clinch the deal, "Detective Dan will be there."

She laughed. "Oh, wonderful! You trying to convince me to go, or stay away?"

He was puzzled. "Well, sure. I just figured he'd be at least one other person you would know."

Aiyanna smiled. "Of course, I *know* Dan. What I didn't tell you before was he dated my older sister, Adrianna. Almost married her." She paused. "Yes, I know Detective Dan," she said with a smirk.

He grimaced, afraid he'd blown it. "Oh, I see. Sorry about that."

"Not a problem. Or I should say, no longer a problem."

Proceeding cautiously, he continued, "So, uh, it's a date, er"—he quickly corrected himself—"*deal*, then."

A smile spread across her face. "Sure! What the hey! I'd be happy to. But only if you grill the brats in beer and butter."

"With onions?"

"Is there any other way?" She gave him a fist bump. "You got it! What time do the festivities begin?"

"Around one o'clock. That okay?"

"Sounds good!"

Aiyanna turned to retrieve some specimen bags from the SUV, her enthusiasm for the hunt having apparently returned. "Okay, so let's get these cornfield soil samples. Never know what we'll find, right?"

Luke forced a smile. "Right!"

Chapter Fifteen

JAKE'S STORY

Sunday, June 28, 2015

3:00 a.m. Scott Emery woke to moans and muffled screams coming from his father's bedroom. This wasn't the first time it had happened. Ever since his stepmom had gone missing in the fall, the nighttime outbursts were a recurring occurrence. But it seemed to be getting worse. And more frequent.

When Scott got to his father's room, Jake was sitting on the side of the bed, sobbing, bent over with his head in his hands. Scott approached his dad and placed a reassuring hand on his shoulder. Jake reached up and took his son's hand, shaking his head in disbelief.

"Can't figure it. No way. Just can't figure it," he repeated over and over.

Scott sat down next to his dad. He thought carefully before speaking.

"Dad, did you tell the police everything about that day?"

Jake shook his head. "They'd never believe me, son. Never believe a man suspected in the disappearance of his first wife. 'Pure fabrication.' That's what they'd call it. Pure fabrication."

Scott sighed. "So, do you want to tell me, Dad? What actually happened that day?"

A few minutes later, Jake and Scott were sitting at the kitchen table.

A cigarette hung by sheer will from Jake's lower lip. Scott had put on a pot of tea. Chamomile. Good for the nerves.

Jake took a deep drag on his Camel. "Well, son. It began like I told them. Gloria and I had gone into town for groceries. The bank. On the way home, we stopped at a farmers' market to pick up some apples, peaches, corn. But Gloria didn't like the corn. Said the ears were too shriveled."

Jake parked his cigarette between two fingers, hugged the hot cup of tea, and took a sip.

Scott leaned forward. "Right. And that's what you told me when I returned home the next day from a fishing trip with Seth. I found you on the front porch in an agitated state. You told me that Gloria stayed home while you went out to get more corn. When you came back, she was gone. You said you thought maybe Mabel had come by and picked her up. On Monday, when she still hadn't returned, that's when I reported her missing."

Jake took another sip of tea, followed by a long drag and a slow exhale.

"Well, it didn't exactly happen that way, son," he said in a whisper. "Ya see, we didn't come home after the farmers' market."

Scott was puzzled. "And there was no Mabel?"

Jake nodded. "That's right. No Mabel. Ya see, son, on the way home we passed a field of sweet corn just busting with ripeness. Up nort' on Route 57 toward Johnsonville. I remember, there was a GMO corn sign."

"GMO corn?" Scott repeated.

"Yeah. Gloria saw the sign and told me to pull over one time. Said she would pick her own corn, GMO or not." He looked up and broke a smile. "She was just that way, ya know. Once she got something in her head, she wouldn't let go."

He took a drag and continued.

"Well, I told her to hurry up. Looked like a storm was brewin'. Comin' in from the west. She said not to worry. She'd be real quick like. I said, 'Okay, knock yourself out.'" He sighed. "So, I waited there by the side of the road, engine idling. And Gloria, well, she disappeared down a tractor path in the cornfield with an empty burlap sack." He paused for a few seconds and chuckled. "And then this here dog, a golden retriever I think, comes out of nowhere and follows her into the field. Must've been chasin' a rabbit or something." He took a big gulp of tea. "And that's the last time I saw her."

Scott squirmed in his seat. "And that's what you told the police?"

There was a long pause.

"'Course not. They'd never believe me." Jake took another drag. "And fer sure I didn't tell 'em what happened next. Sure as hell never would've believed me!"

Scott perked up.

"Ya see," Jake continued, "not five minutes after that dog ran into the field, I heard this commotion." Jake stared blankly straight ahead, like he was reliving it in real time. "Couldn't believe it. Or understand it. I heard Gloria scream. Startled the hell outta me, dontcha know! So I got out of the truck and looked. And there, about fifty yards down this tractor path and off to the side, just inside the thick rows of corn, was a cloud of dust, with torn stalks of corn being tossed into the air. Like maybe a bomb went off or something. Only in slow motion, like. I shouted out her name and ran down the path toward the commotion. Her screams became sorta muffled. I thought there must've been someone there waiting for her. That's all I could think about. Someone there lying in wait. Didn't make no sense otherwise."

Scott was wide-eyed. "Dad, you never mentioned any of this before."

Jake sat back and smiled. "Heh, heh, no way. 'Cause they'd have locked me up in the looney bin fer sure and thrown away the key!" He took a sip of tea, becoming a little more relaxed now, like a weight had been lifted from his shoulders. Or maybe the tobacco and tea combo was working.

"Well, when I finally got to where all the commotion was, all I found was a patch of open ground, all churned up and covered with uprooted, broken stalks of corn, like someone had taken a plow to it. The cornstalks still standing were all twisted, kinda like in a circle pattern. I shouted out Gloria's name, but... nothing. No sign of her." He paused and took a deep breath. "Just the empty burlap sack she was carrying. There lying on the ground, 'n so."

Jake poured himself another cup of tea and looked up. "Got any whiskey for this tea?"

Scott was in a daze. "Uh, oh yeah. Sure, Dad." He went to the liquor cabinet and came back with a bottle and shot glass.

"Well, after a frantic search of the area, I got to thinkin' that maybe a sinkhole swallowed her up. Like I saw on the news. Happened down in Florida or somewhere. Swallowed up the whole damn house! The only thing I could think to do was grab a shovel from the pickup and start diggin'. Must've dug a three-foot hole. Kept digging even after the storm kicked in. Mud, sweat, and tears! That's all I can remember." He stifled a laugh. "Gotta wonder what the farmer must've thought when time came to harvest the corn."

Scott considered this, trying to put the pieces together in his head.

"So, you're saying that Gloria just... *disappeared*? Into thin air? Or a sinkhole?"

Jake stared ahead at the flowered wallpaper, fondling his shot glass.

"C'mon, Dad. Ya gotta admit that's a pretty strange story. I mean, what do you think *really* happened to her?"

Jake shook his head. "That's what's been haunting me these many months." He looked into his son's eyes and sighed. "But I'm glad I finally got it off my chest. Thank you, son."

"No, you don't get off that easy, Dad!" Scott said, raising his voice. "We need to report this to the police real quick! I mean, we gotta close the loop. Ya know, maybe they can do their forensic thing and come up with an answer, 'n so!"

Jake took another sip of tea.

Growing increasingly frustrated, even infuriated, by his dad's seeming nonchalance, Scott straightened up and blurted out, "I mean, maybe she's still lying out there somewhere! Ever think of that?"

Jake stiffened, clearly startled by his son's outburst.

"Hmm. Maybe you're right, son." Jake poured himself another shot and drank it straight down. "Maybe you're right," he repeated. "Maybe we need to tell someone. But..."

"But what?"

"Well, I don't wanna go to the police, that's fer sure," Jake said. He couldn't get that GMO corn sign out of his mind. "Uh, maybe that reporter fella that's been writing about this GMO corn shit." He looked up. "And that molar they found in a box of corn flakes. Read about that?"

Scott was puzzled. "Nah. Can't say that I have. Don't know nothing 'bout no tooth or GMO corn! So, what are you saying we oughta do, Dad?'

"Hmm. Give that fella a call. Maybe he can investigate it without getting the police involved."

Scott shook his head. "I don't know, Dad. Don't see how no reporter is gonna help us find Mom. Maybe we should hire a private eye."

Jake appeared to be weighing the options.

"Nah! The reporter fella. That's who I wanna call," he said at last.

Scott exhaled sharply through pursed lips. "Okay, Dad. If that's what you want to do, I'm okay with it."

Scott poured himself a whiskey and joined his dad at the table. Ruminating. Just ruminating.

Chapter Sixteen

BREAKTHROUGH IN MADISON

Monday, June 29, 2015

Luke pushed aside the rough draft of his second installment on the GMO series and his stomach rumbled, telling him it was lunchtime. Yet he had other things on his mind besides food. Reaching into his desk drawer, he produced a voluminous paperbound book with the unassuming title *The Winnebago Tribe*, by anthropologist Paul Radin. Ever since his first meeting with Aiyanna in Cedarburg, Luke's interest in local Native American culture and history had been piqued, and his inquiries directed him toward Radin's work. Originally published as an annual report of the Smithsonian Institution's Bureau of American Ethnology in 1923, *The Winnebago Tribe* had since become what was considered by many to be the definitive and single best authority on the subject, covering all aspects of tribal history, culture, customs, legends, religious beliefs, and shamanistic and medicinal practices.

Luke was engrossed in the chapter covering religious beliefs—in particular, those pertaining to magical ceremonies, herbal remedies, and reincarnation—when his desk phone rang, abruptly drawing him back into the real world.

"Luke Kramer, *Sheboygan Dispatch*. How can I...?"

"Luke! This is Aiyanna!" Her tone was bubbly and supercharged. "You have to come down to Madison and see for yourself... The soil samples from our field trip have given amazing results... Can't wait to..."

"Whoa. Slow down!" Luke interrupted. "I'm barely getting any of this."

She took a deep breath. "I've got some interesting results from the soil samples we collected this week, and I've just got to share them with you. Ready for this?" She paused. "We definitely identified a giant mushroom variety of the genus *Armillaria*. No doubt. But there's more."

Luke picked up his pen and scribbled on his notepad to get the ink flowing.

"Okay. So, what's up?"

"Well, I can't show you over the phone, unless we do a video call. But I'd like to do this face-to-face."

Luke raised an eyebrow. "I see." He glanced at the wall clock. "Okay. I think I can break loose and be down there by two thirty or so. Will that do?"

"Great!" she replied, obviously ecstatic. "Can't wait to show you."

He figured it was about a two-hour drive from downtown Sheboygan to Madison by way of Plymouth and Fond du Lac. He had packed up his notepads and GMO maps and was heading toward the door when his desk phone rang again. It was an unfamiliar Plymouth number. The call was routed directly to voice mail.

It was a lovely day for a road trip, and Luke welcomed the break and the chance to get out of the office. He made good time and beat his own estimate by ten minutes. Aiyanna, dressed in a white lab coat, her hair pulled back in a careless bun, greeted him in the lobby of Agriculture Hall, the epicenter of the College of Agriculture and Life Sciences, and escorted him to her lab.

"I came down as fast as I could. Afraid the specimens might die before I got here," he quipped.

Aiyanna smiled. "Here, take this," she said, handing him a lab coat as she opened the door to her lab. "Protocol."

"No problem," Luke replied. "I think the last time I wore one of these was in high school chemistry lab."

He did a quick survey of the room. Lab benches and glass-front cabinets were arranged in parallel across the room, crammed full of laboratory glassware and paraphernalia of every type he could imagine and even those he could not: microscopes, bench scales, water baths, beakers, test tube holders, magnetic stirrers, and larger test apparatuses he couldn't make head or tail of.

"So, what are these... machines?" he asked. *Machines* was the only name he could think of to describe them.

"This one's a gas chromatograph," Aiyanna replied matter-of-factly. "That one over there is a mass spectrophotometer. And these two *machines*, as you put it"—she moved to a table on the far side of the room —"are our pride and joy."

She placed her hand on what could pass as a large coffee maker. "This is our DNA analyzer. And this one"—she shifted to the next machine— "is our PCR test apparatus."

Luke perked up. These things he knew about, being a devout *Forensic Files* fan.

"Wait! Don't tell me!" he replied. "Polymerase chain reaction machine. Used to amplify trace DNA samples that are too small to analyze by themselves."

Aiyanna was wide-eyed. "Well, I am surely impressed, Luke. How did you know that?"

He explained his interest in forensics and TV crime shows. Now, his interest was truly piqued.

"And what are those glass-front cabinets over there?" he asked, pointing.

"Ah, yes. They are incubators," she replied. "Environmentally controlled. Temperature, atmospheric composition, humidity."

"Cool!" was all he could say.

"No, not cool. Actually, thirty-seven degrees Centigrade, or roughly body temperature."

He smirked. "I meant... well, you know what I mean."

She let out a laugh. "Okay, so let's get down to it."

She led him into a larger, adjoining room filled with tables and what appeared to be terrariums or miniature greenhouses: soil beds contained within clear plastic tents fitted with flexible tubing. A row of glass-front cabinets lining one side of the room appeared to contain similar soil beds.

Taking a deep breath, she turned to him. "This is our inner sanctum for mushroom research," she said, not without a small measure of pride in her voice.

"What's all the tubing for?" he asked, pointing to the plastic tents.

"Oh, that provides ventilation for temperature and humidity control of the soil beds. And those biosafety cabinets do the same." She pointed to the row of glass-front cabinets. "Only they're also equipped with controlled lighting, from daylight to red or blue, or even ultraviolet."

Luke took a closer look at one of the tabletop beds.

"I don't see any"—he paused to be certain—"mushrooms," he said, almost apologetically.

Aiyanna smiled. "Don't you remember what I told you? The mushroom lives in the soil, below the ground. What we see aboveground are just the occasional fleshy spore sacs that the organism sprouts up when conditions are right. They are the reproductive portion, or organ, of the mushroom. Right?"

He nodded. "Oh, yeah. I remember now."

She moved to one of the biosafety cabinets.

"Come over here," she said softly, like she didn't want to disturb whatever was growing inside.

He approached the cabinet and stood beside her. A handwritten sign posted to the side of the cabinet read ARMILLARIA SHEBOYGANSIS.

"Like I said over the phone, Luke, I believe we have a new species of giant mushroom on our hands. Mycelia and spores isolated from soil samples taken over a five-square-mile area encompassing the region of the Sheboygan Marsh have demonstrated identical genetic makeup. The results are irrefutable!"

He nodded. "Amazing!"

"Yes. Of course, not all samples demonstrated genetic similarity," she continued, "but there were enough matches to enable us to map out a four-square-mile region containing this single organism. And it could even be larger. We'll need more samples for that."

Luke pointed to the posted sign. "And you've dubbed this new species *Armillaria sheboygansis?*"

"Exactly!" She turned to face him. "And now comes the really exciting part."

Aiyanna pressed a switch and turned a dial on the cabinet's interior light control panel. Inside the biosafety cabinet, daylight turned to violet, then ultraviolet. As she did this, the soil took on an unmistakable dull green glow.

Luke took a small step back. "What the...?"

Aiyanna grinned. "Neat, huh?"

Taking a small apparatus from a nearby lab bench that looked like an electrician's voltmeter with two wire-connected probes, she lifted the front sash of the cabinet enough to reach in and insert the two probes into the soil at opposite ends of the soil bed.

"I'm utilizing a modified soil moisture analyzer that places a charge on the soil probes and measures the change in electrical resistance based on moisture content," she explained. "The control box is used to adjust the voltage and charge on the probes. In my case, I don't really care about moisture content. I'm mainly interested in applying a charge to the ground." She turned to the control box. "Now watch this!"

As she pressed the "DC Volt" button on the handheld apparatus and adjusted the voltage knob, the green surface glow began to pulsate, with a kind of slow rippling effect progressing from one end of the box to the other. It reminded Luke of a liquid wave-generating tank he had once seen on an episode of *NOVA*, the science TV show. As she increased the voltage, the rippling increased in speed and intensity, with shorter and shorter wavelengths. As she backed off on the voltage, the waves slowed and faded, ceasing altogether as she withdrew the probes.

Turning to Luke, she smiled. "You can close your mouth now."

True. This little demonstration had rendered him speechless.

"Have you ever seen this kind of thing before?" he finally asked.

"Nope! Never!" She returned the apparatus to the lab bench. "And what's more," she added, "this unusual behavior was only observed on the samples taken from *your* cornfield. Remember? One of the last samples we took from that cornfield you asked to sample. See, I told you that you'd bring me good luck!" She laughed and hugged Luke's arm.

Her touch sent a delightful tingle up his back. Just like those electric probes.

"Uh, oh yeah, sure. The GMO cornfield," he said, regaining his composure. He couldn't bring himself to say *my sister's cornfield.*

She pulled back like a light bulb turned on in her head. "Yes. It was GMO corn, wasn't it?"

"You think there might be some connection?" he asked.

"Hmm, can't say for sure. But definitely calls for follow-up study."

"And more samples," he said.

She referred to her notebook. "Yes. We need to sample a wider area. And include more cornfield samples. Yes, definitely! We may need to get permission from the farmers in the area. Can you arrange that?"

Tilting his head, he opened his stash of GMO cornfield maps. "Sure, I know several of the families in this area," he said, pointing. "That shouldn't be a problem." He thought a moment. "Say, listen. Maybe we can break away this weekend. After the cookout at my mom's."

She drew a quick breath through pursed lips. "Oh, yes! This Saturday is the Fourth! Brat fry at your mom's place, right?"

He nodded. "Yes. You didn't forget, did you?"

"No, of course not!" She quickly added, "Uh, what time did you say it was?"

"One o'clock, give or take. But I'll be getting there around eleven to help my mom set up." He tore a page from his notebook and took out his pen. "Here, I'll write it down. And draw a map."

She took the map. "Can I bring anything?" she asked, almost apologetically.

"Nope. Just yourself. And maybe your favorite brew. The only way to enjoy brats."

Aiyanna smiled. "Leinenkugel! You got it!" She paused a moment. "Hey, maybe I can get there early, too, and help your mom set up."

Luke bit his lip. He thought it best not to divulge the fact that his mom was "very much" looking forward to meeting her.

"That'd be nice. I'm sure she'd appreciate the help."

Chapter Seventeen

UNLIKELY BEDFELLOWS

Tuesday, June 30, 2015

Luke brought his RAV4 to a slow stop on the shoulder of the road outside Plymouth and checked his watch: 1:52 p.m. A large sign with an arrow pointed the way up a gravel driveway on the left:

EMERY REFUSE REMOVAL

AND

SEPTIC TANK SERVICING

The voice message from yesterday's mysterious caller from Plymouth said it was urgent, that he "needed to speak to the guy doing the GMO corn story." When Luke had returned the call as soon as he returned from Madison that night, the young man on the other end hesitated before speaking in a clear, rehearsed voice: "My father and I need to speak to you about my stepmom's disappearance ten months ago." The young man identified himself as "Scott." He said it was important that the police not be contacted at this time. "I will explain everything when you get here," he said, then gave Luke directions. They agreed to meet the next day at two o'clock. Putting the pieces together wasn't difficult. Luke knew this was all about Gloria Emery.

While the engine idled, Luke gathered his thoughts and wondered if he was doing the right thing. As a feature news reporter investigating a potential criminal case, he knew he was operating out of his assigned comfort zone and could potentially be called on the carpet for it. But he justified it as being related to his GMO article series. After all, did not the caller insist on speaking to the "the guy doing the GMO corn story"?

He checked his watch again: 2:00 p.m. Putting his SUV in gear, he wended his way up the driveway, passed the office trailer, and came to a stop in front of a barn that appeared to double as a garage for the Emery family business.

A tall, skinny young man in greasy T-shirt, worn jeans, and motorcycle boots emerged from the barn and approached Luke's SUV.

"You must be the reporter from the *Dispatch*," the young man said, reaching out his hand through the open window. "I'm Scott, the one you spoke to on the phone."

Luke reached across and took his hand. "Luke Kramer. Nice to meet you, Scott," he said with a smile.

The young man exhibited a firm, almost desperate, grip and continued to hold Luke's hand. "Yes, sir. So glad you were able to come all the way out here." He appeared nervous and unsure of what to say or do next.

Luke tried to relax his hold. "Uh, mind if I get out?"

Face flushing, Scott backed off. "Oh, yeah, sure. Uh, sorry."

Luke grabbed his notebook and followed Scott on foot past an assortment of vehicles parked at sundry angles, up a dirt path that led around the barn to a white chipped-paint clapboard house. Luke could just make out the shadowy figure of an older man seated on the front porch in a wooden rocker, rocking slowly. *Must be Jake.* The rocker continued its slow cadence as they approached the porch and Luke could begin to make out the man's features. He was squinting, staring straight at him, almost through him, Luke thought, like he was trying to get the measure of this young stranger.

Scott mounted the porch steps and broke the silence.

"Uh, Dad. This here fella is the reporter I talked to the other day. Name is, uh, Luke."

The rocking stopped. Jake Emery continued studying Luke with piercing blue eyes. It was like time itself had frozen.

"Tell me, young man," he said at last, "are you someone I can trust?"

His words were slow and deliberate, his voice deep and grainy.

Luke stood firm, meeting his stare without so much as a blink. "Yes, sir," he said. "What you say to me will be held in the strictest confidence." He paused. "Unless, of course, it crosses the bounds of criminality."

After a beat, Jake nodded and motioned for Luke to have a seat in the rocker next to him. Luke sat down, tried to get comfortable, crossed his legs, and opened up his notepad.

Before beginning, Jake let out a deep sigh. "I assume, Luke, you read about my wife, Gloria, who went missing last September."

"Yes, sir." He paused. "But only what I read in the papers."

Jake smiled. "Well, you probably know that the *authorities* suspect I had something to do with her disappearance. Suspect me of 'foul play,'" he said, drawing quotation marks in the air. "Them were their words, ya know."

Jake didn't wait for a response. "Let me tell you what *really* happened, young man. What I never told the police, mind you."

Jake proceeded to tell Luke his story.

"Well, when I finally got to where all the commotion was," he concluded, "all I found was a patch of open ground, all churned up and covered with uprooted, broken stalks of corn, The stalks still standing were all twisted like. I shouted out Gloria's name, but nothing. No sign of Gloria. Just the empty burlap sack she was carrying, there lying on the ground."

Luke had stopped taking notes as a pall descended, setting him adrift in his own thoughts and tearful memories of that terrible day in August of '99...

...Alice's sparkling laughter carried on the wind, her taunting chants floating back across the cornfield...The screams continued...clouds of dust mixed with torn shards of cornstalks were flung high above the distant tassels...

Coming out of his trance, Luke met the blank stares of Jake and Scott.

"Uh, you dropped your pen, son," Jake said. Leaning down, he picked it up and handed it to Luke.

Scott seemed uneasy. "Are you okay, sir?"

Luke wiped his brow and repositioned himself in the rocker. "Y-yes, I'm fine," he said. "Just fine... thank you."

Out of the blue, Jake shook his head with a scowl, slapped his thigh, and let out an angry guffaw. "Well, I'll be damned! Either you think I'm a blithering idiot, son, or you're bored to tears. In either case you probably haven't heard a word I said. Or maybe you're just too polite or too scared to call me out as a liar! Which is it?"

Luke was stunned. But Jake's outburst forced him to quickly regain his composure.

"None of the above, Mr. Emery. I assure you, sir, that I heard and believe *every* word you said. And I have good reason to believe you. Let me tell you why."

Luke began to relate his own traumatic boyhood event. It happened in a cornfield not far from where Jake had his experience. And the details were remarkably similar. Even the part about the approaching storm.

Jake and Scott appeared stunned, at a loss for words. After a time, Jake stood and approached Luke. Resting his right hand on the young man's shoulder, he smiled. "Let's go inside once and have ourselves a drink, son. I owe you that for starters, eh?"

Chapter Eighteen

CLOSURE

That Same Afternoon

Sitting around the kitchen table, it only took a few shots of rye and a couple of beer chasers for Luke to hear Jake's entire life story. Jake didn't seem to leave anything out, from his dubious past and tumultuous early years growing up in Milwaukee, including his time served for burglary and statutory rape, to the disappearance of his first wife seventeen years earlier. He was an open book. In no time at all Luke had become confidant and confessor. Luke suspected that even Scott was hearing some things for the very first time.

Luke and Jake were now on a first-name basis.

"So, Jake, what do you say we take a ride and talk to that farmer. See what he remembers. Maybe he knows something."

Jake sat back, eyes narrowing.

"I promise," Luke continued, "I will be very discreet. I'll introduce myself as the reporter doing the story on GMO corn. Which, of course, is absolutely true. No false pretenses there. I promise, I won't mention anything about your missing wife."

Luke gave Jake a moment before he went on. "Tell me, Jake. Have you ever been back to that field since... well... since that day?"

Jake shook his head. "No. Never could get up the nerve to go back."

Luke placed both hands on the kitchen table and leaned forward, feeling very confident in himself. More confident, he realized, than he'd felt his entire life.

"Then I suggest we take that ride, Jake. Ya know, it just may help bring closure, so to speak."

Unlike the time spent around the kitchen table, the ride east on Highway 23 and up Route 57 toward Johnsonville was quiet, even somber, like they were going to a funeral, with only the occasional words of direction: "Turn left at the next stop 'n go light... go straight... slow down... okay, almost there!" In a way the funereal mood was fitting, Luke figured, as he sensed they were visiting the final resting place of Jake's wife—his *second* wife—Gloria.

"Okay, slow down, eh?" Jake blurted out. Beads of sweat effused from his furrowed brow. "Right here! That's where it happened. Pull over!"

Luke slowed down and brought his RAV4 to a stop on the right shoulder of the road by a vast field of newly planted corn just inches high. A shallow grassy ditch was all that separated them from the first rows of corn. Obviously not the same corn that Jake encountered ten months earlier, but the same field. And there was that same signpost identifying this as GMO corn. In his rearview mirror, about a hundred yards back, Luke could see a driveway leading to a handsome farmhouse and barn nestled in a stand of ash and willow.

Turning to Jake, he said, "Let me check my map. It'll tell me the name of the farmer." He thought a moment. "I'll introduce myself to the farmer. If he asks about the two of you, I'll say I'm giving you a lift back into town."

Jake paused a moment. "Why not just drop us off here while you go talk to the farmer?" Pointing to a small grove of trees in a shallow ravine a few hundred feet down the road, he added, "We can stay hidden in that grove over yonder until you get back, 'n so." He gave a little chuckle. "But don't forget about us, eh?"

Luke agreed.

When he steered up the driveway, he encountered a man he assumed was the farmer coming out of the barn, closing the door behind him. He was a middle-aged man of medium height and strong build. Removing a ball cap from his balding head, he paused to wipe his brow on a shirt sleeve as he turned to study the approaching SUV. Giving a cautious but friendly smile, he asked, "Good day, young man. What can I do fer you?"

Luke checked the name on the map one more time, then smiled and held out his reporter badge through the open window.

"I'm Luke Kramer, a reporter from the *Sheboygan Dispatch*. Would you be Calvin Mertz, the proprietor of this handsome farm?"

The man smiled. "Well, yeah. That would be me." Approaching the vehicle, Calvin pulled a rag from his back pants pocket, wiped his hands, and repeated his original question. "So, what can I do fer you, son?"

Luke explained that he was doing a series of articles on GMO crops —corn in particular—and asked if he wouldn't mind being interviewed. Calvin consented, saying he needed a break anyway, and invited him into the house.

The interview was short and covered the essentials: how long had he been growing GMO corn, what varieties had he planted, was there any cost benefit to the farmer, and so on. Luke mentioned he was collaborating with a PhD agricultural botanist from UW Madison and asked Calvin if would mind if they returned to take soil and corn samples for their research. Calvin was "happy to oblige."

"Uh, just one more thing," Luke asked, feigning an afterthought as he closed his notepad. "You haven't experienced anything... unusual in recent years. I mean, as far as the cornfields are concerned. Anything out of the ordinary?"

Calvin tightened his lips and squinted. "Hmm. Don't know if I catch your drift, young man."

Calvin's wife walked in the room with a tray of iced tea and an assortment of dessert bars. "Thought you two might like some refreshment," she said with a smile. "The bars are fresh out of the oven this morning."

Luke beamed. "Lemon bars! Yum, my favorite! Thank you, ma'am!"

Calvin sat back, letting Luke take the first pick. "Yessir, my Lydia makes the best bars in these parts. A family recipe she got from her mom."

"My *grandma*, actually," Lydia said, correcting her husband with a tap on the shoulder. "My mother wasn't much for baking. But Grandma's creations would always place at the county fairs," she stated proudly.

Calvin turned to his wife as Luke was helping himself to a second bar.

"Say, honey. Young Luke here was just asking about any strange occurrences here on the farm in the recent past. I can't say I can recollect anything out of the ordinary."

Lydia looked surprised. "Why, don't you remember last year, Cal? All that fuss over that *crop circle* in the north cornfield? I think that's what you called it. Don't you remember? That was about the same time our Molly went missing."

A light seemed to go off in Calvin's head. "Oh, yeah!" His head bobbed in sudden recollection. "Molly, our golden retriever. We were heartbroken over that. Never could figure out what happened to her. Just... disappeared one day. Never came back. Never found her." His voice trailed off in a wistful lull.

"Uh, about the crop circle, sir," Luke said, trying to get things back on track. "What can you tell me about it?"

"Oh yeah," Calvin said. "Well, Lydia's right, Luke. You see, last fall— guess it was mid-September or so—I went to harvest the north field of corn." He pointed out the side window. "Just this side of that stand of trees you see there in the distance, down a tractor path, I was surprised to find a large swath of trampled and ripped-up corn. In a spiral pattern. Like those crop circles you see on the History Channel. Only much smaller. Maybe thirty feet round, 'n so. But at the center was a large hole in the ground. Like someone took a shovel to it. Didn't know what to make of it at first."

Luke's heart skipped a beat. *Looks like Jake was telling the truth.*

"Did you report it to the police?"

Calvin laughed. "Hell no! I figured it was a teenage prank. Ya know, like maybe a beer party. Those kids will do the damnedest things, dontcha know. I've chased them away partying in my fields more than once. Even threatened to call the police one time." He took a sip of tea and calmed down. "But I know how it is," he said. "I was a kid once!"

He patted Lydia's hand as she squeezed his shoulder.

Luke forced a smile. "Calvin, would you mind taking me to where this disturbance occurred? I mean, I'm sure you're right. Probably just a bunch of rowdy kids blowing off steam." He went out on a limb. "But you see, I'm also investigating what I'd like to call... similar disturbances in the county. Possibly... uh, sinkholes or some other geological phenomenon." He was improvising now.

Calvin sat back and smiled. "So, you've heard about the others, too?"

Luke was taken aback. "The *others?*"

"Sure. This ain't the first time. Other farmers around here have talked about these circles. Small to be sure. Nothing to get all riled up about. Become almost commonplace. But this was the first time I ever seen one. Haven't seen any since, though."

Luke swallowed hard. "I understand." His hand trembled a bit as he jotted down a few notes. "So, you said you could take me there? Where it happened?"

"Sure. I can take you there. But that was ten months ago. The field's been plowed and replanted since then."

"Hmm. Sure, I understand. But I'd really appreciate it."

Luke followed Calvin's pickup truck in his SUV, which, not surprisingly, pulled off to the side of the road right where Luke had been forty minutes earlier. The corn was only inches high, so navigating the field was an easy matter. About fifty feet into the field, Calvin waved his arms, describing the extent of the "disturbance," which covered an area of about twenty feet round.

"So, as you can see, there's not much to see now," Calvin said.

Luke pondered. "Yes, of course. But, if you wouldn't mind, when I return with my botanist friend... er, my consulting scientist... we might want to do a little digging of our own." He was now thinking about his deputy-detective friend as well. "Maybe even a little GPR surveying. That is, if you wouldn't mind."

"GPR surveying?" Calvin repeated with a puzzled look. "What exactly is that?"

"Ground-penetrating radar, useful for locating buried objects and underground geological formations," Luke explained. "You know, things like 'sinkholes' and such."

Calvin rubbed his chin. "Well, I guess that would be alright. As long as I get compensated for any damaged corn. That *radar* thing. That's not gonna harm the corn any, is it?"

Luke shook his head. "No. It's perfectly safe." The wheels were already turning in his head on how best to approach Dan on this one without divulging the original source of his information: Jake and Scott Emery.

Back at the farmhouse, Luke and Calvin shared contact information.

"I'll give you a call to arrange a return visit," Luke said. "Probably sometime next week, if that's okay."

Calvin merely nodded, and they shook hands. Luke doffed his hat to Mrs. Mertz. "Ma'am." After accepting a bag of lemon bars "for the road," he thanked her before turning and heading for his SUV.

Back down the road, Jake and his son were already waiting for Luke by the GMO sign. Luke briefed them on his encounter with the farmer and his wife and his plans to return with his botanist friend... and the ground-penetrating radar. They questioned him about the radar and where was he going to get hold of a machine like that. "I got my sources," he told them. Believing that discretion was the better part of... well, discretion, he left out the part about contacting his friend Detective Dan Meyers of the Sheboygan County Sheriff's Office.

BACK ON THE FARM, Calvin had followed Luke out into the barnyard. Walking down the driveaway, he caught a glimpse of Luke's SUV stopping by the GMO sign. Squinting and shading his eyes, he observed two other men, one older, one younger, exchange some words and looks of recognition with Luke before getting into the vehicle and driving off together.

"Hmm. Wonder what that's all about," he mumbled, scratching his head.

THAT EVENING LUKE phoned Aiyanna to tell her about his visit to the Mertz farm under the cover of his ongoing investigations into GMO corn, crop circles, and sinkholes. He said he had good reason to suspect there might be a connection with the Gloria Emery missing persons case but wasn't free to divulge his sources at this time. Aiyanna acted a little put off by this but in the end conceded "a reporter's right to confidentiality."

"I told Mr. Mertz I'd like to return with my consulting scientist to take soil and corn samples and maybe do a little GPR scanning to check for sinkholes and underground anomalies."

"Hmm. By 'consulting scientist' I assume you mean me," Aiyanna countered with a touch of sarcasm in her voice.

"But... of course," he stammered. "We're a team, right?"

"Uh-huh. If you say so."

"Listen, sorry about the confidentiality thing. But it will all come out in the end, I promise."

Luke said he planned to discuss the use of ground-penetrating radar with Dan but wasn't sure how to go about it without divulging his sources. He had promised to keep their identities confidential. At least for the time being.

"Well, you'd better be careful how you tread with Dan," she said. "He can usually, well, see *through* things pretty easily. Or, I should say, see things the way he chooses to see them."

He wasn't exactly sure what she meant by that but figured it probably had something to do with his failed relationship with her older sister.

"Okay. Well, I'll figure something out," Luke said. "We can talk more about it at my mom's brat fry this weekend."

"I'm looking forward to it," Aiyanna reassured him.

DIGITAL PIN MAPS

Wednesday, July 1, 2015

9:15 a.m. Detective Dan Meyers was absorbed by what he was seeing on the computer screen. Seated beside him, young Deputy Sam Riley was at the controls, flipping pages and windows and navigating the cursor with the ease of a millennial raised on video games and the internet. It was in their DNA.

"So, what am I looking at here?" Dan asked with the acumen of a baggage handler entering an air traffic control tower.

Sam responded without missing a step. "Basically, using the Rigel software, and a few innovative database macros of my own, I've transformed your wall map into a digital model incorporating all variables associated with missing persons cases going back twenty years. It's a data-based linked model that projects a three-dimensional probability distribution map. See the hills and valleys? They represent probability distributions."

Dan nodded. "Okay. If you say so."

Sam clicked a few more times and a new window appeared. Dan smiled as he recognized this map. It resembled the pushpin map on the wall, a two-dimensional geographical representation of Sheboygan County with shaded areas that changed color depending on the variable Sam clicked.

Impressed, Dan turned to Sam. "You've picked up this Rigel software pretty quick. What does it tell us?"

Sam sat back, taking his hands off the keyboard and mouse for a moment. "Well, right now it doesn't tell us much more than your pin map on the wall over there. We need to feed it more information. More variables. We still haven't established a usable pattern." He pointed to the screen. "See all that blue area?"

Dan squinted. "Yeah. Covers about two-thirds of the screen."

"Right," Sam said. "That's all the area we've been able to narrow down as the perp's base of operation with the information we've fed into the database so far."

Dan pondered this. "So you're saying we need more data. More information relating to the missing persons cases."

"Right. I've weeded out all the known and solved cases. What we lack is more information on the *unsolved* cases. The *cold* cases. One interesting thing that most of these cases have in common is the perp seems to favor the warmer weather. About eighty-five percent occurred between May and October."

"Hmm. Cold case. Warm weather," Dan said. "Okay. Well, at least that's something."

Dan's phone rang. It was Luke.

"Well, hello, Sport! To what do I owe a call from our city's most illustrious new member of the free press?"

Luke explained that he possessed some new information that might prove useful in the county's missing persons cases. Dan's eyes widened as he sat down behind his desk. "You have my full attention, Luke."

There was a slight pause. "Uh, I think it's something that's better discussed in person, Dan."

Dan considered this for a moment. "Okay. How soon can you be here?"

"How 'bout thirty minutes?" Luke replied without hesitation.

"Great! See you soon."

~

9:45 A.M. When Luke entered Dan's office, he found Dan and a fellow officer huddled in front of a computer screen. They didn't seem to notice him approaching as he came to stand directly behind them. Peering over Dan's shoulder, Luke took a moment to study the screen before speaking.

"Nice piece of software you have there, Dan."

Dan continued staring at the screen. "Don't you know better than to sneak up behind an officer of the law?" he deadpanned with a touch of feigned reproach in his voice. Turning slowly, he asked, "Know anything about geographic profiling, Luke?"

Luke thought a moment. "Just what I learned on the crime show channels."

"Hmm. Figured as much. Yes, well..." Dan started, then turned to his deputy. "Why don't you explain it to him, Sam."

"Sure." Sam paused. "But, uh, aren't you forgetting your manners, Dan?" He turned to Luke and held out his hand. "I don't believe I've had the pleasure. Name is Sam Riley. Deputy Sam Riley."

Luke shook his hand. "Luke Kramer, reporter for the *Sheboygan Dispatch*."

Dan harrumphed as Sam took over to explain the Rigel software in the most rudimentary terms, which was enough to satisfy Luke. He explained how they were hoping the software would help with their investigations into the backlog of unsolved missing persons cases and described in detail their progress so far.

"But what we really need is more correlating data to feed the computer model," Sam explained.

A light went off in Luke's head. He had spent all morning mulling over how best to broach the topic of Gloria Emery. Now he jumped at the opportunity.

"Well, maybe I can help with that," he said.

Dan and Sam traded curious looks.

"Well, please do, my young Luke Skywalker," Dan replied. "And may the Force be with you."

Luke ignored the left-handed remark and proceeded to recount his recent encounter with farmer Calvin Mertz and his wife in the context of his research into GMO corn.

"And then, as we were wrapping things up, almost as an afterthought," Luke continued, "they described a strange occurrence that happened last September. Something about a crop circle in their cornfield where the ground was partially dug up, like someone had taken a shovel to it. Said it was a pretty good-sized hole. They couldn't narrow it down to the exact day, except a possible two-week window in early to mid-September. Well, I got to thinking. Wasn't that around the same time Gloria Emery went missing?"

Dan straightened up. "Gloria Emery? Yes!" He turned to the map on the wall. "Show me where this crop circle digging occurred."

Luke went to the wall map, took a red pushpin, and inserted it at the location of the Mertz farm, off Route 57 between Plymouth and Johnsonville.

Dan slowly nodded. "Hmm, not far from my red 'Gloria Emery' pin, her last-known location just outside Plymouth." He turned to Luke. "So, what else did this farmer have to say?"

"Uh, well, he said there had been reports of *other* so-called crop circles circulating among farmers in that area, going back some years, 'n so. He said no one took any particular note of them, figuring they were all just some teenage pranks."

Luke turned around and walked slowly back to the map, eyes focused, zeroing in on the region he knew all too well, the region near his boyhood farm outside Elkhart Lake. He slowly raised his hand and pointed to one yellow cold case pin in particular.

"Tell me, Dan. What missing persons case does this pin represent?"

Dan took a shallow breath and placed a reassuring hand on Luke's shoulder. "I think you know too well, Luke. The Klausman farm. One of our oldest and *coldest* cases."

"Sure, I know," Luke said. He paused a moment. "You must remember that day, Dan. The *crop circle*... if you want to call it that. More of a *mini* crop circle. So, maybe—just maybe—there's some kind of correlation here."

He was hoping Dan would put the pieces together. It seemed to work.

"Hmm," Dan muttered. Pausing a moment, he took a stiff breath, turned to Sam, and began barking orders. "Sam, I want to you to research any and all instances of these so-called mini crop circle cornfield events in the county over the past, oh, let's say... twenty years or so! And enter that information into our database."

Sam's jaw dropped. "Twenty years!"

Dan relented. "Okay, let's start with seventeen years."

But Luke didn't stop with the crop circles. Producing several maps from his briefcase, he pushed aside some loose papers and pens on a nearby table and laid out the maps. "And if it's not too much trouble," he said, "would it be possible to add this GMO corn crop information into your computer model? They give the locations of all GMO and non-GMO cornfields in the county over the past fifteen years."

Dan and Sam both stared at him in seeming disbelief, but Luke challenged them right back. "Come on! You said you were looking for correlating data. Right?"

Dan finally gave in. "Okay, okay! Sam, you know what to do." Turning back to Luke he added, "Can you leave the maps with us? This may take some time."

"Sure. Have at it!" Luke said, then thought for a moment. "You know, I could do an article on these reported crop circle sightings. It might help flush out more first- and secondhand accounts. I can have the readers report their crop circle experiences to my attention at the *Dispatch* before handing them over to you guys for proper vetting."

Dan nodded. "Good idea. That'll help weed out the wackos, so we don't waste our time chasing down aliens or Bigfoot," he said, laughing.

"You got it. And one more thing," Luke continued. "The farmer said Aiyanna and I could return for soil and corn samples as part of our GMO and mushroom studies. He also agreed to our doing some digging of our own and the use of ground-penetrating radar as part of our scientific investigations—you know, to look for sinkholes and other geological anomalies. But of course"—he added with a wink—"with the Gloria Emery case, you never know what else we might find."

Dan grinned and patted Luke on the back. "So, Luke, have you suddenly turned criminal investigative reporter?"

"Well, I just figured you'd welcome the opportunity, Dan."

Sam chuckled. "Looks like he's doing your work for you, boss."

Dan gave a twisted smile. "Well, I must admit, he's laid the *ground-work* for me. Pun intended. Har har!"

Chapter Twenty

WORTH THE SQUEEZE?

Friday, July 3, 2015

Luke was running thirty minutes behind, and no sooner had he taken a seat at his desk Friday morning than two notifications on his computer screen alerted him to one missed call and an urgent chat message from Ted Holtz: "I want you in my office as soon as you get in. ASAP!"

He gulped, at a loss as to what could be so urgent. Maybe a new assignment. Or a raise! Nah, he'd only been with the paper less than five months.

When Luke entered the editor's office, Ted was on the phone with his back turned. Still talking, he motioned with a backward wave of his hand for Luke to have a seat. *Eyes in the back of his head*, Luke thought.

"Okay, okay. I understand. I'll be sure to talk to him," Ted barked into the phone. "Not to worry. Yes. I can vouch for him. He's a very upstanding and trustworthy sort... You betcha. And a good day to you too, Mr. Mertz! And have a very happy Fourth!"

Ted turned around slowly in his swivel chair and leaned forward. Resting both elbows on the desk with hands clenched under his chin, he took a few moments. At last, letting out a long sigh, he leaned back, chair squeaking, his fingers interlaced behind his head, and spoke.

"Luke, I just got off the phone with Calvin Mertz."

He waited for a response.

"Uh..." Luke's voice faltered. "Did you say Calvin Mertz?"

"Yes. Calvin Mertz. *Farmer* Calvin Mertz." Ted folded his hands and leaned forward. "Luke, I went out on a limb and vouched for you. I hope I did the right thing."

Luke nodded. His heart was racing. "Yes. Thank you, sir. You did the right thing."

"He said you paid him a visit the other day," Ted continued. "Something about"—he paused to check his notes—"crop circles and sinkholes and digging up his cornfield with ground-penetrating radar?" He looked straight at Luke with an accusatory stare. "Said that after you left the farm, he saw you picking up two other fellas down the road, like you knew them. The one appeared to him to be, shall we say, an 'unsavory sort.' He said he became suspicious and got to thinking, 'What would they be looking for and hoping to find in my cornfield?'"

Luke swallowed hard. "Well, you see, my visit was part of our ongoing investigation into GMO corn."

Ted nodded. "Yes, he did say that. But he said the subject then turned to these infernal crop circles. What in tarnation is that all about?"

Luke squirmed in his seat. "Yes, Ted. But that was *after* he mentioned them first. Actually"—he took it up a notch—"it was his *wife* who first brought up the subject." Luke played innocent. "You see, considering the timing of this event, having occurred last September, I made the connection between the occurrence of this crop circle and the disappearance of... what was her name... Gloria Emery. You remember. It was in all the news. That unsolved murder case."

"Oh my God!" Ted guffawed. "So now you've become a criminal investigator! I don't recall assigning you as sheriff's office liaison."

"Uh, no. You're right, of course." Luke spoke quickly, almost tripping over his own words. "But I *have* become acquainted with Detective Dan Meyers, who is actively investigating this case. We met a month ago at Duke's Bar and, well, hit it off actually. He was the one who put me in touch with the botanist from Madison. You know, the one who—"

"Whoa! Slow down, son!" Ted snapped, raising his voice enough to elicit a startled look from a passing clerk outside his office door. "Let's just put the brakes on!"

Luke was taken aback. He nervously signaled to the clerk through the glass wall partition, indicating *everything was alright*.

Drumming his fingers on the desktop, Ted regained his composure and took a different tack. "Luke, my boy, you are a good reporter. I really like you. And I am certain you will go far in the newspaper business. But I think you are way over your skis on this one! And I'm asking you—no, I'm *telling* you—to back off! Please! Just do your job. 'Special features' reporter, remember?"

Luke cast a sullen glance at the floor, and for a moment they both simply sat there.

The ringing phone broke the silence.

Ted raised an index finger as if to say "Give me a minute" and picked up the phone.

"Hello, Ted Holtz, Editor. *Sheboygan Dis...* oh, good morning, Detective. What can I do for you?"

There was a long pause, followed by an occasional nod, accented with a "yes, sir" or "absolutely." Luke had never witnessed such quiescence from a man so accustomed to dominating a conversation. Ted concluded with, "Thank you, Dan. I'll see what I can do. Absolutely! You betcha! I'll let him know. Have a nice day!"

Ted remained silent for a while after hanging up, tapping his desk blotter with his pen as he gathered his thoughts. His whole demeanor had changed.

"Well, that was Dan Meyers. *Detective* Dan Meyers of the county sheriff's office." He took a deep breath before continuing. "It appears he has corroborated your story and has a shared interest in these so-called crop circles and sinkholes. Said you put him on to it, and, after some initial investigation, they've managed to hit pay dirt. He said he wasn't able to get hold of you, so he called me."

Luke breathed a sigh of relief. "I see," was all he could think to say, failing to suppress a smile.

Ted gave a wan smile in return. "Yes, well, let's hope the juice is worth the squeeze, my friend." His tone became conciliatory. "Okay, son. You've got my permission to pursue this story." He jabbed the air with his index finger. "*Just* as long as it doesn't detract from your ongoing assignments. *Verstehen sie?*"

"Yes, Mr. Holtz," Luke said, beaming inside. "Understood."

"Detective Meyers said for you to give him a call. Didn't want to tell me," Ted said in a huff. "So keep me posted on any further developments. We need to figure out how to report on this moving forward."

Luke nodded. "Yes, of course, Ted."

But, of course, Luke had no intention of revealing the true source of his information: the Emerys. For now, he planned to keep this from Detective Dan as well. There was a term for that, he recalled: confidential news source.

On leaving Ted's office, Luke was whistling a happy tune as he walked back to his desk with a jaunty bounce to his step, which did not go unnoticed by his fellow workers. He acknowledged their blank stares with a polite nod and a smile.

Immediately he phoned Dan, but his call went straight voice mail. *Damn it! Missed him.*

"Hi, Dan. This is Luke. Sorry I missed your call earlier. You can reach me on my cell at any time. Many thanks."

Luke spent the remainder of the morning with Pam reviewing the final draft of the latest installment of their GMO corn story to be published in the Sunday supplement. Though he liked it, one detail Pam had inserted at the last minute bothered him.

"Hmm. Are you sure you want to include the part about the tooth in the cereal box? Take, for example, 'This human tooth find indicates further negligence that only reinforces the case against GMO corn producers.' Don't you think that's, well, uh... *stretching* things a bit?"

Pam cocked her head and glared back at him defensively. "No, not at all! I think it's a perfect segue into the final concluding paragraphs."

Luke sat back and shook his head. "Look," he said, with a conciliatory smile, "I like the story. But maybe we can soften it a little. Keep the cereal box incident, but let the readers make their own connections, draw their own conclusions."

In the end, Pam gave in. She set about rewriting that portion while Luke continued copy editing the remainder of the draft.

After lunch Luke got the return call from Detective Dan that he had been anxiously awaiting. Dan said there was a breakthrough in the Emma Hauptmann missing persons case and wanted to give Luke the chance to break the story.

"There's also some developments in this crop circle business that Sam's been looking into that I think you'll find interesting."

"Well, that's great, Dan. And I surely appreciate your giving me first dibs on the Emma Hauptmann story. Thanks for thinking of me." An idea came to him. "How about we get together at Duke's later on for their Friday night fish fry? My treat. Kill two birds at once, eh?"

They agreed to meet at seven o'clock.

After the call, Luke pondered tomorrow's Fourth of July celebration at his mom's. He was in the process of exchanging emails with his childhood friend Albert Hollander to confirm that he was coming and to give him directions ("Yes, Clara and I are very much looking forward to it!"), when his mom called him.

"Sorry to interrupt you at work, son, but I wanted to ask if you wouldn't mind picking up some sweet corn for the brat fry tomorrow on your way up."

She spoke in a slow, purposeful way, like she was measuring each word, with her classic 'Scansin accent on full display.

"Sure, Mom, no problem. How much should I get?"

She paused. "I think three dozen ears should do the trick."

Luke jotted a note to himself as a reminder. "Okay, no problem. Can do."

Another pause. "And I do hope your new lady friend will be able to make it," she added.

Luke rolled his eyes. "She's a professional coworker, Mom. Not my *lady* friend, as you put it."

"Well, yes, of course. But she *is* a lady, isn't she? And she *is* your friend, right?"

Luke bowed his head. "Sure, Mom. Have it your way. And yes, she is coming. She even offered to get there early to help set things up."

"Oh, that's so nice of her. I do so look forward to meeting her, Luke."

"And she you, as well."

After hanging up, a thought came to mind. He quickly punched in Aiyanna's work phone number. *I hope she hasn't left for the day.*

"Hello. This is Aiyanna-Nez Black Bear."

Perfect! "Hello, Aiyanna. This is Luke."

After exchanging pleasantries, he asked if she still planned on being at his mom's early the next day to help set up.

"Sure. If that's okay."

"Yes, most definitely okay!" Luke replied. "Listen, I have to pick up some sweet corn on the way, and I know the perfect place to do it. I was wondering if you could meet me in Plymouth, so we can take one car."

She didn't hesitate. "Sure, I could do that."

Luke explained that he planned to stop by the Mertz farm stand to pick up the corn. A perfect opportunity to introduce her to Calvin Mertz and his wife and set up a future field trip. "You know, like I was telling you. Those so-called crop circles. I think meeting you would help smooth things over with the Mertzes."

He related this morning's conversation with Ted Holtz and Calvin's apparent irritation over this whole business.

"Okay. Where in Plymouth do you want to meet?"

"How 'bout the Pony Bar and Grill? Like before. I mean, you know where it is. We could leave your car there and take my SUV to Mom's place... I mean, *my* mom's place."

He closed his eyes and bit his knuckle for sounding so presumptive, but she didn't seem to mind.

"Sounds like a plan," she said. "I'll bring some soil sample bags along just in case we get the opportunity."

"Sure. Just in case."

"Great! See you tomorrow."

Chapter Twenty-One

FRIDAY NIGHT FISH FRY

Friday Evening, July 3, 2015

Later that evening, right after work, Luke took his usual three-mile circuit run along the shores of Lake Michigan, enjoying the steady cool breeze coming off the lake amid the squawk of seagulls and other shore birds feeding at the water's edge. As he jogged south along North Side Municipal Beach, his route took him past Sheboygan's Deland Park and the Harbor Centre Marina, within easy view of one of Sheboygan's most prominent landmarks: the breakwater lighthouse located about a thousand feet offshore at the tip of the north pier jetty.

Passing the US Coast Guard station at the mouth of the harbor, he turned west, picking up the Riverfront Boardwalk, which followed the river through the city's revitalized harbor area, with its long string of wharfs and recreational fishing boats moored on the left and restaurants and other commercial establishments on the right.

In contrast to the beach and jetty, there was a notable absence of bird droppings, and the seagulls were nowhere to be found. Looking up, he saw the reason why. Attached high atop a pole were two mechanical birds—hawks to be precise—flying in endless circles on a tethered rod supported from the pole's center, emitting an occasional squawk to alert nearby seagulls of a clear and present danger. Luke smiled. *Looks like Randy's mechanical scarecrows really work!*

Continuing along the harbor path as it approached the Eighth Street Bridge, he circled past Duke's Tavern and concluded his run by heading north along Riverfront Drive back toward his condominium.

After a long, leisurely shower and a brief look at his emails, he checked the time: 6:30 p.m. *Perfect!* Stuffing his notebook in his back pocket, he headed out on foot, backtracking down Riverfront Drive to Duke's Tavern for his seven o'clock rendezvous with Detective Dan.

Once he arrived at Duke's, a pretty, auburn-haired hostess with braided pigtails and a charming smile greeted Luke at the door, with menu in hand.

"Are you here for the fish fry?' she asked, with an unmistakable Scottish brogue.

"Sure am." He gave her a closer look. "Haven't seen you here before. Are you new to the area?"

"Not the area," she replied. "Just the tavern. This is my first night."

Luke took the menu and nodded. "Oh, I see. Well, please, 'lead on Macduff!'"

She cocked her head and gave him a vacant stare.

"Lord Macduff, the Thane of Fife?" he added for clarity, but it seemed to only add to her confusion.

"I'm sorry," he said, somewhat embarrassed. "Just a silly... Shakespearean reference."

"Oh, sure." She giggled.

Clearing his throat, he quickly changed the subject. "I'm supposed to meet a friend here." He checked his cell phone: 6:50 p.m. "He should be here any minute now. Can you please give us a booth by a window overlooking the harbor?"

"No problem," she said. "Just follow me."

Luke took a seat and looked over the menu. Scotch eggs was on the list of appetizers. *Hmm, gotta try them!* he thought. He figured he owed it to the pretty Scottish hostess.

He flagged down a passing waitress, an older woman with a hefty frame and a dour expression.

"What can I get for you, young man?" she asked as she flipped open her order pad.

"I'd like to try one of those 'Scottish Eggs,'" he said. "And could you bring me a Leinenkugel?"

"Are you twenty-one, son?"

Luke grinned. "Last time I checked, yes ma'am."

The woman leaned on one hip. Clearly, she did not see the humor in his remark.

"You can ask Lil," he added. "She'll vouch for me."

"Well, Lil is not working tonight. You'll have to deal with me, dearie," she replied with the willfulness of a prison guard.

Defeated, he was forced to reach for his wallet and produce his driver's license. She was satisfied.

Fifteen minutes passed. Luke enjoyed the egg and was sipping his beer, studying a large charter fishing boat as it made its lazy way upriver and maneuvered into its waiting berth, when he heard a familiar baritone voice from behind.

"Is this seat taken?"

Luke turned. "Evening, Dan. Ten minutes late. Gotta dock your pay for that."

Dan took the seat across from Luke. "Hey, I thought you'd be halfway through your fish fry dinner by now," he said with a smirk.

"Nah, that would've been impolite. But like I said, the dinner is on me tonight... if the information you have is worth the meal."

Dan growled. "Of course. I wouldn't let you down, my friend."

The fish fry was not a disappointment. Washed down with your favorite brew, it was the perfect way to end your workweek in Wisconsin.

Getting down to business, Luke pulled the notebook from his back pants pocket and clicked his pen.

"Okay, so what is this new breaking development?" he asked. "Are you speaking on the record, Dan?"

Dan assured him that he was—except for certain details that would jeopardize the case if made public—and proceeded to divulge the latest findings. It seemed that Adam Emery, Jacob's eldest son, had gone from being a "person of interest" to the primary suspect in the May 8 disappearance of Emma Hauptmann. After scouring Adam's pickup truck for evidence, the Plymouth Police Department's forensic team located a bloodstain in the truck bed that matched Emma's blood type, along with a bunch of empty beer cans. A DNA check produced a match between the bloodstains and hair samples taken from Emma's comb provided by her parents. DNA from the beer cans also matched Adam's DNA, which wasn't surprising but was consistent with his use of the truck. Adam insisted he didn't know how Emma's blood got in the bed of his pickup truck.

"And then there's Milly's testimony," Dan continued.

"Milly?"

"Adam's wife," Dan said. "Apparently, Milly has changed her testimony. She originally stated that Adam was home by seven that evening, right after dropping Emma off at the Pony Bar and Grill near her home in Plymouth. *Now*, however, Milly says Adam didn't return home till well past midnight. He told her he spent the evening at the Pony with some old friends. But when the police questioned the folks at the bar, they couldn't recall seeing him there that night. And of course, they'd already stated that Emma never showed up either."

Luke considered this. "So, let me get this straight. Adam's original story was that he dropped Emma off in Plymouth after work, then went straight home, which Milly corroborated. Now it seems he never showed up at the Pony, like he told his wife, and never made it home till after midnight. So, what was he doing during all that time? Is that right?"

Dan smiled. "That about sums it up."

Luke looked up from his notes. "So, what made Milly change her story?"

Dan leaned forward. "Well, when she walked into the police department last Wednesday, the officers said she was pretty well bruised up around the eyes and arms. She declined to say how it happened, but they suspect it was Adam. He has a long history of domestic abuse. So maybe Milly just had enough and decided she wasn't going to cover up for him any longer."

"I see," Luke said as he made some additional notes.

"But Luke, that last piece of information is off the record. We don't want to publicize it to protect the witness. No telling what Adam would do if he knew his wife was changing her story."

Luke nodded. "Yes. I understand." He paused. "But tell me, what took the police so long to come up with that piece of blood and DNA evidence? You'd think they'd have discovered it on the initial investigation."

Dan sighed. "Well, you know there's always a question of jurisdiction in cases like this. Who takes the lead in the investigation—the local police or the county sheriff's office? Or even the feds in certain cases. It just took... well, a little while to sort things out."

Luke sipped his beer. "Lucky the bloodstain wasn't washed away in the meantime," he said softly.

Dan nodded with a barely audible grunt.

Luke turned a page in his notebook. "I want to thank you, Dan, for sharing this with me. I promise to treat it with all due respect. Can I use your name as my source?"

Dan smiled. "Most definitely, my friend."

Luke realized, of course, that he was being used as well, but that was okay. This way, Dan would get the scoop on the Plymouth police as the source of information.

"Thank you, Dan. You may want to check the Sunday morning edition of the *Dispatch*."

Dan smiled as they clicked beer mugs.

Sitting back, Luke looked at him pointedly. "So tell me. What about this other development you mentioned with the crop circles?"

Dan's demeanor became more relaxed, like the hard part was over and now the fun would begin.

"Well, first of all, Sam input that GMO crop field map information you gave him Wednesday morning into the computer model, and the results were *somewhat* encouraging."

Luke raised his eyebrows. "Boy, Sam's a fast worker!"

Dan chuckled. "Yeah, like a bloodhound on the trail! Doesn't give up once he's got the scent of the game." Clearing his throat, he leaned forward. "So, according to Sam, the model shows a correlation between the GMO cornfields and the last-known location of the unsolved missing persons over recent years."

"Well, that's good, isn't it?"

"Yeah, well..." Dan squirmed. "Except it also shows a similar correlation with *non-GMO* cornfields."

Luke pondered that. "Is there a statistically significant difference?"

Dan sat back. "Well, not much, according to Sam."

Luke was disappointed. He shook his head. "That's too bad."

"But remember," Dan explained, "these were last-known locations, not the actual site of the crime. So, there wouldn't necessarily be a close correlation even if there were somehow a connection between the two."

"Hmm. Guess you're right."

"However!" Dan continued, perking up. "After a preliminary investigation into these so-called mini crop circles, he's finding a much closer correlation. A greater than ninety percent match with your GMO cornfield locations! Of course, he's just getting started with a handful of recent sightings that he's been able to corroborate since Wednesday." Dan checked his notes. "Also, he connected the time and place of *two* missing persons to two separate crop circle events. And of course there are the two cases we're already familiar with, namely Jake's wife, Gloria, last fall, and"—he paused—"the case of your own sister sixteen years ago. The key parameters here are time and location of the crop circle event, which we are hoping to match with the time and last-seen location of a missing person. With this correlation we think we can establish the crop circle locations as the actual crime sites, then use this information to perform a probability mapping of the perp's base of operations."

Luke blew out with puffed cheeks. "Wow, that *is* something! But sounds like a rather convoluted and arduous undertaking."

Dan nodded. "Yes. But with computers, anything's possible. And I think Sam is up to the challenge."

"Maybe Aiyanna's research will eventually shed more light on this."

"Perhaps," Dan said. "But one other thing I'd like to do is expand our area of search up nort' into our neighboring counties. Up around Kiel. But I'll need to talk to Sheriff Bradley in Manitowoc to get permission. I suspect our perp is no respecter of county lines."

Luke and Dan finished off the evening with another round of beer. Checking the time, Luke reluctantly excused himself.

"Got to get to work on this article right away if we want to get the scoop," he said.

"Most definitely." Dan nodded. "Go burn the midnight oil, Sport! Time's a wastin'!"

As he was leaving, Luke did a quick about-face. "Oh, yes. I hope you'll be able to make the brat fry tomorrow at my mom's place, Dan."

"Does a bear crap in the woods? Wouldn't want to miss a good brat fry, now, would I? What time should I be there?"

"Any time after one o'clock, 'n so."

Dan raised his mug. "See you there!"

Chapter Twenty-Two

SONS AND DAUGHTERS OF GERMAN IMMIGRANTS

Friday, July 3, 2015

Cynthia Kramer shut the doors of her Anything Goes Antique Barn earlier than usual on Friday afternoon to get a jump on the Fourth of July weekend celebration she was hosting for family and friends. Cynthia, Luke's mother, had sold the family farm, moved to nearby Elkhart Lake, and opened the antique barn less than four years prior, one year after her husband of twenty-five years, Hermann, passed away following a brief but desperate fight with lung cancer. A farmer at heart, Hermann worked the fields right up to the week before he died. Though he was never a smoker, the doctors said it was probably all the chemicals and fertilizers that took him.

Of sturdy Germanic peasant stock, blond-haired Cynthia Einsbach Kramer boasted a solid but pleasing frame and austere disposition, in seeming contradiction to her love of music, dancing, and festive social gatherings. Friday nights would find her and Hermann at the local fish fry with friends, and Saturday nights at their favorite dance hall, their polka dancing prowess on full, energetic display.

Both Cynthia and Hermann were direct descendants of the first wave of German immigrants to the region in the 1840s. For the most part, their forebears were not met with open arms by the local inhabitants, Yankees from New England who had recently settled the area less than ten years earlier. Privation and hardship marked the lives of these early settlers, Yankees and Germans alike. But for the "Dutch" newcomers, the hardship was worsened because they were generally looked down upon as unsophisticated and ignorant foreigners, not an uncommon experience faced by each new wave of immigrants over the course of America's history. To compound the situation, the Germans tended to keep to themselves, retaining their language and customs, which included "beer drinking, dancing, card playing, and Sunday amusements," much to the horror of their established Puritan hosts. But, with steadfast resilience and perseverance, the population grew and eventually prospered.

What drew Cynthia to the town of Elkhart Lake was the same thing that attracted so many to the lakeside resort town during the past 150 years: Great Elkhart Lake. With pristine beauty, the clear, spring-fed, turquoise waters of Great Elkhart Lake shone like a jewel under the midday sun amid the thickly forested Kettle Moraine region of Sheboygan County. Surrounded on three sides by high wooded bluffs, the one-square-mile lake gave the appearance of having been carved from the earth with a giant ice-cream scoop and backfilled with water. Given that it was gouged from the kettle-pocked earth by retreating glaciers from the last ice age, that metaphor was not without merit. Having no inlet, the lake was spring-fed from below and outflowed into the vast nearby Sheboygan Marsh.

Cynthia occupied a modest three-bedroom, single-story bungalow on the outskirts of town, adjacent to the antique barn which she owned and operated. With an innate entrepreneurial spirit and business acumen, she managed quite well and in under four years had acquired five part-time employees and a full-time supervisor capable of managing the store in her absence.

A fastidious homemaker, Cynthia took great pride in her home, yard, and flower gardens, both front and back, complete with trellised redbrick walkways, a central gazebo, firepit, and a dual-stone charcoal grill. Not the gas variety, mind you, which she abhorred. Only the real thing would do, a genuine charcoal and mesquite briquette grill. Her kitchen with adjoining sunroom exited onto a two-tier wood deck complete with porch swing, umbrella table and chairs, hanging plants, and other decorative accoutrements. The sunroom was the epicenter of card-playing activity on Thursday nights, when she hosted her lady friends for an evening of Sheepshead, Schafkopf, and Hearts. Her "card clutch," as she referred to it.

But more than card playing, Cynthia's greatest passion was bird watching. Her backyard contained an eclectic assortment of hanging bird feeders, all within easy viewing from her sunroom and kitchen windows. They attracted a wide variety of native bird species, including the American goldfinch, northern cardinal, blue jay, black-capped chickadee, a variety of woodpeckers, and on certain occasions her favorites, the ruby-throated and rufous hummingbirds on their yearly migratory journeys from Mexico.

The driveway to the right of the house led back to a two-car garage and adjoining shed, which she had cleared and set up with picnic tables and chairs to provide cover from the sun or rain, whichever weather condition decided to prevail. Fortunately, the forecast for the coming weekend called for fair skies with seasonal temperatures and low humidity.

LATER THAT FRIDAY EVENING, after removing the final batch of dessert bars from the oven and putting the finishing touches on her coleslaw and family-favorite German potato salad, Cynthia adjourned to the living room, took a DVD from her classic movie collection—*Oklahoma!*, her favorite musical—and placed it in the DVD player. She paused in front of the entertainment center to adjust the family photos symmetrically arranged on the top three shelves, studying them for a moment with a pleasing sigh before sitting in her favorite recliner with a hot cup of ginger tea as she settled in for an evening of TV movie entertainment.

On the top center shelf was a bifold picture frame with photos of Cynthia and Hermann: their wedding day on the left and their twenty-fifth anniversary on the right. The difference was stark, a young and vigorous Hermann on his wedding day in contrast to the pale and drawn latter-day Hermann on the right. That picture was taken a mere four months before his passing.

On the third shelf down were three pictures. In the center was a young girl, vibrant and smiling, in pigtails and a calico dress: young Alice, only weeks before she went missing on August 20, 1999. To the left was Alice's baby picture, adorably cute with a pink bow topping a mop of auburn hair. To her right was brother Lukas's lone and solitary, unsmiling, college graduation picture.

The second shelf was filled with a gallery of pictures of another young man in various poses. In one, he was running track and field. In another, he was holding a trophy, posing with a younger Hermann, smiling and shaking hands. In yet another, he was a newlywed, posing with his wedding party and strikingly beautiful blond-haired bride. The most recent had him kneeling in front of a fishing trawler hovering over a prize-winning West Coast bluefin tuna. This was Cynthia and Hermann's eldest child, thirty-year-old Stan Kramer.

Lying on the coffee table in front of Cynthia was a postcard from Stan she'd received the week prior. Postmarked San Francisco, it announced that he would be in Chicago this week attending a conference and was planning to drop by this holiday weekend for "good old-fashioned Wisconsin brat fry." Cynthia reached down and picked up the postcard, shook her head, and let out a sigh. She hadn't told Luke about this for fear he might not show up if he knew his older brother was planning to be there. And the fact that Luke had invited a female friend to the brat fry made her that much more nervous. She feared the perfect storm and secretly hoped Stan's business in Chicago would detain him and keep him from showing up.

Considering this, she got up again and slowly approached the entertainment center. Pausing a moment, she took Stan's wedding picture from the shelf, crossed over to the credenza, and placed the picture facedown in its center drawer.

Chapter Twenty-Three

THE BRAT FRY

Saturday, July 4, 2015

Saturday morning found Cynthia up with the sun to put the calico baked beans in the Crock-Pot. It was another family recipe favorite of unknown origin handed down from her grandmother and her grandmother before that. "The bacon rind is what gives it that certain je ne sais quoi," she would say. She then set about making final preparations for the day's event, setting out the tablecloths, plastic utensils, and napkins and packing the ice coolers with beer and soft drinks. She was depending on Luke to bring the corn, set up the grills, and prep and grill the brats and corn.

Now the only thing left to do was wait for Luke and Aiyanna. She was looking forward to meeting Aiyanna. Luke spoke so highly of her.

It was a few minutes past eleven when Luke and Aiyanna pulled into his mom's driveway. She was standing there waiting for them. Luke scanned the scene and smiled. He had never seen the place—or his mom— looking better.

Cynthia greeted him with a warm hug, then turned to Aiyanna with a smile.

"So, you must be Aiyanna. I'm so happy to meet you," she said, reaching out with both hands and cupping Aiyanna's outstretched hand.

"Thank you, Mrs. Kramer," Aiyanna replied, "but the pleasure is all mine." She looked around. "You have such an adorable place here. I just love the gardens."

Luke spoke up. "Aiyanna is a botanist, Mom. I told her about your gardens and she couldn't wait to see them."

"Oh, that's lovely, my dear. I must show you around. But you must call me Cynthia. *Mrs. Kramer* is just too formal." She comically postured like a staunch Prussian general.

Aiyanna laughed. "Certainly... Cynthia."

Luke opened the tailgate to retrieve the three dozen ears of corn he and Aiyanna picked up earlier that morning from the Mertzes' farm stand as planned. They were fortunate to have arrived in time to speak with Calvin and his wife, Lydia, before they closed the stand for the day. Lydia warmed up right away to Aiyanna, and that was enough to seal the deal. They set a date—Wednesday, July 8—to return for the soil sampling and GPR survey.

"Where do you want me to put the corn, Mom?" Luke shouted out.

Cynthia waved her arm in the direction of the garage. "Over there by the trash cans will do fine, son. We can shuck them later."

As Luke was readying the grill, loading it with charcoal briquettes, his mom spoke up. "Don't forget the mesquite, Luke. Adds flavor."

"Got it covered, Mom."

As an afterthought, she added, "Oh, yes, I almost forgot. Can you please go by Piggly Wiggly once and get some ice for the coolers? Be sure to get enough. There's plenty of room in the chest freezer to store the extra ice."

Luke looked at the coolers. "Three coolers. Got it covered, Mom."

CYNTHIA CONTINUED SETTING up while Luke was out getting ice. She took this opportunity to chat and get better acquainted with Aiyanna. Cynthia learned that Aiyanna had an older sister and two younger siblings—identical twin brothers actually. She'd grown up in Black River

Falls, Wisconsin, a three-hour drive to the west, where her parents still resided. Her father, Larry Black Bear, was a respected elder and active in tribal affairs, boasting greater than 90 percent Native American blood. Her mother was of mixed Native American and French American descent, hence her hyphenated first name, Aiyanna-Nez, to honor her mother's French heritage and family name.

"You know," Aiyanna said, "it was Jean Nicolet, a French explorer, who was the first European to set foot in Wisconsin and make contact with my Native American ancestors. I think it was in 1634, up in Red Bank near present-day Green Bay."

Cynthia expressed surprise and laughed. "Oh, my! I didn't realize the French were here before the Germans."

She was joking, of course. Remnants of French influence were scattered about the state in the form of names for places and rivers, like "Fond du Lac" and "Prairie du Chien," which translated to "Lake Bottom" and "Prairie Dog," respectively.

Cynthia reciprocated with her own, mainly German family history, "with a wee bit of the Irish and Scots thrown into the mix," she said, laughing, making her best attempt at a Scottish brogue. She was the fourth eldest of a large farming family of ten children. A younger sister died of polio at the tender age of two. Only Cynthia and two other brothers had continued in the farming tradition, and they were all now scattered about the Midwest, from Green Bay to Saint Louis to Minneapolis–Saint Paul. One older brother, Clarence, and a younger sister, Edna, still lived close by.

"In fact, you should get to meet them this afternoon," she added.

Passing by the parlor, Aiyanna paused and peered inside.

"Those are lovely pictures, Cynthia," she remarked. "I recognize Luke's graduation picture, but who are the others, if you don't mind my asking?"

"Oh, no, not at all," Cynthia replied.

She put down the dish she was carrying and accompanied Aiyanna into the parlor and over to the entertainment center.

"This one is me and my late husband, Hermann—Luke's father—on our wedding day, thirty-one years ago this past March. And this one is on our twenty-fifth wedding anniversary"—she released an audible sigh—"just weeks before he passed away."

Aiyanna took Cynthia's hand. "Yes, Luke told me about that. It was... lung cancer, was it not?"

Cynthia nodded as she moved on to the next picture. "And this..."

She paused as a tear came to her eye.

Aiyanna finished the sentence for her. "...must be Alice. Luke's younger sister?"

Cynthia took a tissue from her pocket and wiped her eyes. "Yes, our little angel," she said softly, trying to control the tremor in her voice.

Aiyanna put her arm around Cynthia. "Yes, I know about Alice. Luke had trouble telling me about her, but he did manage. He took it pretty hard."

Cynthia nodded. "Yes, we all did. We all took it *very* hard. She was only six years old, you know."

Aiyanna went to the next shelf. "And who is this robust-looking lad?" she asked in a more perky tone.

"Oh, that is Stan, Luke's older brother. He..." She hesitated. "You may actually get to meet him today. He is in Chicago on business but said he'd try to make it up for the Fourth."

"Oh, I see! Luke never told me he had an older brother," Aiyanna replied.

Cynthia frowned and turned away. "Well, I guess I'm not surprised. The two of them never really got along. Sibling rivalry and all that," she said, trying to brush it off. Fact was, she didn't want to get into the thick of it with Aiyanna. Certainly not now. This wasn't the right time. Though she wasn't sure if there would ever be a right time.

"Well, there is still lots of work to be done," she said, eager to change the subject. "Aiyanna, can you please help me get the bratwursts out of the fridge and rinsed off? We need to soak them in cold water before grilling."

Aiyanna grabbed a pack and read the label. "Johnsonville Brats."

"Yes, of course! Only Johnsonville's or Meisfeld's bratwursts will do," Cynthia said proudly.

∽

After returning with the ice, Luke resumed the task of preparing the grill. His mom joined him with a can of starter fluid.

"Here, you're going to need this," she said, offering him the can.

She paused.

"You know, I had a lovely conversation with Aiyanna while you were gone. She is such a nice person. A fine young lady."

"Mm-hmm," Luke said, preoccupied with the grill.

"And such an interesting family history," she continued. "Did you know she has younger twin brothers?"

"Uh. No, I didn't know that."

"And that her mother is of French descent, and her father a leading member of the Ho-Chunk Nation tribe? They live in Red River Falls."

Luke turned to his mom. "No, Mom, she never mentioned any of that."

Cynthia cocked her head. "And you never bothered to ask?"

He could no longer contain his annoyance.

"Mom, please try to understand. Aiyanna and I are... professionals. I like her and all, don't get me wrong. But, well, we aren't exactly *dating*, you know."

His mom shrugged and let out a huff. "Well, maybe that's why you never..."

But she didn't finish her sentence. He knew where she was going with this and took a slow, deep breath.

"Yeah, Mom. I know. Let's just leave it be, okay?"

Sure, he had trouble connecting—starting with himself and his own feelings. He knew that much about himself. In fact, unbeknownst to his mother, or anyone else for that matter, he had sought counseling in college during a particularly stressful period in his life. The therapist told him he needed to confront the person or "objective source" of his pain; but he was never able to find the courage to follow through.

By 2:00 p.m., everyone who was going to show up had shown up, or so Luke thought. There were Aunt Edna, her husband, Tom, and their son Ralph and his young family. Tom and Ralph worked for the Kohler

Company—a major manufacturer and employer for the region—and lived in Kohler, the very prestigious "factory town" that had grown up around the facility located right outside Sheboygan. And then, of course, his uncle Clarence Einsbach, who would never miss a party if he could help it. He and his wife, Doris, owned a farm outside of Kiel. Their son, Mark, managed a farm supply store in Howards Grove, about eight miles northwest of Sheboygan. Luke had to admit it was nice reconnecting with his relatives, having been away from the area for so long. He and his cousin Mark had always gotten along growing up, and they were eager to catch up on things.

And then there were Cynthia's card-playing lady friends—her "card clutch." And of course Dan Meyers, and Albert Hollander with his young pregnant wife, Clara, and their three-year-old son, Al Jr. The Hollanders were the last to show up, with Albert texting Luke to apologize for "a late start and what with all the bathroom breaks along the way. You know how it is with a pregnant wife and a kid in potty training." Luke had to chuckle. No, he really didn't know how it was, he was forced to admit. Life sure had changed things since their treehouse days.

As the afternoon progressed, people gravitated to their comfort zones, generally congregating in one of three groups. Cynthia's close friends and the "card clutch bunch" claimed the deck early on. Luke's relatives mainly occupied the tables set up in the garage and driveway; while the gazebo and its round center table became the refuge for Luke's friends and associates: Aiyanna, Dan, Albert and his wife, as well as Luke's cousin Mark Einsbach.

Cynthia, meanwhile, assumed the role of the gracious roving host, wine cooler in hand, visiting and conversing with each of her "honored guests," as she referred to them. Stopping by the gazebo, Luke introduced her to Detective Dan Meyers and reintroduced her to Albert ("you remember Al, Mom, my childhood friend from the old days"), Clara, and Al Jr.

Addressing Clara, Cynthia remarked, "My, you are looking radiant, my dear! When is the baby due?"

"Thank you, ma'am. Just two more months. Al Junior is looking forward to his baby sister."

"Yes, I'm sure," Cynthia said, patting her gently on the shoulder.

Al Sr. remarked on her fine assortment of yard bird feeders. "You must be a pretty serious ornithophile, Mrs. Kramer."

Dan had a puzzled look. "*Ornithophile?* Uh, isn't that... against the law?"

All eyes were on Dan. Even Luke didn't know whether to take him seriously.

It was Aiyanna who spoke first. "I think you mean *pedophile*, Dan. An *ornithophile* is a lover of birds... a bird-watcher," she explained, assuming a professorial tone. Luke thought she seemed to take particular delight in correcting Dan.

This was followed by a round of lighthearted laughter.

"Sure. I knew that," Dan deadpanned. Without so much as a flinch, he took a slow sip of beer, wiping the suds away from his mouth with his sleeve.

Cynthia smiled, politely dismissing this latest repartee. "Yes, Albert, I do certainly enjoy the company of birds. Especially in the early-morning hours when the chorus of song is *so* overwhelming and comforting."

Aiyanna agreed, saying she was often awakened by those delightful sounds. "Even with my bedroom window closed, the sound still comes through."

Cynthia smiled. "But you must please excuse me." She motioned to the folks on the deck. "Gotta keep those card sharps entertained—and honest!" she quipped. Then she was off.

Dan hugged his can of beer as he peered squinty-eyed at Aiyanna seated across from him.

"So, Aiyanna, how is your sister doing these days?"

"Adrianna?"

Dan sighed. "Of course. Who else?"

"Adrianna is doing just fine, thank you, Dan," Aiyanna replied, stony-faced. After a moment's pause, she added, "She is seeing someone new now. A real *nice* gentleman—with Native American roots."

Dan nodded slowly, then took another sip of beer. "Please tell her I was asking for her and that I wish her the very best." He lifted his beer in the manner of a toast.

With the steely exchange ended, Luke broke the tension with a nervous laugh. "So, Dan, let's talk about those crop circles!"

Dan was staring blankly ahead. "I'm sorry, Luke. You were saying?"

"The crop circles, Dan. Remember? The Mertz farm? Aiyanna and I spoke with Calvin and his wife this morning and got permission to return for soil and corn samples, with a tentative date set for this Wednesday, the eighth."

Dan's mouth puckered. "Hmm. Sounds good," he said. "So, we're talking about that possible *dig* site you were telling me about related to..." Stopping short, he looked around the table. All eyes were on him.

"Yes, Dan. Of course!" Luke interjected, quickly realizing maybe this wasn't the right time—or audience—to talk about digging for missing persons. But he decided to finish what he started. "Do you think that's enough time to get hold of that ground-penetrating radar equipment?"

"Uh, yeah," Dan stammered, "we should be able to arrange that with our friends at Geo-Services." He pulled out his cell phone and tapped something on it.

"Did I hear you say something about crop circles?" Mark chimed in.

Luke cast an inquiring look at Dan. Dan gave a nod, so Luke figured it was safe to confide in Mark and Albert about their current investigation into this so-called crop circle phenomenon. He was careful, though, not to say anything about the missing persons cases and the possible connection between the two.

"Heck, I seen something like what you described on my dad's farm in Kiel a couple summers back," Mark said. "A pretty large patch of corn trampled down in this spiral pattern, just like you described."

Dan perked up.

"Kiel, you said?"

Luke could almost see the wheels turning in Dan's head. He knew that Dan had been wanting to expand his area of search north into neighboring Calumet and Manitowoc Counties, and now seemed to be the perfect opportunity. After some careful cajoling, Mark agreed to ask permission from his dad for them to visit the family farm for soil and corn samples.

Just then Mark was summoned by his dad to meet some friends who had recently arrived. Albert's wife, meanwhile, had joined Mrs. Kramer on the back deck, where little Al was entertaining himself with a set of giant Legos that Cynthia had pulled from an old toy chest in the spare bedroom. That left Luke, Dan, Aiyanna, and Albert at the table. Luke and Albert locked eyes and seemed to have the same thought.

"You know, Luke," Albert said almost in a whisper, "that crop circle thing brings to mind something that happened a very long time ago, eh?"

Luke briefly met Dan's eyes, then turned back to Albert. "Nacits" was all he said.

Albert's eyes widened. "Nacits! Exactly!" He began opening up over the events of that August day in '99. "You know, there was something peculiar in the air that day." He took a deep breath. "Ozone! I remember the weather was changing rapidly. Pressure dropping. I could feel it in my ears."

Experiencing a sudden *eureka* moment, Luke turned to Dan.

"Say, Dan, you were looking for additional correlating data for that... investigation you are working on. Do you think...?"

Luke paused to give Dan a chance to catch up.

"Yes, I remember you now," Dan said as he cast a narrow-eyed stare at Albert. "You were that tall, freckle-faced kid with a talent for predicting the weather. Hmm, small wonder you went on to become a meteorologist."

Albert laughed.

Dan leaned forward. "Listen, Al," he continued in a low, gravelly voice. "Can we confide in you?"

Albert shrugged. "Well, sure. I always considered myself a trustworthy sort. Just what are we talking about?"

Dan and Luke went on to explain their ongoing investigations into the string of missing persons cases that had bedeviled the sheriff's office these past twenty years. They elaborated on their latest computer modeling efforts with geographical profiling software in an attempt to pinpoint a probable suspect in what they assumed was a serial killer case. The most recent correlations involved these crop circles, "which I am thinking may be some kind of calling card left by the killer," Dan explained. For Luke, this calling card theory was a new twist that he, in fact, was hearing for the first time. But it seemed to make sense.

"From what you say, Al," Luke continued, exchanging confirmatory eye contact with Dan and Aiyanna, "we are now wondering if it might be some weather-related phenomenon as well."

"You know, like full moons bringing out the worst behavior in some people," Dan offered.

"Like werewolves?" Albert said with a grin.

Dan frowned. "Okay. I know it's a stretch. But, hey, it's worth a try."

For Luke, however, this didn't seem to be a stretch at all—but for different reasons. He was thinking about that day in Aiyanna's lab and the response of her mushroom culture to electrical stimulation. This was the same new mushroom species that appeared to be associated with the GMO corn crops in the area. Maybe it was all related somehow. In the natural world, he figured this electrical stimulation could easily come from an approaching thunderstorm. Aiyanna would later confide to him that she had the same thoughts.

"Of course, I'm quite familiar with computer modeling," Albert said. "We use sophisticated computer models routinely to predict the weather."

Dan sat back with a self-congratulatory smile.

"Okay, then. So, I am asking you to help us with this investigation, Al. I would like you to input your weather data and the associated geographical information into the twenty-year timeline we've been modeling. Do you think you can handle it?"

Albert beamed. "No problem! More than happy to help."

Aiyanna and the three men raised their bottles and toasted their new partnership.

Their celebration was suddenly interrupted by a voice coming from the deck. It was a voice from the past. Luke's past. A familiar, though unwelcome, voice that sent a chill up his spine, a visceral reaction to dark memories resurrected.

"Hello, Mother! I bet you thought I'd never make it, eh?"

Luke turned to see his brother, Stan, on the back deck, giving their mother a big hug. He stared daggers at his mom as he met her eyes peering over Stan's shoulders. *Mother, why didn't you tell me he was going to be here?*

Chapter Twenty-Four

BARNS AND ATTICS

Midafternoon, July 4, 2015

"Close the door," Luke said without turning around. It was not so much a command as a soft admonition to Aiyanna as she followed him at a distance into his mother's antique barn.

The unexpected appearance of his brother, Stan, at the brat fry had elicited a kind of fight-or-flight response on Luke's part. He'd chosen "flight" as the discretionary better part of valor. Yet he quickly realized that his decision to abruptly stomp off in the direction of the barn—with Aiyanna in anxious pursuit—had taken everyone off guard, including his brother, who up until that time had seemed totally oblivious to his presence.

Inside the barn, walking slowly past rack after rack of glassware, pottery, kitchen utensils, and all things ancient, Luke paused in front of a modern wicker rocking chair incongruously set beside a nineteenth-century horse-drawn carriage. Wiping the dust from one of the wagon wheels, he looked around at the vast array of articles from bygone eras, each bearing witness to humanity's artistic and inventive nature, reflecting the ofttimes homespun and curious state-of-the-art technologies of their day: a spinning wheel, a wheelbarrow; a coffee mill here, an apple corer there; a horse-drawn plow and other farming implements and tools that often harbor mysteries to the modern observer as to their original intended use.

Luke took a seat in the rocker and began a slow rocking motion, his feet planted firmly on the creaking floorboards, his hands grasping the worn armrests. The wicker weave squeaked under the strain of the unaccustomed weight.

"Why is it," he began slowly, "that *old* things... like *memories*... have that stale, dusty, musty smell." He paused and pinched his nose to clear the dust from his nostrils. "Just like our attic growing up on the farm."

Aiyanna was leaning, almost seated, up against a rolltop pigeonhole desk across from Luke.

"Hmm. Not all memories," she said softly.

Staring into the void past her, he replied, "Yeah, I know." He cleared his throat with a raspy cough. "Just the *bad* ones."

There was a moment of awkward silence.

"So, Luke," Aiyanna finally said, "why didn't you ever tell me about your brother, Stan?"

Luke met her eyes with a sudden aggressiveness. "Well, I could ask you the same thing," he bellowed. "Why didn't you tell me about your younger twin brothers? Or your mom's French heritage, and your dad's important tribal connections?"

A startled Aiyanna stiffened and crossed her arms in a defensive stance. "Well, maybe because you never thought enough to ask me about my family!"

He ceased his rocking and sat back. "Oh, I see. So it's all on me!" he said, pouting like a hurt schoolboy.

She let out a commiserating sigh. "Listen, maybe it would help—help us both, actually—if you would open up about your brother. Maybe there is nothing I can do about it. Except to lend a sympathetic ear."

After considering this, he nodded. "Well, okay then. But remember, you asked for it. Better make yourself comfortable. It's a long story."

Aiyanna pushed herself up and took a seat on the desktop.

"Okay, where should I begin?" The question was really for himself. He took a slow deep breath. "As a child, growing up, I was rather short and chubby. The other kids would tease me and called me 'Pudge,' a name that stuck well into my teenage years, even after I grew up and slimmed down."

He described himself as clumsy and awkward, not at all like his older brother, Stan, who excelled at sports at an early age, was popular in school, and was voted "most likely to succeed" in his high school graduating class.

"In a small town, that goes a long way," he said. "Stan was my dad's golden boy." He grunted. "I was more like... an *embarrassment* to him. And my little sister, Alice, well, she was the gem of the family. A real angel. Everybody loved sweet, little Alice. *I* loved Alice." He looked straight at Aiyanna to drive the point home. "I guess being a middle child didn't help my situation."

Luke had already explained to Aiyanna the trauma of losing Alice and how his dad blamed him for her disappearance. "You were supposed to watch over her!" his dad had said. "How could you let this happen? She was depending on you!"

It was after that his dad fell off the wagon and retreated into the bottle, exploding at the slightest provocation, resulting in constant tension at home. Stan in turn blamed Lukas for his dad's violent outbursts and drinking problem and never ceased to put him down.

"Whenever I was being scolded or put down, it was 'Lukas this' or 'Lukas that.' Not 'Luke,'" he said. "Well, somehow I got through my high school years. And college finally offered me a welcome refuge from the living hell at home. By then, of course, I had grown up, slimmed down, developed my own interests and outlook on life. Never the athletic sort, I turned to academics and developed a love for writing, majoring in journalism with a minor in English literature."

He swallowed hard before continuing.

"In my freshman year"—he stared off into space once again—"I met a girl from Racine. Her name was Karen. I liked her a whole lot. And I thought she liked me. For spring break, I asked her home, mainly to meet my mom. Somehow, that really set my dad off. Thinking back, I think Karen brought back memories of Alice. Anyway, he disappeared on a three-day drinking binge. No one knew where he went. Some folks reported seeing him as far away as Green Bay," he said with a wave of his arms.

Luke paused to gather his thoughts.

"Well, my brother Stan was going to law school at the time and decided to stop home for spring break too. Apparently, he took a real shine to Karen. I later learned the attraction was mutual. That summer, unbeknownst to me, she spent a week with him at Lake Geneva. Then" —he slapped his thighs—"one month later he announced their plans to marry!" He looked up and forced a humorless laugh. "Funny, huh? Right under my nose!"

Aiyanna shook her head and winced. "Well, maybe it was all for the best."

"Yeah, all for the best." He sighed. "Well, the following summer they did marry, as planned. I didn't bother going to the wedding, which upset my dad even more, of course." He chuckled. "But I managed to get the last laugh. Six months later she filed for divorce! Not sure of the circumstances. Couldn't care, really."

Neither Luke nor Aiyanna spoke for the longest while.

Eventually, Luke looked up and stared at her. He smiled, like he was seeing her in a new light for the first time. When he next spoke, it was as if a great weight had been lifted from his shoulders.

"Follow me upstairs, Aiyanna," he said in a pleasing, dolce tone. "I want to show you something."

She hesitated but ultimately agreed. "Okay. Lead on."

The wooden staircase was wide enough for the two of them, but they proceeded single file all the same, Luke in the lead with Aiyanna close behind. The boards creaked, and the air became heavy and even more stuffy as they ascended. Cynthia had turned off the AC for the weekend, though the attic fans were still on, which helped a little. Luke could already feel his nose clogging up with the dust kicked up by the stale, circulating air.

The attic space was partitioned into smaller rooms or cubicles, each dedicated to a particular theme. There was one for child's toys from bygone days; books and magazines; house furnishings; knickknacks and lamps, both electric and kerosene; and so on. At the far end, Luke finally came to a stop in front of one of the smaller cubicles. There on various tables and shelves was a generous assortment of arrowheads and other

Native American artifacts contained in locked glass display cases. A posted sign read NOT FOR SALE.

"This is my mom's 'museum,' as she likes to call it," Luke said proudly. "She began collecting them as a little girl. Many she dug up herself. Others she traded for other merchandise."

Aiyanna's jaw dropped as she approached the display cases.

"Nice! *Very* nice, actually!" she said. "I had no idea. No wonder your mom was so interested in my family history."

"Uh-huh. And just so you know, I've become interested as well."

He went on to explain how he had become engrossed in Paul Radin's great work, *The Winnebago Tribe*.

"You've heard of it, yes?"

"Yes, of course! It's required reading where I come from," she said with a low chuckle. "I'm impressed, actually, that you would take such an interest."

"But of course. Why wouldn't I?" he replied. "The parts that truly fascinate me are the chapters covering your religious beliefs. In particular, the magical ceremonies, herbal medicine, and the belief in *reincarnation*."

"Really?" She cocked her head to the side. "But why should you find that so unusual? Reincarnation is a basic tenet of many Far Eastern religions, like Buddhism and Hinduism."

"Yes, of course," he replied. "Maybe that's why I find it so interesting. I just never expected to find the belief so…"

"So close to home?" she suggested, finishing the statement for him.

"Yeah, I guess you could say that."

Aiyanna picked up from where she left off. "While reincarnation may be a shared concept, considered a normal cycle of nature, the way various beliefs view it can differ. Unlike the Eastern religions, which hold that reincarnation is more of an automatic, endless cycle of death and rebirth, the Ho-Chunk believe that the departed spirit, if deemed worthy enough, *may* be granted the request to return to a carnal existence in whatever life form it desires."

"So, what determines this *worthiness*?" Luke asked.

"Good question. In the old days a warrior who died in battle was automatically considered worthy. A man who had lived a spiritual life might also have been considered worthy. And the reason for wanting to return to Earth is also considered before granting this request."

"Interesting," he said, scratching his head.

"You know, if you really think about it," she continued, "one could argue that the Christian belief in both the afterlife *and* the resurrection are opposing concepts. I mean, if there is a permanent afterlife for the worthy believer, then why the need for a resurrection? And vice versa. But by combining the two in that precise sequence—birth, death, afterlife, resurrection—don't you have a kind of de facto one-time reincarnation?"

He rubbed his chin. "You really got my head spinning on that one."

"I think I got my own head spinning, too!" She laughed. "Anyway, as in all religious traditions, I think there is ample room for doubt or at least differences of opinion when it comes to the details. Just like, I suppose, certain aspects of Christian dogma may not be taken literally the same way by every practicing Christian."

"Hmm. You have a point there. But our shared beliefs do embody the broader and more important aspects of our value systems that govern our lives," he offered. "You know, things like 'the Golden Rule' and 'love your neighbor as yourself.'"

Aiyanna smiled. "Likewise, for my people. Success, happiness, and long life! These are the core values that empower our religious experience."

Not about to let go of the topic, he asked, "So, what about the ceremonies and herbal medicines?"

"Yes, well, our shamans *do* continue to practice such things, in concert with modern Western medicinal remedies, of course. They both have their place and serve a positive purpose for healing the body *and* the spirit."

"Whatever works, right?"

"Hmm, I suppose so."

The moment turned awkward as the two of them stood there, Aiyanna fidgeting with a button on her blouse, Luke nervously clearing his throat.

She spoke first. "Say, listen! How 'bout we get back to your mom's brat fry and try to *resurrect* that party?"

"Sounds like good medicine," he said.

As the two headed back toward the stairs, Luke thought of something his mom had said about showing more interest in a relationship.

"Tell me about your sister," he said.

"My sister? Adrianna?"

"Yes. What happened between Dan and Adrianna? Just curious. I know it's none of my business, but—"

She cut him off with a laugh. "But you're just dying to know!"

"Sure. I mean, Dan seems like a nice guy. And I'm certain your sister is a very nice person too. So—"

Aiyanna let out an audible sigh. "Well, it had a lot to do with what we were talking about."

Luke stopped in his tracks. "Religious differences?"

"Yes." She nodded. "But more than that. Dan, shall I say, didn't share the same interest in our cultural heritage as, well, you apparently do. He couldn't handle—how did he put it?— 'all the baggage' that came with a deepening relationship with someone like Adrianna. And my father, he sensed it too. So one thing led to another. Until one day, my sister had enough and decided to break it off."

"Hmm. That's too bad," he said. "I am disappointed. 'Baggage,' that's how he referred to your heritage?"

"Uh-huh. But life goes on. Adrianna is now dating a real nice guy. One of our *own kind*."

"I see."

They continued down the stairs, side by side this time, Luke's hand resting lightly on Aiyanna's shoulder. Bursting from the barn into the bright light of day, he took a deep, refreshing breath of clean country air, clearing his lungs of the musty remnants of attic and barn. A cathartic experience. *Like being born again!*

Chapter Twenty-Five

MYSTERY KERNELS

Late Afternoon, July 4, 2015

It was almost four o'clock when Luke and Aiyanna returned to the brat fry. Some of Luke's relatives had already departed for the day. But Luke and Aiyanna were able to rejoin their friends, who had all remained, in the gazebo.

"So, where have you guys been?" Dan asked.

Luke squirmed in his seat. "Well, you see..."

Aiyanna spoke up, relieving the tension. "Luke had promised to show me his mom's antique barn. Remarkably interesting, I must say. Especially her prized collection of Indian artifacts. I must remember to compliment her."

"I'm quite sure," Dan said with a sly smirk.

Luke looked over to his mom and brother, who were now seated with the remnants of their relatives in the garage. He caught his mom's eye and smiled. She did the same. This apparently did not go unnoticed by Aiyanna. She motioned with a twist of her head and, mouthing the words, indicated he should perhaps pay his brother a visit.

Luke cleared his throat and stood. "Excuse me, guys. There's something I must do."

Luke walked over to his mom's table, where Stan was seated with his back to him.

"Hello, Stan!" Luke said in the most amiable tone he could muster.

Stan turned, looked up, and smiled. "Well, if it isn't my long-lost brother." He reached out his hand. "How the hell are you, Luke? Can't remember the last time I saw you."

Luke reached out and took his hand. "Yeah, I know. It's been a while," he said, knowing it was well before Stan's wedding.

Stan invited him to join them. Luke pulled up a chair and sat directly across from his brother.

"Mom's been telling me about your new job," Stan said. "That's good! Sounds exciting. I'm happy for you." He seemed surprisingly genuine.

For the next fifteen minutes or so they caught up on lost time. Luke learned that Stan had been accepted as a full partner with his San Francisco–based law firm and was now dating a woman from Walnut Creek, a single mom with a young child.

"I must confess," Stan said with a bent smile, "things seem to be getting pretty serious." With a sip of beer and a pointed glance at the young woman seated at the gazebo, he turned the tables on Luke and asked about his own love life. Luke took a deep breath and explained that his relationship with Aiyanna was "strictly professional."

Stan winked. "Sure, I know. That's how it starts out," he said. "Maryanne—that's my woman friend—was a clerk working in our office when we started dating. She's now taken a job with another firm... to avoid appearances of impropriety."

Just then their cousin Mark, who had been tending the grill in Luke's absence, announced, "Hey, just to let you all know there are some brats and corn over here looking to get eaten. Any takers?"

Stan turned. "Sure, I could use a second helping." He turned back to Luke. "How 'bout you, brother?"

Luke shook his head. "Nah, I'm good."

As Stan left the table, Luke's mom took his hand with both of hers and squeezed hard. "Thank you, son. This means so much to me."

He gave her a crooked smile. "Yeah, Mom. I know."

A minute later there was a commotion over by the grill as Stan's voice rang out. "Hey, what the hell! What is this?"

Everyone turned to see a bewildered Stan holding an ear of corn in disbelief and staring down at his plate. He held up the ear up for all to see.

"I bit down and hit something hard. Almost broke my tooth!"

He laid the half-eaten corn cob on his plate next to a pile of half-chewed corn he'd just spit out.

Luke, Dan, and Aiyanna reacted in unison, quickly making their way to the grill. Dan looked at Stan's plate, took a fork, and began separating the contents of the half-chewed corn.

"Looks like you lost a tooth, my friend," Dan said as he picked up an intact tooth—a molar, to be precise—for all to see.

Stan checked his mouth for missing teeth. "Hell no! That's not my tooth."

Dan examined the half-eaten ear of corn. Taking a fork, he tapped two kernels that appeared different from the rest. Aiyanna and Luke joined him. In the end, they were all forced to admit the impossible. There was indeed what appeared to be two human molars embedded in the cob of corn where kernels ought to be, like they had grown straight out of the cob itself! Aiyanna took a magnifying glass from her purse for a closer inspection.

"Well, they appear to be genuine." She tapped the objects with the butt of her glass. "Real enamel," she concluded.

"So you think someone planted them in the cob as a practical joke?" Dan suggested.

Aiyanna shook her head. "I suppose that's possible. But why in the world would anyone go to such lengths?"

"Maybe"—Dan hawed—"to capture the headlines. Discredit the GMO corn industry!" He turned to Luke with a suspicious glare.

"Aw, come on, Dan! You're not suggesting..."

"Hey!" Dan put both hands in the air. "I just call it like I see it. That's what I do for a living." He paused. "Where did you say you got this corn?"

Aiyanna answered for Luke. "We picked it up from a farmer's stand on the way over here this morning."

"Which farmer?" Dan pressed.

"The Mertz farm," Luke replied.

"Calvin Mertz? The place we plan to visit this Wednesday?"

"That's right," Luke and Aiyanna answered in unison.

Dan considered this for a moment. "We need to take this corn cob as evidence," he said. "Need to have forensics take a look at it. Maybe they can get DNA samples from the dental pulp, which may tell us something if we can find a match. Calvin Mertz would be first on my list. I may just pay Farmer Cal a visit Monday morning. Explain the situation and see if he has any trouble providing a DNA sample."

"Can you get intact DNA from a cooked ear of corn?" Luke asked. "I mean, wouldn't the heat destroy it?"

"Not necessarily," Dan replied. "If DNA can be recovered from the bone and teeth fragments of cremated remains, I'm confident we can extract enough intact DNA from these grilled teeth for profiling."

"I'd like to pull samples from the corn kernels, too," Aiyanna added. "Plant DNA can survive normal cooking conditions. It may be degraded and partially fragmented, but we have the means of piecing things together in the lab. I'd like to see exactly what corn variety we're dealing with."

"Well, the sheriff's office has first dibs on the corn," Dan said. "I'm declaring this a forensic case until we know otherwise."

Aiyanna opened her mouth like she was about to protest when he added, "But, you can borrow the samples once we're finished with them."

"Try to keep the teeth intact," she said, backing off. "You should be able to bore through the enamel without destroying the integrity of the sample."

"I know my business," Dan said with a smirk. "We'll only sample what we need." He paused and looked around. "Let's take a look at the other uneaten cobs for further evidence. Maybe there's more teeth to be found."

After careful examination, the other corn cobs were clean. No anomalies found. On Aiyanna's suggestion, Dan took them as evidence anyway, as "control samples," she said.

Dan asked if he could get some plastic bags to hold the specimens. Stan retrieved several plastic ziplock bags from his mom's kitchen and handed them to him.

"Thank you, Stan. I appreciate it."

"Look," Stan offered with a pasted-on smile. "If you need a lawyer for this investigation, Detective, you can always call on me." He drew a business card from his wallet and handed it to Dan.

Dan took the card and stuffed it in his shirt pocket. "Thanks. I'll keep that in mind. But I may want to get a statement from you before you leave. Just for the record."

Stan looked befuddled. "Sure. No problem."

Things calmed down after that, but the whole episode put a bit of a damper on the festivities. By six o'clock most everyone had said their goodbyes and departed, leaving Stan—who was planning to stay overnight in his mom's spare bedroom—Luke, Aiyanna, Dan, and Mark.

"Anyone sticking around for the fireworks?" Stan asked in an upbeat tone, likely trying to salvage some measure of celebration from the day's events.

There were no takers.

THE INVESTIGATION

Chapter Twenty-Six

THE BEAR HUNT

Wisconsin Wilderness

The long, warm days of summer were now upon Akecheta and his people as they basked on the shores of the Great Lake, taking inventory of the season's harvest of whitefish, which had proven bountiful. Nearing the end of their seasonal encampment, the men of the village prepared for the homeward journey while the women fashioned additional baskets to secure their harvest.

The return trip was arduous but without incident. Only once did Akecheta's advance party of Bear clansmen detect the presence of enemy scouts from Illiniwek tribes to the south—they had ventured north into the shared hunting grounds of the Ho-Chunk, Menomonee, and Potawatomi peoples. From the simple calculus of numbers, the interlopers considered it not worth the risk of engagement, even with the promise of much bounty to be gained.

Once again in their inland villages, secure high atop the bluffs overlooking the Sheub-wau-wau-gum marshlands, the Ho-Chunk women set about tending their crops and gathering berries and mushrooms from the fields while the men set out to replenish their stores of deer, rabbit, beaver, wild turkey, and waterfowl.

For Akecheta and other men of the Bear clan, with the summer came thoughts of one of the greatest hunting opportunities of the season. It was the time of year called *hiruci'c*, when the black bear was drawn to groves of hickory and red timber oak to feed on their burgeoning yield of acorns and nuts. The bears, satiated from their feast and taking rest in the open clearing of the grove, would become easy prey to the experienced hunter who knew where to find them.

"Always approach them downwind," Akecheta told his son, Enapay, "so they do not pick up your scent. And take care not to kill all of the resting bears."

"And never kill a breeding bear," Matoskah added. "If you value your own life, never go after a breeding bear!"

Akecheta laughed. "Yes, most definitely. That is rule number one!"

Enapay looked up at this father. "Can I come with you on the hunt this time, Father?"

Akecheta patted his son on the head and smiled. "In time, my son, in time. Perhaps next season you will be ready."

Akecheta selected ten of his most experienced hunters and two young first-time braves for the hunting party. This way, the older, experienced braves could mentor the young in the proper and safe methods for hunting bear, which, along with bison, constituted the most covetous and dangerous animals to pursue. In preparation for the hunt, a ceremony would be performed, called *wanantce're*—which translated to "concentration of the mind"—to prepare the men mentally and spiritually and to ensure some measure of success by magically conjuring or attracting the attention of the bear.

That evening, Akecheta invited the others to join him in his lodge. A kettle of food, consisting of corn and dried fruit, was placed on the fire as a feast offering to the bear. Tobacco and red feathers were also placed in small bark vessels as additional offerings. When all was ready, Akecheta as host began singing and rubbing two ceremonial sticks together while the others ate. This he continued to do until he attracted the attention of the bear's spirit, as indicated by a small flame that jumped from the fire to the offerings.

In the morning, the men made final preparations for the hunt, which included chewing special hunting medicines that they then rubbed onto their arrows. Preparations complete, they set out with Akecheta leading the way toward the hunting grounds where the hickory and oak trees grew and the bears gathered for their summer feast of acorns and nuts.

As the sun passed its zenith, they came at last upon a clearing among a stand of red oak where they expected the bears to be feasting. From a distance, there appeared to be nothing more than rocks jutting out from the ground. When one rock moved, the men froze in their tracks. Akecheta counted the number of bears and held up four fingers. Then, holding up two fingers and pointing to the two closest bears on the right, he signaled his men to spread out and proceed quietly, taking note of the wind direction, which was in their favor. Once positioned, Akecheta raised his hand slowly. Then, with a swift motion he lowered it, unleashing a swarm of arrows from the bows of his companions. The clearing erupted in a flurry of growls and moans. *Swish!* A second volley of arrows streamed forth and found their marks. And then a third.

The two targeted bears lay mortally wounded, while the other two fled to the safety of the thick surrounding forest.

Akecheta smiled. "This is good," he said, pleased that not all the bears were killed.

The men approached the wounded bears carefully, which they dispatched safely and quickly with spears and knives.

They spent the next several hours field dressing the bears and preparing sleds to transport them back to the village. One group of men assembled the sleds, while the second focused on dressing the bears, which began by making two long incisions, one on each side of the chest. Through their collective experience and collaborative efforts, they performed the tasks efficiently and quickly. The two novice braves watched and assisted as they were instructed, eager to learn.

Upon returning to the village, Akecheta and his men received a less than enthusiastic reception. He thought it strange at first but quickly learned from a fellow clansman of some disturbing news circulating through the village. It appeared that in a neighboring village, a hunting party had returned earlier that same day with the mutilated remains of one of their braves. After speaking with the leader of the hunt, Akecheta learned that the young man had made the tragic mistake of tracking and attacking a breeding grizzly bear, generally larger and more ferocious than black bears. The man failed to make that distinction and suffered the dire consequences.

"He was operating alone," Wambleeska, their leader, explained. "We heard his cries for help and came to his aid as quickly possible, but the bear was already upon him, tearing him to pieces. We attacked the bear and were finally able to drive it off. But the damage was done. By the time we returned to the village, the young brave's spirit had departed from him."

Akecheta shook his head with grief. "I am so sorry it ended that way." He laid his hand on the man's shoulder. "He died a brave warrior's death. We will provide him the proper burial."

For a member of the Bear clan, a proper burial meant a ground interment in keeping with the custom of the manegi ("people of the earth") clans, as opposed to being laid to rest on a raised platform or scaffold, as was the practice of the wangeregi ("people of the sky") clans.

Following the custom of friendly pairing of clans from the opposite divisions, Akecheta reached out to a member of the Thunderbird clan to preside over the preparation of the body for burial and to take charge of all burial rites. This person was responsible for extending invitations to those wishing to attend the feast and for selecting the warriors who would pay tribute.

As a fellow Bear clansman, Wambleeska was chosen to prepare the body. Akecheta stood by as Wambleeska lay a red mark across the forehead of the deceased warrior, then a black charcoal mark immediately below. His entire chin was daubed in red to simulate a smiling face eager and unafraid to enter the spirit world.

Wambleeska addressed those present, explaining the meaning of the marks: "That he may be recognized by his relatives in the spirit land." He then spoke directly to the deceased with words of encouragement and instruction. Following this, the clan songs were sung—songs the original Bear clansmen were said to have sung when they first came upon Earth— and the body was carried to the grave. They placed food at the grave site to sustain the spirit over the four-day period of the wake. After the sun went down, the chief mourner took a lighted stick made of hard wood and planted it at the east end of the grave site.

It was believed that the spirit of the deceased remained hovering above the place for a period of four days before proceeding to the spirit world to rejoin his ancestors. For this reason, the wake that followed continued for four nights, being an extended celebration of the life and death of the man. Food was shared and much tobacco smoked, and those present continued to eulogize and share stories of the deceased.

Akecheta then rose up and addressed the gathering to recount the "journey myth of the departed soul to the spirit land," describing to the deceased in detail what he would encounter along the way.

"First, you will come to a lodge having one door facing the rising sun, the second facing the setting sun. In the lodge you will encounter an old woman who will challenge you with questions. Her task is to convince you that you are indeed a spirit now, for up till now you hadn't realized you are dead.

"You will be faced with many tests and obstacles along the way. You will encounter the lodge and fire of Herecgu'nina, chief of the bad spirits, who will seek to seduce you. But with your war club you will counter and strike all bad spirits that cross your path. From there the road will lead to a beautiful place of flowers and fields where friendly souls will reach out and escort you to the lodge of the Earthmaker, who waits for you with great expectation. There, after presenting offerings of tobacco and correctly responding to a final series of questions, you will be successfully reunited with your ancestors who have been eagerly awaiting your arrival, greeting you with robust and joyous shouts of salutation: Haho!"

Chapter Twenty-Seven

NEWS SCOOP

Monday, July 6, 2015

Monday morning the newsroom was abuzz with the latest breaking news of the Emma Hauptmann missing persons case, and Luke had become something of a celebrity. Friday evening, after returning home from his fish fry dinner meeting with Dan, he quickly penned the article that would be Sunday morning's leading front-page story in the *Sheboygan Dispatch*: "DNA Links Adam Emery to Disappearance of Plymouth College Student."

A smiling Anita approached Luke's desk with a cup of coffee in one hand and a bottle of Florida fresh-squeezed orange juice in the other.

"Here, this is from Ted," she said as she set the bottle down with a thud right in front of Luke. "He said you'd understand the 'squeezed juice' reference."

Luke jumped. "Ah, yes, very good!" He took the cup of coffee and chuckled. "Thank you, Anita."

"Has Ted talked to you?" she asked, taking a seat on Luke's desk in her form-fitting designer capris, legs crossed. Luke gulped at the sight of her bare calves and visible curve of her thighs, almost choking on his coffee, before reminding himself that she was a married woman.

"Yes, I spoke with him first thing this morning. He's a changed man."

"A born-again Lukas fan!" she said, laughing.

"Well, I wouldn't go that far."

Just then Pam walked by. Either she hadn't gotten the news or was deliberately avoiding him. After all, Luke's breaking news story had eclipsed Sunday's GMO series installment. *She's probably blaming me for going soft on her "tooth in the cereal box" connection.* He considered dropping by to share Saturday's bizarre find at his mom's brat fry. *Who knows, maybe there's some weird connection between the teeth-on-the-cob and the molar in the cereal box. It was a box of corn flakes, right?*

"Well, gotta get back to work," Anita said, hopping off the desk. "Enjoy your juice!"

"I will. Thanks again."

Luke leaned back in his chair, folding his hands behind his head as he considered his next move. Reaching forward, he made a few keystrokes and a new blank Word document opened up. He began typing: "Mini Crop Circles Baffle Local Farmers." The article almost wrote itself, with Luke making only an occasional reference to his handwritten notes.

Local farmers have been hard-pressed to figure out the origins and meaning of what they are calling "mini crop circles" that appear from time to time in cornfields throughout the county. Calvin Mertz of Johnsonville blames it on teenage pranksters looking for a good time. "Those kids will do the darndest things," he told this reporter. "I've chased them away partying in my fields on multiple occasions. Even threatened to call the police one time."

But others aren't so sure and suggest bizarre and even sinister causes for these mysterious events. A few farmers went so far as to blame it on space aliens! Whatever their origins, there's no doubt they have been showing up on a regular but seemingly random basis over the past fifteen years...

...If you or someone you know have ever encountered one of these strange occurrences, you are invited to share your story. Contact the writer at the email address below. Your name and contact information will be held in the strictest confidence and only divulged upon your approval.

Luke hoped to have the article ready for tomorrow's edition. He smiled as he gave it another read.

"Nice! Let's see how many fish I can lure with this one."

It was close to eleven o'clock when he received a surprise call from Plymouth. He recognized Jake Emery's number, and his heart raced. *Must've read Sunday's headlines about his son, Adam. Probably pissed off!* Slowly he reached for the phone.

"*Sheboygan Dispatch*. Luke Kramer speaking," he said in as calm a tone as he could muster.

There was a moment of silence. Just heavy breathing on the other end. And then, "Good morning, Luke." More silence. "This is Jake Emery."

Luke was baffled. Jake sounded calm, almost serene.

"Uh, yes, Jake. How are you doing this morning?" Wincing, he wished he could take those words back.

Jake replied with a short, gruff laugh. "How am I doing, you say?" Then a pause. "You mean, before r after I saw yesterday's headlines?"

Luke rubbed his forehead as he considered his response.

"Yes, well, I am so sorry about your son, Jake, but—"

"*But* don't enter into it," Jake interjected. "There are no *buts* about it."

Luke was confused. "I... I don't understand. What do you mean?"

"I mean," Jake replied, "if Adam did what they say he did, well, he ain't no son of mine!"

Luke held back a sigh of relief. Bringing his hand back down, he picked up a pen and notepad.

"Listen," Jake continued, "I feel I can trust you, Luke. I don't wanna go running to the police. But I feel I can trust *you* to do the right thing."

Luke bit the end of his pen. "I see. So what exactly do you mean?"

"Well, you see," Jake began, "I got a call from a customer saying that one of our trucks showed up unexpectedly the night of May 8th, the same night that Emma went missing. The driver of the truck told him that they were scheduled for a service call the next day but decided to drop by now because of the weekend rush, or some other bullshit story. I asked him who the driver was. He said it was my son Adam. And that he was alone."

Luke was taking this all down. "Is that so unusual, Jake? To make a service call late at night?"

"Well, it sometimes happens. But only in the case of an emergency. Like a backed-up or overflowing septic tank. Happens more often with a simple holding tank. But you would never go alone. In this case, there was no emergency request, and there was no record of it in the truck's log. And no receipt in the account ledger. If the customer hadn't called me direct, I never would have known about it."

Luke pondered this. "And you think there may be something amiss?"

Jake guffawed. "Amiss! When I approached Adam about it, he flew into a rage. Never seen him behave like that before."

"So, what is it you want me to do, Jake?"

There was a moment's silence on the other end of the phone before Jake spoke again. "You gotta do what you think is best, son. But if someone were to examine the tanker truck that Adam used that night and just happened to inspect the contents of a certain farmer's septic holding tank, well, that someone just might find something of interest."

Luke sat back and took a slow breath. "I see. And how long have you been keeping this under your hat, Jake?"

"Well, actually, since the next day after it happened, when I got the call from the customer. I didn't think so much of it at the time." He paused. "Until yesterday, that is, when I saw the headlines. That's when I made the connection. And that's when I confronted Adam and he almost threw me across the room!"

Luke realized he was up to his neck in this thing now, and there was no turning back. He felt bad for Jake, though, and his other two sons, Scott and Seth. He was certain they weren't involved and that Adam had acted alone.

"Jake, can you tell me the name and address of the customer?"

"No problem. Got a pencil?"

Luke fidgeted with his pen. "Ready when you are."

After taking down the name and address, Luke repeated it, to be sure he got it right.

"Thank you, Jake. I promise... to do the right thing. But I know it's not going to be easy for you and the boys."

"Well, it is what it is," Jake said.

Immediately after hanging up, Luke rang the sheriff's office.

"Hello. This is Luke Kramer of the *Dispatch*. I'd like to speak with Detective Dan Meyers, please... No, please don't put me on hold! This is an urgent matter!... Yes, thank you."

Chapter Twenty-Eight

GRISLY FIND

Later That Same Day

Detective Dan Meyers sprang into action the moment he got off the phone with Luke Monday morning. He had pressed Luke for the source of his information, but Luke held fast to protecting his confidential news source.

No matter, Dan thought. If he found what he hoped to find, it wouldn't matter who blew the whistle.

The first thing Dan did was secure two search warrants, one for the Emery premises and the second for a farmer in Waldo, the customer Adam serviced the night of Emma Hauptmann's disappearance. This took him till almost two o'clock, as he had to wait for the judge to return from lunch to sign the warrant. In the meantime, he set about rounding up a posse. First, of course, there was Sam Riley, his trusty new deputy; followed by a forensic expert, Steve Kelly; a two-man HAZMAT team; and finally, Deputy Jimmy Collins and his cadaver dog. He notified the Plymouth Police Department out of courtesy, but since this was outside city limits, it was technically a county matter.

"Okay, guys. You know the drill. Let's mount up!"

Dan and Sam led the way in his police cruiser, followed by the forensics-HAZMAT team van, with Jimmy Collins and his dog bringing up the rear in his paddy wagon. Picking up Highway 23, they headed out of town toward Plymouth, about fifteen miles due west. Just this side of the city limits, they turned south on Route 57 toward the small town of Waldo.

"Hey! Now I know 'where's Waldo?'" Sam quipped.

Dan groaned and shook his head. "Bet you've been waitin' all day to spring that on me, eh?"

About five miles down the road—halfway to Waldo—they reached their destination, a small farmhouse on the left. Dan could see the mound and protruding vent of the buried septic holding tank in the backyard.

Dan and Sam approached the front door of the farmhouse and knocked. A woman in a house dress, probably in her thirties, with a baby in her arms greeted them.

Dan doffed his hat. "Sorry for the intrusion, ma'am." He presented his badge and paperwork. "But I have a warrant to search the premises. Is this the home of Jedediah Heilbroner?"

"Why, yes, it is."

"Is your husband home?"

"No, he's not," she said. She seemed a bit flustered. "Um, he's at work. What's this all about?"

"Not to worry, ma'am. We're just following up on a lead we received from... an anonymous source. Doesn't directly involve you or your husband. But we will need to inspect the premises. More specifically, your backyard and your septic holding tank."

"Omigosh! Well, by all means. Be my guest!" she chortled. "Never been asked by anyone to look at our septic tank before."

"Thank you, ma'am." Dan tipped his hat again.

Directing the remainder of his team up the driveway into the backyard, he took a moment to size up the situation. The hatch on the tank was smaller than he'd expected. As they began suiting up, the HAZMAT officer in charge was apparently having the same misgivings.

"Ya know, that hatch looks awfully narrow," he said. "But we'll give it a try."

A tripod with a hoist was set up over the hatch to permit confined entry. The "lucky" man going in would be equipped with a respirator mask and oxygen tank on his back.

Dan asked the woman when the tank was last serviced. She answered that it was less than a week ago. He was thinking that could be good, in that there wouldn't be so much waste to wade through. But it could also be bad, if the body had decomposed to the point of being turned to sludge and pumped away. *I guess we'll find out soon enough.*

A noxious plume enveloped the team as the HAZMAT leader removed the top hatch, forcing them to turn their heads away.

"Here." Dan handed the leader a gauging stick. "Let's take a measure before sending anyone in."

The officer inserted the stick all the way until it touched bottom, then pulled it out.

"Looks like just under two feet," he said.

"Good. Those hip boots over your HAZMAT suit should do the trick," Dan assured him.

They made a preliminary inspection by lowering a floodlight and video camera into the interior. A quick survey revealed nothing out of the ordinary at first. Then, "There! See it?" shouted his partner at the video screen. "That hazy bulge in the surface."

The lead officer nodded. "Yeah, I see it." The two men looked at each other. "Okay. So who goes in?"

"Draw straws, guys!" Dan offered with a grin.

The leader turned to his partner.

"Okay, ready. Rock, paper, scissors... Go!"

"Damnit!" his partner called out. "How 'bout best of three?"

The leader laughed. "No way! You're going in!"

Dan turned and cast a petulant look at the dueling duo. "Come on, ladies. Get a move on! Time waits for no man."

"Short-straw" donned the bulky air-breathing apparatus, consisting of a respirator mask, air tank, and back harness. With the lead officer's assistance, he hooked his body harness to the hoist and began the slow, controlled descent into the foul, dark void. Almost immediately, they ran into a problem. Given the man's girth and bulky air tank, he wasn't able to get through the open hatch.

"Not gonna fit," he said.

"Nah, you can make it!"

But try as he might, he was about two inches short of squeezing through. Reluctantly, the lead officer agreed to give it a try, being a little slimmer. But he, too, had trouble.

"Hmm." Dan puzzled.

"How 'bout we contact the Plymouth HAZMAT team?" Sam offered. "Maybe they have someone, or the right apparatus, that can fit."

Dan grimaced at the thought of having to involve the locals. In the end he was forced to come to the same conclusion. They only had a few hours of daylight left. *Time waits for no man!*

Dan got Police Chief Bill Preston on the cruiser radio.

As expected, Bill Preston gloated over the opportunity to come to the assistance of the county sheriff's office. "We'd only be *too* happy to bail you out of this one, Dan." He paused. "*If* you give us first rights to reporting the find."

Dan was seething but managed to keep his cool. He took a deep breath and swallowed his pride. It went down hard.

"Okay, Bill. You got it."

"Yeah, well, it so happens we have this one guy who does a lot of sport diving. Ever hear of a hookah diving system?"

Dan was growing impatient. "No, can't say that I have, Bill."

"Well, he's got one. And I can assure you he'll have no problem getting to the *bottom* of your problem!" Bill let out a guffaw that came across the radio as a static choke.

Dan winced. "Thank you, Bill. Over and out."

About forty minutes later, the Plymouth Police team arrived. Dan checked his watch. "Okay, guys. Time's a wastin'!"

The officer who finally succeeded in entering the tank was a little wiry dude who looked like a high school cross-country runner. Of course, the hookah surface-supplied breathing system he brought with him went a long way. A battery-operated air compressor located at ground level pumped surface air to the diver—or rescuer in this case—through an umbilical line connected to the man's respirator mask, so the only thing that entered the tank was the man and his mask, with the umbilical trailing behind. He was able to get through the twenty-four-inch hatch with six inches to spare.

"Hell, I could've gotten through that hatch if I had one of those," Dan's HAZMAT officer grumbled.

"Gotta get us one of those," his leader mumbled back.

Dan harrumphed.

It only took a minute for the officer to confirm the find.

"We got ourselves a body down here!" he shouted out.

Dan exhaled. Seemed like he'd been holding his breath this whole time.

"That's great!" He turned to Sam. "Get me one of those rubber body bags, Sam. They're in the van."

They lowered the bag to the officer.

"Damn! There's not much left here to recover." Dan could barely make out what he said. "But I'll do the best I can."

"We only need enough to identify the remains," Dan shouted back.

He noticed Sam giving him the evil eye.

Dan turned back to the officer in the tank. "But try to get as much as you can. We gotta think of the girl's family. May want to come back later with a tanker truck and pump to get all possible remains."

Sam nodded, apparently satisfied.

They managed to recover a good portion of the remains, including the skull and about 80 percent of the bones. Most of the soft tissue had decomposed and dissolved into the sludge, however. But Dan was hopeful they could make a positive identification through DNA testing and profiling of the bone marrow and dental pulp samples, along with matching dental records.

As his men were cleaning up, Chief Preston turned to Dan. "So, can you give me the name and number of that reporter you've been speaking with? I'd like to give him a call... if you catch my meaning."

Dan hemmed and hawed. "Sure," he finally said with a dejected look. "After all, a deal's a deal."

Tearing a page from his notepad, he wrote down Luke's business number. "His name is Luke Kramer," he said, handing Bill the piece of paper. "Works for the *Sheboygan Dispatch*."

Bill stuffed the note in his shirt pocket. "Thanks. I'll be sure to give him a call tomorrow."

Dan simply nodded.

As the chief was turning to go, Dan added, "I would suggest you have your boys pick up Adam Emery as soon as possible for questioning. We can only hold him so long without a warrant, but we don't want him to go running off when he catches wind of what's going on here. I'd do it myself, but we'll be busy impounding that vehicle and running tests in the lab."

"Can do," Bill assured him.

With the presumed remains of Emma Hauptmann secure and on their way back to the Sheboygan crime unit along with most of the investigative team, Dan, Sam, and Steve Kelly, their forensic expert, remained behind to take a statement from Jedediah, who by this time had returned home and was anxiously awaiting the outcome of the search.

Dan took out his pen and notebook as he turned to Jed.

"So, Mr. Heilbroner. Mind if I ask you a few questions?"

"Does this whole thing have anything to do with the night of May 8th?" Jed asked.

"As a matter of fact, it does," Dan replied, surprised by his opening question.

"Well, I thought something was suspicious when that tanker truck showed up that night, 'n so," Jed said. "Unusual thing to happen."

"That so? And who was the driver of the truck, Jed?"

"Adam Emery. Jake's oldest son. He's always serviced our account. But never late at night, showing up unsolicited and unannounced."

Dan nodded. "I see. And did you notice anything peculiar in his behavior that night?"

Jed paused. "Well, he seemed to be staggering a bit. But that wasn't too unusual for Adam. He was never one to shy away from the bottle, if ya catch my drift," he said snidely.

Dan smiled. "Uh-huh. I understand." He made some notes.

"So, was it you who phoned the *Sheboygan Dispatch* to report the matter?" Dan asked, trying to get a fix on who the tipster was.

"Nah. Not the *Dispatch*," he said. "I phoned Jake Emery the next day. That's who I called."

A light went off in Dan's head. "Very interesting. Thank you, Jed. Now, if you wouldn't mind," he continued, handing Jedediah some paper forms and two clipboards, "I'd like you and your wife to make separate written statements of the events that transpired that night and any follow-up action, to the best of your recollection."

Jed took the clipboard. "Sure. Be happy to." His wife peered over his shoulder. He turned and looked back at the septic tank now surrounded by yellow crime scene tape. "Hard to believe," he said. "What a ghastly way to end up." He turned back to Dan. "So, it's the Emma girl, right?"

Dan perked up. "Now, why would you say that, Jed?"

Jed smiled. "Well, I just figured. Putting two and two together, 'n so. I mean, after reading yesterday's paper naming Adam as the chief suspect in her disappearance."

Dan nodded. "Hmm. Well, I'd appreciate it if you'd keep this under your hat. But I'm sure you'll read about it in the papers soon enough."

"Sure, not a problem." Jed scratched his head. "And to think it all happened right under our noses, in our own backyard."

"Yeah. Hard to believe what some people will do," Dan said.

Having secured the area and taken the Heilbroners' statements, Dan thanked them for their time and assistance, then gathered up his team and proceeded to their next destination.

WHEN DAN and his team drove up to Jake's place, there was ol' Jake sitting in his rocker on the front porch. Almost as if he was expecting them.

"What can I do for you fine gentlemen of the law?" he said as Dan stepped up onto the porch. Sam lagged a few feet behind while Steve remained in the yard doing a quick visual survey of the surroundings.

Dan presented the search warrant and explained the reason they were there.

"Well, you will find that tanker truck Adam used that night parked right over yonder. It's only been used once since that night."

"And when might that have been, if you don't mind my asking?"

Jake spit a wad of chewing tobacco on the front lawn and wiped his chin with his shirtsleeve. "I can tell you exactly when it was. Five days ago at the Heilbroner farm south o' here near Waldo."

Dan and Sam looked at each other.

"So, Jake, can you give us the keys to the truck?"

"Don't need to. It's open."

Dan squinched his eyes, thinking it rather strange that Jake would be so calm and compliant.

"Thank you, Jake. If you don't mind, I'd like you to make a written statement while we inspect the truck."

Jake just continued rocking. "No matter," he said, taking the clipboard from Dan's outstretched hand.

A full inspection of the truck turned up a few tantalizing pieces of evidence. Under the driver's seat was a plastic bag containing a pair of woman's panties, producing raised eyebrows from the trio. From the glove compartment, Steve recovered a woman's compact case with a used tube of lipstick inside. "Perfect!" he said, as he placed the case in a plastic specimen bag.

Sam strung a ribbon of yellow crime scene tape around the truck as Dan headed back to the porch.

"I want to thank you, Jake, for your cooperation."

Jake handed him the completed form.

"Happy to oblige," he said, though his words sounded hollow.

"Of course," Dan added, "I'm gonna have to impound that truck for a more complete search." He turned and pointed to the truck. "Need to check the contents of that tank, for starters." He scratched his head. "Although I'm not sure how much we're gonna find after two months."

Jake grunted.

"So, I'll have the boys return tomorrow morning with a tow truck to pick it up, just so you know."

Jake sighed. "Do what you gotta do."

Dan tightened his lips. "Right. So, I guess that should do it for now, Jake. You, uh... have a nice evening, eh?"

As they drove away with Sam at the wheel, Dan looked back. There was Jake still on the porch, continuing to rock.

Chapter Twenty-Nine

FUGITIVE FROM THE LAW

Tuesday, July 7, 2015

9:30 a.m. Dan was going over last-minute details with the team assigned to impound the Emerys' tanker truck when Sam peeked his head into the briefing room.

"Hey, Dan. Turn on Channel Six news. I think you'll find it interesting."

Dan looked up. "Can it wait, Sam? I'm trying to wrap up this briefing and get the team on the road."

Sam shook his head. "No, I think you better take a listen."

Dan sighed, mildly perturbed at the interruption. "Excuse me, gentlemen. My deputy requires my attention."

He picked up his cup of coffee and joined Sam in the next room. Sam handed Dan the remote and he turned up the volume.

"...and there are continuing developments in the Emma Hauptmann missing persons case," the newscaster said. "And for that we take you to Tom Kovac reporting live from city hall in Plymouth."

Dan's jaw dropped as he drew closer to the TV. A young man with a microphone was standing outside the police headquarters addressing the TV camera.

"Thank you, Ed. This is Tom Kovac of Badger-3 News. The Plymouth Police Department announced a possible major breakthrough in the

Emma Hauptmann missing persons case with the grisly discovery of human remains late yesterday afternoon, recovered from a septic holding tank at an undisclosed location near Waldo, Sheboygan County. And here to tell us about it is Police Chief Bill Preston."

The camera panned to the chief. Dan couldn't believe what he was seeing. "Just couldn't wait for the evening papers, could you, Bill?"

A gloating Bill Preston addressed the camera. "That's right, Tom. But first I want to extend kudos to the men of the Plymouth Police Department for their dedicated professionalism in making this discovery possible. I also wish to thank the county sheriff's office for their assistance in this matter."

Dan almost choked on his coffee. "For 'their assistance in this matter'? What unadulterated bull! The unmitigated gall of that man!" He could barely contain himself.

"...and as we speak, my boys are heading out to pick up Adam Emery for questioning," Bill continued. "As you know, Adam is the principal suspect in this case. We plan to hold him until the forensic testing is completed."

"That's good work, Chief," the reporter replied.

The interview continued for another minute or so, with the reporter concluding, "This is Tom Kovac, Badger-3 News, reporting live from Plymouth, Wisconsin. Now back to you, Ed."

Dan turned off the TV and it was all he could do to keep from throwing the remote across the room.

"What the hell! Talk about telegraphing your next move! Why not just send the guy a get-out-of-jail-free card!"

DAN WASN'T the only one watching the Badger-3 News report with his morning coffee. As Milly Emery poured her husband, Adam, a second cup, she noticed an abrupt change in his demeanor. The newscaster was wrapping up his report when Adam suddenly stiffened in his chair. With the blood draining from his face, he went into panic mode and without so much as a word, sprang from his chair, rushed into their bedroom, threw some items into a knapsack, and bolted out the front door. She followed him to the door, and the next thing Milly heard were the spinning wheels of his pickup coughing up rooster tails of gravel and dust as he took off for parts unknown.

Less than ten minutes later, three Plymouth police officers were knocking at her front door.

~

WHEN DAN LEARNED of Adam's escape, he went ballistic. He immediately got Chief Preston on the phone and read him the riot act for "putting publicity and personal notoriety before public safety!"

"I should've done it myself!" Dan growled.

Bill tried to assure him that everything was under control. The state police were notified, and it wouldn't be long before Adam was apprehended.

But it was all Dan could do to calm down and refocus on the tasks at hand: impounding the truck and following up on the forensic test work.

And then there was the DNA testing of those human molars seeming to grow out of that ear of corn! That one *really* had the boys in the crime lab stumped. When Dan instructed them to look for a match against known missing persons, they just exchanged blank stares. "Sure, anything you say, boss."

Chapter Thirty

CEREAL KILLER

Tuesday, July 7, 2015

At the same time Dan was reaming Bill Preston out, Luke and Pam were collaborating on the next installment of their GMO exposé. After giving it some careful thought, Luke had decided to share Saturday's strange "teeth-on-the-cob" episode with Pam.

"Oh my God!" she exclaimed. "That is *so* weird! It definitely trumps my 'tooth in the cereal box' story. Were they molars?" She stifled a laugh.

"Well, yes, actually they were," Luke said. "Three molars in fact. But you know, this is pretty serious stuff, Pam. The sheriff's office is following up with DNA testing. They plan to go through their database to try to come up with a match."

"A match?" Pam asked. "A match for what?"

Luke decided it was time to bring her into the loop.

"Well... any match at all, really. But mainly for missing persons."

He explained how he'd been working with Detective Dan Meyers of the county sheriff's office with his investigation of a string of missing persons cases going back over sixteen years.

"Dan thinks there may be a connection with other strange events that have been baffling area farmers. Stories of crop circles occurring in cornfields that seem to coincide with these disappearances. He thinks it might be 'calling cards' left by the killer."

Of course, Luke didn't go into his own personal history and the common experiences he shared with the notorious Jake Emery. That really would have blown her mind... as well as the "confidential source" arrangement he had with Jake.

Pam leaned back and grinned, like the wheels were already turning in her head. "So, you think we might have a 'cereal killer' on our hands, eh?"

"Serial killer? Yes, perhaps."

She laughed. "No, I mean c-e-r-e-a-l killer, dummy!"

Shaking his head, he groaned. "Ugh! That's really bad, Pam. Only you would come up with something like that." He reconsidered. "But you know, on second thought, I like that. 'Cereal Killer!' Would make a great headline, eh?"

Luke then explained how he and his botanist friend from UW Madison were going to meet up with Dan tomorrow in a cornfield out near Johnsonville to do some snooping around.

"You got permission from the farmer?" she asked.

"Sure. No problem."

She appeared deep in thought.

"You know, since you told me your strange story, I can tell you mine. Just found out yesterday, in fact. They might be related."

Luke's ears perked up. "Really? What is it?"

"Well, it's about that tooth found in the cereal box. I got a report back from the State Ag Department that's been looking into it. They were actually able to trace the origins of the corn that went into that box of corn flakes."

"That so?"

"Yes. But you better sit down. You're not going to believe this."

Luke took a seat. "Okay. Shoot!"

"The corn came from a co-op up near Kiel. You know, north of Elkhart Lake just across the county line."

Luke's jaw dropped. "No way!"

"Yes way!" she replied.

He immediately thought of his cousin Mark and his account of a crop circle on his dad's farm outside Kiel.

～

LATER THAT AFTERNOON, Luke finally got the call from Dan he'd been waiting for since yesterday morning.

"Hey, Sport. You sittin' down?" Dan began.

"Sure. What's up?" he said with feigned detachment.

"First off, I want to thank you for that tip you phoned in yesterday morning. It really paid off. Big time!" Dan said, enunciating each word, his baritone voice resonating with delight.

Luke could almost see the broad smile on his face.

Dan went on to describe exactly how things went down at the Heilbroner farm and Jake's place.

"Of course, we need to wait on the DNA tests. The remains, the panties, the lipstick. They all had to contain DNA."

"And the dental records?"

"Yeah, that too. I'm confident we're gonna get a match for Emma Hauptmann. And as soon as that happens, we'll issue a warrant for Adam's arrest. In the meantime, we'll have to track down and find the bastard!"

He explained the situation, how Chief Preston's "moment of glory" in front of the TV news camera managed to tip off Adam, who made his escape minutes before the police came knocking at his door.

"Hmm, that's too bad," Luke said.

"Yeah, well, there is one more thing. Tell me, have you received a call from Chief Preston yet?"

Luke was puzzled. "No. Don't think so. But I can check my voice mail. What's up?"

Dan explained the deal he made with Bill, that he could report the story and take credit for the find. "But that's all, just the find!" he emphasized. "The follow-up at Jake's place, well, that's my story! And I'll be sure to have the last word when the DNA evidence comes in and it's time to issue a warrant for Adam's arrest."

Luke thought it funny, the two jurisdictions battling over control of a case... and the publicity. But he supposed that happened all the time.

"Okay, Dan. If I don't hear from Bill soon, I'll give him a call. Check tomorrow's headlines."

"Thanks. And by the way," Dan added, "I'm pretty sure I know who the anonymous caller was who tipped you off."

"Really?"

"Of course! I know it wasn't Jedediah Heilbroner or his wife. And it certainly wasn't Adam." He paused. "It had to be Jake Emery himself."

Silence.

"Well, you just might be right," Luke was forced to admit.

Dan laughed. "That's okay. That's what we detectives do. The power of deductive reasoning and the process of elimination," he said, patting himself on the back.

Smiling, Luke reminded Dan about the next day's rendezvous at the Mertz farm and the ground-penetrating radar. They agreed to meet at one o'clock.

"Not a problem! Outlook would never let me forget. I got the GPR lined up with my friends at Geo-Services. And by the way, remember that soil sample we took off Jake's shovel last fall when we ran the initial investigation on his wife's disappearance?"

Luke had to think about it. "Yeah. What about it?"

"Well, I plan to take soil samples from the Mertz crop circle site tomorrow and get a forensic soil expert to compare the two samples. Calvin Mertz said it looked like someone had been doing some digging there, right? Maybe we can link Adam to that disappearance as well."

Of course, Luke had no doubt there would be a match. It was simply a matter of who Dan would pin it on, Jake or Adam. But he decided to play along.

"So, Dan, you think Adam might be the serial killer responsible for all these unexplained disappearances?"

"He could be. I know it's only a hunch at this point. But it's starting to add up."

"Even going back seventeen years?" Luke challenged.

Dan took a few seconds. Luke could imagine him doing the quick math. "Sure. I mean it is possible," Dan said. "Adam was nineteen when Jake's first wife, Laura, disappeared. And then your sister, Alice, just one year later." There was a momentary pause. "I mean, think about it. Laura's gold wedding band shows up at the site of your sister's last-known location. A souvenir or trophy taken by Laura's killer the year before. Leaves it at the site of your sister's abduction as a calling card or something. Along with a twisted crop circle of corn."

Luke put his head in his hands. "I don't know, Dan. Doesn't make any sense. How would Adam know where to find Alice that day in the corn-field? And why in the world would Adam want to murder his own mom? And then his stepmom fifteen years later?"

Silence.

"Don't know, Luke. Just gotta go where the evidence leads, is all. Motive comes later."

After hanging up, Luke shook his head. He next texted Aiyanna to remind her about tomorrow. They agreed to meet for lunch at the Pony Bar and Grill around noon and head out together to the Mertz farm.

Luke put down his cell phone and leaned back, hands folded behind his head. He let out a sigh as he wondered how long he could maintain his confidentiality with Jake Emery over Gloria's disappearance. Sooner or later, Dan would figure it out. And he was starting to feel a sense of—call it duplicity—for not sharing this with Aiyanna.

Chapter Thirty-One

CROP CIRCLES AND SINKHOLES

Wednesday, July 8, 2015

It was a little before noon when Luke rendezvoused with Aiyanna in Plymouth. He had just enough time to treat her to a quick lunch before meeting up with Dan and his investigative team. They took an interior booth.

Aiyanna seemed pleased. "Weather is perfect! It rained last night, so the ground should be good for digging."

"You always wear that amulet." He pointed at the bear amulet hanging around her neck. "You had it on at the brat fry too."

She reached up and fondled it. "Yes. It brings me luck."

Luke smiled coyly. "Funny, a scientist talking about *luck*."

"Not at all," she countered. "Luck, serendipity, providence—call it what you may, it has played a significant role in a great many scientific discoveries."

He shrugged. "I suppose."

Sitting back, she took a more pensive pose. "Tell me, Luke. Exactly what are you hoping to accomplish today?"

His lips tightened. He wasn't at liberty to tell her about his encounter with Jake, so he did the next best thing.

"Well, you remember what I told you about how my sister disappeared. How the area was torn up with the corn in a kind of spiral pattern?"

She closed her eyes. "Yes. Crop circles and sinkholes. That's what you and Dan called them."

Luke nodded. "Yes. Well, it turns out, according to farmers in the area, this crop circle thing is not so unusual. Happens from time to time going back quite a few years."

She smiled. "Yes, I did read your article in yesterday's *Dispatch*. Very entertaining. Any response yet?"

"Quite a few, actually. I need to check them out before forwarding them to Dan and Sam." He shifted in his seat. "You see, my theory is that there might be some geological basis for the phenomenon that generates a kind of sinkhole that can swallow a person whole, then closes up somehow."

Of course he couldn't divulge that it was Jake who first suggested the sinkhole theory, which is what drew him to the Mertz farm in the first place. But Luke grabbed onto this theory as the only rational explanation for what happened to both his sister and Jake's wife, Gloria, what with Jake's personal account being so much like his own sixteen years earlier.

With a small shrug, he continued, "But of course, as far as Dan is concerned, it has nothing to do with sinkholes at all, but everything to do with someone taking a pick and shovel to the ground to dispose of a body!"

"Hmm. Sounds like Dan," she said. "But one way or another, you both think that the crop circle event at the Mertz farm *might* have something to do with the disappearance of Jake's second wife ten months ago. They both occurred at about the same time."

Of course, Luke had no doubt about there being a connection. He spread his arms out across the back of the bench seat and nodded. "Exactly! But the GPR will tell the story. Sinkholes. Or buried body."

Their eyes met. Hers was a penetrating, hypnotic stare. "And you're hoping that it may also bring some kind of closure to what happened sixteen years ago."

Pausing, he blinked and turned away. "Yeah, I guess you could say that."

Aiyanna reached out and lightly touched his hand. "I hope so, Luke. For your sake."

Luke gave a wistful sigh. "So, what d'ya say we hit the road and test out our theories?"

~

AIYANNA HAD PACKED her red Blazer with all the necessary field trip paraphernalia: trowels, sifters, buckets, pots, plastic sample bags, jars, dissection kit, magnifying glass, and even a microscope for a more thorough field examination of specimens should that prove necessary. When she and Luke arrived at the Mertz farm, they found Dan and his team already there. A flatbed truck with a backhoe was parked alongside the road just ahead of the driveway; Dan's cruiser and a van with the word GEO-SERVICES emblazoned on the side panels were parked side by side in the yard.

Luke and Aiyanna joined Calvin and Dan in the yard.

"Good day, Mr. Mertz," Luke said, holding out his hand.

"And a good day to you, son, and to your pretty assistant," Calvin replied as he shook Luke's hand, giving Aiyanna a wink.

Inwardly she groaned.

"I've been discussing with Calvin what we plan to do," Dan chimed in. "I assured him that if any corn were damaged, he would be properly compensated."

Luke gave a reaffirming nod. Dan then introduced Luke and Aiyanna to Deputy Jimmy Collins and their forensic expert, Officer Steve Kelly.

"Okay, then. Let's get started," Calvin said, and climbed into his pickup. "Time's a wastin'. Follow me."

The caravan made its way down the road and parked on the shoulder right past the GMO corn sign. Leaving their vehicles, they proceeded single file into the cornfield with Calvin leading the way, followed by Dan, Luke, and Aiyanna with their backpacks loaded with sampling and testing paraphernalia.

"The corn's grown some since your last visit, Luke," Calvin called out. "I hope that's not a problem."

The corn was still less than a foot high, so they had no trouble getting through. But the Geo-Services technician who brought up the rear found navigating the rows of corn with his GPR rig a bit more of a challenge. The rig resembled a four-wheel rotary lawn mower with over-sized back wheels, the radar unit mounted low to the ground where the engine should have been, and a computer video screen mounted on the push handles at eye level. In the end, they were forced to clear several narrow paths through the field to establish a grid pattern to accommodate the rig.

About twenty-five yards into the field, Calvin turned and motioned with his arms.

"This is about where it happened," he said.

Dan surveyed the area and started giving orders to the technician to scan the area in roughly ten-foot swaths until he had mapped out an area about the size of a baseball diamond.

At the same time, Aiyanna began taking soil samples along with several whole stalks of corn, roots and all, which she transplanted into individual pots. She was hoping to keep them alive and growing back in the horticultural lab at Madison.

What immediately struck her was the white gauzy look of many of the soil samples, especially those closely associated with the corn roots.

"See this?" she said to Luke, pointing out the cotton-like appearance of the soil samples. "Fungal mycelia," she noted. "Same as the samples we retrieved from your sister's field two weeks ago."

Luke nodded as Dan happened by and paused to peer over Aiyanna's shoulder.

"Hmm. Those soil samples," he said, scratching his head. "Funny, they look an awful lot like the soil samples I collected sixteen years ago. Where your sister went missing, Luke. Remember?"

Aiyanna noted Luke's anguished expression, then glanced up at Dan. "Do you still have those soil samples?"

"Hmm. Should still be in the evidence lockers. I can double check when I get back. You interested?"

"Definitely! That would be an interesting check over time. Would I be able to get a sample for testing?"

"If we still have them, I'll see what I can do," he replied.

Just then the GPR tech called out. "Hey! I think I found something over here!"

The others rushed to join him around the video screen.

"See there! That shadow. An anomaly. Doesn't look like the other surrounding geological formations. Not very big, though. Maybe three feet long."

"How deep is it?" Dan asked.

"Uh. One point two two meters."

Dan groaned. "In normal terms."

"Okay. Approximately four feet."

"Perfect!" Dan said. "Let's dig it up. We can use shovels for this."

It took the four of them less than twenty minutes to exhume the "anomaly." They all stood around, hovering over their find.

"It's just a dog," Dan declared, unable to hide his disappointment.

"Still wearing a neck collar," the technician added.

"Not *just* a dog!" Calvin butted in with a tearful ring to his voice. He knelt down beside the decomposed, almost mummified, remains of the poor animal and took hold of the steel name tag on the collar. It read "Molly."

"That's our Molly! Oh my God! Those damn kids! They must've done this to her!"

Dan tried to console him. "I'm sorry, Calvin. I truly am. I had a 'Molly' once, as a kid growing up."

Aiyanna shook her head and rolled her eyes.

Calvin looked up. "Actually, I guess I need to thank you guys for finding her." He wiped his eyes with his shirtsleeve. "Now at least we can give her a more fitting burial. In our backyard."

Aiyanna couldn't help but notice the profusion of hyphae penetrating the canine's remains. She proceeded gingerly. "Mr. Mertz. I don't mean to be disrespectful, but would it be possible for us to examine the dog more thoroughly?"

His voice quivered. "You mean... like an autopsy?"

Aiyanna responded with a sympathetic smile. "Yes, Calvin. Like an autopsy, so we can determine exactly what it was that ki... well, you know. How she died."

He nodded. "Yeah. I suppose that would be possible."

No sooner had Aiyanna wrapped up poor Molly and placed her in the back of her Blazer than the technician let out another cry.

"Okay, guys! I have another find over here. And this one is much bigger!"

Dan perked up.

"How deep?"

"Much deeper," the technician replied. "About... fifteen... no, twelve feet! Sure looks like..." He hesitated until they had all gathered closer so he wouldn't be shouting.

"Looks like what?" Dan pressed.

"Well, see for yourself."

They all peered at the monitor screen. "Definitely could be a body," Dan said coolly. "Twelve feet, you said. I think we'll need the backhoe for this one."

～

AN HOUR later Dan and his team found themselves staring down at the near mummified remains of what appeared to be a woman's body, about five feet, two inches tall, slight build.

"Damn!" Dan exclaimed as he examined the body more closely. "She's covered with that same white downy material, just like the dog and those soil samples."

"Amazing!" Aiyanna said. "I've never seen mushroom hyphae penetrate to this depth before. I need to get samples."

"Ah, not so quick!" Dan interjected. "This is a coroner's case now. You will get your samples, but first things first. We need to perform a complete postmortem, establish her identity and cause of death before we do *anything* else."

Aiyanna backed away. "Sure, Dan. You're right of course. Nothing from the body. But I need surrounding soil samples from this depth. Could help with the case too."

Dan thought a moment. "Okay," he said. "Take your soil samples. But double up on them. We'll need them for forensic evidence as well."

Dan phoned in for a backup medical van to transport the Jane Doe to the county morgue in Sheboygan while Aiyanna and Luke continued taking samples for her mushroom research from other parts of the cornfield and a few control samples from the fallow field across the road.

Dan also secured his own soil sample for his forensic geologist to examine for a possible match with the soil recovered from the Emerys' shovel. Returning to the field, he overheard Luke asking the GPR tech whether there was any sign of a sinkhole.

"Nah. Didn't see anything like that," the tech responded. "But it's all been recorded on the hard drive. We can take a closer look back at the lab."

"Mm-hmm" was all Luke said.

By five o'clock the team had pretty much wrapped things up, both figuratively and literally. They thanked the Mertzes for their cooperation and assured them they would be compensated for all their trouble.

Luke turned to Dan as they were preparing to leave.

"So tell me, Dan. Twelve feet under. Why would anyone go to such lengths to conceal a body? I mean, how is it even possible with no more than a shovel?"

This one had Dan puzzled. "Hmm. Good question."

But Dan sensed there was something else on his Luke's mind.

"So, what's really bothering you, Sport?"

Luke took a slow, deep breath. "Well, I was thinking. Would it be possible to use this GPR rig to examine the site where Alice went missing sixteen years ago? The Klausman farm. I mean, if she were... twelve feet under, d'ya think there'd be enough of her remaining to be detected?"

Dan took a moment. He knew what Luke was seeking: closure. "Well, it's certainly worth a try," he said as he put a reassuring hand on Luke's shoulder. "I'm sure I can convince the sheriff to reopen your sister's case. I'll go ahead and contact Ed Klausman to arrange a visit."

Luke nodded. "Thanks, Dan."

"Don't mention it. This case is kind of personal for me, too, dontcha know." He paused. "Hope we can both find a resolution on this, Luke."

Chapter Thirty-Two

AIYANNA'S DREAM

Later that Evening

Back in her Madison lab with the day's booty of field samples, Aiyanna worked late into the evening sorting, cataloging, planting, and otherwise doing all the things a well-trained and disciplined scientific investigator does to document and preserve her find. The DNA testing and microscopic examinations would have to wait until the next day.

When she finally returned to her apartment around ten o'clock, she was feeling a little light-headed. She realized she hadn't eaten since lunch, so she brewed herself a pot of ginger tea, retrieved a leftover Chinese takeout meal from the fridge, and plopped it in the microwave. "Waste not, want not," as her father always said.

Retiring to her bedroom, she removed the bear amulet from around her neck and hung it on a hook over the dresser next to a picture of her mom and dad. She then took the small buckskin pouch clipped to her belt and placed it in a humidor emanating the faint scent of tobacco. She wasn't a smoker. But she maintained a measure of her people's traditional beliefs in the palliative and guardian effects of this ancient weed. "Carry it with you at all times," her father would tell her as a young girl, "as an offering to unseen spirits, to facilitate passage through an uncertain world." Some might call it superstition. But, as with the amulet, she likened these things to the Saint Christopher necklaces, holy water, or rosaries of the Catholic faith or the prayer beads of other religions.

After a hot, cleansing shower, she donned her PJs and climbed into bed. Her mind continued to mull over the events and images of the day. One thing that continued to haunt her was Luke's talk of sinkholes and the mysterious disappearance of his sister sixteen years earlier. As she drifted in and out of that hypnagogic state of half-sleep where thoughts and images melded into an amalgam of the surreal, sleep finally overcame her.

And with sleep... a dream.

IN HER DREAM she found herself wrapped in a soft, cool mist, permeated with diffuse white light. She had a sense of being in a large, enclosed space, with the syncopated sounds of water droplets echoing from nearby unseen sources. Like dripping water faucets. Directly ahead through the mist there came a shadowy form. Barely discernible at first, it approached in a slow, deliberate, but nonthreatening manner. It was the unmistakable form of a man. As he emerged closer out of the mist, his features became better defined. Now standing but two arm's lengths away, the image was clear. He was a Native American man, average height, dressed in the ancient manner of the Ho-Chunk people, buckskin leggings, breechcloth, jacket vest with bone-weaved breastplate. His hair was combed straight back with two long braids and topped off with a roach porcupine headdress set off with three turkey feathers.

The man smiled and spoke.

"You wear your bear amulet very well, Aiyanna."

His voice was firm but gentle. While Aiyanna was fluent in Hocąk, she found the man's dialect something of a challenge. Perhaps an older form of Hocąk.

She looked down, realizing only now that she was wearing the necklace and amulet. She smiled in return.

"Thank you, sir. It was... a gift from my father, passed down through... generations."

The man gave a gentle laugh. "Yes, I know its origins, my child."

He came closer, reached out, and touched the amulet.

"It has been many, many moons since I last wore this," he said with a tear in his eye.

Aiyanna was dumbfounded. "I... I don't understand."

The man stood back. "I am Akecheta," he announced proudly, "leader of the Bear clan. Your father was right to give this to you. You have a true heart and hold dear the traditions of our people."

Aiyanna responded timidly. "Are you... my ancestor?"

Akecheta laughed. "Why, of course! That is why I come to you in a dream."

The mist had gradually cleared while they spoke. It was only now that Aiyanna realized where she was, in the belly of a great cavern, surrounded by crystalline rock formations of many shapes and sizes. Small rivulets trickled down the walls of the cavern, joining a larger stream that flowed beyond her ken, while other waters dripped from the dome of the cave high above, having the proportions of a large, roofed coliseum.

"Where are we?" she asked.

Akecheta surveyed the cavern. "It doesn't matter where we are," he said. "You only need to know why I come."

She hesitated. "And why is that?"

He breathed a deep sigh. "My child, you will be faced with a choice. You must choose wisely. You must not forget the ways of our people. You must search your heart. That is the only way you will succeed."

With these words spoken, Akecheta nodded and turned to go.

"Wait!" Aiyanna shouted out. "Please, do not go!"

Akecheta continued to walk away into the new gathering mist. As he did, other shadowy figures appeared farther off in the distance, seeming to beckon him on.

"Do not forget the ways of our people. That is the only way," he repeated, looking back over his shoulder.

Aiyanna was powerless to move and could only watch as her ancestral leader of the Bear clan slowly faded into the growing mist, leaving her as she began. Alone in a cool, white void.

When Aiyanna awoke, she found herself lying on her back on the floor and staring straight up at the ceiling. Shaking, she tried to comprehend the meaning of the dream. *Was it a dream?* It seemed so real, so vivid. She forced herself to sit up and looked over at the dresser. The amulet had somehow fallen from its hook onto the floor. She got up, went over, and picked it up, studying it with her eyes and fingers.

She repeated the name, *Akecheta*, many times. After placing the amulet back on its hook, she paused as she was turning to go to bed. Retrieving the necklace, she returned to bed, placing the amulet under her pillow.

It was four o'clock in the morning. Still time to catch two more hours of shut-eye. She grasped the amulet and hugged her pillow. She had no trouble going back to sleep. And this time there were no dreams.

Chapter Thirty-Three

THE EVIDENCE IS IN

Tuesday, July 14, 2015

Forensic test results were coming in fast and furious and confirmed what everyone had strongly suspected, linking Adam Emery to what had now evolved from a missing persons case to a kidnapping, rape, and first-degree homicide case. Luke's front-page article in Tuesday's edition of the *Dispatch* summed it up nicely.

Detective Dan Meyers of the Sheboygan County Sheriff's Office issued a warrant for the arrest of Adam Emery of Plymouth for the felony counts of kidnapping, rape, and first-degree murder of Emma Hauptmann, missing since May 8 when she never returned home from the Emerys' Refuse and Septic Servicing Company, where she worked as part-time clerk. DNA samples from the bone fragments and teeth of the remains recovered from a septic tank in Waldo, as well as the lipstick and undergarments found in Adam's tanker truck, matched Emma Hauptmann's DNA, as did earlier blood samples from Adam's pickup truck. The dental records also confirmed the body to be that of Emma Hauptmann. When the county's forensic team examined the contents of the tanker truck, they also found bone fragments with matching DNA. The clincher was Adam's own DNA, found on the woman's undergarments.

Satisfied with his day's work, Luke turned on Badger-3 News that evening to see a replay of an earlier televised interview with Detective Dan Meyers.

"Yes, Tom," an ebullient Dan Meyers announced to the world. "We're sure we have the right man and a slam-dunk case with the forensic evidence that has piled up over the past two weeks. We are even looking into possible links between Adam and other long-unsolved missing persons cases that could go back as far as 1998."

"That's amazing, Detective Meyers!" replied the TV reporter. "I wish you well in your ongoing investigations." He then turned to the camera. "That's all for now. This is Tom Kovac from outside the Sheboygan County Sheriff's Office reporting for Badger-3 News. Back to you, Ed."

Luke shot a text message to Dan, congratulating him on his "Emmy Award–winning TV performance." Dan thanked him. Luke asked whether there was any new information confirming Gloria's remains from the Mertz farm.

Luke watched three dots dance on his screen for a few moments before Dan's next message popped up.

Dan: *Still waiting on matching DNA results from hair samples taken from the Emery place. Jake was very accommodating.*

Luke: *Not surprised. I think he's just wants to know the truth .*

There was a thumbs-up emoji from Dan.

Luke: *And what of those corn cob teeth from the Fourth? Any luck with the DNA testing?*

More dancing dots.

Dan: *We were able to get enough DNA for profiling. Farmer Mertz came up clean. And no match with the database. But tell Aiyanna we were able to draw DNA from each tooth without destroying the samples!*

Luke: *Great!* (with two emoji smiling faces)

Dan: (Thumbs-up emoji)

Luke: *Are we still on for tomorrow at the Klausman farm?*

Dan: *You got it. See you tomorrow!*

The previous Friday, Dan had called to say he'd spoken to Ed Klausman and was able to arrange a visit for Wednesday, the fifteenth, to survey for Alice's remains. Luke now planned to rendezvous with Dan's team at the sheriff's office the next day at 9:00 a.m. before heading out to the farm together. Dan described Ed as "very accommodating." While Ed didn't own the farm at the time of Alice's disappearance, he did recall the incident reported in the papers and was glad to do whatever he could to "help solve that cold case."

Luke went to the kitchen and heated up some leftover casserole. Grabbing a beer from the fridge, he was returning to the living room when his cell phone alerted him to a new email. It was from Aiyanna.

Hi, Luke,

We need to talk. I've got some exciting new developments to share with you from last Wednesday's field trip. Can you come down to Madison one day this week? The sooner the better. And if convenient, could you please bring down those soil and specimen samples that Dan promised me? Also, I'm collaborating with a colleague from our horticulture department. I told him about the mysterious corn kernels from your mom's brat fry and he is *very* interested. Would it be possible to bring the corn cob down as well, along with a normal "control" cob from that day?

Oh, BTW, that's great news on that Emma Hauptmann case! Please offer Dan my congratulations.

Best,

Aiyanna-Nez

Luke replied immediately, saying Thursday would work best for him. He'd come down first thing in the morning and do his best to bring those specimens from Dan.

After their email exchange Luke sat back, hands folded behind his head, and pondered. *Maybe I should have told her about our plans to visit the Klausman farm tomorrow.*

But since Aiyanna had already taken samples from that site on their first field trip together, he figured it wasn't necessary. And he didn't want to take her away from her important work in Madison. On the other hand, if they did find something, well, it would be nice having her there for moral support.

He reached for his phone, then reconsidered, second-guessing himself a second time. Not a good idea, he finally concluded, springing this on her at the last minute.

RETURN TO THE SCENE OF THE CRIME

Wednesday, July 15, 2015

9:00 a.m. Luke's heart was beating a little faster than normal when he arrived at the Sheboygan County Sheriff's Office, 525 North Sixth Street, in downtown Sheboygan. Dan met him in the lobby and escorted him to a small briefing room where the other members of the team were already assembled. He knew Sam, of course, and recognized Deputies Jimmy Collins and Steve Kelly and the Geo-Services tech, Jeff Seibert, from his visit to the Mertz farm the week before.

Luke gave a nervous smile as he greeted the team. "Good morning, gentlemen. I greatly appreciate this opportunity and hope we can finally close this 'cold case,' as you call it. For me, of course, it's anything but *cold*. Rather, it's very warm and personal."

The men exchanged nods and expressions of sympathy.

"Yes, Luke," Dan replied. "We are all hoping close this one, being one of the oldest open missing persons cases in our files."

After formally introducing Luke to the team, Dan reviewed the game plan. It would pretty much mirror the same approach taken a week before at the Mertz farm. Dan assured them all that the farmer, Ed Klausman, was expecting them.

Luke turned to the Geo-Services tech. "Jeff, I know this GPR can pick up sinkholes and other voids below the service. Correct?"

"Yes, that is correct."

Luke thought for a moment. "So, just how far down can it penetrate?"

Jeff sat back and folded his arms. "Well, depending on the nature and conductivity of the substrata, it can go as deep as a hundred feet. Clay soil tends to limit its penetrating power, but sandy soil and granite are a piece of cake."

Luke nodded. "I see."

"Okay, girls. Science lesson over." Dan smirked. "The flatbed and backhoe are parked out front waiting for us." He checked his watch. "Okay, let's mount up! We should be there by ten o'clock, barring any unforeseen delays."

~

10:05 A.M. THE team arrived at their destination. For Dan it was a return to the scene of the crime. The field seemed eerily unchanged after sixteen years, even though the farm had passed to new ownership since then.

"Good morning, gentlemen," Ed Klausman said as he greeted them in the driveway with his golden retriever, Kelsey, by his side. Ed was a tall, sinewy, affable fellow. His sunbaked leathery skin attested to a lifetime of farming.

"Good morning, Ed," Dan said, shaking hands. "This here is Luke Kramer, from the *Dispatch*. He's the brother of Alice. The girl we're looking for."

Ed reached out and took Luke's hand. "So sorry for your loss, Luke. This must be... pretty hard for you." He backed up. "Sixteen years ago," he said, rubbing his chin. "Hard to believe."

Dan recounted his own involvement in the case as a young deputy who had recently joined the force. "So, it's pretty personal for me, too," he said with a nod to Luke.

"I understand," Ed said. "Well, time's a wastin'. Let's get started, eh?"

Dan knew the way, like it was only yesterday. Heading down the dirt road about a hundred yards, they parked their vehicles by the Tenderbrooke Farms Co-op GMO Corn and Soy sign, then hoofed it into the field, Jeff's GPR rig trundling before him. With most of the sweet corn having been recently harvested in this part of the field, they made rapid progress over the remaining stubble toward the site of Alice's disappearance.

Dan did a quick visual survey of the area. He wasn't able to precisely pinpoint the location of the crop circle but managed to stake out an area that he felt was sufficiently large enough to encompass it. About half the size of a football field. Luke nodded in agreement. Dan gave a thumbs-up sign to Jeff to power up the GPR rig and begin the scanning process. The software automatically recorded the GPS location as Jeff easily negotiated the spent rows of corn, generating a three-dimensional subterranean map of the area to a depth of about forty feet.

Fifteen minutes into the scan, Dan started to fidget. "See anything yet, Jeff?" he shouted out. But Jeff probably couldn't hear him over the echoes coming through his headphones as he focused on the computer screen to his front. After about thirty minutes he came to a stop, removed his headphones, and took a deep breath.

"Well?" Dan asked.

Jeff wiped his forehead with his shirtsleeve. "Not a darn thing," he said at last. "Just the usual substrata of soil, loose sediment, and broken rock."

Dan looked at Luke and saw his own perplexed feelings mirrored on the young man's face.

"I'm sure we got the right field," Dan said, turning to Jeff. "You say you saw... *nothing?*"

Jeff cocked his head. "Well, not anything that you'd be interested in. No anomalies. I mean, nothing that could be taken for a body."

Luke jumped in. "How about... sinkholes? Maybe something deep in the ground. Strange rock formations, or something."

Jeff scratched his head. "Well, I was focusing mainly on the first forty feet or so." He looked at Dan. "I can go deeper if you'd like."

Dan paused. "Sure, let's do it again, but deeper this time."

"Okay. Whatever you say. You're the boss."

Jeff put his headphones back on, made some adjustments, and repeated the search.

This time the results proved interesting. Halfway through the field he stopped and called the team over. They gathered behind him and studied the screen.

"See those shadows, and that larger clear area?"

They all nodded.

"The clear areas are voids. A cavern or cave of some kind beneath the bedrock. And see there?' He pointed to an anomaly in the computer image. "There's a fissure in the rock that opens into the cavern."

"Hmm. How far down?" Luke asked.

"About seventy feet, give or take."

"Interesting," Luke said. "Do you think it might have generated a sinkhole at some point in the past?"

"I don't know. It's hard to say. But I suppose it's possible."

In the end, they hadn't recovered their corpus delicti, but there was at least the *possibility* of a sinkhole of some kind occurring in the past.

"Of course, there's always the fallback possibility that Alice was... abducted," Dan offered.

Luke shook his head. "I don't know, Dan. There just wasn't enough time for that. Remember, I was there."

Dan paused. "Well, you know how time can distort one's recollection of things, Luke. It happens all the time."

Luke turned to Jeff. "Can you finish mapping out the whole area, and perhaps some of the surrounding field as well? I'd like to see how far that deep cavern goes."

Jeff looked at Dan, who gave him an approving nod.

Next Dan handed Luke three plastic specimen bags. "Here," he said, "don't forget your girlfriend in Madison. I'm sure she'd appreciate some soil samples to compare to the ones we took sixteen years ago."

Luke thanked Dan with a smile. Of course, he and Aiyanna had already sampled soil from this farm three weeks prior during their first outing. But more specimens couldn't hurt. And, coming from Dan, he appreciated the gesture.

ON THEIR RETURN TO SHEBOYGAN, Luke rode shotgun with Dan as they discussed the potential significance of the new find: caverns far beneath the surface, but not so far below that they couldn't have perhaps played a part in the formation of sinkholes, or some other anomalous event. Dan remarked that the cornfield where the presumed body of Gloria Emery had been recovered exhibited no evidence of sinkholes or deep caverns. Although he admitted that the GPR scan was not set up to penetrate so far into the ground during that survey.

"I was surprised how extensive the caverns were," Luke said. "They covered the entire survey area in length, and then some. And no telling how far beyond they extend."

"Mm-hmm. That was interesting," Dan said. "I think I'm gonna be hitting the road with my GPR road crew to explore all known sites where crop circles have been reported. Sam has been making significant strides with his computer modeling in correlating all this information." He turned to Luke and grinned. "But don't tell him I told you so. Don't want him getting a swelled head over this."

"Cross my heart." As an afterthought, Luke added, "Mind if I drop by the office and see for myself?"

"Hmm. Don't see why not. Of course, we're not ready to publish any of this, so it's *all* off the record for the time being."

Luke nodded.

Back in the sheriff's office, Luke joined Dan and Sam in front of the computer screen. Sam seemed eager to show off his most recent findings. He started off by bringing up the digital pin map, which Luke was already familiar with from his initial visit two weeks earlier. Since then, Sam had expanded Dan's original red, blue, and yellow color-coded pins into a rainbow of colors representing years going back to 1997.

"Now watch this," Sam said.

After a few clicks of the mouse, the map on the screen was overlaid with a large area of transparent yellow.

"This is the mapping of GMO cornfields for the county taken from the yearly information you provided, Luke. If I change the date, you can see the overlay change shape."

"Sure," Luke said. "The fields changed over time. I can understand that."

"Okay, now watch this!"

An array of seemingly random circles now filled the screen map. As Sam changed the year, the circle locations also changed.

Dan explained. "Those are the locations of mini crop circles reported over the past ten years, Luke. And I gotta say, your series of articles on these events really helped flush out previously unreported cases. Made our job a whole lot easier compiling this information."

"Well, I'm glad I was able to help," Luke said, rather pleased with himself.

"Also, searching the newspaper archives and back issues," Sam added, "we were able to uncover the first reported instances of these events going back seventeen years. I'm still compiling this information, so it's not yet in the model's database."

Sam turned their attention back to the computer screen.

"Now notice that for any given year, the circles all fall within the GMO crop areas, with the exception of a few outliers, which could be explained by misreported cases, or perhaps the GMO map isn't a hundred percent accurate. But in general, the correlation is quite good. Almost ninety-five percent!"

Luke raised a brow. "That's quite amazing."

"Okay, now here comes the best part," Sam said, fidgeting in place like he was getting ready for a 3-2 pitch.

As Luke watched, the map became awash in scattered patches of light that changed with time.

"Looks like a radar weather map over time," he said.

"Bingo!" Dan exclaimed. "That's exactly what it is. It represents the data that your meteorologist friend, Albert, gave us this past week."

"Right," Sam added. "And if I synchronize the GMO corn and crop circle information with this weather data, I can play it back, like a movie, for the past ten years, which is all the weather data we have at the moment. But what it does show is an excellent correlation over time between areas of thunderstorm activity and the occurrence of these crop circles. Again, about a ninety-five percent correlation."

"So, you think there's something about thunderstorm activity that triggers these events?" Luke asked.

"Don't know about cause and effect. But there definitely is a correlation."

Luke was thinking about the storm that preceded his own experience with his sister's disappearance. And Jake's account of the approaching storm preceding Gloria's disappearance. Of course, that last piece of information was something Dan and Sam weren't aware of. But now they were watching it play out right in front of their eyes on the computer screen.

"I gotta hand it to you, Sam, you're quite the hacker. I take back half of all the bad things I've ever said about you." Dan added with a smirk, "But double down on the other half!"

Luke had to chuckle. He stood back and folded his arms. "So, what about the missing persons data? How do they correlate with the crop circle information?"

"Yes, well, that's really the good news," Sam said. He was beaming now, and clearly on a roll. "I've been able to directly connect about eighty percent of unsolved missing persons cases in the area to specific mini crop circle events. The real key to these correlations is the timing of these events, together with proximity and timing of last-seen missing persons. So, we think these crop circle sites represent the actual crime sites.

"But just to clarify, not *every* crop circle—and there have been quite a few in the course of time—is linked to a missing person. Otherwise, we'd have an avalanche of missing persons cases on our hands," he said with a laugh. "However, most of the unsolved missing persons—about eighty percent—can be linked to a mini crop circle event. The remaining unsolved cases seem totally unrelated, like your average runaway."

Luke was shaking his head. This was too good to be true.

"So, what about the perps?" he asked. "The Emerys? How do they enter into this... computer model?"

"Ahem!" Dan jumped in. "Yes, well, that was the whole reason we delved into this geographical profiling software in the first place." He tapped Sam on the shoulder. "Show Luke the perp profiles that you've come up with."

With a few more mouse clicks the map changed to a 3D profile map with peaks and valleys.

Sam explained. "This is a three-dimensional probability distribution map showing the probable location of a single perpetrator's home base for a grouping of crimes, in this case, missing persons. Starting with the basic last-known location data and neglecting the time element, you can see the probability distribution is fairly flat over a wide area encompassing Plymouth all the way up to Elkhart Lake and out to Johnsonville."

"So, in this case," Dan interjected, "we either have a roaming serial killer living off the land—in other words, has no permanent home base of operations—or there are multiple perps located throughout the area operating over the same period of time, a possibility we had considered from the very beginning. Actually, that makes sense considering the fact that the victims don't fit any particular profile—man, woman, child, young or old."

Sam continued. "But, if we incorporate the crop circle crime sites for the past seventeen years, you can see the probability curve start to take shape, peaking in and around the Elkhart Lake area, which becomes more pronounced over time."

"So, what are you saying, exactly?" Luke asked.

Dan sighed. "Well, unfortunately, this fails to point an accusing finger at the Emerys or anyone else we may have been considering in the Plymouth area. And there have been more than a few, I might add. At the moment, we have no known suspects in the Elkhart Lake area. Of course, we haven't yet explored the area around Kiel. It's my guess that the map would extend into that region as well."

Luke leaned back against a desk. To tell the truth, he was pleased with the outcome. He felt confident that the perp, serial killer or otherwise, wasn't Jake. And he found it hard to believe Adam would have killed his own mother and stepmother. Then a light bulb went off in his head.

"You know what I think?" Luke said.

Sam and Dan turned their heads.

"I think we need more correlating data. And I know just where to go for it."

Dan smiled knowingly. "Wouldn't happen to be your *girlfriend* in Madison, now, would it?" He winked at Sam.

Luke sighed with feigned annoyance. Fact was, he was beginning to like that possibility, despite Dan's repeated sophomoric innuendos.

"You mean my *collaborator*, Miss Aiyanna-Nez?"

"Of course," Dan replied. "Anyway, the next time you see your *collaborator*, Miss Aiyanna-Nez, please give her something for me. Something I've owed her since our trip to the Mertz farm."

Dan left the room and returned in a few minutes with one cold-pack container labeled FORENSIC BODY SAMPLES – MERTZ FARM, and a second smaller container labeled SOIL SAMPLES – KLAUSMAN FARM, AUGUST 20, 1999.

"The Mertz samples are last week's Jane Doe body samples from forensics. The other bag contains a sixteen-year-old soil sample from the site of your sister's disappearance. She said she wanted to compare them with recent soil samples from that area."

Luke nodded and reached for the containers.

"Not so quick," Dan said. "Before I relinquish them, you will need to sign these chain of custody forms. Aiyanna will need to sign them too. She can have the samples only if she promises to give me a full report of her findings. For our forensic files."

"Well, I'm sure she'll have no problem with that," Luke said as he signed the forms. "Uh, there is one more thing." He handed the signed forms back to Dan. "Would it be possible to *borrow* the corn cobs taken on the Fourth? Aiyanna said she'd like to do some testing of her own. One of her colleagues from the horticulture department is eager to study this strange phenomenon, quite apart from any forensic significance."

Dan rubbed his chin. "Well, since we have the tooth DNA samples, I suppose that would be okay if she agrees to share her results. But we'll need them back as forensic evidence if we find a DNA match."

Dan motioned to Sam to retrieve the evidence and additional chain of custody forms.

"Thank you, Dan! And Aiyanna thanks you as well."

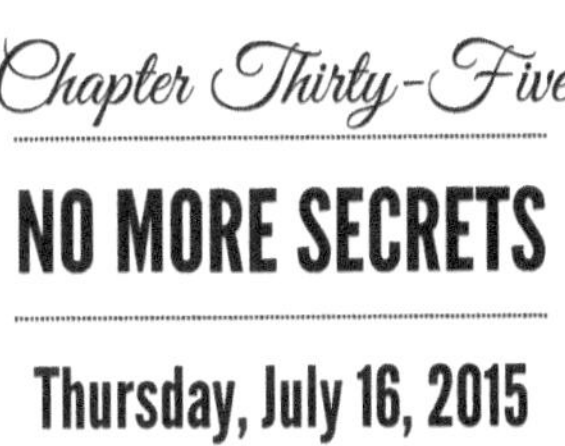

NO MORE SECRETS

Thursday, July 16, 2015

It was another lovely day for a road trip. Luke got an early start and in no time at all, it seemed, he was climbing the steps of Agriculture Hall on the UW Madison campus, carrying a leather satchel containing the soil and specimen samples Dan had promised Aiyanna. Once in the lobby, he texted her. "Be there in a sec," she texted back.

When Aiyanna met Luke, she wasn't alone. A tall, gaunt fellow with wire-rim spectacles, draped in a lab coat one size too large, accompanied her carrying an iPad, with a rolled-up newspaper tucked under his arm.

"Good morning, Luke," Aiyanna said in a chipper tone. "I'd like you to meet Dr. Nathaniel Greene of our horticulture department."

"Good morning, Doctor," Luke said as they shook hands. "Luke Kramer, reporter for the *Sheboygan Dispatch*."

Aiyanna smiled. "Not to worry, Luke. I've told him so much about you I think he knows you already!"

"Please, call me Nate," the doctor replied. "It is certainly a pleasure to meet you in person, Luke."

The doctor's voice was bold and confident, which belied first impressions based on physical appearance. But he exhibited a haughtiness that troubled Luke. Academicians sometimes came across that way, he reminded himself.

Nate unrolled the newspaper he was carrying. "I found especially interesting this article in last Thursday's edition of the *Dispatch*." He held it up and read the title aloud: "'Cereal Killer or Freak of Nature.' It talks about a human tooth found in a cereal box and certain 'mystery kernels' found on an ear of corn. 'Teeth-on-the-cob' is how they put it."

Luke's jaw dropped. He wasn't sure if the doctor was serious or just playing with him.

"Yes, uh, well, that article was the brainchild of my coworker, Pam York. I've been collaborating with her on a series of articles on GMO corn, and well, she decided to embellish things a bit."

The doctor smiled. "Yes, well, the style does smack of a tabloid exposé. I especially liked the part, let's see, how did she put it"—he read directly from the article—"'the only cob of corn that bites back!' My, how poignant!" he said with a wry grin. "But I do, in fact, take the subject matter seriously."

Luke exhaled slowly, wondering where Nate was going with this.

"I would have passed it off as a prank," Nate continued, "if it weren't for Aiyanna's eyewitness account of this bizarre happening. It occurred at your mother's Fourth of July cookout, I understand."

"That's right, Doctor. As a matter of fact, Aiyanna and I picked the corn up from the Mertzes' farm stand earlier that morning. The same Mertz farm we investigated last week that has become associated with a potential homicide case. Of course, I'm not at liberty to discuss the details of that case."

"Yes, of course. I understand you're working with the sheriff's office on this," Nate said, with a confirmatory nod toward his colleague. "Tell me, has forensics come up with anything on the 'teeth-on-the-cob'?"

Luke explained that they were able to recover DNA but had not yet found a match with anything in their database.

"Well, based on our findings with the corn and soil samples Aiyanna brought back last Wednesday," Nate said, "I think there may be a curious link. Were you able to bring the actual specimen with you today?"

Luke reached down and patted the satchel. "Got it right here, along with the soil and specimen samples you asked for, Aiyanna. The specimens and corn cob are cold-packed, so you may want to store them away before we do anything else. But I can assure you that the corn cob and two of the three teeth remain intact. The third being the half-eaten specimen, of course, which you'll find in a separate bag."

Nate beamed. "Excellent! I was hoping that would be the case."

Aiyanna reached for the satchel. "Let me get these in the freezer for safekeeping. Excuse me, gentlemen."

Grabbing the satchel, she retreated to her lab. It only took a few minutes before she returned with the empty satchel.

"Thank you, Luke," she said. "And please, thank Dan for me."

"Are we ready, then, Aiyanna?" Nate asked.

"Lead the way, Doctor!"

Nate turned to Luke and smiled stiffly. "It's just a short walk from here. Down the road a piece. Shall we?"

Dr. Greene led them out of the building and up the walkway heading west along Linden Drive. On the way, Aiyanna explained her findings from the soil samples taken from the Mertz farm. She was happy to report that *all* the samples containing mycelial growth were a positive match for the new giant mushroom species she had dubbed *Armillaria sheboygansis*. Not just the same species, but the same sprawling organism! Even the soil samples taken from sixteen feet under evidenced this new giant mushroom species.

"And what's even more interesting," she said, "is that the mushroom soil samples taken from Mertz's GMO cornfields exhibited the same pulsating bioluminescent response to electrical stimuli as the samples we retrieved from your sister's cornfield three weeks ago! However, the mushroom soil samples taken from the fallow field across the road did not exhibit this characteristic, even though they were genetically identical to the GMO cornfield samples, being one and the same organism."

"Yes," Nate chimed in. "We think there is some kind of epigenetic response going on resulting from a special symbiotic relationship this mushroom species enjoys with genetically modified corn."

Swoosh! Like a supersonic jet, that last remark flew fast and high over Luke's head!

"Can you please explain that last statement in layman's terms."

"Certainly," Nate replied. "A symbiotic relationship is one in which..."

"No. I understand the concept of symbiosis," Luke said, "but the term 'epigenetic' eludes me."

Nate cleared his throat, apparently not happy with the interruption.

"Yes, well, *epigenetic* is when something from the environment activates, or turns on, one or more genes in an organism, triggering the expression of an observable trait, or even illness. The classic example in the insect world is royal jelly, which is fed to selected bee larvae by the nurse bees to activate the genes responsible for turning the young developing bee into a new, fertile queen."

"I see," Luke said. "So, in our case, you think there is something about the GMO corn that turns on this bioluminescence response. Which is why we don't see it with non-GMO corn soil samples."

"Precisely! And it doesn't end there, as you will see in a few minutes."

Not far down the road, they crossed over and headed up a walk leading to an ivy-faced redbrick three-story building. This was the home of the UW Madison Horticulture, Plant Science, and Agronomy Departments. Nate led them inside and toward the rear of the building to a large adjoining solarium that contained rows of both open and covered beds along with several greenhouse structures. He explained that each greenhouse was equipped with its own ventilation system designed to control the temperature and humidity and contain what was growing inside.

"Over there," Nate said, pointing to two larger greenhouses on the far side of the room.

A sign posted by the door of the first greenhouse read "Experimental Station 6A, Non-GMO Corn." The second greenhouse was labeled "Experimental Station 6B, GMO Corn from Mertz Farm." The first greenhouse contained a raised soil bed but otherwise appeared empty.

"So, what's going on in the first greenhouse?" Luke asked.

"Well, that's our control test bed," Nate replied. "I can better explain that after I show you the next station."

Nate led them into the second greenhouse through a small anteroom or foyer, "designed as a means of double containment," Nate explained. Inside was a raised soil bed—Luke estimated it to be eight feet long by four feet wide and four feet high—with two rows of growing cornstalks spaced at roughly one-foot intervals. Luke counted ten stalks in all, five stalks per row.

"Well, Aiyanna, I see you managed to keep your specimens alive," he remarked. "They seem to be thriving."

"Yes, fortunately. Owing to Dr. Greene's tender loving care."

"And *Green* thumb, no doubt," Luke added.

He could see Aiyanna wince. Luckily, Nate didn't seem to hear. Or perhaps just pretended not to hear. He picked up where he'd left off.

"You see, in this bed we hoped to duplicate the conditions encountered in the field on the Mertz farm—and other farms in the area, according to Aiyanna. What we found was quite remarkable. Beyond exhibiting the bioluminescence response, what we have observed is a direct symbiotic, rather than parasitic, relationship with the corn plant.

"Typically, when a pathogenic mushroom species invades a host plant, like a tree, it sends its hyphae along the plant's root system excreting digestive enzymes that destroy the host. *Armillaria ostoyae*, for example, is responsible for killing off large swaths of conifers in many parts of the United States and Canada. But, as Aiyanna may have explained to you, *Armillaria* has the ability to extend flat shoestring-like structures, called *rhizomorphs*, that bridge the gap between food supplies—in our case, between fields of corn—allowing it to expand its coverage over enormous areas of ground. Hence the moniker *giant mushrooms*.

"Now, with our newly discovered species, a rather unique symbiotic relationship seems to have developed, whereby the mushroom hyphae penetrate the roots and stem of the corn host, extending all the way to the tassels and silk and even into the developing kernels of corn, without damaging the plant. Rather, it appears to derive its nourishment from the plant while providing the plant with water, minerals, and added resistance to insect infestations."

Nate paused to demonstrate this point by brushing away the soil from the base of one of the cornstalks to reveal the white cottony mycelial growth associated with its root system.

"What's even more remarkable," he continued, "is that there may even be a kind of neural network at play here, with cornstalks capable of communicating in a rudimentary fashion with other cornstalks in the field via this subterranean network of mycelial growth. Exactly what purpose this serves is something we are continuing to explore."

As he spoke, he moved to a control box similar to what Luke had seen before: a DC voltage regulator hooked up to two electrodes inserted into the soil at opposite ends of the soil box. Only this regulator was larger and powered off an AC/DC adapter plugged into the 110 AC house current.

"Now, watch this." Nate flipped the switch and slowly turned up the DC voltage.

Luke observed a faint pulsating green glow emanating from the soil. But this time, rather than producing a series of evenly spaced green waves traveling from one end of the box to the other, as he had previously witnessed in Aiyanna's lab, the pulsations traveled from stalk to stalk at different frequencies and wavelengths, but in a seemingly coordinated fashion. As Nate had suggested, what came to Luke's mind was something akin to a neural network of synapsing brain cells he'd once seen on a PBS *NOVA* show.

"Keep watching," Nate said as he turned off the voltage regulator.

Luke was surprised to see the pulsations continue, bouncing from stalk to stalk.

"It's almost as if... they're *hunting*, or expecting to find something," Nate said, in a very subdued, deliberate but guarded tone.

Hunting? "Hunting for what?" Luke asked.

"Good question," Aiyanna replied. "That's what we hope to find out in our next series of experiments."

The pulsations were only now beginning to fade as Luke ventured a suggestion.

"What would happen if you placed a living thing among the cornstalks and turned on the power?"

Luke noticed Nate and Aiyanna exchanging looks of surprise.

"Well, that is an interesting thought," Nate replied. "What kind of living thing did you have in mind?"

"Well, maybe something small to start out. Like a... cricket or something. Or maybe a mouse. The kind I used to feed my pet boa."

"You had a pet boa?" Aiyanna asked. She seemed surprised.

"It was part of my high school science project."

She gave a little smile. "Well, that is actually something that I have also been considering."

Nate raised an eyebrow. "Really? And I thought you were an animal lover, Aiyanna," he said, with an ill attempt at humor.

Changing the subject, Nate diverted Luke's attention back to the first greenhouse.

"So, you were asking earlier about the other greenhouse."

"Yes. There doesn't appear to be much going on in there," Luke said.

Nate explained, "In that soil bed, our control, we have cultivated the same mushroom species from GMO soil samples taken from the Mertz farm and have planted two rows of *non*-GMO corn from seed. We hope to determine whether this symbiotic relationship, once triggered in the fungus, can be replicated with the non-GMO corn."

Luke nodded. "I see."

Before heading back to Sheboygan, Luke offered to take Aiyanna to lunch, his treat. She gladly accepted.

"Do you have a favorite spot?" he asked.

Five minutes later, they found themselves at the Forager, a popular gastropub featuring farm-to-plate comfort food located on South Pinckney Street, which also offered a superb view of the state capitol and surrounding park square. People were out in force enjoying a sun-soaked lunchtime break or leisurely stroll through the park.

"So, what do you recommend?" Luke asked, perusing the lunch menu.

"Oh, I could close my eyes and point and not be disappointed. But if I were forced to choose, I'd go with the Bibimbap Burrito. But, of course, you can never go wrong with the Forager Burger."

"Bibimbap it is, then," Luke said, motioning to the waitress.

"So what do you think of Dr. Greene?" Aiyanna asked after placing their order.

"Hmm. A bit of an enigma," Luke offered as he assumed a pensive pose, his right hand bracing his jaw with index finger extended to his cheekbone.

Aiyanna leaned forward. "How do you mean?"

"Well, he is obviously well informed but appeared a little bit... *stiff*.

Like he was maybe hiding something?" he responded, turning it into a question.

She laughed. "I grant you the *stiff* part. He can be imperious at times. But I don't know what he could be hiding."

Luke sat back. "Where did he work before coming to UW Madison?"

"He came from industry. Worked for a major agricultural chemical company. Not sure which one. But he's been with us for the past five years."

"I see," Luke said.

The waitress arrived with their order. "Would there be anything else, Aiyanna?"

"No, that's all for now," she replied. The waitress whisked away.

Luke looked at her quizzically. "A friend of yours?"

"She knows me. I come here all the time," she explained.

He cleared his throat and took a more serious tone. "Listen, Aiyanna. I need to tell you something. The reason I couldn't make it down yesterday."

"Oh, there's no need to explain."

He squirmed. "Maybe not. But it is something you should know. And I feel bad for not telling you sooner."

She cocked her head slightly. "Okay. You have my attention."

Luke started slowly. "Well, yesterday I returned to the cornfield where my sister disappeared sixteen years ago. You remember, the one we visited three weeks ago outside Elkhart Lake. This time Dan accompanied me with his GPR crew. Hoping to find her remains, you see. To seek closure."

Aiyanna hesitated, obviously hurt. "And... you didn't want to tell me this?"

"No, it's not that. It's just that... I knew you were very busy, and I didn't want you to have to decide between your work and—"

"And what? Our friendship?"

"Well... yeah, I guess," he said, at a loss for words.

Silence.

"So... what did you find? Unless you don't want to tell me for fear of upsetting me," she said briskly.

Luke's lips tightened. "There were... no remains. We found nothing."

Aiyanna's countenance relaxed. "Well, that's something." Her expression morphed to curious consternation. "So what do you think really happened to her?"

Luke went on to describe what they did find. A large cavern, deep in the ground that extended possibly for miles.

"I'm thinking maybe a sinkhole swallowed her up into the cavern. I know that sounds crazy, but it's the only explanation I can come up with. Of course, Dan still believes she was abducted, but I just couldn't..."

He paused midsentence. Aiyanna's face had turned to stone.

"Aiyanna, what is it?"

"A cavern? You said a cavern deep underground?

"Uh, yes. That's what the GPR revealed."

Aiyanna proceeded to relate her dream from a week ago. It was the same night, in fact, they'd returned from the Mertz farm after discovering and exhuming Gloria's presumed remains.

"The dream, it was so vivid. It seemed so real," she said.

Luke was mesmerized. "Do you believe he really was your ancestor, this man, Akecheta, who you encountered."

Aiyanna paused. "Yes. I truly do believe it. Our religion teaches that such things are possible. You must know this from your reading."

Of course, Luke knew this.

"And the cavern that you found yourself in. Did it have a name? Or location?" he asked.

"No. Not that I can recall. Only, it was beautiful. Surrounded by colorful rock crystal formations and the sound of flowing water. And there were other figures, off in the distance, through the mist. I can only assume they were my ancestors as well."

"And what did this man actually say to you?"

Aiyanna was looking off into space, like in a trance. "He said, 'My child, you will be faced with a choice. You must choose wisely. You must not forget the ways of our people. You must search your heart. That is the only way you will succeed.'"

She turned to Luke. "But I'm not sure what it all means. I just have this gut feeling that there is a connection between my dream... and what you discovered yesterday."

A thought popped into Luke's head.

"In his chapter on shamanistic and medical practices, Radin describes two types of magical ceremonies," he said. "One of them, *waruka'na*, has to do with knowing something by 'exerting one's powers,' I think is how he put it. He even gives an example of a man who was trying to find his missing son. He goes to a shaman, makes an offering of tobacco, and asks him to 'exert his powers' to locate his son. Coming out of his trance, the shaman directs the man to a remote place and, sure enough, he finds his son, just as the shaman said."

Aiyanna smiled. "I guess your people would call this 'psychic power.'"

"I suppose so," Luke said. "But even today, crime investigators have sometimes used psychics to their advantage." He paused. "So, a thought came to me. Do you think one of your tribal shamans could help me locate my lost sister?"

Aiyanna leaned back. "Well, that is an interesting thought."

She paused for a moment.

"It's a long shot," she said at last. "But I think something could be arranged. Let me talk to my father."

He raised an eyebrow. "Your father? Your father is a shaman!"

She laughed. "No, but he is close friends with one. And besides, it would also give you a chance to meet my..."

"Okay, pick a date!" Luke said quickly, not giving her a chance to finish.

His attention had already turned to the calendar app on his smartphone when he heard her sigh. Looking up, he thought he caught a look of frustration on her face.

"What?" he said, a bit bewildered.

Aiyanna shook her head. "Oh, nothing. Nothing at all," she said, seeming to brush it off. "I'll just have to get back to you with a date. After all, I can't speak for my father."

"Oh, yeah, sure. Of course," Luke replied apologetically, not sure why he should feel like apologizing. He repocketed his phone. "But I have a certain feeling about this."

"Hmm, yes. A certain feeling, I'm sure."

After lunch, Luke suggested a walk through the park in the Capitol Square. He had something else on his mind he wanted to discuss. He was thinking, *No more secrets with Aiyanna.*

"Ya know, there is one more thing I need to confess to you, Aiyanna."

She stopped in her tracks. "Uh-oh! You're going to tell me you have a wife and child back in Philly?"

He blushed. "No, it's nothing like that!" He gathered his thoughts. "It is something that, once divulged, would break the confidentiality I have established as a reporter with a certain individual. But I feel compelled to share it with you."

Luke proceeded to recount the *true* story of Gloria Emery's mysterious disappearance as told to him by her husband, Jake. Jake had reached out to Luke in trust, and Luke in turn was reaching out to Aiyanna.

Her eyes widened. "Well. That is quite a story. And you believe him?"

"Yes, I do," Luke said in all sincerity. "Because it so closely resonated with my own personal experience. So now you know the real reason I went to the Mertz farm in the first place. Not to pursue my GMO story, but to find Jake's missing wife."

Aiyanna took Luke's hand and squeezed it.

"Crop circles. Sinkholes. Missing persons," she said. "I'm beginning to consider the possibility there may be something truly amiss in the natural world. Something beyond our current understanding."

"Hmm. Maybe Pam was right," Luke replied. "Maybe there really is a *cereal killer* out there on the loose."

"Right under our scientific noses!" Aiyanna added.

THE NEXT AFTERNOON Luke got a call from Aiyanna to say she had spoken with her father.

"My dad said Uncle Lobo would be available the second weekend in August to meet with us."

"Uncle... Lobo?" Luke asked. "Is, uh, Uncle Lobo a... shaman?"

"Of course! His full name is Charlie Graywolf. But he usually just goes by 'Lobo.' He's a close friend of the family. We call him Uncle Lobo."

"Oh, yeah, sure. Okay, I understand."

"So, I figure you can come down to Madison Friday morning on the seventh to discuss our research, then drive out together after work. Black River Falls is about a two-hour drive from here. We can spend the weekend at my folks' place. They're, uh... really looking forward to meeting you."

Luke was quick to respond. "And I am looking forward to meeting them as well."

Chapter Thirty-Six

DATA OVERLOAD

Thursday, August 6, 2015

The past three weeks had seen an avalanche of new or confirming information resulting from forensic testing and Dan's ongoing missing persons investigations. First and foremost, the Jane Doe remains exhumed from the Mertz farm were confirmed to be that of Gloria Emery, missing since September. A positive DNA match was made between the recovered bone and teeth fragments and the hair samples provided by Jake Emery from Gloria's comb and brush. The cause of death, however, could not be determined with any certainty, and the location of the body twelve feet underground would also pose a dilemma for prospective jurors trying to convict Jake Emery... or any living person for that matter.

Also, soil samples taken from the Mertz farm showed only an 80 percent probable match with the samples recovered from the shovel in Jake's pickup truck, according to the forensic geologist's report. So, while the evidence appeared to point a guilty finger at Jake Emery, there wasn't sufficient evidence to issue a warrant for his arrest. He remained a person of interest.

"And for all we know, it could just as well have been Adam, or any of Jake's sons," Dan was forced to acknowledge.

The geo-forensics expert did note in his report that upon microscopic examination, there was a strong similarity between the mycelial fungal filaments found in the two soil samples. However, he conceded that he'd have to defer to a botanical forensics expert to make this final determination. Of course, Dan knew exactly who to contact for this analysis.

"Most of the soil samples from that region contain a similar floral profile, particularly with regard to fungal species," Aiyanna reported back, citing her new *Armillaria sheboygansis* mushroom variety as the predominant species in the area. "Sorry, I can't help you there, Dan."

But when Dan was given the final DNA results of the corn-tooth specimens by his forensic expert, Steve Kelly, he nearly choked on his coffee.

"This can't be right," he said. "Must be a mistake."

"No mistake, sir," Steve was quick to reply. "We ran the tests in triplicate. They all came back the same. A twenty-five percent positive match with Gloria Emery's DNA. This is what one might expect from persons related as first cousins."

"Yes, I know about the matching scenarios between relations. But that doesn't make any sense. So, you're saying Gloria and this corn-tooth sample are directly related... as first cousins!" Dan exploded in laughter. "That's absurd!"

"I know," said Steve. "Sounds crazy. But having exhausted the search of our DNA database, we decided to run this comparison as a last resort, kind of on a dare, taking bets on the outcome. And guess what? I lost!"

Dan shook his head. "I'll have to consult with the folks in Madison on this one," he said. "See what sense they can make of it. So, what the evidence is telling us is that someone planted a molar—no, three molars!—from one of Gloria's first cousins in a corn cob at a remote farm stand in Sheboygan County. Is that what you're telling me, Steve?"

"Er, well, the three teeth actually gave three separate mappings, but they were all a twenty-five percent match."

"Wait a minute. You're suggesting that the teeth came from three *separate* first cousins! That's what you're saying?"

"Not me, sir. The test results are saying that."

"Oh my God! Is that the best we can come up with, Steve? What jury is gonna buy that? Sure muddies the waters against the Emerys. Or anyone else for that matter."

Dan's GPR road trips did, however, yield much more positive and useful results and served to corroborate the validity of Sam's computer model. To cover more ground more quickly, he set up three separate GPR teams working in parallel. Of thirty-three crop circle sites examined for matching missing persons predicted by the model, seven turned up the actual human remains of missing persons, which Dan's forensic team was able to identify through DNA matching. As with the case of Gloria Emery, however, postmortem examinations were not able to identify the exact cause of death for any of the seven bodies recovered.

Two of the sites that yielded no bodies did turn up some interesting artifacts, however. In one case, they found a woman's compact case inscribed with the word "Nancy," the name of the missing person actually linked to that site by the computer model. And in a second case, they discovered a man's gold wedding band.

"Gold wedding band. That has a familiar ring to it," Dan deadpanned.

"Yeah, and there's another bizarre coincidence," Sam noted. "The missing person in that gold ring case was Ed Hauptmann, reported missing by his family ten years ago. Ed happened to be the uncle of Emma Hauptmann, the murdered college student."

Dan's eyebrows raised. "My! That *is* bizarre."

When Dan shared this information with Luke, Luke posed a poignant question.

"Can you tell me, Dan, which of these sites gave evidence of hidden caverns?"

Dan was initially flummoxed by the question, but Sam had an answer within minutes.

"Well, Luke. It seems that the twenty-six sites that produced no human remains—including your sister's site and the Ed Hauptmann and Nancy sites—demonstrated a network of caverns deep in the geological rock formations. The seven recovered human remains sites demonstrated no such geological formation."

Dan had to admit that was an interesting find.

"Probably just another coincidence," he said. But he suspected Luke wasn't buying into that.

MEANWHILE, over this same three-week period, Aiyanna intensified her field survey work to determine the full range of this new giant mushroom species. As a courtesy to Dan, she relayed this information as it was developed to Deputy Sam Riley for his computer model. Together they were able to map out an irregularly shaped area that went far beyond the original Elkhart Lake site, extending as far north as New Holstein in Calumet County, south to Random Lake above the Sheboygan County line, and west just beyond Plymouth, including nearly the entire Kettle Moraine State Forest area. If correct, she estimated the total area of coverage to exceed 200 square miles, or 128,000 acres!

"This is an amazing find!" she said. "It far surpasses the 2,384 acres occupied by Oregon's *Armillaria ostoyae* single mushroom organism."

She acknowledged that she would need to go back and verify her genetic findings to ensure that this was indeed a single organism. But single organism or not, it did represent a new species of the *Armillaria* honey mushroom.

What's more, the recent soil and root samples taken from the Klausman farm evidenced the same mushroom species from sixteen years ago, establishing that this giant mushroom had been around for at least sixteen years!

Aiyanna's mushroom field data filled in the final pieces of the puzzle for Sam's computer model, just as Luke had suggested.

ON THURSDAY, August 6, Aiyanna showed up at the Sheboygan County Sheriff's Office to review the latest findings with Dan and his team. Luke also joined them in the briefing room.

"There! I think that does it!" Sam declared with a click of the mouse.

The computer map was now overlaid with a new transparent lavender pattern as numbers flashed across the bottom the of screen.

Crop Circle/Missing Persons Correlation: 40%
Missing Persons/Crop Circle Correlation: 80%

Crop Circle/GMO Corn Correlation: 95%
Crop Circle/Thunderstorm Correlation: 95%
Crop Circle/Armillaria Correlation: 95%
Missing Persons/Armillaria Correlation: 80%

"The lavender overlay represents the mapping of your new giant mushroom species, Aiyanna," Sam explained. "*Armillaria sheboygansis.*"

"Hmm. How do I read these numbers, Sam?" she asked.

"Okay, so taking the first entry you would read, 'Forty percent of crop circles are associated with unsolved missing persons cases.' The second entry would read, 'Eighty percent of missing persons cases are associated with crop circles.' And so on."

"So, why are these first two correlations so different?" Luke asked.

"Well, that's because most crop circles are isolated events in nature that do not involve humans. And not all unaccounted missing persons are related to this crop circle phenomenon or part of a serial killing. Runaways, for example. They don't necessarily fit any pattern. What is surprising is that this number—eighty percent—is as high as it is. Here, this Venn diagram shows it better:"

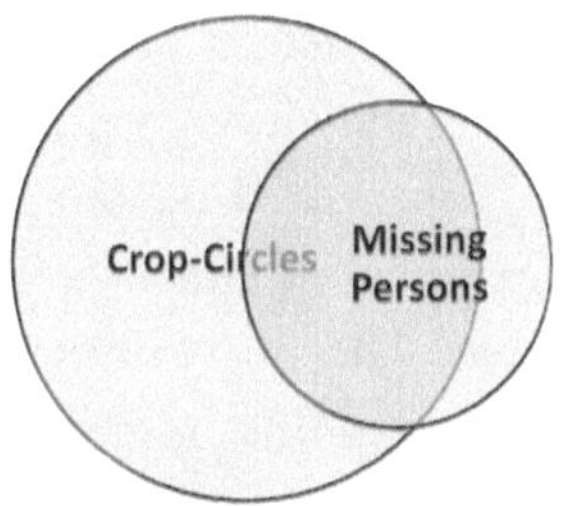

Sam continued. "But as the other numbers show, there *is* a very strong correlation between the four parameters—GMO corn, crop circles, thunderstorm activity, and mushroom locations—for predicting the time and location of unaccounted-for missing persons."

Luke rubbed his chin. "Uh-huh. Can you bring up the perp probability distribution you showed me two weeks ago, Sam?"

With a few clicks of the mouse, the screen was filled with the familiar 3D probability map with its peaks and valleys. When Sam set the timeline at the bottom of the screen for August 1997, the curve was virtually flat. As he moved the timeline counter forward in time to the right, a peak developed in the Elkhart Lake area. As he continued to move the counter to the right, the graph expanded toward the south, the east, and eventually to the west and north. The peak area continued to grow and fatten in the Elkhart Lake region, resembling a growing octopus as it extended its tentacle reach over an ever-expanding area until it reached its current state in July 2015.

Aiyanna was amazed. "The dynamic timeline graph has all the appearance of an expanding life form." She pursed her lips for a moment. "It's too bad we don't have a complete timeline model for the spread of this *Armillaria* species," she said. "Only the current point-in-time mapping data and the sample taken sixteen years ago at the Klausman farm. It would be interesting to see if the rate of expansion of *Armillaria sheboygansis* matches the rate of expansion of your missing persons data field."

Sam looked at her quizzically. "So, what are you suggesting, Doctor?"

She smiled. "That we may indeed have a serial killer on our hands, but not of a human sort, originating and operating out of the Elkhart Lake and Sheboygan Marsh areas."

Dan did a double take. "Whoa! Wait a gosh darn minute! Are you suggesting that this... *mushroom* is somehow responsible for these disappearances?"

"... and crop circles," Sam added. "Don't forget the crop circles, which we know correlate very well with many of these disappearances."

Aiyanna struggled to make her point, forgetting that she was not addressing a gathering of scientists at a professional symposium, but rather a group of law enforcement officers who, however sincere and dedicated they may be, tended to seek simple, pragmatic solutions to potentially complex and novel problems.

"You might as well blame it on *alien abductions*!" Dan blurted out after she tried to explain the results of their recent laboratory findings, linking mushrooms and GMO corn in a potentially lethal and totally unprecedented way.

"Okay, Dan. So, how do *you* explain the Gloria Emery DNA results for the 'tooth-on-the-cob' find?" she countered. "All practical or reasonable explanations go out the window, wouldn't you say?"

A thoughtful Sam chimed in. "And don't forget the computer 3D Perp Map," he said, pointing to the computer screen. "It didn't point to the Emerys, but rather to the area around Elkhart Lake where Aiyanna first discovered this new species of giant mushroom." He looked at Aiyanna.

She nodded.

A tight-lipped Dan muttered something unintelligible and threw up his hands. "I don't know!" he said. "Maybe there's someone else in the Elkhart Lake area we are overlooking. Ever think of that? A real person! Not some Mario Brothers toadstool run amuck!" He exhaled like a blowtorch as he turned to Aiyanna. "So, what do you suggest we do, Doctor?"

Aiyanna took a deep breath and counted to ten. "I'd like to invite you, or someone you designate, to come down to Madison tomorrow to witness what we've discovered." She looked at Luke. "Luke will be coming down in the morning. So you'd be in friendly company."

Seeming to mull it over, Dan turned to Sam. "Okay, Sam. You can go. But you'll be off the clock on this one. If that's okay with you. Don't want to waste valuable department resources on some fantastic witch hunt."

"Sure," Sam responded sheepishly. "I guess I could use a day off."

Chapter Thirty-Seven

SYMBIOSIS REVEALED

Friday, August 7, 2015

Luke made a point of getting an extra-early start Friday morning. He didn't want Sam getting to the Madison campus before him, mainly because he had something he wanted to discuss with Aiyanna—alone. So instead, he had arranged to meet her in a nearby coffee shop at seven o'clock. Of course, he had also arrived packed for a weekend getaway to Black River Falls and was more than a little nervous about meeting Aiyanna's folks and Shaman Lobo.

"I want to apologize for getting into such a huff with Dan yesterday" were the first words out of Aiyanna's mouth when he met up with her in the coffee shop.

Luke shrugged it off. "You needn't apologize to me," he said. "I know how Dan can be. And I know you and he are not exactly—how should I say—on the best of terms."

They grabbed a pot of coffee and retreated to a table by the window.

"So, what did you want to talk about, Luke?"

He hugged his cup. "Well, I've been doing a little digging of my own into this Dr. Greene fella. Now, I know he is a respected colleague and member of the scientific community, but…"

"But what?"

"Well, did you know he was originally employed by a large US-based

GMO company before being recruited by the Santoma Corporation in 2006?"

"Well, I knew he worked in the public sector before coming to the university. And he does get grant money from industry for his research."

Luke grimaced. "Ah, yes. But did you know he is *still* on the direct payroll of Santoma?"

Aiyanna blinked. "No, I didn't know that."

"Well, wouldn't that be regarded as a conflict of interest?"

She sat back. "I don't know. I guess it depends on how his contract reads."

"Well, I'd be a little bit—I don't know—perhaps a little wary of this guy. He struck me as someone who is hiding something."

Aiyanna simply laughed it off. "I think you're making much ado about nothing. You saw the work he's doing. And after today I'm sure you'll change your mind. We've got a lot to show you—and Sam. I just hope Sam leaves his badge at home and comes here with an open mind."

Luke suppressed a laugh. "Yeah, I don't think he was all too happy about giving up a day of leave to come down here today. Dan put the squeeze on him."

Luke's cell phone buzzed with an incoming text message. He looked down. "I think our buddy Sam is waiting for us."

After linking up with Sam outside of Agriculture Hall, the three of them headed down the street to the horticulture building, where they met up with Dr. Nathaniel Greene in his office. Nate greeted them with a tepid smile and exchanged introductions and perfunctory pleasantries with the deputy. It was obvious Nate was less than enthusiastic about sharing his research with "an outsider," but Aiyanna had convinced him that transparency was in their best interest as their findings could potentially impact the ongoing missing persons investigations and could even benefit from them.

Nate handed each of them a white lab coat. "You'll need these. It's a matter of laboratory protocol."

"I hope you brought your notebook, Sam," Luke said.

"Can I take pictures?" Sam asked.

Aiyanna and Nate looked at each other. Nate cleared his throat. "No, I'm afraid pictures are not permitted. And if you wouldn't mind, I'd like you to please leave your cell phones here in my locked drawer. They'll be safe, I assure you."

Luke hadn't remembered Nate being so fussy on his previous visit. He eyed Sam. *Must be the new outsider among us.*

"Sure. Not a problem," Sam replied.

"And one more thing," Nate said as he produced several official-looking documents from his desk drawer. "I'd like the two of you to sign this nondisclosure agreement. It basically says that anything you learn or see here is not to be made public or shared with anyone but is the sole intellectual property of the University of Wisconsin."

He nudged the documents forward and held out two pens.

Luke looked at Aiyanna. She was biting her bottom lip, as if to say, "I wasn't expecting this."

Sam sought clarification. "When you say, 'not share with anyone,' I assume you mean anyone outside of the sheriff's office."

"Yes, of course," Nate replied in a gruff, matter-of-fact fashion. "After all, we need to protect the interests of the university."

And the Santoma Corporation, Luke thought.

In the end, Luke and Sam agreed to sign the documents.

With their signatures obtained and their phones secure, Nate led the team down the hall toward the solarium at the rear of the building. On entering, they encountered two other researchers tending a row of shrubbery in a raised open bed. They exchanged smiles with Dr. Greene.

As the entourage approached the two larger greenhouses, Luke noticed a change right away. The first greenhouse—the "control bed" as Nate had previously described it—now contained a three-week's growth of cornstalks, which he remarked upon.

"And what else do you see?" Nate asked.

Luke pressed against the greenhouse glass and looked closely. "If I'm not mistaken, I see a few yellow buttons—mushrooms—growing from the soil."

Aiyanna smiled. "Yes, as we've discussed, they are the fruiting bodies of the mushroom." She turned and spoke directly to Sam. "These are what people typically identify as *mushrooms*, Sam. It's the job of these fruiting bodies to produce the spores that, once released, are capable of generating more mushroom plants."

"Are they edible?" he asked.

"Yes, quite so!" she replied. "The fruiting body of *Armillaria* are commonly called *honey mushrooms*. Rather sweet and tasty. The Indigenous peoples of Wisconsin—my ancestors—relied heavily on them and other mushroom varieties for sustenance."

"Now, if you will please follow me," Nate said as he directed them to the second greenhouse. Luke noticed immediately that the stalks were now towering at six feet, nearly ready for harvesting. Nate led them, one at a time, through the double-contained entranceway. Once inside, he made sure he had their attention before proceeding.

"Now look closely," he said. "What is different about this soil bed?"

Sam was the first to respond. "Well, I don't see any... *fruiting body* mushrooms. Not like the other greenhouse."

"Precisely!"

Sam reacted with a self-congratulatory smile.

"You see, corn is a *monoecious* plant, meaning it grows both male and female flowering parts." As Nate spoke, he began setting up a video camera mounted on a tripod, which he trained on the center of the soil bed. "The tassels," he continued, pointing to the tops of the stalk, "are the male flowers, which produce the pollen. The ear is the female organ or flower. Pollination occurs when pollen grains fall on the silk, which serves to guide the pollen tube toward the egg. Once fertilized, the egg develops into a kernel, or seed, of corn."

Nate reached out to one of the developing ears of corn and exposed the kernels inside. "Now, what we have here are fertilized ears of corn, so the tassels and silk have done their job. Ah! But in our case the story does not end there!"

Removing a penknife and what appeared to be a coffee filter from his pocket, he proceeded to tap and scrape the nearest tassel with his penknife, resulting in a small deposit of what looked like brown powder on the coffee filter. He held out the filter for all to see.

"What we have here are mushroom spores."

Luke and Sam shared blank stares.

"There are many symbiotic relationships in the plant world. Some are parasitic in nature. Others mutually beneficial to one or both of the species involved. But the symbiosis that has developed between *this* species of Armillaria and *this* particular variety of GMO corn is like nothing I've ever seen before. The cornstalk now serves as the fruiting body of the mushroom! The mushroom allows the corn to complete its fertilization process before it commandeers the reproductive apparatus of the corn plant for its own reproductive purposes. Which is why you don't see any mushroom fruiting bodies growing above the soil in this soil bed."

There was a moment of silence as Luke tried to process this remarkable new information.

"My, that is amazing!" he said at last.

"Yes. But the fun is only beginning," Nate replied with the giddy delight of a schoolboy.

Aiyanna was already at work setting up the next demonstration. Retrieving a small cage from beneath the soil bed, she removed a white mouse and held it in her hand. The mouse was equipped with a tiny harness and tether—like a miniature dog's leash. Placing the mouse at the center of the soil bed, she attached its leash to a stake securely planted in the ground, then retreated and turned on the video camera. The mouse began to explore the immediate area within the confining radius of its leash.

"Experiment 6-B-080120-01," Aiyanna said, speaking into the video microphone.

As she did this, Nate repositioned a lab cart containing the DC voltage regulator and connected its lead wires to the two electrodes buried in the soil, same as before.

"Luke, I think it was you who suggested the hunting experiment, was it not?" Nate said.

Luke raised an eyebrow.

Nate reached for a box on the cart and produced four dust masks, which he held out to the others. "Here, I'd like you to put these on."

"Uh, what are these for?" Sam asked nervously as he fiddled with the mask.

"It's just a precaution," Nate assured him. "You'll understand in a moment."

Nate donned his own mask and watched as the others did the same.

"Now, watch very carefully!" he said, and flipped the power switch.

As Nate turned up the voltage, the ground began to erupt in a dull green pulsating glow, same as the one Luke had previously observed, traveling from stalk to stalk and back again in seemingly random fashion. But this time, the pulsations quickly became focused on the mouse, which was apparently oblivious to any impending danger. The stalks closest to the mouse swayed under the influence of the pulsations, bending over in a generally spiral pattern toward the ground, surrounding their furry prey. To Luke's surprise, the ground around the mouse began to move, to actually undulate in synchrony with the pulsations. At the same time, faint puffs of brown dust could be seen, seeming to burst forth from the corn tassels lying closest to the mouse.

"Did you see that?" Nate asked. "Now keep your eyes on the mouse!" Even the mask couldn't conceal his exuberance.

The effect of the dust cloud on the mouse was clear. The creature became immobile, its breathing slowed, its eyes closed. All at once, the ground erupted in a flurry of plant roots protruding upward, reaching out, "hunting" as it were, for the mouse. They exhibited that same cottony white appearance Luke had seen before from multiple soil and root samples taken in the fields. In no time at all, the mouse became completely entangled as the roots continued to envelop and pull the animal downward into the now roiling soil, stirred and loosened by the displaced root system. Luke saw Nate flip off the power switch, but still the hunting continued, and within less than a minute the animal was completely submerged. The green pulsations gradually diminished until finally all commotion ceased. The mouse was nowhere to be seen. Just a small, tethered leash disappearing into a patch of stirred-up soil.

Luke and Sam exchanged jaw-dropping looks of astonishment.

"What did I just see?" Sam said with a whimper. "Please tell me I didn't see what I just saw."

FOLLOWING THE LIVE DEMONSTRATION, Luke was still trying to process what he had witnessed as Nate led the somber group back into the main building toward a small conference room near his office. From the look on Sam's face, Luke could tell he was grappling with the same thing.

The conference room was equipped with a large video screen that had network and plug-in capability. Powering up his laptop, Dr. Greene launched a PowerPoint presentation with the esoteric title SYMBIOTIC BIOELECTRICAL TERRESTRIAL EVENT PHENOMENON.

He quickly went through the first set of slides, which basically repeated what they had witnessed in the solarium.

"What was that brown dust cloud we saw?" Sam asked.

"Mushroom spores," Nate replied. "Containing a nerve toxin. Meant to paralyze or incapacitate its prey. Amazing, is it not?"

Sam nodded.

"Ergo, the need for the dust masks," Luke offered.

"Precisely!" Nate continued, "So you see, we believe that the mycelial network actually serves as a kind of information pathway, essentially a neural network much like the nervous system of higher animals. The predator response is activated or turned on by an external electrical stimulus of some kind. In nature, this could be provided by an approaching electrical storm. In the lab, we can induce it artificially with a DC power generator."

"You mean, like Frankenstein?" Luke suggested.

Nate gave a wan smile. "Yes, I suppose you could say that."

The next series of slides presented the results of microscopic examinations showing the hyphal growth associated with the corn root system and vascular tissue extending far into the stalk, which was not surprising in itself, except that the tissue remained completely intact and undamaged by this mycelial advance.

"As you can see, we have demonstrated hypha growth that reaches into all parts of the plant, but primarily the reproductive parts—the tassels and ears. Even, on occasion, into the unfertilized eggs of the immature cob. The plant does not appear to be adversely affected by this relationship. On the contrary, it now aids and abets the mushroom's search for prey."

Luke posed a question. "So, the mushroom no longer attacks the plant for nourishment?"

"That is correct. What we have found is that, somehow, the enzymes secreted by the mushroom for digestion have shifted from starch- and cellulose-digesting enzymes—amylases and cellulases—to protein-digesting enzymes, or proteases. The fungus now draws its nourishment from the rotting animal flesh."

"So, we have something like a Venus flytrap?" Sam offered.

Nate smiled, like he was responding to a classroom student. "Very good, Sam! Yes, just as the Venus flytrap feeds on insects that become entrapped via a mobile response mechanism, our mutated—or epigenetically modified—species has developed an elaborate mechanism of entrapment that enlists the aid of the corn plant—primarily its root system—to capture, incapacitate, and consume its small mammalian prey. The mechanics of this response is not yet understood, but we feel it is likely hydraulic in nature, similar perhaps to the folding response of mimosa leaves after being touched."

As Nate spoke, Luke passed a handwritten note to Sam that read "Small prey? How about dogs and people?"

Sam gave a confirming nod and wrote back: "How am I going to explain any of this to Dan without photos or video?"

Sam ventured another question. "So, Doctor, what have you been able to determine regarding the corn-tooth mystery, if you don't mind my asking?"

Nate paused. "Yes, well, that is quite the conundrum." He drummed the tabletop with his fingers. "When Aiyanna told me that your county sheriff's office made a positive DNA match with the recent victim of foul play taken from the same cornfield, I was flabbergasted." He turned to Aiyanna. "Can you please elaborate for the deputy?"

Aiyanna cleared her throat. "Well, the tooth pulp DNA was shown to be a recombinant hybrid of three sources of DNA: mushroom DNA, corn DNA, and human DNA—or more specifically, Gloria Emery's DNA. A twenty-five percent match, in fact, for Gloria's DNA, corroborating what the sheriff's crime lab came up with."

Dr. Greene picked it up from there. "Yes, it appears that somehow, the victim's DNA became *entwined*, if I may employ that expression, with both corn and mushroom DNA, which found its way to the female cob egg."

"So what was the percent composition of the three DNA sources in each of the three tooth samples?" Luke asked.

"Good question," Nate replied.

He presented a series of slides showing the actual chromosomal mapping patterns of tooth pulp DNA samples.

"We've color-coded the three DNA sources, as you can see here." He demonstrated with his laser pointer. "Gloria's blue DNA and the mushroom's red DNA each account for twenty-five percent, while the yellow GMO corn DNA makes up a full fifty percent. The other two teeth specimens show different mapping patterns, but they exhibit the same percent compositions," he said as he quickly went through the two remaining mapping slides.

Nate took a deep breath, folded his hands on the table, and eyed his audience. "What I am hypothesizing is that the Gloria DNA and mushroom DNA recombined first in a vegetative fashion, followed by the sexual recombination with corn DNA during the corn's normal reproductive process. This suggests that hyphae assumed the male role normally performed by the corn's pollen tubule. Upon fertilization of the cob eggs, it expressed itself *not* as a normal seed, or kernel of corn, but as differentiated human dental tissue." Nate scratched his head. "The only thing I can compare it to is certain human cancers, solid tumors, which often exhibit strange growths resembling disparate organ structures."

He was met with blank stares.

"So you're saying this is a form of... *cancer*?" Luke asked.

"Just by analogy. What we do have is an *aberrant* form of genetic expression. Aberrant even for the novel system we are considering."

Sam ventured a guess. "In other words, a *freak* of nature."

Nate sat back and folded his hands. "Well, yes. I suppose that would sum it up nicely."

AFTER THEIR EXTRAORDINARY LABORATORY VISIT, Luke invited Sam to join him and Aiyanna for lunch at the Forager, which Luke had taken quite a liking to on his last visit. This time he tried the Forager Burger and ordered a round of beer for everyone.

"What are you going to put in your official report about this visit, Sam?" Luke asked.

Sam grunted. "Nothing! Don't you remember? I'm off the clock, on my own time. I owe Dan nothing—officially!" he said with a wry grin. "But I may want to reexamine the computer model. It looks like you may have identified the culprit and base of operations after all."

Luke was puzzled, but Aiyanna knew the possible implications.

"Yes," she said. "I was thinking the same thing when you demonstrated your dynamic perp map yesterday with its origins around Elkhart Lake and expanding outward from there. This giant *Armillaria* mushroom seems to demonstrate the same geographical origins and growth pattern over time." She took a sip of beer before continuing. "And with this mycelial neural network thing going on, perhaps the equivalent of a *head* or *brain* actually exists in the Elkhart Lake area, reaching out to the far reaches of the county—like the arms of an octopus!"

Luke's phone buzzed as he received an email from Calvin Mertz, the Plymouth farmer. He gave it a quick read.

"Hmm. Interesting."

"What is it?" Aiyanna asked.

Luke pressed his lips together. "Well, guess who is suppling GMO corn to the farmers in the area?"

She shook her head. "Dunno."

He smirked. "Why, none other than Santoma." Looking at Aiyanna, he asked, "Any wonder your good friend Dr. Greene is so interested in this case?"

Sam seemed confused. "Santoma? Who or what is Santoma?"

Luke and Aiyanna went on to explain the connection.

"Well, that explains the NDA," Sam said. "No wonder he wants to keep this under wraps."

Chapter Thirty-Eight

THE BLACK BEAR FAMILY LODGE

Friday Evening, August 7, 2015

Luke and Aiyanna got a later start than expected out of Madison, so they didn't reach Black River Falls until almost nine o'clock. Aiyanna had phoned her folks earlier to say they were running late and not to expect them for dinner. They had to settle for a fast-food meal on the road.

"It's too bad," Aiyanna said. "I was hoping to treat you to some authentic home-cooked Native American cuisine."

"Well, there's always tomorrow," Luke offered.

Black River Falls, population just under 4,000, was located on the Black River about 130 miles from Madison. It served as the county seat for Jackson County but was also the headquarters for the Ho-Chunk Nation, which regulated all tribal affairs for its nearly 8,000 members.

The Black River region had been a longtime sanctuary of the Ho-Chunk people from time immemorial and so became a natural mecca for the returning remnants of the tribe following their federally imposed mid-nineteenth-century relocations to the future Western territories of Iowa, Minnesota, South Dakota, and Nebraska. Initially discouraged from returning by federal authorities, they were eventually given permission to resettle in their ancestral home of Wisconsin. However, as a people they continued to struggle economically and with federally enforced programs of cultural assimilation.

A century later, things slowly took a turn for the better. The Indian Reorganization Act of 1934 finally gave the Ho-Chunk the right to petition the US Courts for past redresses, and in 1963 they drafted their first constitution for self-rule. The constitution was revised in 1994, establishing three branches of government and officially restoring the traditional Ho-Chunk Nation tribal name. At long last, 1975 marked the welcome demise of the federal assimilation policy, resulting in a resurgence of teaching of the Hocąk language and culture to Ho-Chunk youth.

WHEN LUKE and Aiyanna arrived at the Black Bear residence—a modest modern rambler located on the outskirts of town on the bank of the Black River—Aiyanna's parents, Larry and Rachel Black Bear, greeted them with open arms.

"Welcome to our humble lodge!" said Larry Black Bear, with the broadest of smiles.

"Please make yourself at home, Luke," Rachel joined in. "I know you and Aiyanna have already eaten, but I have prepared a nice evening snack for you."

A compact, robust, middle-aged woman, Rachel was all of five feet tall, with a radiant smile and a soft, pleasing voice. Her burly husband towered over her by more than a foot and possessed a similar gentle demeanor.

Adjourning to the family room, dominated by a large stone fireplace and entertainment center with large-screen TV, they settled in for an evening of relaxation and conversation. The room, finished in rustic decor with bare timber ceiling rafters, was tastefully appointed with Native American accents, artwork, wicker weave baskets, and fine crafted articles of copper, silver, and bone. A large bearskin rug covered the floor in front of the fireplace.

The twins—Aiyanna's seventeen-year-old brothers, Alex and Carl— were absorbed with video games but took time out to politely make their introductions. Tomorrow, Luke would get to meet Aiyanna's older sister, Adrianna, and her fiancé, Adam White Eagle.

Larry Black Bear took a seat in a large, leather-upholstered swivel rocker. With legs crossed he began a gentle side-to-side motion. In his buckskin sandals, loose-fitting chinos, and casual linen button-down shirt with bolo tie accent, he struck Luke as the epitome of relaxed confidence, the unquestionable master of the house.

"So, Luke," Larry began, "Aiyanna tells me that you are a reporter for a Sheboygan newspaper. And a darn good one at that!"

"Thank you, sir." Luke tried his best to match his host's calm demeanor. "I've been with the *Dispatch* less than six months now, but I think I've managed to turn a few heads with my articles," he said. "And I understand, sir, that you are a respected elder in the tribe."

Larry chuckled. "Well, I hope that to be the case. I do my best."

Rachel and Aiyanna entered the room with trays of petit fours, dessert bars, and frosted glasses of iced tea. As they served their guest first, Luke responded, "Thank you, Mrs. Black Bear. They wouldn't be lemon bars, would they?"

She smiled. "Aiyanna told me they were your favorite."

He gave Aiyanna a surprised look. "My, you don't miss a trick, do you?"

Gentle laughter followed.

Rachel asked Luke about his family. He talked mainly about his mom and growing up on the farm, his high school and college days, and his life in general, highlighting the good parts, eschewing the traumatic. When the conversation turned to the business of the tribe, Larry took the lead.

"As you are probably aware, the economic fortunes of our people took a dramatic upturn with the advent of the gaming casinos." Larry took a sip of tea and sat back, setting the glass on the adjacent lamp table. "It all began with the opening of a tobacco store in a trailer in Wisconsin Dells in 1982. Before then we were, for all practical purposes, a welfare state, subsisting largely on state and federal hand-outs. Since then, through enterprise and daring, our gaming industry has grown in dramatic fashion and has completely transformed our society's economic and social well-being. We now own and operate six gaming casinos in the state," he stated proudly, "generating over two hundred million in profit annually, which has given us total economic independence. As an elder, I help regulate the casinos and participate in the day-to-day operations of our local casino here in Black River Falls."

Luke was impressed. "I had no idea. I mean, I knew about the casinos but wasn't aware of its impact on tribal affairs."

Larry nodded with a serene expression. "Yes, it has certainly made a difference."

Luke then tried to guide the conversation toward culture and religion, but Larry seemed to know where he was going.

"Yes, Aiyanna has told me of the tragic loss of your sister. And of her own mysterious dream."

Larry took a slow deep breath and glanced skyward, then looked at Luke with a calming smile.

"We have a very close friend—also works at the casino—who happens to be a respected shaman," Larry said. "He is schooled in the traditional healing arts and religious practices of the Ho-Chunk people. He is also very much involved in our schools, teaching our children our Native culture and language, carrying on the ancient traditions of our people. His name is Charlie Graywolf." He smiled. "But most often he just goes by the name Lobo"—he turned to Aiyanna with a smile—"or Uncle Lobo, to our children."

Larry took a sip of iced tea before continuing. "I have invited Uncle Lobo to our cookout tomorrow. You will have a chance to meet and speak with him. And I am hopeful that you will find him... quite helpful."

Luke thanked him. His attention then turned to something that had been intriguing him since his arrival that evening. Against the wall to the left of the fireplace stood a glass case, the kind you might find in a museum. The case contained a seemingly odd assortment of paraphernalia, artifacts, a buckskin wrap, and the dried remains of various birds laid out on two glass shelves.

"I am very interested in your glass case display, Larry," Luke said with a nod toward the case.

Larry looked pleased. "Ah, yes! That is our Bear clan war bundle. I am its custodian, as it was passed down to me from my father, and his father before him."

He invited Luke to take a closer look and joined him in front of the case.

"Yes, I've read about the war bundle," Luke said, "but never thought I'd actually see one."

Larry explained that the war bundle was the centerpiece of the tribe's most important ceremonial feast, the *Wagigo*, Winter Feast, or War Bundle Feast. It started out as a feast primarily to ensure success in war but later developed into a general ceremony of thanksgiving to the spirits set in midwinter. The details of the feast varied slightly between the twelve clans, but the war bundle generally contained the same elements.

"First, there are the eagle feathers, the deer-tail headdress, and the war club, all items worn when on the warpath. The flutes you see are associated with different spirits and are used to accompany the clan songs during the actual ceremony. In battle, they were said to have a paralyzing effect on the enemy, making him easy prey. The four bird bodies include the eagle and two kinds of hawks, said to give the possessor the characteristics of these animals in times of war. And then there are the special stench-earth medicines, to empower the user and ensure success in war."

"That's fascinating," Luke said. "The War Bundle Feast itself, how does that work?"

Larry groaned. "Oh, that is quite an involved affair," he said. "Better left for another day. Suffice it to say the ceremony actually consists of three separate parts: the Sweat Lodge Ritual, the feast in honor of the Earthmaker or the Thunderbirds; and the feast in honor of the Night Spirits."

Suddenly Rachel called out, chiding her husband in a loving way, "So, are you going to monopolize Luke for the entire evening, Larry? I'd like to learn a little bit more of his family story, if you don't mind."

"Ah, forgive me, my dear. I was only responding to his natural inquisitiveness. But you are right, of course." He turned to Luke. "I defer to my better half. Shall we please rejoin the ladies? I, too, would like to learn more about you and your family history."

Chapter Thirty-Nine

SHAMAN LOBO

Saturday, August 8, 2015

The next day started out cloudy. There had been a light rain overnight, but as the morning sun rose higher, the clouds began to break up. No matter, Larry Black Bear was up at six o'clock firing up the smoker in the backyard.

When Luke joined him two hours later for coffee, the meat was already loaded and well on target for a three o'clock rendezvous with the master's carving knife.

Larry greeted him briskly. "Good morning, Luke! I hope you slept well?"

"Like a baby," he replied with a yawn and a steaming cup of coffee in hand.

"Tell me, have you ever had bison?" Larry asked.

Luke paused. "Bison? You mean buffalo?"

Larry tried not to laugh. "No, I mean 'bison.' Buffalo live in Southeast Asia. Bison are the bearded variety native to North America." He opened the smoker to check on his brisket. "Always white fat side up," he explained, "so the fat can melt down into the meat to keep it moist and tender."

The mouthwatering aroma of mesquite and rendered fat filled the air.

"Of course, unlike old times," Larry continued, "we don't have to hunt for bison meat anymore. They're raised on farms these days, like domestic cattle." He smiled. "A trip to a good butcher shop is all the hunting we need to do. But I get mine direct from a ranch not too far from here."

He explained that when Europeans first arrived, great herds of bison roamed throughout North America as far east as western Pennsylvania, Virginia, and the central piedmont of North Carolina. Today, the wild herds were limited to the Great Plains and northward into Canada.

"Farms and ranches now supply our needs. By my last count, there are at least twenty in Wisconsin alone."

"That's news to me," Luke said. "Maybe I should do an article on that."

Larry smiled. "That would be nice."

AIYANNA and her mom remained in the kitchen preparing breakfast and making final preparations for the afternoon cookout. Aiyanna went over the list of Native American dishes Rachel had come up with to complement the smoked brisket of bison that Larry was serving up: wild rice and cranberry salad; corn and bean succotash; roasted butternut squash with a mix of cinnamon, allspice, butter, and maple syrup; and a hearty loaf of acorn nut corn bread, all topped off with a sweet cornmeal pudding dessert.

"This is perfect, Mom! I'm eager for Luke to sample our Native American cuisine."

Rachel smiled.

Around eleven o'clock, Aiyanna greeted Adrianna and her fiancé, Adam, who had made the trip from La Cross, less than an hour away to the west.

"Just in time to help out in the kitchen," Rachel said as she handed them each an apron.

IT WAS ALMOST two o'clock when Charlie "Lobo" Graywolf made his appearance. At least, that's who Luke assumed him to be by Adrianna's earlier description. A large, barrel-chested man with a round face and wizened features. By large, you could even say huge—and add powerful! He reminded Luke of the "Chief" character in *One Flew Over the Cuckoo's Nest*. Luke was hoping that his spiritual prowess would come close to matching his apparent physical strength.

"Good afternoon, Larry. It is good to see you again," Lobo said.

His soft, almost lilting, voice projected a confident, calm reassurance, belying any outward appearance of surliness.

Larry smiled and took Lobo's hand. The two embraced with a hug.

"I'm so happy you were able to join us," Larry replied.

After greeting the other members of the family, Larry introduced Lobo to their guest of honor, Luke Kramer.

Lobo extended his hand. "It is so nice to meet you, Luke," he said with a knowing glint in his eye.

"*Pinagigi*," Luke replied, taking his hand. "The pleasure is all mine."

"Well, you are quite welcome!" Lobo replied wide-eyed. "My! It appears I have a new Hocąk-language student!"

Everyone laughed. Luke could see that his response even took Aiyanna by surprise.

"You know," Rachel boasted, "Aiyanna is quite fluent in Hocąk."

"And has a passing familiarity with other Native dialects as well," Larry added. "Notably Algonquian and Miami."

"Oh, Dad!" Aiyanna said, sounding like an embarrassed schoolgirl.

Luke had to chuckle. "Hey, I think that's great! I wish I had retained more of my German growing up."

ACROSS ALL CULTURAL TRADITIONS, shared food and games provided the perfect occasions for bonding, lubricating the gears of social interaction and discourse. And this afternoon provided ample opportunity for both. A friendly game of horseshoes or ring-and-pin (similar to the European game of cup-and-toss) gave everyone a chance to test their dexterity while engaging in friendly conversation as they eagerly awaited the feast to come.

Larry's brisket was a resounding success, as were the accompanying side dishes and desserts prepared by the women of the house.

"So, how did you enjoy the brisket of 'buffalo'?" Larry asked Luke in a friendly, chiding fashion, using air quotes on "buffalo."

"Excellent!" Luke exclaimed with a wink. "A gastronomical delight!"

As the heat of the day gave way to the soothing coolness of twilight, the emerging fireflies were Larry's cue to fire up the firepit for an evening of roasted marshmallows, relaxed conversation, and storytelling. One by one, the family gathered around the fire, recounting the events of the day, boasting of victories at horseshoes and moccasin games, and jostling for the best ember position to ensure the perfect roasted marshmallow.

After a few moments of anticipatory silence, the stage was now set for the storyteller.

"Uncle Lobo, please tell the story of the origin of the Bear clan," Adam pleaded.

Though not blood related, Lobo, a member of the Wolf clan, was considered a part of the family, a courtesy often extended to members of the Wolf clan.

The Ho-Chunk oral tradition embodied a wealth of stories and myths that served to enshrine their beliefs and instruct their people on the proper way to conduct one's life. Originating in ancient shamanistic and tribal traditions, the stories were passed down from generation to generation and tended to evolve over time, often adapting to current needs and sometimes impacted by the influence of the white man's Christianity.

The origin myths varied from clan to clan, with multiple versions even existing within the same clan. However, while they differed in the details, they did incorporate certain common elements and themes. Most notably they all traced their origins to Red Bank (*Moogaŝuc*) located on the northern shores of Green Bay (*Te-rok*), with Ma-ona the Creator, or Earthmaker, playing a key role in later versions.

And so, Lobo began his story.

"In the beginning, the Earthmaker instructed the animals to select and send one of their own from across the waters to gather in council at Red Bank. These would become the first human ancestors of the Ho-Chunk clans. The four spirit bears chose the youngest among them to go. As the young bear spirit neared the shores of Green Bay, he turned into a raven. Some say he even took the form of white foam as he came ashore, which is why the Bear clansmen have so much life and the power to heal. Over his head was a halo of lightning and thunder, and with his appearing, the winds ceased to blow and the day stood still. Earthmaker had endowed the bear with such great powers. While walking on the shore, he came upon a Wolf and together they entered the great Council Lodge, whose four doors opened to the four cardinal points. They sat at opposite ends, facing each other. To this day they called each other friends, or 'he who sits opposite me.' They both agreed that, as long as they both should live, when either asked a favor of the other, it would be done."

THERE WAS a long pause as Lobo concluded his tale. Luke noticed Aiyanna signaling her sister, Adrianna, who nodded and turned to her fiancé. "Adam," she said, "let's go help my mom clean up inside. We can rejoin the campfire later."

The twins had already adjourned to the family room, where they resumed their video games from earlier in the day.

As the sun set beyond the grove of birch that bordered their back-yard, Luke sensed a subtle shift in mood toward things spiritual as typically embodied in the nighttime sky. A light breeze gently fanned the flames and glowing embers as one by one the stars appeared in the now cloudless sky.

"So, Aiyanna. Your father tells me you had a dream," Lobo said softly. "Please, tell me."

Aiyanna proceeded to relate her dream of being visited by her ancestor, Akecheta, a tribal leader and head of the Bear clan in his day.

"He told me that I would be faced with a choice. That I must choose wisely and not forget the ways of our people. That is the only way I would succeed."

She held out the bear amulet necklace for him to see.

Lobo gently massaged the amulet and remained silent as he appeared to contemplate the meaning of the dream.

"Revelations may come in the form of a dream," he said at last. "But this dream is meant for you alone. It is not a communal revelation. You must search for its true meaning. If you concentrate and search your heart, you may find the answer." He paused and considered it further. "But I sense it has something to do with your work and your quest for the truth... as it relates to others close to you."

Aiyanna gently nudged Luke to get his attention, mouthing the words "tobacco offering."

Luke reached into his pocket and produced a small leather pouch.

"There is one other thing, Uncle Lobo," Aiyanna said, turning to Luke. "Luke has a story to relate to you that involves a special request."

Lobo nodded and smiled, making eye contact with Luke. Somehow, Luke thought Lobo already knew what was coming.

He proceeded to tell the story of his missing sister, Alice, and spared no detail, even the part about being blamed by his father for her disappearance. At last, he concluded with the most recent find deep in the cornfield where she'd disappeared sixteen years earlier, the sinkhole or caverns that he suspected had "swallowed her up," and the strange association between a certain breed of giant mushroom and genetically modified corn that may also have played a part in her disappearance. Aiyanna clarified this point by briefly describing the research she was involved with at the university.

"I was hoping you might employ the magical powers of waruka'na to ascertain my sister's location," Luke concluded. "Was she abducted, as some people think, or... somehow swallowed up by the earth? A sinkhole, perhaps."

"Hmm. That is a most peculiar tale," Lobo responded. "With many possible implications, the worst of which I would not choose to contemplate."

Luke anxiously awaited his response.

"Are you prepared to make an offering?" Lobo said at last.

Luke fumbled with the pouch and produced a large wad of tobacco.

"This is all I have," he said.

Lobo took the tobacco. "That will do."

Lobo divided the tobacco, packing a portion into a smoking pipe and tossing the remaining tobacco on the fire. As the smoke from the fire wafted upward into the night sky, he held out his arms and began to chant in Hocąk, praying to the spirits as his gaze followed the smoke up into the sky. He then lit the pipe, took several puffs, and offered it to Luke. Luke received the pipe and took a puff, then passed it to Aiyanna, who did the same before passing it to her father.

Lobo sat on the ground with legs folded beneath him as he appeared to go into a trance, chanting all the while. Several minutes passed before he spoke.

"I see a field of corn. Beneath the corn, deep in the ground, there is a cavern. A large room filled with beautiful rock crystal formations. A stream runs through the cavern leading to... a distant lake surrounded by green meadow fields. A village. With people tending to a little girl..."

Lobo trembled as he resumed his chanting.

"But there is danger nearby," he continued. "Giant beings that threaten the safety of the child. Yet she is shielded by the people as they encircle the village with offerings of food and tobacco..."

Lobo resumed his chanting. Suddenly, the chanting ceased and he came out of the trance.

For a time, he just sat there ruminating.

"Your sister is alive," he said at last. "Even now. She was not abducted."

Words and tears could not express Luke's relief.

"That's wonderful news! So, where is she, exactly? How do I find her?"

"Well. That is a difficult question." Lobo paused. "I sense a disturbance in the natural order of things. Something I have never known before."

Aiyanna took Luke's hand and squeezed it.

"As you may or may not know," he continued, "we believe the cosmos consists of four worlds that are layered one beneath the other: Heaven, the Sky, Earth, and the Underworld. Ma-ona the Creator, or Earthmaker, rules the Heavens, which is also the domain of Thunderbird, the most revered and approachable of the Ho-Chunk deities. Trickster, another of

Ma-ona's creations, rules the Sky World; and Hare is in charge of the Earth World, which is basically our world, or the world of the living.

"The Underworld is a vast region immediately beneath the Earth World. It is largely a water-filled realm ruled over by Turtle, another of Ma-ona's creations. Black Wolf, White Wolf, and Green Wolf are its protectors, just as their fourth brother, Gray Wolf, the progenitor of my clan, is the protector of the human race in our Earth World."

Lobo took a deep breath before continuing.

"However, the Underworld is also the dominion of the Great Serpent and its evil minions. By some, it is called the Underwater Panther, as it is believed to be part feline in nature. Just as the Ice Giants of old terrorized the Earth World and its inhabitants, the Great Serpent and its minions terrorize the Underworld. It is believed that these powerful beings are even capable of entering our Earth World through natural portals, like springs, rivers, and lakes, which are connected to the Underworld oceans by a system of caverns, to wreak havoc on human beings with floods, disease, and other calamities." He paused, giving Luke a moment to catch up before laying the next piece on him. "They are also said to kidnap infants and children."

Luke was enthralled.

"What I sense," Lobo continued, "is a *disturbance* in the Underworld —or more precisely, an *unholy* disturbance in the normal pathway that connects to the Underworld."

Luke finally spoke. "You mean, like a new portal that has opened up communicating directly to this... underworld realm?"

Lobo nodded. "Yes, you could say that."

Luke and Aiyanna shared worried looks.

"So, if my sister is still alive—I mean, in the real natural and physical sense of the word—how do I go about rescuing her?"

Lobo sat back as he emptied the spent embers from his pipe.

"Very, very carefully, I would say. As I said, this is not like anything I've encountered before. It is not recommended that man, in his natural state, enter such realms. It is dangerous to do so." He paused. "Have you ever heard of Eagle Cave?"

Luke shook his head. "No, I haven't."

"Well, I must tell you about it sometime," Lobo said as he stoked the embers with a stick. "Tell me, Luke," he continued absently, "do you have a guardian spirit?"

Luke was puzzled. "A guardian spirit?"

Lobo explained that for a Ho-Chunk boy to enter manhood at puberty, he must go through a period of fasting and focused mental concentration and conditioning for the purpose of acquiring a guardian spirit who will accompany him through life, offering guidance, protection, and strength.

"If you are serious about venturing into this realm," he said, "you do so at your own peril. You must acquire a guardian spirit and put yourself in the proper mental conditioning."

"Which spirit do I choose?"

Lobo chuckled. "Luke, you do not choose the spirit. The spirit chooses you!"

THE NEXT DAY, as Luke and Aiyanna were packing up and preparing to leave, Aiyanna took her father aside.

"So, Father. What do you think about Luke?" she asked timidly.

Her father did not respond immediately.

"It doesn't matter so much what I think of him," he said. "The question is, what do you think of him, Aiyanna?"

She sighed and folded her arms. "Well, I really do like him. In fact, I like him a whole lot. But..."

"But what?"

"Well, he confuses me. I mean, our relationship is strictly... *professional*. At least, that's what I keep telling myself."

"Well, professional or otherwise, relationships can be confusing. Especially where emotions are concerned."

"Still, I'd like to know your thoughts," she pressed.

Her dad became pensive.

"As you know, Aiyanna, I like to fish. Always have. And I consider myself a pretty good angler," he said with a chuckle. "Now, sometimes you reel in the fish, and you keep it. Sometimes, well, for one reason or another, you throw it back." He paused. "Now, Luke, well..."

Aiyanna waited nervously.

Her dad turned to her and smiled with a twinkle in his eyes. "Luke... is a keeper."

She breathed a sigh of relief.

"Thank you, Dad. I appreciate that." She gave him a warm hug, then backed away and folded her arms. "Still, he confuses me. I know he's had trouble with women in the past. But he can be so... *obtuse* at times!"

Her dad perked up. "*Obtuse?* Oh, my!" He tightened his lips. "Hmm. Maybe you just need to try a different bait."

Chapter Forty

SEARCHING HEARTS

Sunday, August 9, 2015

On the ride back to Madison Sunday afternoon, Luke sat in the front passenger seat with the window down, his arm resting on the sill as he welcomed the rush of warm, clean country air across his face and ruminated, trying to digest the events of the weekend.

Turning to Aiyanna, he asked, "So do you *really* think Alice is alive, in the physical and natural sense of the word, as your Uncle Lobo said?"

She didn't respond right away. "I don't know. The *scientist* in me says 'no way!' But my heart, well, it says otherwise."

Luke studied Aiyanna, seeing her in a new light as something stirred within him. "What was it your Uncle Lobo told you? 'If you concentrate and search your heart, you may find the answer.'"

About halfway to Madison they took a short detour off I-94 to stop in Wisconsin Dells to deliver some documents Aiyanna's dad had given her for the manager of the Ho-Chunk-owned-and-operated casino located there.

"Hey, why don't we stick around and have some fun as long as we're here?" she said after making their delivery.

Wisconsin Dells was a popular family tourist destination, arguably the most popular in the Midwest for folks of all ages, boasting a wide collection of amusement and water parks, shops, restaurants, and—as previously mentioned—casinos. The town, which lay on the Wisconsin River, derived its name from the Dells, a scenic glacier-formed gorge noted for the high, majestic sandstone formations and caves that lined its banks.

"I haven't been here since I was a kid," Luke said, forcing back a tear as he thought about that last time. It was sixteen years ago in celebration of his sister Alice's sixth birthday—the same summer she went missing.

But this day turned into a totally different experience, an exhilarating and much-needed lift and the opportunity to finally comes to terms with his inner self and developing feelings toward Aiyanna. Without realizing it, he found himself holding her hand as they strolled the downtown shop-lined streets. Roller coasters had always terrified him. Now, with Aiyanna by his side, he willingly braved the ups and downs of the Dells's signature ride, Mount Olympus, with joyous shouts and hugs. A leisurely duck boat cruise on the Wisconsin River provided the perfect opportunity to snuggle. And there were plenty of selfie and photo ops along the way. At Aiyanna's urging, they topped off the day with a fine meal at one of the town's premier restaurants.

"Here's to good times and good friends," she said as they clicked their wineglasses.

Luke beamed. "Yes. To good friends!"

When they arrived in Madison, he transferred his bags to his parked car before accompanying Aiyanna to the second-floor landing of her apartment. It was a one-bedroom garden apartment located on University Avenue in the Sherwood Hills neighborhood just off Madison's campus, not far from Lake Mendota.

"I want to thank you for the fantastic weekend," he said as she fumbled with the front door keys. "I think your mom and dad are great people. And your Uncle Lobo, well, he is just... amazing!"

"And don't forget the Dells," she said.

"Yes. Definitely the Dells!"

The door opened and she went inside. He remained standing on the landing.

"Well, don't you want to come inside?" she said. "Maybe sit a spell."

"Oh, sure. I didn't want to presume..."

What an awkward moment. He was trying to process the events since

Friday. It had all started on such a professional basis. But now, he was feeling something else.

She laughed. "Nonsense! I've got an unopened bottle of sambuca I've been wanting to try out. But a person shouldn't drink alone. That's a bad sign, wouldn't you agree?"

"Yes, I most definitely agree." Luke stepped across the threshold.

Her apartment was neatly appointed with rustic furniture and wall accents that reflected a combination of her Native American heritage and scientific bent.

"I guess I get my taste for decor from my parents," she said with a chuckle.

Luke looked around. The main living space was efficiently arranged in a typical L-shaped fashion that combined the living room and dining areas and was partitioned from the kitchen with a half wall and countertop. A sofa and love seat combination separated the living room from the dining area and faced a large entertainment center on the outside wall. The dining area contained a small Ikea-style table and chairs combo but was principally set up to serve as a home office space, with a desk and filing cabinets. A short hallway lined with closets for coats, towel racks, and utilities led to the bathroom and bedroom.

"Nice!" he said. "And functional. I like it."

"Thank you. Make yourself at home while I pack away my things and freshen up a bit," she said before disappearing into the bedroom.

Luke checked out her huge CD and vinyl record collection lining the wall, noting the hi-fi stereo console complete with turntable and stackable record changer.

"I see you're a connoisseur of quality audio," he hollered out. "I commend you for your fine collection."

"Yes, I am definitely a fan of the vinyl LP revival," she called back. "But I typically try to maintain backup digital copies whenever possible."

When she returned, she was barefoot and wearing a cutoff pair of denim shorts and a loose-fitting, button-down, V-neck blouse that was quite revealing. Luke swallowed hard as he noticed there was no bra beneath the blouse. She headed straight to the kitchen.

"How do you like your sambuca? Neat or on the rocks?"

"Doesn't really matter," he said. "However you like it."

"See if you can find an Andrea Bocelli LP," she said as she prepared the drinks. "His *Passione* album. I simply adore it."

Luke took several Bocelli LPs from the rack and stacked them on the turntable. Enough playtime to fill the evening. *Passione* would be the last to play.

Aiyanna entered the living room with two snifters of sambuca on the rocks as the lilting sound of Bocelli's signature baritone tenor voice filled the room. She handed a glass to Luke and took a seat on the sofa, her legs folded under her as she signaled him to take a seat next to her. They clicked glasses and took simultaneous sips.

"Hmm. Nice!" she said softly.

The light of day was beginning to fade and the room took on the red hue of the setting sun. Aiyanna lit two candles on the coffee table as they recounted the events of the day, picking up where they'd left off at dinner. Luke put his arm around her, kicked off his shoes, and rested his feet on the coffee table. She drew closer. He nestled his face in her hair, enjoying its softness and scent. They continued to cuddle, sipping their sambuca, reliving the weekend's events, enjoying the sounds of Bocelli as the minutes dissolved into hours and the final light of day retreated from the room. There was only the glow of candles now.

"So, what was your best part of the weekend?" she asked at last. He looked at her. She was radiant as her lips engaged the rim of the glass and she took another sip. His gaze couldn't help but travel downward to her tan cleavage.

"I really enjoyed the visit with your family," he said, "but I must admit, spending the day together at the Dells, just the two of us, took the prize."

She turned to him and met his gaze, her eyes sparkling in the dim candlelight, her visage exuding a soft honey glow.

"Do you know my favorite part?" she asked, almost in a whisper.

He thought a moment. "No. What?"

"Right now," she said. "This very moment. *This* is my favorite part."

She leaned forward and gave him a gentle kiss on the lips, then backed off a few inches as their eyes remained fixed on one another's, savoring the newfound tenderness of the moment.

Placing her glass on the table, she took his glass and did the same. It was impossible for him to conceal his arousal. Looking down, she gently stroked his thigh and confirmed what he already knew to be true.

Reciprocating, he placed his hand inside her blouse, and she helped him by unbuttoning it. An instant later they were locked in a passionate embrace. They kissed long and hard as his free hand gently caressed other parts of her body. She lay back and pulled him down upon her. And there, on the sofa, they made love to the strains of "Anema e Core."

WHEN LUKE AWOKE the next morning, he was initially confused. This was not his bed. This was not his room. Turning, he saw Aiyanna lying close by his side, and it all came back to him. It was a night the likes of which he had never known. But as he lay there, he wondered, *Did I do the right thing?* Worse yet, when she woke up, would she wonder the same? Or was it merely the sambuca and the intoxicating refrains of Bocelli that had led them to this point?

For some time, he lay there admiring her profile in the morning light, studying the rise and fall of her breasts with each breath, until she roused, stretched out her arms, and turned to him.

"So, do you want to make coffee, or should I?" she said with the gravelly voice of newfound wakefulness.

Like magic, the very sound of her voice dispelled all fears.

"I'll do it," he said with a smile.

Pulling on only his jeans, he made his way to the kitchen, found the coffee pot, and groped through the drawers searching for the percolator parts.

"They're in the dishwasher," she said as she joined him. "Coffee is in the fridge. Keeps fresher that way. How do you like your eggs?" she asked as she hugged him from behind, resting her head on the nape of his neck.

"Over medium," he said turning to face her. A thought occurred to him. "Say, I'd better text Anita to let her know I'll be running late."

Fifteen minutes later, they were seated at the table enjoying coffee, eggs, and toast with cut-up bananas and blueberries on the side. "Let's see what's going on in the world," she said as she picked up the remote and clicked on the TV.

"... and here is an update from yesterday's breaking news story," the newscaster blurted out as the name "Adam Emery" scrolled across the screen. "The State Police continue their pursuit of fugitive Adam Emery, wanted for the kidnapping, rape, and murder of Oshkosh college student Emma Hauptmann on May 8th of this year. The Manitowoc and Sheboygan County Sheriff's Offices joined in the search yesterday evening as Mr. Emery escaped on foot into the Kiel Marsh State Wildlife Area just southwest of Kiel, Manitowoc County, following a high-speed car chase by Wisconsin State Police."

Scenes from yesterday's police activity flashed on the screen: road barricades; marked state police, county, and local police cruisers with red lights flashing; scores of police officers and canine teams scouring the countryside.

"And now we take you live to Kiel with Badger-3 News reporter Tom Kovac."

The camera zoomed in on Tom's face as he recounted the main events from yesterday.

"Thank you, Ed. To recap, the state police spotted Adam Emery's pickup truck traveling north on I-43 just south of the city of Sheboygan at approximately ten minutes past six Sunday evening and attempted to pull him over. Mr. Emery refused to stop and led the police on a wild car chase, exiting onto Route 42 and continuing through the town of Howard's Grove up Route 32 toward Kiel. The Kiel police were alerted and set up a barricade east of town. Adam took a quick turn onto Mueller Road to avoid the barricade and ended up in a ditch about a half mile beyond Saints Peter and Paul Cemetery south of town. Police said he continued cross-country on foot, where they believe he's now holed up somewhere in the Kiel Marsh State Wildlife Area."

The camera pulled back, revealing Sheriff Alex Bradley of the Manitowoc Sheriff's Office standing to one side of Tom, with Detective Dan Meyers on the other.

"So, Sheriff Bradley, can you give us an update on the situation?"

The sheriff looked like an older, slightly shorter version of Dan, with crew-cut hair, but he was a little heftier.

"Certainly, Tom," the sheriff responded. "As you probably know, last night's passing storm hampered efforts to pursue Mr. Emery. The canine teams lost his scent as they entered the marshlands. But we have surrounded and cordoned off the entire area, so we feel confident that, with the new light of day and clearing skies, we will be successful in apprehending the fugitive."

"But that does cover quite a wide area," Tom noted.

"No problem," the sheriff retorted. "He has nowhere else to go but into our hands."

Tom turned to Dan. "Detective Dan Meyers of the Sheboygan County Sheriff's Office, do you have anything to add to Sheriff Bradley's account?"

"No, just that we are closely coordinating the efforts of our county and local police departments. We have been pursuing this case for the past three months and feel confident that Mr. Emery will be apprehended in short order."

"Thank you, gentlemen," Tom said, turning to face the camera. "So, there you have it, Ed. A coordinated police effort that is sure to win the day. Now back to you."

Luke and Aiyanna were transfixed.

"Shoot! I better get back to the office and find out who is covering this!" Luke said as he punched a number on his cell phone.

Anita picked up right away and told him that Pam York was on the case. That's good, he thought. We have a pretty good rapport. This gave him time for a quick shower before gathering up his things and heading out. He gave Aiyanna a hug and a kiss on the cheek before leaving.

"I'll give you a call later today to fill you in."

"Sure," she replied, and drew him closer for a longer kiss and embrace. Her body through the soft terry-cloth bathrobe gave him enticing thoughts about delaying his departure.

As he approached his parked car, he turned, walking backward, smiled, and waved. Peering out her garden balcony window, she blew him a kiss.

Chapter Forty-One

THE HUNT IS ON

Monday, August 10, 2015

It was almost half past noon when Luke arrived back at his office. Anita greeted him with a half-smile and handwritten note:

Luke, please see me as soon as you get in the office. –Ted.

"Ted was looking for you this morning," she said. "Wondering where you've been. I told him you were pursuing a new lead on the GMO story." She looked at him askance. "I hope I wasn't lying."

Luke grinned. "No, that's actually true. I picked up some new information in Madison on Friday that could break the story wide open."

She cocked her head. "Really?"

He waved the note in the air. "Sorry, Anita. Better see the boss now. I'll tell you about it later."

Ted was practicing his putting game with a new putter and a paper cup when Luke entered his office. Quietly Luke took a seat on the far side of the room so as not to disturb the golf master.

"Gotta brush up for next weekend," Ted said, his eyes fixed on the ball as he lined up his shot. "Doing a round at Whistling Straits with Tim and some of his sportscasting friends from Badger News. You know Tim, our sports editor?"

Ted concentrated and took his best shot. The ball meandered its way to the cup over the green throw rug and scored a direct hit.

"Yes!" he said triumphantly, pumping the air with his club. Turning toward Luke, he took a seat on his desk, resting both hands on the handle of his club.

"So tell me what you've been up to, Luke. I was looking for you this morning to cover the two o'clock press conference in Kiel. After all, it was you who broke the story linking Adam Emery's DNA to the Emma Hauptmann missing persons case. I couldn't find you, so I sent Pam York in your stead."

"That's fine, Ted. I'm confident Pam will do a good job."

"Yes, I'm sure she will." He paused. "But you still didn't tell me what you've been up to."

Luke crossed his legs to get more comfortable and thought carefully before proceeding.

"I'm chasing down a new feature story on bison farms in Wisconsin. Been out in Red River Falls talking to some elders of the Ho-Chunk Nation. Did you know there are about twenty ranch farms in Wisconsin where bison are raised like cattle?"

"Ho-Chunk Nation? You mean the casino Indians?"

Luke bit his tongue. "Yeah, that's right. They own and operate six gaming casinos in the state as the major source of tribal income. But I was thinking more about focusing on the bison farms and tying that into their tribal tradition."

Ted took a moment. "Well, you might get more traction out of the casino angle," he offered. Pausing, he threw up his hands. "But whatever works for you, Luke. I trust your instincts."

Ted set the club down and sat behind his desk. "Tell me. What's happening with the GMO story? Thought you and Pam would've wrapped that up by now."

Luke cleared his throat. "Ahem. Yes, well, there's been a new development there as well."

One eyebrow went up. "Really?"

"I learned something in Madison on Friday that could eventually blow that story wide open."

Luke proceeded to update him on developments leading up to Friday's visit but stopped short of divulging the details of that visit.

"You see, I was asked to sign a nondisclosure agreement with the UW Madison research staff, giving them rights of first publication."

Ted drew back. "You did what?" He appeared visibly shaken and annoyed.

Luke explained that he had to sign it as a condition to proceed further with the interview and tour of their facility.

"Okay, so you signed the NDA. But our legal folks didn't sign it. And you failed to consult them before signing. So, the newspaper isn't under any nondisclosure constraint."

Luke gulped. "Well, by inference, yes, we are. The devil's in the details of the fine print." He produced a copy of the NDA for Ted to examine. "Technically, I was representing the paper when I signed it. I can disclose the information internally, but we can't publish without the review and approval of the university."

After a quick read, Ted threw the document down on the desk and shook his head. "This is rubbish! Flat-out rubbish! I'll have our lawyer take a look at it. They'll shoot more holes in it than Swiss cheese!" he growled. "So, who else was there with you? I mean, besides the folks from the university."

"Deputy Sam Riley"—he paused—"who also signed the agreement."

Ted guffawed. "Well, let's just see how far that goes with the sheriff's office and Dan Meyers!"

LUKE GRABBED a cup of coffee and a sandwich from the vending machine before heading uptown to the sheriff's office to watch the televised press conference. He tried Sam's cell phone, but it went straight to voice mail. Showing his press badge in the lobby, he was escorted to Deputy Collins's office, where he learned that Sam had accompanied Dan in the search and would be attending the press conference.

"So, what are you free to tell me about the search efforts, Jimmy?"

Jimmy frowned. "Off the record?"

Luke nodded and made a cross-the-heart sign. "Off the record."

"Well, the search resumed in earnest early this morning at sunup," Jimmy began. "Canine teams picked up Adam's scent and penetrated the Kiel Marsh Area. But I believe they soon lost the scent at the water's edge. Search parties continued on foot as the east–west perimeter shrank to a tighter and tighter search area, while maintaining a close watch on the north and south exit points. A helicopter search team was dispatched later his morning running crisscross patterns over the entire area. But so far, no luck. Hopefully, we'll learn more at two o'clock."

Jimmy brought Luke a cup of coffee as they settled in front of the TV monitor and tuned in.

Sheriff Alex Bradley made the opening remarks, followed by Kiel Police Chief Bruce Holstein, and finally Detective Dan Meyers, who began taking questions from the press. He took the first question from a short, stocky blond in plaid shirt and jeans seated in the first row.

"Pam York, *Sheboygan Dispatch*. Detective, can you tell us how much of the marshland area your team has searched and whether there is any chance that Mr. Emery may have slipped though the perimeter?"

Dan coughed into his fist and took a sip of water before proceeding. "We estimate that about seventy percent of the area has been searched at this point in time. Some articles have been recovered which, based on the reaction of the canine teams, we feel belong to Mr. Emery. So, we believe we are hot on his trail. And let me assure you, the perimeter is quite secure. Next question."

A heavyset, white-haired gentleman from the *Milwaukee Press* spoke up from the rear. "Can you tell us what Mr. Emery was wearing at the time of his disappearance?"

"Yes, well, there was one eyewitness present when Mr. Emery fled from his car. She described him as wearing blue denim jeans and a green, long-sleeve shirt. She was close enough to see his name tag sewn on the breast pocket of his shirt: ADAM. We assume it was a work shirt used in the course of his father's family business."

Questioning continued for the next twenty minutes and concluded with promises to release any and all pertinent information as it became available.

That opportunity would come less than fifteen minutes after the press conference ended. Luke was about to leave the sheriff's office when Jimmy Collins, with a phone to his ear, motioned for him to stay.

"Uh-huh... Right... Ten-four," Jimmy said, ending the phone call.

"Troubling news?" Luke asked.

"That was the Kiel police. A man phoned in to say he was watching the press conference and remembered seeing a man who met Adam's description walking along a country road while he was out riding his bike early this morning. About three miles *south* of the Kiel Marsh Wildlife Area. He said the man was alone and had just come out of a cornfield munching on an ear of corn. He was described, and I quote, as 'all disheveled, looking like a drowned rat.'"

Luke thought a moment. "So, what are you saying? Adam may have slipped through the perimeter in the rain during the night?"

Jimmy nodded sheepishly. "Could be." He went to Dan's large county wall pin map and studied the area. "So... that would put him about here," he said as he drew a circle in the air with his right hand around an area roughly halfway between Kiel Marsh and Elkhart Lake.

Luke gulped. They both knew that area well. It included the Klausman farm—and Alice's yellow pin—which lay between County Road J and the Sheboygan River.

"So, what are you gonna do, eh?" Luke asked.

Without saying say a word, Jimmy picked up the phone and punched in a few numbers. After a couple of rings, he said, "Good afternoon, Dan. Listen, we just got a news tip. Might mean nothing, but you need to know."

Luke thought he heard the rumbling of distant thunder. Late-afternoon pop-up storms were common at this time of year, so he didn't think much of it.

BACK IN HIS apartment that evening, after the fast-moving storm had passed, Luke gave Aiyanna a call to update her on the day's events. Yes, she had seen the press conference on TV but, of course, hadn't heard the latest developments concerning Adam's sighting beyond the police perimeter.

"Listen, Luke," she said. "I was thinking about last Friday's live test demonstration and wondered if you might be able to arrange a site visit so we could test the hunting theory with a larger prey animal?"

Luke wasn't expecting this. "So, what did you have in mind?"

"Nate and I were thinking of a rabbit this time. We plan on using a more powerful generator and a larger electrical grid area employing several electrodes going deeper into the ground. And we want to use an actual cornfield for our test this time."

Scratching his head, he said, "Sounds interesting. I'll see what I can arrange."

"How about your Uncle Clarence's farm? Keep it all in the family."

He was impressed that she had remembered his uncle's name.

"Sure, I'll see what I can do. If that doesn't work out, maybe we can go back to the Klausman farm. Ed seemed pretty accommodating the last time around."

She paused. "Well, sure. As long as that doesn't... you know... bring back bad memories for you."

"Thanks, but I think I can handle it. Send me a list of things you'll need. A test protocol, I think you scientists call it."

She laughed. "Sure. Not a problem."

After hanging up, he phoned his cousin Mark for his uncle's phone number. Luckily, Clarence was home and answered the phone. Luke framed the request as part of their ongoing investigations into these mysterious crop circles, which Clarence was already quite familiar with.

"We're testing our hypothesis that, under the right conditions, they may be brought on by an electrical disturbance in the environment such as the type produced by an approaching electrical storm. Our apparatus will simulate this electrical disturbance in the field and try to induce a crop circle reaction."

"Sounds interesting," his uncle replied. "Only too happy to oblige and advance the cause of science."

Of course, this was all very true. But it wasn't the whole story. Luke made no mention of the live bait portion of the test, which, of course, was the real driver for their investigations.

"Oh, and one more thing," Luke added. "Can you confirm that this is GMO corn you are growing, as shown on my USDA crop maps?"

"Sure. No doubt about it."

"And where do you source your corn?"

"Hmm, mostly from the Santoma Corporation. Like most of the farmers around here."

Bingo!

"Thanks, Uncle Clarence. Just wanted to confirm for the record."

After comparing their calendars, they settled on the twentieth, a week from Thursday, at 10:00 a.m.

"The corn will be about ready for harvest, so any stalks that are taken down during the test won't go to waste," Clarence explained.

"Sounds like a plan. Thanks again, Uncle Clarence. And please give my love to Aunt Doris."

"Will do. See you then."

Chapter Forty-Two

ON THE RUN... AGAIN

Tuesday, August 11, 2015

10:30 a.m. Detective Dan Meyers was pacing the office like a caged tiger, jumping whenever the phone rang, eager to get some good news on Adam Emery's whereabouts. It had been twenty-four hours since Adam was last spotted on a country road a few miles south of the Kiel Marsh State Wildlife Area, not far from the Klausman farm. And yesterday's late-afternoon pop-up storm only further hampered search efforts.

"Friggin' weather!" Dan mumbled. He turned to Sam. "Any word from the aerial recon team?"

Sam shook his head. "Not since nine. They had to land to refuel."

Dan was frustrated. He had done everything by the book, coordinating with all other state and local enforcement agencies, and still that bastard managed to slip through their perimeter sometime Sunday night. But the ground search parties hadn't given up. They simply shifted their operation south of the Kiel Marsh, setting up a new perimeter north of Elkhart Lake along County Road J to the west and the Sheboygan River to the east.

~

W‍HEN L‍UKE ARRIVED at the sheriff's office at one o'clock that afternoon, he found Sam in the conference room, which had been designated as the command center for this operation.

"Any new information you're able to share with the press, Sam?"

Sam only frowned and shook his head. "Afraid not, Luke. Except that Dan is now looking to charge Adam with the murder of Gloria Emery. I think more out of frustration than anything else. But please keep that under your hat."

Luke nodded. "Well, when they do find Adam, I think you know that charge won't have much chance of sticking."

Of course, Luke knew the truth of the matter and was thinking that now might be a good time to divulge his confidential connection with Jake Emery. He had spoken with Jake that morning and Jake was thinking the same thing. Felt it was time to lay everything on the table and not "muddy the waters" any more than was necessary. If the truth came out during Adam's trial, it would only jeopardize the legitimate case against Adam in the murder of Emma Hauptmann.

When Dan entered the room, Luke's presence managed to evoke a wan smile.

"'Morning, Sport. How are things in the mushroom world?" he asked in a sardonic tone.

Luke hesitated. "Well, I know this may not be the best time to bring it up, Dan, but did Sam happen to fill you in on his visit to Madison on Friday? Some very interesting developments." He cast an inquiring glance toward Sam.

A wry-mouthed Sam responded, "I'm afraid not, Luke. Haven't had the time... or occasion, really."

Dan appeared to perk up a bit. "Well, now is as good a time as any, Sam. Why don't you tell me about it?" Dan perched himself on the conference table and crossed his legs. "Okay, I'm eager for a *good* story for a change. Let's talk corn! I'm all *ears*!"

Sam proceeded to describe what he witnessed, from the green glow and pulsating soil to the capture and interment of the lab mouse in the clutches of the corn's animated root system.

Dan remained silent to the very end.

"That's quite an amazing tale," he said at last. "And quite frankly, I find it rather hard to believe."

"Well, I was there, Dan," Luke chimed in, "and can vouch for everything Sam said as true. I guess you'd have to see it to believe it."

Dan shook his head. "You got that right! And you say they took video of the whole thing?"

"Right. And one more thing," Sam continued, looking askance at Luke. "We were asked not to divulge any of this to the public until they'd had a chance to publish the results."

Dan laughed. "Don't worry, fellas! I wouldn't want to be viewed as an accomplice by going public with *that* story!" He paused and considered it further. "Okay, let's say for the moment that it's true. What do you think it means?"

Luke spoke first. "Well, for one thing, I think it might change how we view these disappearances and their associated crop circle events."

Sam nodded. "I agree."

Dan turned to his deputy. "So, you actually think it's possible for a cornfield to swallow up and devour a human being, just like that lab mouse?"

Sam shrugged. "Dunno. But after what we saw, I wouldn't put it beyond the realm of possibility. And considering that the lack of forensic evidence fails to establish a cause of death or ties anyone to the scenes of the crimes."

"Ah!" Dan asserted with a finger pointed in the air. "Except for the Gloria Emery case! There is circumstantial evidence linking Jake or Adam to her death. That's why I plan to charge Adam with her murder."

Luke was forced to speak up. "Ahem," he said, clearing his throat. "I need to tell you something, Dan. Something you're probably not going to like."

Luke proceeded to tell of his initial encounter with Jake and Scott Emery over a month earlier when Jake recounted the events of that tragic day last September in the Mertzes' cornfield.

Not surprisingly, Dan seemed taken aback. "So," he said, slapping his thighs, "you actually believed Jake and his outlandish story?"

Luke inhaled sharply. "Yes, I did. Because it so closely paralleled my own experience sixteen years ago. You remember how that went down."

Dan took a moment. "Well, did you ever think that Jake was playing you? That he fabricated the story from sixteen-year-old newspaper accounts? Let's face it. He sucked you in!"

Luke looked Dan straight in the eye. "No, I don't think so, Dan. Why would he have reached out to me to begin with? He wanted to talk to someone he could trust to help find his wife's whereabouts. So he reached out to the reporter doing the story on GMO corn. That big GMO corn sign by the cornfield made a helluva impression on him. Tell me, was GMO corn even mentioned in the old newspaper clippings? Was it even mentioned in your own police reports from sixteen years ago?"

Silence.

"No. Nada," Luke continued. "No mention of GMO corn back then. Why would there have been? There was no reasonable connection at the time, so why mention it?"

At that moment, Jimmy Collins barged into the room waving his cell phone.

"Just got a call with an update from the aerial recon officer, Dan."

Dan sighed and crossed his arms. "Okay, Jim. Shoot!"

"Well, the officer was reluctant to mention it at first, but after I pressed him, he said the only thing they managed to come up with was a small crop circle in a cornfield a few miles south of the Kiel Marsh Wildlife Area, about halfway to Elkhart Lake. The officer said he recalled seeing Luke's newspaper article and knew that Sam was investigating these strange events. So I told him to take pictures of it and text them to your cell phone."

Dan opened his text messages and indicated that sure enough, the pictures were there. His eyes squinted for a closer look. "Interesting" was all he said.

"Let me see it," Jimmy said.

Dan handed him the phone.

Jimmy studied the several pictures. "Hmm. That sure looks like the Klausman farm." He tapped the screen and looked more closely. "Yes, no doubt about it. You can even see the name on the mailbox." He touched the screen again. "And there's that GMO corn sign."

All eyes turned to Dan.

He was at a loss for words. Had to be a first, Luke figured.

THE UNDERWORLD

THE BISON HUNT

Wisconsin Wilderness

The long days of summer were now waning as Akecheta and his people planned their most ambitious hunt of the year, a bison hunt that would take them on a many days' journey in search of the great herds that roamed the open grasslands of present-day southwestern Wisconsin. In preparation for the hunt, Akecheta would unite with a neighboring village and select fifty of their best and strongest braves who had proven themselves in prior hunts. As with the earlier summer bear hunt, this would be preceded by a wanantce're ceremony to prepare the men mentally and spiritually and to ensure some measure of success by magically conjuring or attracting the attention of the intended prey—the bison.

However, because they would be entering contested hunting grounds, there was the possibility of encountering enemy hunting parties along the way, particularly those from the Illinois Confederation—the Illiniwek or Illini—to the south. They would therefore be performing a second ceremony, the Wagigo, or War Bundle Feast, intended to ensure success in war. As the leader of the hunting party and custodian of the Bear clan war bundle, Akecheta was responsible for organizing and hosting the feast, a multiday affair that consisted of three separate ceremonies: the Sweat Lodge Ritual, the feast in honor of the Earthmaker or the Thunderbirds, and the feast in honor of the Night Spirits. Offerings of buckskin were made to as many deities and spirits as possible, including the Earthmaker, the Thunderbirds, the Disease-giver, the Sun, the Moon, the Morning Star, and the Night Spirits. The larger the number of deerskins obtained, the greater the number of spirits for whom offerings could be made to ensure a successful war party. In practice, though, enough skins were prepared—typically ten or eleven—to enable as many clans as possible to participate in the ceremony.

The night before the main ceremony, the men entered the sweat lodge, a low-profile, dome-shaped hut constructed of saplings covered with blankets and animal skin. It was basically a purification ceremony intended to prepare the participants for the feast ceremonies to follow. A fire was prepared and rocks placed on the glowing embers. Sage was dipped into a bowl of water and both were sprinkled on the hot rocks. As the lodge filled with steam and the men began to sweat, the host sang and offered tobacco and prayers of thanksgiving and supplication to the spirits.

In preparation for the ceremony proper, close relatives of the participating men constructed a special lodge, extending east to west with a single entrance on the east end. The host sat to the left as you entered, with the guests seated in a line after him, each one opposite a fireplace. At the extreme western end of the lodge sat the women and children.

On the day of departure, the men of the hunting party made their final preparations, gathering their supplies of blankets, pemmican, and hunting gear of bows and arrows, tomahawks, flint knives, and war clubs. Several dog teams would accompany them to assist with their return trip, dragging sleds laden with smoked meat, hides, and other processed bounty from the hunt. After saying their goodbyes, the men headed out in the direction of the setting sun, with Bear clansmen Akecheta and Matoskah leading the way. Wrapped in buckskin and tied with buckskin straps, the Bear clan war bundle was slung across Akecheta's back.

After a four-day journey, Akecheta's hunting party reached the open grasslands and the grazing herds of bison. They had encountered no trouble along the way but did see signs of other hunting parties as they neared their destination.

In the absence of horses, later introduced by Europeans, all hunting was done on foot. For prey animals as formidable as bison, one of two methods of communal hunting was employed: the bison jump or the bison corral.

In the bison jump, the herd of bison was lured toward a cliff and stampeded over the edge, causing them to fall to their deaths below. Since a convenient cliff did not present itself to Akecheta and his men, they were forced to resort to the corral method.

The men set about constructing a large enclosure out of boulders and logs measuring up to fifteen feet high. A similarly constructed walled chute led into the enclosure, intended to funnel the stampeding animals into the "kill zone" of the corral.

Akecheta turned to Matoskah and smiled. "You, my brave friend, are the fastest runner among us. You shall be the lure."

"It will be my honor," Matoskah replied.

When all was ready, Matoskah took a position between the herd and the entrance to the corral chute. Crouching low in the grass to conceal his presence, he began to make the sound of a calf in distress. Once he had attracted the attention of the herd, a portion of the hunting party, disguised as threatening wolves, caused a stampede from behind, waving blankets and shouting. Remaining low in the grass and continuing the plaintive cries of a wounded calf, Matoskah quickly made his way toward the chute's entrance with the herd rapidly bearing down on him. At the last possible moment, he dashed off to one side, barely escaping the gush of stampeding one-ton beasts as they rushed by, the hide of one animal brushing him and propelling him to the ground.

The remainder of the hunting party stood outside the corral wall, waiting with spears and bows and arrows. Once the corral was filled with snorting, confused bison, they let their arrows fly!

Akecheta joined Matoskah when the hunt was done.

"You did well, my friend." He noticed the abrasions on Matoskah's forearm and smiled.

"Just a close brush with death. That's all," Matoskah said with a laugh.

Overall, the hunt went well.

"Twenty-two bison!" Akecheta announced proudly.

This would result in more than 8,000 pounds of dressed meat. Add to that the hides and bones used to construct tools and other useful implements. Nothing was wasted.

They spent the next four days dressing and preserving the meat. Smoking was the preferred method. Two smoking lodges were constructed, with the butchered meat laid out or hung from poles for as long as necessary to complete the smoking process. At the same time the hides, bones, and sinew were prepared and bundled for the long journey home.

After two days of travel, they came to a place of legend and mystery, where a great river ran past high, red sandstone cliffs honeycombed with caves and grottoes too numerous to fathom.

Akecheta turned to Matoskah. "This is the place spoken of by our storyteller. Somewhere in these cliffs lies the legendary Eagle Cave. If we had more time, I would wish to explore these cliffs further." He turned and looked back at the long train of sleds and warriors trailing behind. "But we cannot tarry here. It is fraught with danger."

A place of low water and sandy shoals allowed them to ford the river with relative ease, although the men were forced to off-load the meat from the sleds and carry it across the river on their backs. Akecheta knew this left them vulnerable to ambush by marauding war parties, so he chose to make the crossing in small groups, sending an advance party ahead to scout the banks and wooded interior on the far side before crossing with the main body of men and supplies. Matoskah led the advance party. Once he signaled that all was clear, Akecheta proceeded to cross with the main party.

Now on the other side, Akecheta froze in his tracks, raising his arm to signal those behind him to stop. Cocking his head, he sensed an unnatural stillness in the air, a sense of being stalked, as a hunted deer is alerted to approaching danger. Suddenly, there was a subtle movement in the bushes to his left. Without a moment's hesitation he shouted the command, "Prepare yourselves! We are under attack!"

As he uttered the word *attack*, there was a *swish-zip!* as an arrow whisked by his head, missing its mark by mere inches. He winced as a second arrow grazed his left shoulder, drawing blood. From out of the brush, the enemy descended upon him and his trailing party as war cries filled the air. Adrenaline kicked in as his men instinctively responded in heroic fashion. Akecheta gripped his war club and swung it mightily at the head of an attacking warrior. Blood gushed forth like a fountain from the crushing blow as the enemy's mortally wounded body tumbled to the ground, shaking with the final throes of death until limp.

Akecheta retreated to higher ground, shouting to his fellow warriors to do the same. Finding safe purchase in a hidden grotto, he unraveled his war bundle and produced one of several flutes purported to have the power to paralyze the enemy and render him easy prey. The high-pitched sound penetrated the forest and reverberated off the red sandstone canyon walls. As Akecheta looked down, it appeared that the tide of battle was turning in his people's favor. He spied Matoskah in the clearing yelping and shouting chants of victory as he held up a freshly severed scalp still dripping red.

It was all over in less time than it took to skin a rabbit. Akecheta smiled as he reassembled his war bundle and slung it over his shoulder while still holding the flute. When he was about to move forward, he lost his grip as the rocks beneath his feet suddenly gave way. Reaching out, he grasped a tree limb protruding from a crevice in the rock cliff. But that too gave way with a *cee-rack*! The ground beneath him now opened up and he found himself in free fall, slipping and sliding down a long, steep incline toward an uncertain fate. "Aiyee!" he shouted. But no one could hear him. He continued to fall, caroming from rock to boulder as daylight quickly faded and darkness enveloped him. His thoughts caromed as well, taking him back to the storyteller and the legend of the Big Eagle Cave Mystery. Suddenly, his breath was swept away as he plunged into the bone-chilling depths of a deep underground lake.

Struggling to orient himself in the dark, cold void, it seemed an eternity, his lungs nearly bursting, before he at last broke through to the surface. Gasping and choking, he quickly righted himself in the murky confines of the tomb-like space in which he now found himself.

A dim light shone in the distance. But it was not the light of the outside world. He had apparently surfaced in a different portion of the cavern into which he fell. Swimming hard toward the shimmering light, he could now make out a campfire burning near the water's edge. What fueled the fire was not clear. Pulling himself ashore, he managed to save his war bundle and war club but had lost the flute that had saved him and his men in battle. He drew close to the fire to warm himself, spreading open the buckskin war bundle to dry out its contents.

His attention was suddenly drawn to a flickering shadow cast against a nearby cavern wall. The source of the shadow became clear. Boldly ensconced high on a boulder not forty feet away was a great, black wolf, as still and quiet as the night. Glowing, penetrating green eyes stared back at him, not menacing or threatening in the least. Rather, majestic and noble.

"A Black Wolf," Akecheta mumbled.

Something possessed him to look down at the ground by his side, and there he spied the flute which he thought he had lost. He bent over to pick it up. When he stood back up, the wolf was gone! A smile slowly spread over his face as he heard the distant howl of the wolf reverberating off the cavern walls.

"Yes! *My* Black Wolf! *My* guardian spirit!"

Chapter Forty-Four

FASTING

Saturday, August 15, 2015

Aiyanna doesn't seem to be herself, Luke thought. She had invited him down to Madison for an afternoon of kayaking on nearby Lake Mendota, but she seemed preoccupied, distant. It reminded Luke of the way his old friend, Chuck Evert, behaved the night before he was shipped off to Afghanistan. Luke and some high school buddies had gotten together to give him a farewell party—even smuggled in some beer for the occasion. But Chuck was distant. Like maybe he knew he wasn't coming back. Not in one piece, anyway.

"You okay?" Luke asked Aiyanna as they relaxed on the raised deck of a lakeside restaurant. "I mean, you hardly touched your food."

"Well, I'm on a partial fast," she explained. "Fruits and vegetables. I'm a little concerned about this week's field trip to your uncle's farm and I want to prepare myself. You know, physically and... mentally."

"And spiritually?"

She flinched. "Yes, that too."

"So, what's your concern?"

With a sigh, she said, "Well, I keep thinking about what Uncle Lobo said last weekend about your sister, Alice, still being alive. And the part about a disturbance in the normal order of things opening up an 'unholy portal' into this Underworld realm. You know, growing up I always considered these things to be mere legend and myth. But maybe..."

Luke admitted to having similar thoughts. "I also got to thinking about what your uncle said about nurturing one's spirit and seeking the blessing of a guardian spirit."

"You mean, through fasting, prayer, and meditation?"

"Uh-huh. I admit that's an area of my life I have mostly neglected. But if I were serious about venturing into this underworld realm in search of my sister, I would surely welcome the protection of a guardian spirit." He leaned forward. "I mean, if Alice really is alive, in the real physical sense, shouldn't we be doing everything we can to bring her back? And who knows how many other lost souls there are in that purgatorial realm. Look at all this crop circle and missing persons evidence Sam has been accumulating. Dan insists the culprit is corporeal. A serial killer on the loose. But Pam's *cereal killer* play on words may be much closer to the truth."

Aiyanna smiled. "And I think Deputy Sam is inclined to lend some credence to our theory. You saw how he reacted when Dan came down hard on my mushroom GMO corn hypothesis last Thursday in their briefing room. By the way," she added, "who are the 'Mario Brothers' Dan referred to?"

Luke returned a blank stare. "Seriously? You never played the video game? I grew up with the *Mario Bros.* game and Nintendo 64, a game console. It was a rite of passage in my neck of the woods."

"Well, forgive me for living a sheltered existence. But I never was much for video games growing up. They didn't allow it on the reservation," she said with dramatic flair, then laughed.

Back at her apartment, the two settled down on the sofa in front of the TV sipping sambuca to take in the final two episodes of *Outlander* season one, where Jamie is rescued from Wentworth Prison and the gruesome clutches of the evil Black Jack Randall. Between episodes, they took a short break to stretch their legs and replenish their drinks.

"So, do you think time travel is possible?" Luke asked as he returned to the sofa.

Aiyanna was slow to reply. "Hmm. Perhaps. In some form or another. Who can really say?" She added somewhat cryptically, "Though perhaps not the normal kind of time travel we are accustomed to thinking about."

"Normal?" he asked, baffled. "What do you mean? There is nothing *normal* about time travel, whatever form it takes."

Not trying to explain herself, she took another sip of sambuca.

He decided to change the subject. "Oh, I almost forgot!" He stood and reached for an envelope from his overnight bag and handed it to her. "It's the first installment of my new feature series on bison in North America. Your dad gave me the idea. I plan on five Sunday installments, starting with this one in tomorrow's paper."

Aiyanna beamed. "Oh, wow! That's great! My mom and dad will be so happy. Can you give me an extra copy? They don't get the *Dispatch* out there in Black River Falls."

"Of course. Voilà, madam!" And he handed her a second copy.

She briefly thumbed through the article. "Nice! Pictures and all."

He rejoined her on the sofa as they resumed the final episode of *Outlander*. The story line got Luke thinking again about missions in life. Rescue missions in particular. And the gravity of certain situations that demanded exceptionally bold and decisive action.

Toward the end, he returned to the topic of fasting, prayer, and meditation.

"So, you're serious about that, aren't you?" Aiyanna asked as they cuddled together.

Luke nodded wistfully. "Yes. I think I might give it a try."

There was a pause.

"Tell me," he continued, "is sex allowed during periods of fasting?"

Aiyanna was quick to respond. "Well, from what I've read about it, the jury is out on the subject. It seems to vary by culture and tradition and the extent and purpose of the fast. The Roman Catholic Lenten season is a form of fasting but doesn't necessarily proscribe sexual intimacy. It's largely a matter of mutual consent. However, a prolonged and intense fasting experience can suppress the libido as the body adapts to more of a survival mode."

Luke was surprised. "Whoa! It looks like you've thoroughly researched the topic." He looked into her eyes and drew close. "But we don't have to worry about that tonight, my dear," he whispered as he nibbled gently on her ear. "My fast doesn't begin until tomorrow at the very least."

He took her in a firm embrace. But she gently nudged him away.

"Hmm. But my fast has already begun, my dear. Can we just cuddle?" she said as she snuggled close to him. "As a matter of... mutual consent."

Chapter Forty-Five

FIELD TEST

Thursday, August 20, 2015

9:00 a.m. When Luke arrived at the Pony Bar and Grill in Plymouth, Aiyanna was there waiting with a steaming pot of coffee and two cups.

"Never saw you in cargo pants and a hunting vest before." Luke took the seat across from her. "Very attractive," he added playfully.

"Yes, well, the extra pockets are quite useful at times," she said with an air of mystery to her voice.

Glancing around, he was a bit bewildered. "So, where is your partner in crime, Dr. Greene?"

She cleared her throat. "Ahem. Yes, well, Nate wasn't able to make it today. Something came up that forced him away... on business."

No way was Luke buying it. "Away on business? You mean, Santoma business."

Aiyanna peered down. "Yeah, something like that," she said with a faraway tone. Regaining her composure, she looked up and forced a smile. "But it's nothing the two of us can't handle."

Leaning back, Luke drummed his fingers on the table. She seemed to be hiding something.

"I see. Well, it is what it is," he said finally. "So what's the game plan?"

She produced a quad sketch pad from her briefcase and drew a straight horizontal line across the middle of the first blank sheet.

"Okay, so here we have the edge of the cornfield," she said, labeling the area above the line with the word *Cornfield*. She continued drawing as she spoke. "About five feet inside the field, we'll stake out our twenty-foot-square electrical test grid marked by four ground probe electrodes, one at each corner of the square. From the edge of the field, we'll clear a path to the center of the grid, where we'll locate our bait station." She looked up. "Just a stake in the ground to tether our test rabbit."

Luke grimaced.

Aiyanna continued, "We'll make the path wide enough—about three feet—to provide a clear line of sight from the bait station to our location just outside the cornfield, where our DC power generator and tripod-mounted video camera will be located."

She drew two little boxes and labeled them "EGGS" and "Camera."

"What does EGGS stand for?" he asked.

"Electrical grid generation system," she said with a smile. "Nate and I thought the new upsized DC generator and grid system deserved a special name."

She drew two cartoon people next to the power generator and video camera. "That's where you... I mean, *we*... will be, after I place the live rabbit at the bait station tethered on a leash tied to the stake." She drew a cartoon figure of a rabbit at the center of the square, then took Luke's hands and squeezed hard. He thought he saw tears welling up in her eyes.

"Luke, I need you to control the video camera. And promise me that *whatever* happens—I mean, no matter what—you *must* not fail to capture it on video! It will be our only proof of what happens."

This took him by surprise. "My, that sounds rather ominous. I mean, are you expecting any trouble?"

She tried to correct herself. "Uh, no. Not at all. It's just that, well, since Nate is not here to help, I'm going to have to rely one hundred percent on you."

He pretended to be happy with that explanation. "Not a problem. I think I can handle it."

Sitting back in her chair, she softened her tone and changed the subject. "So how's the fasting coming?"

Luke sighed. "*Fasting* is a misnomer. It should really be called *slowing*. I mean, there's nothing 'fast' about it."

Aiyanna laughed. "Well, it will do you good. And the other part. How's that going?"

"You mean the prayer and meditation? Well, as good as can be expected, I guess. I bought a CD that purports to teach the proper meditation techniques. I'm trying to focus, or 'concentrate the mind,' as your Uncle Lobo put it, to acquire a guardian spirit. Trouble is, I'm not sure how to tell whether I've got one."

Aiyanna smiled. "If and when that happens, I think you'll know."

10:00 A.M. When Luke and Aiyanna arrived at his uncle's farm outside Kiel, Clarence and Doris were in the yard to greet them. His Aunt Doris smiled and gave him a hug.

"It's good to see you again, Luke," Doris said. Turning to Aiyanna, she reached out and took her hand, patting it with her free hand. "And it's so nice to see you again, dear. It's Aiyanna, is it not? Or would you prefer to be called *Doctor* Aiyanna?"

Aiyanna smiled. "Please, Aiyanna will do just fine, ma'am."

Clarence rested one hand on the nape of Luke's neck and drew him closer. "So tell me, Luke. What's the plan? And what can I do to help?"

Luke turned to Aiyanna. "Why don't you explain."

She showed Clarence the sketch of the test setup and explained what they wanted to do—except she left out the part about the rabbit, of course. Luke noticed she had scratched out the cartoon figure of the rabbit in the sketch.

"So, you see, we're studying the effect of direct electrical disturbances on corn crops," Aiyanna said. "We think it may have something to do with the formation of these so-called crop circles."

"Yes, that's what Luke was explaining to me over the phone."

"So, if you can tell us where to set up, that would be great," Luke said.

"I'll do better than that," Clarence replied. "I can help you clear that path through the field you got drawn on your sketch."

Luke and Aiyanna shared looks of concern.

"Not to worry," Clarence added. "After we clear the path, I promise to get out of your way."

"Thank you, Uncle," Luke said with a smile. "We sure appreciate your help."

"Well, I do have an ulterior motive," he added with a grin. "You see, this is grain corn, not sweet corn. Mature and ready for drying and harvesting. So I plan to put you two youngsters to work. Don't want any of it to go to waste. I'll cut the stalks near the ground, while you two kids stack them into shocks for drying."

With the three of them working together, in no time at all they had cleared a straight, three-foot-wide path about eighteen feet into the cornfield.

Returning to the barnyard, Luke looked back down the path. It resembled one of those haunted corn mazes he remembered going to as a kid on Halloween and the fun of "getting lost" in the maze. He looked at Aiyanna. He hadn't noticed it before, but in addition to the buck knife she had strapped to her upper thigh, she was also wearing several buckskin pouches around her waist, and all of her pants and vest pockets were bulging. He laughed. "You look like someone getting ready to go on safari!"

She smiled wanly and mumbled something cryptic. "Gotta be prepared. Never know what you're going to run into."

The two of them unloaded the power generator, tool cart, and video equipment from the SUV. For the moment, the rabbit remained in its cage hidden from view.

"Well, I'm gonna leave you kids to your own business, now, while I tend to mine," Clarence said. "Doris and I will be running into town to hit the bank before it closes at noon and run a few other errands. We'll be back in time for lunch. Doris has prepared something nice for the two of you."

"Oh, that won't be necessary," Aiyanna said. "She shouldn't have gone to all that trouble."

"No trouble at all!" Clarence said. "She's only too glad to help."

And with that Luke's uncle walked over to his pickup truck, where Doris was waiting.

After they drove off, Luke and Aiyanna continued setting up their test equipment in the open field. Luke took a three-foot stake and planted it at the far end of the cleared path to mark the location of the bait station. Centering on the stake, they measured and marked off the perimeter of the twenty-foot-square test grid in the crowded field of corn. Luke drove the four corner probes into the ground while Aiyanna ran the wires to the power generator. In the clearing, Aiyanna set up the video camera and tripod and sighted the bait station through the camera's viewfinder, adjusting the tripod position for a clear line of sight down the path.

"Looks good," she called out, then secured the tripod feet to the ground with tent stakes.

She took a deep breath as Luke rejoined her. "Well, everything is set. I think we're ready for the live bait," she said.

Returning to the SUV she retrieved the rabbit cage and walked it down the path to the bait station.

"I feel bad for the rabbit," Luke said as she removed the animal from its cage.

"It's all in the interest of science," she responded, attaching the rabbit's leash to the stake.

The way she said it, though, was not at all like Aiyanna. Cold. To Luke it seemed she had become hardened to the whole matter, detached, performing in an almost robotic fashion.

Returning to the clearing, Aiyanna made a final inspection of the EGGS generator and test apparatus while Luke took his position behind the video camera.

"Everything is good to go," she said. "Are you ready with the camera, Luke?"

He made a final check through the viewfinder.

"Everything is A-okay," he said, giving her a thumbs-up.

She paused, exhaling slowly. "Okay. Here goes!"

The generator chugged to life as she flipped on the power switch, then began to adjust the supply voltage. As the meter passed the thirty-volt mark she seemed to grow increasingly anxious. Forty volts. Forty-five. "Should've seen something by now," she mumbled. Then, as the meter topped fifty volts, they saw a faint green glow emanating from the ground and noticed some movement of the inner stalks. The ground showed a slight rippling motion. She cranked it up to fifty-five volts. The ripples became more pronounced, forming a circular standing wave between the stalks of corn, like the surface ripples formed in a glass of water placed in front of a loudspeaker.

Beads of sweat formed on her brow.

"You okay?" Luke asked.

She didn't respond but kept her eyes forward, as though in a trance.

Suddenly, the inner stalks bent in unison toward the rabbit, lying down in a spiral counterclockwise pattern as the roots heaved upward, reaching out to ensnare their prey. A faint cloud of brown dust burst forth from the tassels.

"Nerve toxin!" Aiyanna said. "Meant to paralyze its prey. Just like in the lab. Amazing!"

Just as the rabbit was starting to become ensnared, Aiyanna did something totally unexpected. Without warning, she turned to Luke, gave him a big hug and a kiss, and placed something in his shirt pocket. Backing away she said, "I'm sorry, Luke. Please forgive me, but this is something I must do!"

Rushing forward into the test grid, she set the rabbit free and took its place at the center.

"What the hell are you doing?" he shouted, totally flummoxed by her behavior.

"Please, don't let me down, Luke. Keep the camera rolling!" she shouted back.

Suddenly, the ground below Aiyanna exploded upward and outward. Like a giant maw, the earth opened up and began to swallow her whole. One of her waist pouches sprang loose and fell to the ground just beyond her reach.

"Luke, help me!" she said reaching out with her one free arm, the other having become immobilized by the entangled mass of roots.

Abandoning his post, Luke lunged forward, inadvertently brushing against the camera on its swivel mount as he did so. Reaching her, he grabbed her arm as she continued to sink, now buried waist-deep in the roiling soil, roots and stalks conspiring, reaching up to pull her down.

"No! No!" she shouted. "The pouch! Give me the pouch!"

Luke looked away and saw the pouch that was just beyond his reach.

"Please! Get it for me!" she begged. "Put it in my hand!"

"But I have to let go of your arm to do that!" he cried.

"Yes! Let go!"

Reluctantly he obeyed. Releasing her arm, he retrieved the pouch, then returned and shoved it into her open palm. Her fist clamped down on the pouch like a vise.

"Thank you!" she said as her shoulders sank below the surface.

At this point the roots were beginning to take hold of Luke as well.

"I'm sorry, Luke. But you must go!" she cried. "Save yourself!" She then forced a smile. "I'll be fine, Luke. Really!"

It was all he could do to rip the roots away from him, like the tentacles of a giant kraken, then quickly back away on his buttocks like a retreating crab.

The last words Aiyanna uttered before disappearing below the surface were "I love you, Luke!"

And with that, she was gone.

Hysterical, Luke gulped in breaths, his heart racing. Leaning forward on his knees, he clawed at the earth, staining the soil with a mix of blood and sweat, but to no avail. Pounding the earth hard with clenched fists, nails digging into his palms drawing blood, he moaned, "Damn! Damn! Damn! Why did you do this, Aiyanna!? Why?" At last, raising both arms to the heavens, he looked up sobbing, tears running down his cheeks, and cried out, "Oh, God, please hear my prayer! Or whatever spirit is listening. Please, take pity and bring Aiyanna back to me! Or take me to her. Whatever! Please speak to me!"

But there was no response. No sounds. Only the hum of the generator and the distant caws of invisible crows.

It was then that Luke became aware of a bulge in his shirt pocket, something Aiyanna had placed there right before she ran off to meet whatever fate awaited her. He reached in and pulled out a folded sheet of paper—a note in Aiyanna's handwriting:

My Dearest Luke,

Please forgive me for what I am about to do. But I must seek the reality behind the legend. Wasn't it you who said, "If Alice is still alive, shouldn't we be doing everything we can to bring her back?" As both a scientist and a person of faith in search of the truth, I have no choice if I am to remain true to my creed and to myself.

Luke, last week I had another dream. In my dream your sister, Alice, came to me, pleading for help to be rescued from the depths of the Underworld realm in which she had become trapped. She said she is well but feels that her time is running out. So please, take heart. If what I discover is really true and meant to be, then we shall meet again. Perhaps on a different plane, in a different realm, even a different time! But it is a path that I must take. You must search your own heart as to what you must do. Please seek the advice of Shaman Lobo.

Luke, in three short months I have come to know and love you. You are a kind and loving person and have so much to offer, more perhaps than you may ever realize. Please know that I love you with all my heart! And I do this for the two of us. And for Alice!

Please tell my mom and dad, my sister and brothers, that I love them dearly. And God willing we shall all meet again in this life!

And finally, you must PLEASE safeguard the video! It alone will attest to what happened here! I doubt anyone will believe what you have to say. The video alone will tell the story.

Forever loving you,
    Aiyanna

PS: The keys to the SUV and my apartment are under the front passenger seat.

LUKE REMAINED ON HIS KNEES, transfixed by Aiyanna's words. He wiped his eyes with a dirty shirtsleeve to be sure he had read it correctly. The salt from his tears wetted his lips, reminding him of her sweet kisses.

He refolded the note and placed it back in his pocket. Taking his cell phone from his pants pocket, he punched in a number, but the screen indicated no service.

"Damn!"

Gathering his strength, he slowly gained his feet and staggered down the cleared path toward Aiyanna's SUV. Still no service.

He retrieved the keys from beneath the front seat, started the engine, and drove off down the driveway in search of a serviceable cell phone area. After driving a half mile down the road, he pulled over and tried Dan's cell phone number again. This time Dan picked up.

"Hi, Sport. What can I do ya for?"

WHEN LUKE'S Uncle Clarence and Aunt Doris returned to the farm, Aiyanna's SUV was missing from the driveway.

"That's strange," Clarence said, turning to Doris. "Let me go out to the test site so I can check on things."

Clarence gasped at what he saw: a newly formed crop circle right smack-dab in the middle of the test grid!

"Oh my God! It looks like their theories were right after all!" he said aloud.

But there was no sign of the kids anywhere.

"Hmm, maybe they had to go off and get supplies or something."

It was then he noticed a furry white rabbit in a leather harness scampering about dragging a leash. "That's odd," he mumbled. "Looks like someone lost their pet rabbit."

He leaned down and made little rabbit sounds to attract the animal. Obviously tame, it timidly approached and allowed him to bend down and stroke it gently.

"Nice little fella," he said as he took hold of the leash with his other hand. "I'll take you back to the house and give you some fresh food and water." He looked around. "Gotta find out who your owner is."

When Clarence returned to the yard, the SUV had suddenly reappeared, parked with its engine idling.

"Oh, so there you are!" he shouted. As he approached the vehicle, he saw Luke in the driver's seat, slumped forward and hugging the steering wheel.

"So, where is Aiyanna?"

A sobbing Luke looked up, took a shaky breath, and offered a wan reply. "Gone!"

"Gone? What do you mean 'gone'?"

"Just... gone" was all he said.

He was pallid, white as a ghost, and trembling.

Clarence put his hand on Luke's shoulder. Obviously, something had gone wrong. "Listen, why don't we go inside the house. I'll have Doris fix you some hot chamomile tea. You can explain it to us then."

Chapter Forty-Six

GONE AWRY

Later That Day, August 20, 2015

2:10 p.m. Clarence and Doris sat on the parlor sofa observing their nephew seated a safe distance across from them on an ottoman, bent over, sipping a cup of chamomile tea. The color had begun to return to his cheeks, but he remained drawn and detached. Clarence and Doris huddled together, as if they needed to protect themselves from the strangeness that had suddenly transformed Luke from the sensible young man they had known to something other than normal—even scary.

"I am really sorry to put the two of you through this," Luke mumbled. "It wasn't supposed to end up this way. It was... an experiment gone awry."

Clarence exchanged nervous looks with Doris but remained silent. An "experiment gone awry" he could understand. A whole person swallowed up by the earth without a trace? Now, that was something that strained credibility! Surely, he thought, Luke should have been able to come up with a more believable story to explain Aiyanna's disappearance and whereabouts. Maybe he had to drop her off somewhere? Or they had a falling out and she thumbed a ride back to town? Anything but the story Luke was pushing.

"Well, I guess we'll find out when your detective friend and his men get here," Clarence offered cautiously. "You say they have a device that can see what's under the ground?"

Luke nodded. "Uh-huh. It's called ground-penetrating radar, or GPR."

"I see," Clarence and Doris responded in unison.

In the course of the last two hours, their world had been turned upside down as they were forced to entertain the possibility that—just possibly—their nephew was involved in foul play.

"What will Cynthia say?" Doris whispered to Clarence.

He patted her hand. "Shh! Not in front of Luke," he replied under his breath.

Before long, Clarence heard the sound of vehicles coming up the driveway. The Einsbachs breathed welcome sighs of relief. Clarence rose slowly and walked to the front door to greet their visitors while Luke and Doris remained seated.

Opening the door, Clarence counted three vehicles. The Sheboygan County sheriff's cruiser led the way, followed by a van with the word GEO-SERVICES written on the side, and then a second cruiser from the Manitowoc County Sheriff's Office.

Clarence recognized Dan from the July Fourth cookout and forced a smile as the team approached the front porch. "Good to see you again, Detective Meyers," Clarence said as he held out his hand.

Dan shook his hand and returned a twisted smile. "Yes, same here, Mr. Einsbach. Although I wish it were under better circumstances. Tell me, how is the missus?"

"Doris is... well, she's fine," he said with a nervous twinge. "Just a bit shaken up. She's inside with Luke."

"And Luke?"

Clarence frowned and shook his head. "A real basket case, I'm afraid."

"Hmm. Not surprised." Dan motioned toward the door. "Shall we?"

"Oh, yes. By all means," Clarence said. "Gentlemen, please follow me." And he led them in.

Once inside, they made their way to the parlor. Dan tipped his hat to Doris. "Ma'am." And he introduced the other members of his team.

"These are Deputies Sam Riley and Jimmy Collins from our county sheriff's office. And that fellow is Deputy Taylor from the Manitowoc

County Sheriff's Office. Since Kiel is officially out of my jurisdiction, this has become a joint investigation. And Sheriff Bradley has kindly given me permission to take the lead."

Luke stood slowly and set the cup of tea on the coffee table. "Good to see you all again," he said with a fractured smile.

Dan took a deep breath. "I must say, Luke, I've seen you looking better." He glanced around the room, making direct eye contact with Clarence and Doris. "If you don't mind, sir, ma'am, I'd like to speak with Luke alone. To get the facts of the case. Later, I'd like to get separate statements from the two of you. If it's not too much trouble."

"Uh, oh, sure. No trouble at all. We understand." Clarence motioned for his wife to follow as they retreated into the next room and closed the door behind them.

By now Luke had regained the better part of his composure.

"Mind if I record this?" Dan asked as he produced a digital audio recorder from his pocket.

"No. Not at all," Luke said. He took a seat and began relaying the events, starting with his early-morning rendezvous with Aiyanna in Plymouth and ending with Aiyanna being swallowed whole in the cornfield.

"It was just like that mouse in the solarium, Sam," he said, looking straight at Sam for support. "You surely remember that."

Sam nodded. "Yes, of course. Amazing. And downright unnatural, if I do say so."

"We were supposed to replicate the experiment in the field with a rabbit," Luke explained. He looked around the room and pointed to the animal now returned to its cage by the door. "There, you see! My uncle retrieved it from the field. That was supposed to have been the bait."

"Hmm," Dan said, chewing on his lip. "I really am sorry, Luke. If this went down as you say, Aiyanna certainly deserved better. You both deserved better."

They all nodded in confused sympathy.

Luke shook his head. "Thank you, Dan. I appreciate it. But listen, I got the whole thing on video. You'll be able to see for yourself!"

Dan raised an eyebrow. "Video? So, where is that video?"

Luke thought a moment, bewildered by his own oversight. "Uh... I guess it's still out in the field. I... never thought to bring it in."

"That's okay. We'll get it," Dan said. He shut off the digital recorder and addressed the team. "Well, I think it's time we paid a visit to the cornfield to get to the bottom of this."

Within minutes the team joined Jeff Seibert, the Geo-Services technician, who had remained behind in the barnyard to prepare the GPR device.

Luke led the way into the cornfield down the mazelike path toward the test site. It was a jaw-dropping experience for Dan's team. Throughout all of their investigations into this so-called mini crop circle phenomenon, this was the first time they had actually witnessed the direct aftermath of an event. Except for Dan, of course, who was first on the scene along with Sheriff Ben Hodges when Luke's sister disappeared sixteen years prior. "Sixteen years to the day, to be exact," Dan had been quick to point out to the team. The coincidence was apparently not lost on him.

"Jesus!" Sam exclaimed as they entered the test site area. "What a mess!"

Dan turned toward the video camera still on its tripod. "Grab that video camera, Sam!" he ordered. "We'll check it out when we get it back to the office." He turned to Luke. "Sorry, Luke. But we'll need it for evidence. I have no doubt it will confirm your story."

But his tone was less than certain.

Jeff Seibert powered up the GPR machine and established a grid pattern for his geo-survey.

"Make sure you scan deep, Jeff!" Luke said. "Especially any geological anomalies that suggest sinkholes or underground caverns."

Jeff nodded and set about surveying the area.

Ten minutes passed. "Anything yet, Jeff?" Dan asked, growing visibly impatient.

"No. Nothing yet," he shot back.

But hope was fading when, after thirty minutes of scanning and rescanning the area, nothing turned up. No body. No Aiyanna. No nothing. Except, "I do detect a deep fissure over a void that suggests a system of caverns deep underground," Jeff announced. "About seventy feet down."

Luke's heart skipped a beat. *Yes!* Deep down he was hoping this was what they would find—or wouldn't find. No body. No remains. That was good! It could only mean that Aiyanna had found her way into that Underworld realm after all. Of course, there was the other possibility. The one he preferred not to think about: that a sinkhole had simply swallowed her into oblivion into the lifeless void of a deep, hidden, natural abyss.

Luke was alone in his private ruminations, though. Dan never did share his beliefs in such things. Sinkholes, maybe. But not underground worlds, the stuff of fantasies as far as Dan was concerned.

Still, Luke sensed that Sam was on the fence. He knew from his model studies and accumulated data that the lack of human remains associated with certain missing persons cases were often associated with these deep cavern anomalies, although he did not seem ready to commit to any particular theory to explain it.

As the afternoon wore on, it was clear to Luke that Dan had become increasingly distrustful of his version of what happened. Dan seemed eager to get back to the office to examine the video evidence, even as Luke's own thoughts spun wildly in a hundred different directions.

"Listen," Dan finally announced to the team. "I think this about wraps it up in the field." He turned to Luke with a suspicious glare. "Luke, I'm gonna have to impound all this equipment—what do you call it?"

Luke had to think about it. "Electrical grid generation system—or EGGS," he replied weakly.

"Yeah, whatever," Dan shot back. "We need to confiscate it for forensic evidence." He paused. "And Aiyanna's Bronco as well. Uh, just a formality, you understand."

But Luke knew better. "Sure, I understand." With an adroit sleight of hand, he had the presence of mind to detach the car keys from her main key ring, retaining her apartment and other keys. He handed the car keys to Dan.

Dan turned to Sam. "Sam, I'd like you to take Luke back to Plymouth where he left his vehicle parked. Then, I would like everyone—and I mean *everyone*," he said with an eye toward Luke, "to rendezvous back at the office in the briefing room tout de suite. I will meet you there once I've gotten sworn statements from the Einsbachs."

He paused as he looked back at the cornfield. "Gentlemen, I am afraid we have yet another missing persons case on our hands. And this one is especially perplexing and"—he glanced at Luke—"*upsetting*, to say the least."

Chapter Forty-Seven

IMBROGLIO

Late Afternoon, August 20, 2015

4:30 p.m. Sam was the last of the investigative team to arrive and joined those gathered in the briefing room.

Dan looked up. "So, where is Luke?"

"He'll be here shortly, Dan. Had to stop off in the men's room."

Sam sensed it immediately. The mood was somber. You could cut the tension with a knife. A pall of distrust had settled over the small gathering, which included Dan, Jimmy, Steve Kelly—the crime lab expert—and now Sam. Apparently, Dan, Jimmy, and Steve had already seen the video evidence. Dan was tapping his pencil, clearly growing impatient with Luke's tardiness.

At last, Luke entered the room. "Sorry for taking so long, but I needed to freshen up a bit."

Indeed, Luke appeared in much better form than he had an hour ago. But that didn't help the situation—or his case.

With the team seated around the small conference table, Dan leaned forward and folded his hands. "Okay, gentlemen," he said softly, "let's consider the evidence."

With a click of the mouse, the video began to play on the pull-down wall screen. It started out normal enough. Aiyanna explaining the experimental setup. A small rabbit tethered to a stake in a clearing in the middle of a cornfield. The hum of a nearby power generator. The motion of cornstalks, swaying and bowing in a generally circular pattern. Then, the sudden upheaval of the earth beneath the rabbit.

Sam nodded. It all looked quite familiar to him, only on a grander scale. Instead of a mouse, there was the rabbit. Instead of a few scrawny stalks of corn in a laboratory solarium, a lush field of ripened corn. It all seemed to be playing out as Luke had explained.

Suddenly the unexpected happened. Aiyanna was heard mumbling something off-camera, then seen rushing forward into the field of view, freeing the rabbit from its tether. Unintelligible shouts from Luke were heard beyond the visual camera range. Suddenly, the camera angle shifted dramatically, and the frame of action was lost. All you could now see were crowded, swaying stalks of corn. And all you heard were muffled cries and the sounds of an apparent struggle and argument. For a moment all was quiet. Then came the sound of Luke's voice crying out.

Dan paused the video and remained silent for a few moments before speaking.

"It will take some time to analyze the acoustics. Try and make out what was actually said," Dan explained. "But that about sums it up, gentlemen."

Luke was shaking, his head buried in his hands. When he looked up, he was in tears.

"Don't you see what happened?" he cried. "I screwed up! I nudged the camera on its swivel mount when I ran to save Aiyanna! Don't you see?"

Dan shook his head and scoffed. "What I see is... confusion... struggle... turmoil. What I *don't* see is someone being swallowed up by the earth. And what I *don't* see are Mario toadstool people devouring a lady in distress!" he said, his voice rising, rife with biting sarcasm and frustration.

Sam rolled his eyes. *Oh my God! Not the toadstool people again!*

Dan cleared his throat as he tried to regain his composure.

"I'm just trying to put the pieces of a puzzle together, Luke. I'm a detective. That's what I do! First, the two of you show up on your uncle's farm to conduct this so-called experiment. A magician's disappearing rabbit trick! According to your aunt and uncle's testimony, they go off to run some errands. When they return, they find you, Aiyanna, and the SUV gone, and a so-called crop circle generated in your place. There are obvious signs of a struggle. And the video you offer as proof is conveniently turned on its end. But the soundtrack does offer evidence of a struggle of some kind. When you return to the farm, you are alone. The story you tell your aunt and uncle is that Aiyanna has been magically swallowed up by the earth! Okay. Fine. But when we search the area with GPR we turn up nothing! *Nada!*"

Dan sat back and extended his arms. "So, please tell us, Luke. Where is Aiyanna? That pretty girlfriend of yours. Corpus delicti. No body, no murder, right?"

By now Luke had his head buried back in his hands and was rocking back and forth, groaning and sobbing. He looked up and turned to Sam. "Sam, you've *got* to believe me, right? I mean, you saw what happened in the lab!"

Sam opened his mouth to speak, but nothing came out. He just turned to Dan and shrugged, as if to say, "Dunno."

Dan continued his tirade. "I tell you, Luke. This whole mushroom corn thing has gotten a bit too out of hand for my liking. You stage an elaborate scheme and come up with these bogus fake news stories. I'm sorry, Luke, but you gotta do better than that. Is it just to sell newspapers? Jesus! First Jake's fairy tale and now this!"

Pausing a moment, Dan narrowed his eyes in triumph, like he had saved the best for last.

"Or... is it maybe a lover's quarrel gone bad? Is that it, Luke? You and Aiyanna had a falling out? I'd understand that. Believe me, I *know* how these things can happen. Mixed-culture relationships sometimes... well, sometimes they don't work out."

Sam could hear Luke's teeth grinding. Luke bridled and finally spoke up. Wiping the tears from his eyes, he verbally lashed out at Dan.

"So, you tell me, Dan! You never did find Adam's body, did you? And my guess is you never will! That thing about the recent crop circle on the Klausman farm. Think that's a coincidence? Just after Adam breaks out of your secure perimeter. Last seen near the Klausman farm. Think that's all just a coincidence? Let's face it, Dan. You're in denial! Looking for a perp that doesn't exist. At least not the flesh-and-blood kind you think."

Dan bristled, his face boiling red. Sam had never seen him like this before. Pushing back on his chair, a glowering Dan raised two clenched fists in the air and slammed them down hard on the table. Even his seasoned veteran officers all jumped in their seats.

"That's it!" he shouted. "This meeting is over! Go back to your rag paper, Luke. I've got better things to do. But be warned." He pointed and jabbed an accusatory finger in Luke's face. "You are a person of considerable interest in this missing persons case. You know forensics. You know what that means. You're not to leave this county as long as this remains an open investigation!"

LATER, after a dejected Luke had left the building, Dan retreated to his private office, asking not to be disturbed. Breathing a deep sigh, he took a new pin and added it to his missing persons wall map, locating it a little east of Kiel in Manitowoc County. He stood there, breathing hard, arms folded across his chest, contemplating this most troubling turn of events.

"Finally got my wish," he mumbled with a cheerless chuckle. "Expanding this investigation into our neighboring counties."

Dan had considered taking Luke into custody—he certainly had cause to do so—but decided that putting him on a long leash would better serve the investigation. And then too, in the back of his mind— call it intuition, or simply wishful thinking—something was telling him that maybe, just maybe, there was some truth to Luke's version of what happened.

Chapter Forty-Eight

GUARDIAN SPIRIT

Evening of August 20, 2015

When Luke left the sheriff's office that evening, he felt more isolated and alone than he'd ever felt in his life. Wrestling with the demons that threatened to consume him, he struggled to get his emotions under control, gather his thoughts, and develop a plan of action.

For starters, he doubled down on his usual three-mile run along the shore of Lake Michigan and the harbor's riverfront paths, extending the run south to King Park and beyond before circling back. At the conclusion of his run, he paused at the north pier and walked the wave-battered stone jetty out to the breakwater lighthouse. There he took time to meditate and contemplate the majesty of the lake and, yes—even to pray. As he sank deeper into a meditative state, a sense of calm unlike any he'd experienced before came over him. It was only the bellowing of a foghorn from a passing yacht returning to port that roused him from this peaceful state.

Before returning to his condo, Luke stopped at the office to make copies of Aiyanna's letter. He had deliberately avoided showing the letter to Dan for fear it would be confiscated "as evidence." Luke figured he would eventually disclose it, but at the right time. For now, there were others he needed to share it with.

On the way out, he bumped into Pam York, who happened to be working late, taking both of them off guard.

"Well, hello there, stranger!" she said. "Where have you been keeping yourself these days?"

He stammered and groped for a response.

"Uh, well, I've been on... special assignment. Ted knows about it."

"Oh, you mean that bison series you're running in the Sunday supplement. Nice piece!"

"Yes, well, thank you! Thank you indeed! As a matter of fact, I need to follow up tomorrow with an interview in Black River Falls. Can you please tell Ted I won't be in?"

"Sure. You got it!"

"Great. See you later, Pam. Gotta run," he said with a manufactured smile.

Back in his condominium, Luke showered and settled in for the night. Emptying his pockets on his bedroom dresser, he discovered a business card from Deputy Sam Riley. He now vaguely recalled Sam slipping him the card as they were leaving the briefing room. Luke turned the card over. There was a handwritten cell phone number and a short note from Sam: "If you need anything just give me a call."

Luke smiled. *Sam's personal cell phone number. Nice! May come in handy.* He entered the number in his cell phone contact list and put the card in his wallet for safekeeping before crawling into bed for the night.

Lying there awake, he continued to ruminate over the day's events. He must have read Aiyanna's letter twenty times before eventually turning out the light. One line in particular stayed with him: "You must search your heart and seek the advice of Shaman Lobo."

"Yes, that is exactly what I must do," he mumbled weakly as sleep overcame him. As his arm fell limp at his side, the letter slipped from his grasp and floated gently to the floor.

And with sleep... a dream.

~

LUKE WOULD USUALLY TELL people he never dreamed. Or at least, he could never remember any of his dreams. But tonight would be different.

Tonight, his dream would be unique, vivid in every detail, and memorable.

In his dream Luke found himself in a cold, damp, dark place. A cavern, it seemed. A fire was burning at the center of this chamber space, and he drew close to warm himself. As he rubbed his hands over the fire, he became aware of a large, flickering shadow cast against the cavern wall. His eyes were drawn to the shadow's source. Boldly poised high on a boulder not twenty feet away was a great white wolf, the likes of which he had never seen before. That such a beast even existed was new knowledge for him. White, pure as snow, the wolf stared at him with penetrating red eyes. Not a menacing stare or pose, but majestic and bold!

Then the wolf spoke, taking Luke by surprise. At least the words appeared to be emanating from the wolf, though the animal remained as motionless as the lifeless rock on which it stood. The words reverberated off the chamber walls and within Luke's head, embedding themselves deep in his psyche.

"Luke! I am your guardian spirit. Take courage and trust the yearnings of your heart. Seek wisdom and pray for strength. For the journey will not be easy and will be fraught with peril."

These words were followed by a stiff breeze that passed through the cavern, slowly erasing the image of the wolf like a sand painting swept away by the desert wind.

∼

WHEN LUKE AWOKE, he found himself seated in the middle of his bedroom floor, not knowing how he got there. He was not anxious or unnerved by the experience but remained seated, deep in thought, meditating and praying until sleep finally overcame him again.

The morning sun found him once again in his bed as he awoke to greet the new day. Amazingly refreshed, he knew what he must do and prayed he'd be up to the task.

Chapter Forty-Nine

BLACK BEAR POWWOW

Friday, August 21, 2015

For this road trip, Luke decided to rent a car rather than risk taking his own vehicle and being picked up by the police. With orders not to leave the county, he was certain Dan had alerted the neighboring authorities. He even walked to the rental agency rather than drive and park his own vehicle, so high was his level of paranoia.

During the two-hour drive to Black River Falls, Luke wrestled with how best to break the news to Aiyanna's family. He had sent Larry a text message early that morning saying he was planning to be in the area and hoped to spend some time with him and Rachel, and Uncle Lobo if at all possible. Larry texted back asking whether Aiyanna would be with him and that he was looking forward to seeing them. Luke remained silent and did not respond.

When he knocked on the door of the Black Bear residence right before noon, he was greeted by an ebullient Rachel.

"Hello, Luke!" she said cheery-eyed. "It's so nice to see you again. Larry said you would be dropping by." Looking past him toward his parked rental car, she appeared puzzled. "Are you alone? Is Aiyanna not with you?"

"Uh, no, Mrs. Black Bear. Aiyanna is not with me today."

Rachel became concerned. "Well, is she alright?"

Luke hemmed and hawed. "Yes, I believe she is. But, in a manner of speaking, that is, uh, actually what I came to find out."

He cringed at his flailing opening remarks. The words didn't come out the way he had planned.

Rachel slowly backed away. "I... don't understand," she said, pausing. "But please, do come in."

After inviting Luke into the family room, she offered him hot tea and biscuits. He took a seat, fumbling for the right words.

"Uh, I was wondering, Rachel, if it would be possible for Mr. Black Bear and Uncle Lobo to join us." He patted a manila envelope he held under his arm. "I have something we need to discuss, and it would be best if all were present to hear it."

Rachel straightened up and replied soberly, "Yes, Luke. Certainly. I'll see what I can do."

Luke was sipping a cup of chamomile tea when Larry Black Bear and Charlie "Lobo" Graywolf entered the room. It was almost one o'clock.

"We got over here as quick as we could, hon," Larry said as he gave Rachel a peck on the cheek. "You said it was urgent."

Luke stood and turned to Larry. "It's good to see you again, sir."

"Ah, Luke!" They approached each other and Larry gave him a quick hug, then glanced at the manila envelope. "Does this have something to do with your bison story? Aiyanna sent me a copy of your first install-ment, and I must say, you did a very nice job!"

"Well, thank you, sir. But no. I'm afraid it's not about the bison story." His tone turned dour. "This has to do with... Aiyanna."

Larry deflated. "Oh, I see. Well, then, let's all have a seat and talk about it." He motioned to the others.

Larry took a seat in his swivel rocker while Luke and Charlie shared the sofa. Rachel sat on the matching love seat.

Once they settled in, Luke leaned forward, cleared his throat, and began.

"First, let me say, sir, that I believe Aiyanna is... well and safe. But she is, how should I say... missing."

Larry paused, exchanging nervous looks with Lobo. "Does this have anything to do with her... *spelunking* adventure?"

Luke cocked his head and glanced back and forth between the two older men. "Spelunking adventure?" He was puzzled. "What do you mean?"

"Ahem," Lobo interjected. "Aiyanna came to me one day last week to say she was going cave exploring with some friends and wanted me to pray for her and give her some earth medicines to keep her safe."

Luke sat back. Yes, of course! Aiyanna had made no mention of this to him. But it kind of made sense considering what she was planning to do.

"I see," Luke said. "And what did you do?"

"Well, I told her that she must fast, pray, and meditate in preparation for her adventure. I then prepared four bundles of herbs—sweetgrass, cedar, sage, and tobacco—the four sacred herbs of Ma-ona the Creator, and gave them to her in separate pouches."

Luke remembered the pouches attached to Aiyanna's belt and the one he recovered for her just in time as she was about to go underground.

"Uh-huh," he said.

Lobo continued. "Yes, well, I then recounted the ancient legend of the chief who journeyed to the spirit land to bring back his departed wife from the dead. It was a most perilous journey, not something to be taken lightly. These were the same herbs the shaman offered the chief to protect him on his journey." Lobo forced a nervous chuckle in the form of a grunt. "I figured if it was good enough to protect against the perils of the spirit land, it should be good enough for an afternoon of spelunking."

"Yes, I see," Luke said, fidgeting and still wrestling with the best way to proceed. He decided the simple truth was best. "Well, you know about the research Aiyanna was involved in with GMO corn and mushrooms. She briefly described it during our last visit."

They all nodded.

Luke proceeded to elaborate on her findings and the predatory nature of this symbiotic relationship. He described the laboratory experiments in the solarium with white mice, and the follow-up field experiments she was planning with larger animals, like rabbits. This naturally led to a description of the events of the previous day at his Uncle Clarence's farm, which he described in every detail, leaving nothing out.

In the end he likened it to what happened to his sister, Alice, sixteen years ago to the day.

"But I believe with all my heart and soul that Aiyanna is... alive and well," Luke said. "I truly believe that."

He was reaching for the manila envelope when Rachel broke down, sobbing, her face buried in her hands.

Larry immediately got up from his chair and joined his wife on the love seat, embracing and trying to console her but seemingly at a loss for words.

Rachel looked up, speaking through her tears. "My poor baby! Aiyanna! What has happened? Why did she do this?"

Larry began rocking her. "Shh, my love. It's okay. Everything will be alright." After she regained some measure of composure, he turned to Luke. "What makes you think Aiyanna is alive?"

Reaching into the manila envelope Luke produced three copies of Aiyanna's letter and gave each one a copy.

After reading the letter, Larry asked, "Luke, why would she have done such a thing? Just to prove her... scientific theory?"

"I don't know," Luke replied weakly. "But I do believe, in her mind, she was trying to reach out to save Alice. To recover her from this Underworld realm, if such a thing is even possible. Aiyanna said that Alice came to her in a dream. The experience must have been real enough to convince her."

Luke turned to Lobo. "Uncle Lobo, I... er, we need to know if Aiyanna is still alive. And if so, where is she? As you did for Alice, can you perform the magical powers of waruka'na to answer these questions?"

All eyes were on Lobo.

"Well. I can try," he said at last. "But I cannot promise or predict the same outcome." He paused. "Do you have an offering?"

Luke produced a wad of tobacco from his pocket and handed it to the shaman.

"This will do," he said.

Lobo instructed Larry to ready the fireplace while he prepared the pipe for the ceremony. When all was ready, they joined in a circle on the floor, legs folded, seated on the bearskin rug as Lobo lit the pipe and passed it around. He began to chant in Hocąk, praying to the spirits, and raised his arms to the heavens. As he fell into a trance, his eyes rolled up in his head.

"I see a large cavern filled with rock crystal formations," he said. "A stream runs through the cavern leading to a distant lake surrounded by green meadow fields. No... not a lake, but a large sea. It is the domain of the Great Serpent—the Underwater Panther—and its evil minions. I now see a Green Wolf, tending to a woman recently arrived." Lobo paused and a smile came to his face. "It is... Aiyanna! And she is protected, for the moment, by her guardian spirit, the Green Wolf." He paused. "And... there is yet another. A man of ancient origins who has come to her aid. He bears the mark of a Bear clansman." Lobo's tone became fearful. "But there is also danger. From the water. The Great Serpent!"

Lobo resumed his chanting. Then, falling silent, he emerged from his trance. Weary and bleary-eyed he slowly turned to Larry and Rachel.

"Your daughter is alive," he said. "She abides in an Underworld realm. For the moment, she is safe. But her safe return is not guaranteed." He turned to Luke. "I know only that this portal in the cornfield that you described is but a one-way passage, Luke. It is... an *unholy* portal. It offers no return and represents a disturbance in the natural order of things. The return path must be through a natural portal." He sighed. "But its location, or even existence, I cannot ascertain."

"You mentioned a man of ancient origins who has also come to her aid," Luke said. "Who is this man?"

Lobo shook his head. "I do not know. Perhaps the spirit of an ancestor."

Luke thought for a moment. "Could it be the ancestor from her dream? Remember? His name was... Akecheta. I believe that is what she said."

Lobo pondered. "Perhaps."

～

AS THE AFTERNOON PROGRESSED, Lobo's soft-spoken manner did much to ease the tension in the room. In time, Rachel regained her composure. But the afternoon's exchange did take its toll on her.

"I'm sorry, but I simply must excuse myself," she said to Luke. "Please, stay as long as you like."

Getting up, she gave him a hug and adjourned to her bedroom.

With Rachel now gone, Lobo sensed a new urgency in Luke's demeanor.

"You seem to have something else on your mind, Luke."

Luke cleared his throat. "Yes, well, I didn't want to discuss this in front of Rachel. But I understand the nature of this... thing. And I believe I can breach the portal. I need to try to save Aiyanna."

"No, Luke!" Larry responded sternly. "You would be swallowed up just like Aiyanna and your sister. And countless others, if I understood you correctly."

Luke nodded. "Yes. Going back seventeen years at least."

"And none have returned? What does that tell you?" Larry said.

Lobo agreed. "It is much too dangerous for a living human to enter the Underworld, Luke. Unknown perils abide there. Even for us, there is much that we do not know about the Underworld."

Luke paused a moment. "Even for someone who is protected by the White Wolf guardian spirit?"

Lobo's eyes widened. "What do you mean?"

Luke described his recent fasting and praying experience, culminating in last night's dream in which a white wolf appeared to him, identifying itself as his guardian spirit. The dream setting—a cave or cavern—was also similar to what Aiyanna had described in her dream and what Lobo had seen in his vision.

Lobo nodded. "That is quite a story, young man."

Lobo looked at Larry with raised eyebrows.

Larry finally broke the silence. "No! I forbid it! It is much too dangerous!"

"But please, tell me," Luke begged, "what is the significance of the White Wolf?"

Lobo proceeded to tell him the legend of the four wolves and the origins of the Wolf clan to which he himself belonged.

"My name is not Graywolf for nothing," he said with a chuckle. "You see, Luke, the ancestors of the Wolf clan were all wolves. In the beginning, the Earthmaker made four brothers: Green Wolf, Black Wolf, White Wolf, and Gray Wolf. At that time, they all dwelled on Earth's surface in what we call the Earth World, or the world of man. But after a time, all but the Gray Wolf went to live in the realms below Earth as protectors of the Underworld realms. They appear aboveground only on rare occasions. After some time, some of the Gray Wolves became men, the ancestors of the Wolf clan."

Luke appeared transfixed.

"So, that only reinforces the purpose of my dream," Luke said. "I am being called into the Underworld realm by my guardian spirit, the White Wolf, to seek Aiyanna! To save her and my sister, and perhaps others as well."

Lobo pursed his lips. "I cannot confirm or deny this," he said. "You must search your heart for the answer."

Still, Larry remained adamant. "This is not a matter of the heart, Charlie! It is far too dangerous a venture. I absolutely forbid it!"

Yet Lobo could see in Luke's eyes the determination of a seeker of truth. A true warrior!

ON HIS RETURN TO SHEBOYGAN, Luke took a detour through Madison. The wheels were already turning in his head, but he needed Aiyanna's help. He had the strange feeling that she was there with him in spirit directing his thought processes, leading him to her apartment where she kept her notebooks.

It was close to six o'clock when he reached Madison. No problem. He had her apartment keys, which he'd retained when forced to surrender her car keys to Dan the day before.

It was an eerie feeling when he entered her apartment—alone. Quiet as a tomb. He could nonetheless feel her presence. He smiled as he spied two empty glasses and a half bottle of sambuca on the kitchen counter. A copy of his bison article still lay open on the coffee table. With a lump in his throat, he gently fingered a Bocelli album jacket resting empty against the stereo console. Swallowing hard, he refocused on the reason he was there.

Going through her desk drawers and filing cabinet, he found what he was looking for. "Yes!" A three-ring binder with her laboratory notes and detailed plans for the electrical grid generation system, or EGGS. He smiled and looked skyward. "Thank you!" Gathering up her other notes and binders he headed for the door, then paused and turned around for one final look.

"Someday," he said. "I swear. Someday."

Chapter Fifty

PLAN OF ACTION

Saturday, August 22, 2015

8:oo a.m. There was nothing like a good night's sleep to clear the head. Over a hot breakfast and a fresh pot of coffee, Luke began to generate a mental to-do list as he finalized his plan of action. First order of business—a visit to his cousin Mark's farm supply store in Howards Grove.

Mark was a wiz at all things mechanical and electrical. Growing up he was always tearing down, repairing, or assembling one gadget or another, from toasters, computers, and audio components to cars and tractors. You name it; he could handle it. All the local electrical and automotive supply store owners knew Mark.

He was on a ladder tending to something on the top shelf when Luke entered the store. Luke hit the counter call bell, and Mark looked down. "Well, this sure is a surprise, Cuz! Hold on. Be right down."

"Nice place you have here," Luke said as he surveyed the store. "How's business?"

"Great! Couldn't be better," Mark replied as he joined Luke at the counter. "So, what brings you to Howards Grove, Luke? Nothing much to report on here, I'm afraid," he said with a grin.

"Well, actually, I was hoping you might help with a little project I've taken on to assist with Aiyanna's research. You remember Aiyanna from my mom's brat fry?"

"Sure do. Real nice lady. Good looker, too, if you don't mind my sayin'," he added with a wink.

Luke cleared his throat. "Yes, I certainly agree." He breathed a sigh of relief. Obviously, Mark hadn't spoken to his dad about Thursday's happenings at the farm. That was a good thing.

"So, what is it you need help with?" Mark asked.

Luke took some papers from the briefcase he was carrying and showed them to Mark.

"I was wondering if you could help me put together this device?"

Mark took the drawings and laid them out on the counter. After studying them a bit he said, "This doesn't look at all complicated. Mainly just a DC power generator and voltage regulator hooked up to some electrodes. The control box wiring is a little tricky—some kind of rheostat and potentiometer combination—but I think I can pick up what I need from my friend who runs an electrical supply outlet downtown." He turned to Luke. "So, what's it used for, if you don't mind my asking?"

Luke explained what he could without giving too much away.

"Okay, sure," Mark said. "I carry mostly AC generators but do have one of these DC models in stock. Puts out up to five hundred volts DC. Runs on diesel. Is that okay?"

Luke beamed. "That'd be perfect. I only need about sixty volts."

"No problem. I can put this together and have it for you by the end of the day. How's six o'clock sound?"

"Perfect," Luke said. "I can pay for it in full now, if you'd like."

"Nah! There's no rush on that. We're family."

Luke thanked him and spent a few minutes in idle chat before leaving.

"And give my best regards to Aiyanna next time you see her," Mark said as Luke was leaving.

Luke gulped. "Yes, I certainly will... The next time I see her."

Back in his SUV, he took a minute to gather his thoughts, then punched in Sam's personal number on his cell phone. Sam picked up on the third ring.

"Sam Riley here."

Luke cleared his throat. "Hello, Sam. This is Luke Kramer."

There was a slight pause.

"Good mornin', Luke." Another pause. "Uh... how are you?"

"I'm good, Sam. Real good, actually."

"Well, I'm glad to hear that, Luke."

Taking a deep breath, Luke continued, "Listen, Sam. I'm sorry to bother you on the weekend, and after what just happened. But... I really need to talk with you. You said if I ever needed help, to call."

He could hear forced breathing on the other end.

"Sure, Luke... No problem. How can I help?"

Luke explained that he would like to meet sometime later that day if possible. "At your convenience, of course. I've got a favor to ask and feel like it would best be handled in person."

"Uh, sure thing. How about Duke's Tavern for lunch?"

Luke considered it and shook his head. The risk of running into Dan at Duke's was too high. "Hmm. How about we meet on the River Walk down by the Coast Guard station?"

"Okay. I can do that," Sam said. "How does one o'clock sound?

"Perfect! Thank you, Sam. See you then."

TEN MINUTES to one found Luke seated on a park bench overlooking the harbor. Though the sky was clear, blue, and bright, a suffocating gray veil had begun to descend. Focusing on a distant fishing trawler, he didn't even notice Sam approaching until he was seated beside him.

"Ever notice the absence of seagulls along this stretch of the river, Sam?" Luke asked.

His voice was weak and unsteady. Recent events were taking their toll, despite his good night's sleep.

Sam looked up and around. "Yeah, come to think of it, you're right. So, how do you explain that?"

Luke pointed to a pole not thirty feet away with two mechanical hawks in rotational "flight" mounted high atop the pole, letting out periodic hawk sounds.

"Keeps the gulls away," he said. "One of my first assignments when I joined the *Dispatch* five months ago."

Sam looked up, squinting in the noonday sun. "Nice. I think I remember reading about it." Turning to Luke, he said, "Didn't know you covered that story. That was before we met, of course."

Luke became pensive. "Sam, I want to thank you for going to bat for me on Thursday. I could tell that you and Dan weren't, shall we say, on the same page, with all this crop circle stuff and... well, my version of what happened."

Sam smacked his lips. "Yeah, well, Dan and I don't always see eye to eye on things."

"Just off the record," Luke continued, "I was curious about whether there was any follow-up on that crop circle that appeared on the Klausman farm the day after Adam Emery broke through the search perimeter."

"Well, just off the record, we did send the Geo-Services team out there a couple days later." He paused.

"So, what did they find?" Luke pressed.

"There was what appeared to be a collection of human remains, sure enough. One appeared pretty whole and still intact. But they were so deep in the ground, about twenty, thirty feet or so, we figured it must have been an old burial site, like maybe an ancient Indian burial mound. No way they could have been recent—you know, like Adam."

Luke nodded. "I can understand that." But in his mind, he was thinking otherwise.

"So, is that all you needed to know?" Sam asked.

"Uh, no. There was one other thing."

"Okay, shoot!" Sam chuckled. "Figuratively speaking, of course."

Luke paused to gather his thoughts. "This computer model of yours. Is there any way it could be used to *predict* the probability of a crop circle event, for a given location, based on let's say, the weather forecast for that region?"

Sam cocked his head. "Seriously?"

"Yes, seriously. I'm just curious, you understand."

Sam gave it some thought. "Well, the model is *not* a predictive model, you understand. Although it excels at correlating past events from the database I've developed."

"Exactly," Luke responded. "So, based on past history, the model is capable of correlating crop circle events with Santoma GMO cornfield locations and recorded weather data for that location, right?"

Sam thought about it. "Sure. Piece of cake."

"So," Luke continued, "if you plug in a detailed weather *forecast* for a particular GMO cornfield location, it should come up with a crop circle probability forecast. Right? I mean, it should give you at least the best day and time of day for such an event."

Silence.

"Okay. So, what would you have me do, Luke?" Sam said at last. He seemed unsure, nervous.

"Would it be possible for you to get in touch with Al Hollander and have him input the meteorological forecast for this region over the next week or so? The Klausman farm and surrounding area in particular."

Sam rubbed his chin. "Sure, I guess I can do that."

Leaning forward, Sam folded his hands. "Listen, Luke," he continued, speaking in a more somber tone, "I don't know what you have in mind. But as both a friend and a law enforcement officer, I wouldn't want you to go and do something... stupid, ya know?"

"Sure, Sam. Don't worry," Luke offered with a crooked smile. "I've got everything under control."

6:00 P.M. Mark Einsbach was in the stockroom getting something for a customer when he heard the counter call bell. "Be right with you!" he shouted back. He checked his watch. *Almost closing time.* He passed Luke's EGGS DC power generator all assembled and ready to go. *Hmm. Maybe that's Luke now come by to pick it up.*

Mark emerged from the back room with a small box and smiled when he spied Luke at the counter.

"Hi, Luke. Thought it might be you," he said. "Just give me a minute while I take care of this last customer."

Luke gave a wan smile. "No problem. Take your time."

A few minutes later, Mark joined Luke at the counter. "Okay, Cuz. I got your device ready to go. It's in the back room. Wait here and I'll go get it."

"Uh, just a moment, Mark. There's... something I need to talk to you about, and I want you to hear it from me before you hear it from someone else."

Mark cocked his head. "Sure, Cuz. Shoot!"

"Well, it's about what happened at your dad's farm on Thursday."

Luke proceeded to describe their misadventure and Aiyanna's disappearance. At first, he presented it as a possible "sinkhole event." But after showing Mark a copy of Aiyanna's farewell letter, he went on to describe what he really thought happened. Mark didn't quite know what to make of it, all this fanciful talk about underground worlds and caverns. Made his head spin. But it was clear Luke believed it was true, and apparently Aiyanna did as well. Growing up, Mark had always viewed Luke as something of a dreamer. "Marching to the beat of a different drum" is how he once put it. In the end, he ultimately settled on the sinkhole theory and awkwardly expressed his sincere sympathy over Luke's loss.

When Luke asked him how much he owed for the generator, Mark hesitated. "Nah, that's okay," he replied with a nervous twinge in his voice. "You don't owe me nothing." He patted Luke on the back. "It's all in the family!"

Truth was, not knowing exactly how Luke planned to use this device, Mark didn't want to leave any paper trail.

THE NEXT DAY, Cynthia received an unexpected visit from Luke following her Sunday morning church service.

"My, this is certainly a pleasant surprise!" she said, greeting him at the front door. "What brings you out on a Sunday morning, Luke?"

But even as he gave her a hug, she already knew why he had come. She had spoken with her brother Clarence during the church service, and he'd told her about Thursday's events.

Luke grimaced. "I'm sorry, Mom. I should have told you sooner."

Initially, Cynthia received Luke's explanation of what happened with open skepticism, but when he presented a copy of Aiyanna's farewell note, her demeanor changed.

"I believe you, son," she said, giving him a loving, motherly hug. "And believe me, I am so sorry for Aiyanna." She wiped a tear from her eye. "I will pray for her and ask our congregation to pray. I think that is all we can really do."

She had difficulty, however, embracing Luke's theory that Aiyanna was still alive and could somehow be "rescued." Yet she didn't let on... didn't want to dash Luke's hopes, though it all seemed the stuff of fantasy and wishful thinking. That Aiyanna was swallowed up by a sinkhole, disappeared, and perished in a cavern far under ground seemed a much more plausible explanation.

Chapter Fifty-One

SURPRISE DELIVERY

Monday, August 24, 2015

When Luke showed up in the newsroom Monday morning, people greeted him in the usual manner. No one appeared to have any knowledge of what had happened on Thursday, but it took him the better part of the morning to resume his normal routine and get back into the swing of things.

Pam York sensed something different in his behavior, however.

"Are you okay, Luke?"

"Uh, sure. Just feeling a little under the weather, is all."

He tried focusing on the next installment of his bison series and later in the morning checked in with Ted to update him on his progress. But even Ted could tell something was amiss.

"You okay, Luke?" Ted asked. "You seem a little preoccupied."

Luke forced a smile. "No, I'm fine Ted." He tried to make something up. "Just a little setback with Aiyanna, is all."

"Ah! Relationship issues! Well, I promise not to pry. But, if there is anything you think you need to share, you've got a confidential sounding board with me."

"Thanks, Ted. I appreciate it."

After lunch, Luke got that phone call from Sam he had been hoping for. There was heavy breathing at first, like a prank caller.

"Hi, Luke. Uh, listen. I've got that information you were asking for." His voice was guarded and muffled, like he had his hand over the receiver.

Sam began by reiterating his earlier caveat about the model not being a predictive model, then proceeded to describe his findings. After he'd input Al's detailed weather forecast for the week, the model calculated a 38 percent probability peak for a crop circle event for the region in question that coming Wednesday, between noon and three o'clock.

"That's great, Sam," Luke said. "Thank you! I owe you one."

"No problem," he replied. "Like I said. I don't know what you plan to do with this information, but be careful." He tried to lighten things up— "Just don't forget to invite me to the next brat fry. Okay?" Still, his somber tone was unmistakable.

~

WHEN LUKE RETURNED to his condo that evening, there was a FedEx package waiting for him. *Hmm, can't remember ordering anything.* He noted the return address: Black River Falls, WI. Inside were four small buckskin pouches and a note:

Luke,

I could see from the look in your eyes on Friday that there would be no deterring you from your mission to rescue Aiyanna. So I've enclosed some herbs to aid you on your journey: tobacco, sage, sweetgrass, and cedar. Compliments of Ma-ona the Creator. Use them wisely. Continue to pray and fast. May God and the Spirits be with you. And may your guardian spirit, White Wolf, protect you!

Uncle Lobo

Luke gave a little chuckle as he peered out the window toward the setting sun.

"Pinagigi, Uncle Lobo!"

Chapter Fifty-Two

FINAL PREPARATIONS

Tuesday, August 25, 2015

When Luke arrived at the Klausman farm at eleven o'clock, Ed was changing the oil in his tractor and didn't seem to notice Luke's approach until his golden retriever started making a fuss.

"Mornin', young man," Ed shouted out. "I think Kelsey remembers you from your last visit. She never forgets a friendly face—or scent." Ed took a break to greet his visitor. "What can I do for you, Luke?"

Luke returned the greeting as he patted Kelsey on the head. "Well, Ed, I was doing some follow-up reporting on that sudden crop circle event that came on the tail of the recent Adam Emery fugitive hunt. I understand the GPS scan didn't turn up anything useful, but I'd like to see the site and get your take on what happened, if that's okay with you."

"Sure, no problem!"

Luke followed Ed down a tractor path through the cornfield about a hundred yards, ending up a short distance from a copse of trees bordering a stream.

"Looks like the corn is about ready for harvesting," Luke said.

"Yup. I expect to get to it in a week or two, after it's had a chance to dry out some." Ed paused and pointed into the cornfield. "I think you can make it out from here. Just about twenty feet into that stand of corn."

"Mind if I take a picture or two?"

"Be my guest."

Luke took out his cell phone for some pics, then employed his GPS positioning app to get the exact coordinates of the site.

Back at the house, Ed offered Luke a glass of iced tea and asked about the Adam Emery case as they lounged on the front porch.

"Well, as far as I know, Adam Emery remains at large," Luke said.

"Cryin' shame. That young college girl. I sure hope they catch up with that bastard!"

Luke tried not to smile. "Oh, I think Adam will get what's coming to him, if he hasn't already."

He paused briefly to consider how to frame his next question. "Tell me, Ed. When you bought this place twelve years ago, did the previous owner talk about any other crop circle event besides the one involving my sister, Alice?"

Ed massaged his chin. "Well, come to think of it, he did mention something that happened the year before. A crop circle—although he didn't call it that at the time—discovered in the same field as your sister's. He said he didn't make much of it, figuring it was a teenage prank."

"I see," Luke said.

"Yeah," Ed continued. "He also mentioned it was around the same time the police found a car abandoned off the side of the road not far from here. Said it belonged to the missing wife of Jake Emery. Later he got to thinking there might have been a connection. I mean, after what happened to your sister, and all."

Luke pondered. *Makes sense. That explains Laura's gold wedding ring showing up a year later.*

"And he never mentioned any of this to the police?" Luke asked.

"Hmm. Can't really say."

"Interesting. Thanks for sharing that, Ed."

Politely declining a refill on his iced tea, Luke shook hands and thanked Ed for his time and assistance before heading back to his SUV.

Taking a left out of the driveway, Luke continued about a hundred yards down the road and pulled off onto the gravel shoulder, engine idling. Retrieving the USDA crop map from his briefcase, he marked his current location and the copse of trees by the stream that bordered Ed's field. According to the map, there should have been a small dirt road up ahead to the left that traversed the adjacent field, accessing the stream and same trees from the opposite side. He looked up and squinted, shielding his eyes from the sun. There it was! Just down the road on the left. You'd easily miss it if you didn't know it was there.

"Perfect!" he said. "That's where I need to be this time tomorrow."

Luke made several stops before heading home: the Walmart on the south side of town and two sporting goods stores he was familiar with. He took a shopping list and began checking off the items one by one: cargo pants; boots; helmet; hunting vest replete with zippered pockets; buck knife and sheath; water purification tablets; first aid kit; matches in waterproof container; flint and steel fire starter kit; two pocket canteens; and a generous supply of pemmican, peanut butter, and assorted high-calorie trail mix bars. Between the cargo pants and vest, there were plenty of pockets for storage. In addition, he added a small backpack containing a dozen glow sticks and flares and a few mountain-climbing essentials: eighty feet of climbing rope, assorted carabiners and belay devices, and removable rock anchors. Plus a chest harness, which he planned to wear under his hunting vest.

When he got home, he laid everything out on his bed and took inventory. Oh yes, and not to forget the most important items: the four buckskin pouches from Uncle Lobo containing the tobacco, sage, sweet-grass, and cedar!

Chapter Fifty-Three

UNHOLY PORTAL

Wednesday, August 26, 2015

1:00 a.m. Luke peered through the tripod-mounted video camera's viewfinder, focusing on the far end of a newly cleared path in the field of ripening corn, not far from the stream and copse of trees that bordered the back of the Klausman farm. Positioned in the tractor lane on the edge of the field, he had made the path wide enough to accommodate a second backup camera alongside the first. Both cameras were aligned and locked in their swivel mounts, their tripod legs staked to the ground—lessons learned from the failed first attempt with Aiyanna.

Luke's SUV lay concealed on the far side of the stream. An hour earlier, he had sent Sam Riley a text message marked URGENT with some GPS coordinates and instructions.

Sam responded: "What's this all about?"

Luke replied: "You'll know when you get here."

He powered down the phone and secured it in his right thigh pocket inside a waterproof case. Leaving his wallet and keys in the SUV, he finished setting up for what he hoped would be the *final* field test.

Luke had chosen this field as the most likely location for triggering a symbiotic bioelectrical terrestrial event, as Aiyanna had dubbed this bizarre phenomenon. Geographical, biological, and meteorological forensic evidence all supported a good likelihood for this time and place.

A 38 percent chance, to be exact, based on output from Sam's software model.

Yet Luke had brought something else along to help tip the odds in his favor: the homemade electrical grid generation system, or EGGS, which his cousin Mark had assembled based on the plans from Aiyanna's lab notebook. Following Aiyanna's previously developed protocol, the four EGGS soil probes were positioned at the corners of a twenty-foot-square grid, their lead wires connecting to the terminals of the EGGS power generator. Everything checked out. Everything was ready.

Luke donned his backpack and helmet and patted himself down, taking a final mental inventory of his supplies. Buck knife strapped to his thigh: *check*. Buckskin pouches containing the four sacred herbs of Maona—sweetgrass, cedar, sage, and dried tobacco leaves—securely attached to his belt: *check*. Backpack with journal, food, glow sticks, climbing gear, change of clothes, first aid kit: *check*.

The air had become thick, like a storm was brewing, as the tallest of the silk tassels began to sway in a gentle breeze. The overhead sky was clear, but there was a faint, unmistakable scent of ozone in the air.

"Nacits!" Luke said.

This was the moment of reckoning. He took a deep breath, paused a second, and set the two cameras to Record. Going to the EGGS generator, he turned it on and slowly adjusted the power output to fifty-five volts DC. Quickly, he jogged down the narrow path and positioned himself at the center of the test grid—the "bait station."

He waited, nervously muttering in a flashback moment the lyrics from "Oh, What a Beautiful Morning," an old musical number from his high school senior class production of *Oklahoma!* It had something to do with golden meadows and fields of high-growing corn.

He stopped midsentence, startled by a sudden movement at his feet —a slight tremor at first. He looked down. There it was! That same spiral ripple pattern and pulsating green glow that had by now become so familiar. *The EGGS is working!* The stalks nearest him bowed in the direction of the spiral, bending inward, closing in on him while the roots beneath his feet heaved upward, ensnaring his feet with a grip as strong as braided steel. Like sentient beings, the stalks played out their ballet of death, a coordinated attack of roots, leaves, and stems.

Even if he had chosen otherwise, Luke was powerless to resist. The strong musty scent bursting forth in a brown cloud of dust at the onset of tassel motion had done its job. He remembered what Aiyanna had said: *Nerve toxin! Meant to paralyze its prey.* First his fingers and toes went numb, then hands, feet, arms, and legs. It seemed only his peripheral nervous system was affected, as he had no trouble breathing, hearing, seeing—or thinking. It had all happened in a matter of seconds.

Now, looking down he saw the ground below him open up in a churning maelstrom of detritus, while above him, a swirling vortex of soil, uprooted stalks, and dismembered cobs and leaves clouded the otherwise clear blue sky. He was in the eye of a storm and felt no pain. He sensed a downward movement and could see, fast approaching, an ever-widening maw in the earth's surface. He took a deep breath, fearing it may be his last. Plummeting through the open ground, he gasped as the light of day disappeared, plunging him into total darkness, into the very throat of Mother Earth!

Something pulled him downward through an ever-narrowing passage, drawing his body though a labyrinth of twisted roots and tentacles that tugged at him in all directions, threatening to rip him apart. Surprisingly, a kind of peace overtook him as he resigned himself to almost certain death. Then suddenly, as if on command, they released their life-threatening grip and let him pass. Descending ever deeper, he had the sensation of being squeezed, like toothpaste from a tube. Or better yet, a mouse passing through the alimentary canal of his pet boa! No sight, no sound, only the choking, pungent scent of dust and mold, like the stale, attic air of his mother's antique barn, damp and sooty, closing in on him.

The twisted passage forced Luke's head to the right, and there before him was the appalling image of a rotting human corpse enveloped in a green glow. He tried to scream, but no sound came out. Was it real, or just a terrifying hallucination? The corpse was wrapped in a cottony filamentous web that seemed to throb with its own life force. *Fungal hyphae drawing nourishment from the rotting flesh, just like Nate said!* Continuing his slow but inexorable descent, Luke became bathed in the low-intensity glow of the web's self-made light as pulses of green bioluminescence bounced from one synapsing strand to the next, creating a nexus of higher-order communication and function. Amazing! *A fungal neural network! So Aiyanna was right. The fungus is not only huge and alive, but also a thinking, sentient being!*

Luke gasped in horror at what he saw next: fragments of a drab green work shirt draped over a hollow chest of rotting flesh. The name tag and stenciled lettering on the shirt were still readable: ADAM – EMERY REFUSE REMOVAL.

Leaving Adam behind, he continued downward as the earth slowly loosened its grip, gradually widening to allow his passage. As he descended, he passed through a region of mixed human and animal remains that turned increasingly indistinguishable, in the end becoming mere fragments of bone and dust. The green glow faded, the fungal mass evanesced, and Luke became enveloped in a suffocating darkness as he faded in and out of consciousness. And then... *what is that?* A dim, white light with shades of red directly below him. Faint at first, it quickly grew in size and intensity, taking on the features of an open fissure structure in the looming solid rock formation below. A horrifying thought went through his mind: *Oh my God! Subterranean lava flow!*

That was Luke's last thought before passing out.

Chapter Fifty-Four

APOLOGY

Later That Day, August 26, 2015

Wednesday afternoon found Dan busy at his desk, buried in paperwork, when Sam Riley walked into his office. He knew it was Sam by the sound of his walk. Without looking up he asked, "What is it, Sam?"

"There's something you gotta see, Dan."

There was a strained urgency in Sam's voice. Not at all like him. Dan looked up.

"My God, Sam! You look awful! Like you just saw a ghost."

Sam leaned forward on Dan's desk. "Yes. You might say that."

Dan straightened up in his chair. "Well, that doesn't sound good. Tell me. What happened?"

"Well, I think it would be best if I... showed you."

"Uh, okay. Sure. Where do you wanna go?"

"The briefing room. On my laptop. I'm already set up."

Dan followed Sam into the briefing room. The laptop lay on the table plugged into the wall-mounted video screen. Dan took a seat at the table across from Sam.

Without a word Sam made a few clicks of the mouse and the screen lit up. There was Luke Kramer on full display standing in a small clearing surrounded by ripened stalks of corn.

"Oh, Jesus! Not this again!" an exasperated Dan blurted out. "My God, he looks like a Navy SEAL on a secret mission! What is this?"

"Shh! Just watch," Sam retorted.

As the action played out on the screen, Dan slowly became transfixed, studying the screen through steepled fingers. He thought he heard Luke humming and singing a little tune.

But things escalated quickly. When the critical part at last came—only minutes into the video clip—and Luke was swallowed up by the earth, Dan let out an audible gasp. "Oh my God! What the hell!"

"Here's another." Sam played a second video clip from the backup video camera Luke had set up. It basically showed the same thing, but from a slightly different angle, confirming what the first video recorded.

Dan took a deep breath and exhaled slowly through pursed lips. "So, do you think these videos are... authentic? I mean, haven't been tampered with or artificially generated?"

Sam shook his head. "Two videos of the same thing from different angles? I don't think so. Anyway, I can have the forensics experts analyze them. But honestly, I don't think Luke is, shall we say, sophisticated enough be able to pull off something like that."

Dan considered this, trying to make sense of it all.

"How the hell did you come by these videos, Sam?"

By this point the color had returned to Sam's face. He sat back and explained as much as he could, showing Dan the text message he'd received from Luke around ten o'clock that morning:

SAM. URGENT! PLEASE GO TO KLAUSMAN FARM AT THE GPS COORDINATES GIVEN BELOW WHERE YOU WILL FIND TWO VIDEO CAMERAS MOUNTED IN CLEARINGS IN THE CORNFIELD. WE ARE EXPECTING RAIN SOON, SO PLEASE, HURRY! LUKE.

"When I got there," Sam said, "I first checked with Ed Klausman to see if he had spoken to Luke or knew anything about this. He said Luke dropped by yesterday to ask about the recent crop circle discovered during the Emery fugitive hunt and was doing a follow-up story. Ed said he showed him the location. But that was all. He hadn't seen Luke since then."

Sam then related his meeting with Luke over the weekend. He said Luke was inquiring about the Rigel software and its ability to predict coming events based on weather forecasts.

"So you helped him with that?" Dan asked.

Sam squirmed a little. "Well, sure. I didn't think there was any harm in that. And anyway, I told him the model was not a predictive model, but it might possibly shed some light on near-future events."

Dan looked back at the screen. "So, where is Luke *now?*" he asked, trying—but failing—to control the tremor in his voice.

Sam produced a manila envelope from his briefcase and laid it on the table, pushing it over to Dan.

"I was wondering the same thing. So I contacted Jeff Seibert at Geo-Services. I remained at the Klausman farm until he showed up an hour later. He ran multiple GPR scans of the area at difference depths, and…"

Dan's eye twitched. "And…"

Sam shook his head. "Nada. Nothing. Not even a dead rabbit. Except, there was that strange deep layer anomaly. You know, the deep void with a fissure, like maybe a sinkhole or deep cavern or something."

Silence.

"So, what do you think?" Sam asked.

Dan brought his hands up to his face, forming a tent with his fingers and pondered. "Well, for starters, it appears that I owe Luke—and Aiyanna—both an apology." He let out a deep sigh.

The two men remained there for some time without a word, each lost in their own thoughts. Finally Dan blurted out, "But why the hell would he go and do such a stupid thing?"

Sam raised an eyebrow. "Hmm. Maybe to find and rescue Aiyanna?" he said softly. Like he was in church.

Dan slowly shook his head. "Damn! Ain't love grand!" he said with a sardonic twist of the mouth. "I liked Luke. You know, I really did!"

Sam swallowed hard. "Yeah, me too."

∾

THAT EVENING FOUND Detective Dan Meyers at Duke's Tavern and Sports Bar, drowning his sorrows as he lamented the loss of a good friend. One of the hardest things he ever had to do was drive out to Elkhart Lake late that afternoon to break the tragic news to Luke's mom. Sam had asked to go along, but Dan insisted this was something he needed to do by himself.

Of course, Cynthia was devastated.

"Anything I can do to help, ma'am, you know you just need to give me a call" were Dan's parting words.

Chapter Fifty-Five

HERO'S QUEST OR FOOL'S ERRAND?

The Underworld Realm. Day One

When Luke regained consciousness, he found himself lying on the ground in the midst of a cool, damp, open subterranean space, a cavern of some kind, lit by a dim white light. His senses recovered, he sat up and looked around. The source of that light was now apparent, emanating from giant crystalline rock formations protruding from the cavern floor, walls, and ceiling into the space surrounding him. He likened it to being at the center of a gigantic geode. Quartz crystals, he figured. A low-frequency hum accompanied the white light, something like the quiet buzzing of a fluorescent lamp. With his eyes slowly acclimating to the dim light, he noticed the crystal formations changing colors, from red to green to violet, all the colors of the rainbow. As the colors changed, the frequency of the hum changed as well, resulting in an orchestrated mix of frequencies and harmonies. A veritable light show.

"Awesome!" he whispered, mesmerized by the sights and sounds of the crystal forest.

Gathering his strength, he slowly gained his feet and assessed his physical condition. *No apparent broken bones, thank God!* Only sore and bruised. While he brushed off the dirt and remnants of roots and fungal fibers, he looked up to see from where he had fallen. The ceiling of the cavern was dotted with numerous crevices and recesses, and it was difficult to determine from which one he had come. But it didn't matter. It was a good twelve-foot drop from any one of them. His backpack and helmet lay several yards away.

"Oh, well. So much for protective gear!" he said with a chuckle.

Fortunately, his wristwatch, which he had safely tucked beneath his shirtsleeve, managed to survive the fall, as did his cell phone. Checking the time, he saw that less than fifteen minutes had passed since this adventure began. So he could not have been unconscious for very long.

Taking inventory of his other supplies, he found that everything was intact. His buck knife remained secured to his thigh, though the straps had loosened up a bit. His vest had suffered a minor tear but was otherwise okay. His backpack and helmet had, likewise, endured only minor damage.

He strained to hear the sound of trickling water, tilting his head. Approaching the nearest wall, he could see tiny rivulets coating the rocks and flowing to a narrow stream on the floor of the cave. He followed the burbling flow about fifty feet downstream to where it widened into a small, shallow pool of crystal-clear water. He spotted movement in the water and bent down for a closer look: small shrimplike creatures swimming right below the surface.

"My God, there is life down here!"

With those words, he realized there was something he had to do. Opening one of the buckskin pouches on his belt, he removed a pinch of dried tobacco and offered it to the spirits of the water and cave, asking for protection and permission to proceed further. As he did this, he was startled by the faint sounds of howling reverberating through the cavern. It was the howl of a wolf.

Luke looked up and smiled. "The White Wolf! My guardian spirit!"

In a sudden moment of awareness and triumph, he proclaimed, "I am alive! I actually made it into the Underworld!"

He studied his surroundings more carefully. The cavern was not very wide at this point—perhaps twenty yards across—but appeared to extend indefinitely in two opposite directions. The direction of the flowing stream seemed to follow the main chamber or vein of the cavern. He recalled the words of Shaman Lobo: *A stream runs through the cavern leading to... a distant lake surrounded by green meadow fields. A village. With people tending to a little girl...* So that's what Luke decided to do—follow its downstream course to whatever fate awaited him.

Picking himself up he set out, keeping a constant lookout for any telltale signs of Aiyanna's passing as he went. Perhaps she left a clue knowing he would soon follow. He actually had no idea as to what her plans had been for finding Alice but figured she must have harkened to the same words of the shaman. Perhaps she was further guided by her dreams.

As he continued through the cavern, it became clear he was on an ever-descending course that was taking him to deeper realms. He could feel his ears popping with the changing pressure. At times, the stream turned into a series of small waterfalls, even rapids, forcing him to negotiate some tricky ledges and steep vertical inclines. The rock formations were changing as well, becoming less crystalline and more amorphous, like granite and limestone. At various points, there were lateral passageways that disappeared into darkness. But surprisingly, the main path remained lit. He soon realized that the water itself was a source of light. Perhaps it was some form of bioluminescence, or because the streambed retained a largely crystalline composition.

For eight long hours, Luke trudged on, pausing only once for a quick meal of pemmican and trail bars. Averaging about a ten percent downward grade, he reckoned he had descended well over two miles into the earth's interior by this time. Now the path began to level off as the cavern became more expansive, with the stream widening into a slower-moving pool. Up ahead there was a brighter, different kind of light accompanied by what sounded like the rush of a waterfall as the cavern took a slow turn to the right. Luke was totally unprepared for what he encountered around the next bend.

There before him stretched a scenic vista that took his breath away as the stream plunged over a steep cliff to an immense body of water below. It had to be a good five-hundred-foot drop. A vast lake—you could even call it a sea—stretched as far as the eye could see, bordered by green marshlands pockmarked with occasional dry patches of land overgrown with shrubs and stubby, gnarly trees, the kind you might find above a mountain timberline. The far walls of the cavern were difficult to discern in the perpetual dim twilight of this new realm but seemed composed mostly of pillars of marble and granite. His eyes followed the cavern ceiling upward as it arched to indeterminable heights, forming a great dome, studded with protruding light-emitting quartz crystal formations that gave the appearance of a star-filled night sky.

"I must be in the watery Underworld realm of Ho-Chunk legend!"

But it was nothing like he'd envisioned it from his discussions with Aiyanna's Uncle Lobo, and those words came back to him: *Even for us, there is much that we do not know about the Underworld.* Whatever, he was here now and, for better or worse, this was the stark reality he was forced to deal with.

Luke considered his next step. He could either take the long way down—a long, narrow path that continued to the left of the waterfall— or he could employ his limited climbing skills and rappel down the face of the cliff. He decided upon the former, figuring that was likely how Aiyanna would have proceeded, and that way, he might pick up a clue indicating her presence.

His watch told him it took him about sixty minutes to reach the bottom. He did so without incident. Neither was there any evidence of Aiyanna's passing. Continuing on, he picked up a path that took him through a marsh toward higher, drier land. The climate at these lower depths had turned more temperate and humid, and he felt almost over-dressed. He observed the water to be crystal clear and teeming with aquatic life of various forms and sizes, from schools of those tiny shrimp-like creatures to larger swimmers resembling catfish and pike.

Luke kneeled down at the water's edge for a closer look. Initially, the fish seemed to take an interest and approached to investigate. All at once, in unison, they darted off into the distant depths of the sea as Luke sensed a large, looming presence from behind him. Then came the rustle of sedge grass and an ominous hiss. *Not good.* He slowly turned his head, and his heart skipped a beat at what he saw: a huge creature, black with feline features, penetrating eyes glowing red, coiled serpent tail, and the talons of a bird of prey. The creature towered an intimidating fifteen feet or more by Luke's quick reckoning and was at least twice as long, consid-ering the tail. *Oh my God! The Great Serpent! The Underwater Panther of Ho-Chunk legend!* Luke reached for his buck knife.

The panther arched its back and issued a hideous hiss. There was no place for Luke to go or hide. He would have to stand and fight.

"So, is this how it all ends?" he stammered as he brandished his knife, waving it back and forth, waiting for the beast to strike.

Suddenly, from out of the shadows—perhaps the same shadows from which the beast had emerged—a great White Wolf leaped, interposing itself between Luke and the beast. The wolf took a staunch defensive stand as it faced the beast and snarled a fearsome growl. The beast hissed and backed off momentarily. Adjusting its position to face this new threat, it seemed unaware of the two other figures Luke now spied lurking in the shadows. Just then, one of the figures sprang forth, swinging a war club at the beast's head, while the second—a great Black Wolf—lunged forward and went for the throat of the panther. The beast leaped up, flailing its talons at the attackers as it let out a fearsome cry that resounded with ear-piercing effect off the cavern walls. Luke recognized the one swinging the war club as a Ho-Chunk warrior, adorned with war paint in ancient Native American battle dress. The struggle did not last long, as the beast must have realized it was now outnumbered and outpowered. It quickly sought its escape into the waters of the lake, seeking the safe depths of the Underworld sea.

The White Wolf turned to Luke and nuzzled him affectionately. Luke reciprocated, bending down to pet and embrace the creature.

"Thank you, great White Wolf! Truly my guardian spirit!"

Luke looked up. The warrior who had come to his rescue was standing there, smiling, with a great Black Wolf sitting by his side. He said something Luke did not understand and reached out his hand. Luke stood and smiled as he took it.

"Pinagigi!" Luke said.

The warrior looked surprised and responded in Hocąk.

Luke pointed to himself and said, "Luke."

The warrior nodded and patted his chest. "Akecheta."

Luke recognized the name immediately and was overtaken by awe and wonder.

"Aiyanna! Do you know Aiyanna?" he asked.

Akecheta's eyes grew wide as he smiled, nodding. "Aiyanna," he repeated. He then took Luke's arm and bade him follow.

With the White Wolf by his side, Luke followed Akecheta and the Black Wolf as they negotiated the marsh wetlands toward higher ground. The trail took them through a narrow canyon passage to a distant rise overgrown with scrubby pine concealing a hidden alcove in the cavern wall. Arm outstretched, Akecheta motioned for him to enter. Reluctantly, Luke entered the dark space and spied a figure in the shadows seated on a rock on the far end, with what appeared to be another wolf lying by the figure's side. It was the figure of a woman. She looked up.

"Oh, my God! Luke! Is that really you?"

At the sound of her voice, Luke's heart skipped a beat.

"Aiyanna!"

She rushed to him with open arms. They met and embraced long and hard, each fearing to let go lest the other vanish into thin air.

"I can't believe I found you!" He held her at arm's length and studied her tear-drenched face. "Let me see you. Yes! It is really you!"

"I'm so sorry, Luke. To leave you the way I did. The reason I didn't tell you beforehand was I didn't want you to talk me out of it!" She laughed through her tears. "Tell me, how did Dan and the others react to the video?"

Luke turned sullen and bowed his head sheepishly, like a puppy who had failed his master.

"I'm sorry, Aiyanna. But I... I screwed up."

He recounted the events that immediately followed her disappearance: the failed video and how he was actually suspected of foul play by the authorities. Dan in particular.

"Except Sam," he said. "I know he believed me. And in fact, he actually helped me with my plan to rescue you."

"Good old Sam," she said. "I liked him from the start. But Dan?" She sighed. "Well, Dan's a different story."

Luke looked down at the noble beast lying by her side. "So, who is your companion?"

Aiyanna smiled. "My protector and guardian. The Green Wolf, of course!" She kneeled down and hugged him. "I wouldn't have made it this far without him."

Standing, she turned to Akecheta and said something in Hocąk. He said something back.

"I just told him that I thought it was time to get something to eat, and he agreed."

After they enjoyed a fresh fish catch grilled over an open fire, with roasted tubers that could pass as potatoes, Aiyanna explained what she had been able to glean from Akecheta since her arrival six days earlier. Actually, she had to ask Luke how long it had been as there was no way to count solar days down there.

"You see, from what Akecheta tells me, they measure time by the ebb and flow of the sea tides, with two tides corresponding to a single twenty-four-hour-and-fifty-minute lunar day. The higher of the two tides marks their evening, or eventide. The other or first high tide marks the start of a new day, corresponding to our morning. Seasons are measured in terms of the periodic semiannual flooding of the fields— one major and one minor flooding—which provides nourishment for arable land. Something akin to the flooding of the Nile in ancient times."

"Wait a minute!" Luke said, trying to play catch-up. "Who are *they*?"

Aiyanna sighed. "Ah, yes. I forgot. You haven't met the local inhabitants," she said, laughing. "Actually, neither have I! But Akecheta has had more time to get acquainted."

Luke looked at Akecheta, then back to Aiyanna. "So tell me, how is it that your ancient ancestor is with us *now*? I mean. Is that *really* him, or just... you know... in *spirit* only?"

Aiyanna took a deep breath, clearly struggling to frame her thoughts.

"Yes, this is the strangest part, Luke. And I must admit I had trouble coming to grips with it at first." She paused. "It appears that this Underworld realm in which we now find ourselves, while not *supernatural* or spiritual, is definitely something *more* than natural. I would call it *preternatural*."

"Preternatural?" Luke repeated. "What do you mean?"

Removing a notebook and pen from his backpack, he began taking notes.

She chuckled.

"A reporter always comes prepared," he said haughtily, then winked. "Please continue."

"Yes. Well, from what I've been able to gather, this is a special place or plane of existence, where all time, from all eras, appears to intersect. Ancient times, modern times, even future times, I suspect."

He scratched his head. "I don't understand."

"Well, for example, Akecheta told me how he was leading a bison-hunting party when they came upon a hostile band of Illiniwek. A battle ensued. In the struggle, Akecheta happened to stumble into a crevice and fell into a deep underground cavern lake. When he reemerged, he found himself in a separate underground chamber from which he was unable to recover. There he encountered his guardian spirit, Black Wolf, who guided him through an Underworld labyrinth to the very place we now find ourselves. He has since learned that if he were ever able to return to the Earth World from which he came, he would be placed back into his former time. Likewise, if we are able to return, we would also find ourselves back in our own originating timeline. Until then, we all share this common time and place. He learned this from the people who inhabit this realm."

"So, how long has Akecheta been here?" he asked.

"Hmm. Well, the best I've been able to tell, we both arrived around the same time but only found each other less than two tidal days ago. He was initially taken in and cared for by the native people of this realm. I told him why I had come, and when he stumbled across you, he was getting ready to take me to their village to meet them... and hopefully link up with your sister."

"I see. And how did the people of this realm come to be here in the first place?"

Aiyanna smiled. "That is a story for another day, or should I say, another *tide*. Suffice it to say, judging by their dialect, Akecheta believes them to be direct descendants of a very ancient people. Perhaps a common ancestor to the Ho-Chunk."

Following their meal, she produced a pinch of tobacco from one of her buckskin pouches and offered it to Akecheta with a few Hocąk words. Akecheta nodded and produced a smoking pipe from a rolled-up buckskin wrap—which Luke immediately recognized as a war bundle—and proceeded to pack it with tobacco. Just as Shaman Lobo had done, he tossed the remaining tobacco on the fire as he began to chant.

"He is making an offering to Turtle, the principal deity of this Underworld realm," Aiyanna explained. "Praying for safe passage and protection from evil spirits. And he suggested that we do the same."

Aiyanna and Luke each took a pinch of tobacco from their pouches and followed Akecheta's example by throwing it on the fire. The ancient Bear clan warrior then lit the pipe and shared it with Luke and Aiyanna.

Chapter Fifty-Six

WRITING ON THE WALL

The Underworld Realm. Day Two

With the coming of the next day's first high tide, following a period of much-needed sleep, the three Underworld travelers prepared to set out for the village. Luke and Aiyanna were eager to meet these denizens of the deep in hopes they could lead them to Alice.

Luke looked around, puzzled. "What happened to the wolves?"

Aiyanna smiled. "A guardian spirit is not a constant companion," she explained. "They come and go as needed. Sometimes quite unexpectedly, as I'm sure you have discovered."

As they began their journey, the landscape opened up, presenting a much wider vista than Luke could ever have imagined. It brought to mind the stories of Jules Verne and the esoteric myths espoused by certain modern "hollow earth" theorists that postulated the existence of vast new worlds and subterranean civilizations. At the same time, the ambience became brighter, more like twilight or an overcast day on the surface. Or perhaps his eyes were just growing accustomed to the dim light of this world.

Luke checked his watch. They had been walking for six hours when they reached the outskirts of a human settlement. Resembling a Polynesian fishing village in many respects, it consisted of groupings of thatched-roof huts situated in and around the wetlands bordering a large freshwater sea. The huts appeared to be constructed of a type of bamboo covered with a reed matting material. Those on and near the water were elevated three to four feet off the ground, with a single doorway accessible by ladder.

The bustle of human activity became more evident the closer they drew to the village. Surprisingly, even small dogs scampered about. Boats and rafts constructed entirely of reeds lay upon the shore, similar in appearance to Peruvian reed fishing boats Luke recalled seeing in a TV documentary. Later that eventide, Luke would make the following entry in his journal:

I was immediately struck by the physical attributes of these people. Small to medium in height and stature, they exhibit a trim, lean, and agile nature. Remarkably light skinned with gray to white hair, they possess no facial hair and, from what I can tell, little to no body hair. They have deep-socketed, penetrating eyes, ranging from blue-green to hazel in color. Assuming they share a common ancestor with their distant Native American cousins on the surface, Aiyanna believes these differences may be the result of their bodies having adapted over the ages to the conditions of this Underworld realm.

The women of the village wear a tunic-like dress made of a rough-textured, woven cloth material. Many complement this with a richly patterned hooded blanket or poncho and face scarf. The men wear loincloths and leggings of the same material and are, for the most part, bare-chested, although open vests are not uncommon.

The cloth material appears to be a form of woven flax, like coarse linen. For some of the men—presumably, those of higher ranking in the village—the cloth leggings and vests are replaced with fox, beaver, or muskrat fur, or even buckskin, which I was told is a rare find in this realm.

Sandals, fashioned from snakeskin leather, are worn by men and women alike. Akecheta confirmed that snakes of various species are plentiful in both the marshes and the adjoining sea. Snake leather is also used to create straps and laces for various utilitarian purposes. We were told that flax, bamboo, and reeds grow in abundance throughout the surrounding marshlands. Bamboo and reeds form the major construction materials for their huts and vessels.

The women wear their hair in elaborate braided patterns and accessorize with stone bead necklaces and precious gems mined from the cavern walls. The men favor carved bone ornaments and nose and ear piercings, with their hair drawn up in a single bun at the back of their heads.

A common accessory for both men and woman, adults and children alike, is a single clear quartz crystal pendant worn about the neck. Akecheta says the crystals are believed to possess curative powers, ward off disease and evil spirits, and support a general sense of well-being.

As the three entered the village proper, an elder of the tribe greeted Akecheta. Judging by his smile and relaxed demeanor, the two had obviously met before under friendly terms. After a brief exchange, the elder motioned for the three of them to follow him. They immediately attracted the attention of the villagers, the children in particular, who gathered about in growing numbers as this entourage came to resemble a parade, complete with yapping dogs responding to the excitement of their masters.

He led them to one of the larger lodges on higher ground and introduced them to Chief Hotah and his council. Akecheta was able to understand enough of their language to communicate, filling in the gaps with hand gestures and sign language, and oftentimes resorting to drawing pictures on the ground. Aiyanna would then translate into English for Luke.

"They appear to speak a very ancient dialect," Aiyanna whispered to Luke. "The best I can tell, a mixture of Sioux, Algonquian, and Miami."

During this session they were guaranteed protection, shelter, and food. Asked how they came to be among the Underworld, they explained the best they could. Chief Hotah nodded, seemingly unfazed by what Luke would have considered a rather disconcerting disclosure. The chief explained that from time to time, in the past, they would be visited by strangers from the "world above."

"Some, like Akecheta," he said, pointing to the warrior, "would arrive by accident, having stumbled into a chasm or sinkhole that connects to our world. Most often, however, they would be infants or young children brought here against their will by the evil workings of the Great Serpent. They would come from various eras and cultures, as evidenced by their dress and appearance. If they survived the passage—and many did not— they would be welcomed, cared for, and assimilated into our society.

"But lately, there have been a rash of newcomers or otherworldly visitors—'lost souls' we call them—who appear to have simply fallen through the dome"—he pointed upward—"through unnatural portals that have opened up in more recent times."

Luke pondered this. *Unnatural portals? Perhaps a better translation would be "unholy portals," the term used by Shaman Lobo.*

Luke asked if it would be possible to meet these lost souls. "You see, we have much in common. Aiyanna and I count ourselves among them."

The chief met Luke's eyes and slowly nodded, then turned to one of his council members and spoke a command. The man bowed and backed away. Luke noted it was the custom to never turn your back to the chief when leaving his presence.

Aiyanna next asked the chief about the origins of his people: how they came to be in this Underworld realm, which she thought, from all her teachings, was never intended as a dwelling place for human beings.

The chief said he understood her confusion and offered to arrange a special visit for his new guests to the Stone Garden and the Wall, two sacred locations where his people went to pray, meditate, and connect with their ancestors.

"Our shaman will meet you there and address your questions."

ON THE WAY to the Wall, the group passed a series of lagoons tended by men and woman of all ages. In one lagoon, Aiyanna noticed they were harvesting what appeared to be freshwater seaweed. In another they were bringing up basketfuls of what resembled catfish. The lagoons were laid out in grid patterns that extended well into the sea.

"Looks like they've learned the basics of aquatic farming," she said.

Beyond the lagoons, in nearby marshes, teams of women gathered wild rice in reed canoes, using ricing sticks and basket techniques similar to those followed by the ancient Ho-Chunk, as attested to by Akecheta. And beyond the marshes were what looked like fields of cultivated crops: corn, squash, and beans. The people had apparently picked up some rather sophisticated irrigation techniques, creating artificial ponds by diverting and damming the trickling flow of fresh runoff from the steep cavern walls and controlling its flow into the fields with a system of canals and sluice gates.

Off in the distance, Aiyanna saw something she hadn't noticed before, or perhaps had just overlooked as a mirage. Luke followed her gaze as they stopped to observe.

"Looks like a cloud," he said.

Aiyanna agreed. "Yes, that's what I thought. Apparently, this underground world is vast enough to generate its own weather system. Classic water cycle. Evaporation, cloud formation, and possibly rain. Localized geothermal heating may also play a role. Amazing!"

As they were leaving the village limits, the trail sloped upward to a rocky plateau that overlooked the sea and village. Continuing on, they passed an area of underground chambers, or *kivas*, similar to those found among the Pueblo Indians of the American Southwest. Measuring ten to fifteen feet in diameter, the chambers were topped with domed earthen roofs supported by a system of bamboo crossmembers and reed matting. Like the Pantheon of Rome, there was a center hole for ventilation and to let in the light. Their guide explained that they were used mainly for religious ceremonies and also served as "sweat lodges," something Akecheta expressed familiarity with.

Beyond the kivas, the trail wound its way among an odd assortment of giant, carved pillars of stone strewn in seemingly random fashion across a barren field of rock and sand. Sculpted to resemble real or imaginary creatures of nature and other forms, no two effigies were alike. Through Akecheta's interpretive efforts, they came to understand these effigies were carved by "the Ancient Ones" when this world was first inhabited by humans in ages long past. The area was known to the locals as the Stone Garden.

At the far end of the field stood a solitary figure of a man where the path exited the garden between two pillars. He wore a long robe of a fine linen weave bordered with ermine fur—which in itself seemed unusual for this realm—and was holding a long staff made of cedar, also a rare find. Taller than most of his people, he had long, flowing, snow-white hair, pale skin, and pink eyes. Albino, Aiyanna thought.

Their native guide approached the man with veneration and respect and introduced him as the village shaman, one called Howahkan, which translated as "mysterious voice."

Shaman Howahkan nodded and motioned for them to follow him as they headed toward a sheer-faced granite cliff wall. To the left was a deep recess, protected by an overhanging ledge that effectively turned it into a sheltered grotto, measuring approximately fifteen feet wide by ten feet deep and ten feet high. Once inside, as one's eyes adjusted to the shadowed interior, the inner and side walls of the grotto came alive with densely packed carved inscriptions and painted images that resembled a combination of Egyptian hieroglyphics and ancient petroglyphs of the US Southwest. The locals simply referred to this place as *the Wall*.

The shaman turned to his guests and proceeded to explain, in a voice that was both calm and commanding. Aided in part by sign language and the wall images themselves, Akecheta did his best to interpret the ancient dialect, which Aiyanna then translated into English. She hoped not too much was lost in the translation:

In ancient times, as ancient as the wind, our people once lived on the surface, in the Earth World, at a time when ice covered much of the world. This was a time of great peril when Ice Giants from the north were free to roam Earth and devour humans. Our people, the Ancient Ones, who lived in the north country, were most vulnerable to their attacks. We offered prayers to the Creator Earthmaker to save us from annihilation. Earthmaker heard our prayers and sent Hare and Turtle to our aid. Turtle opened a portal into his Underworld domain and created a special realm into which we were able to escape, every man, woman, and child, along with selected beasts and crops, including our canine companions, beavers, rabbits, foxes, deer, corn, beans, squash, and tobacco. Before the Ice Giants could follow, the portal was closed and forever sealed. To further confuse the Ice Giants, the Creator declared that Time itself would remain *frozen* [or *floating*, depending on translation] in this realm so that the Ice Giants could never know when or where to find us. But this world was not without its own manner of peril. The Great Serpent and its minions, who have dominion over this World, remained a constant threat. So, the three wolf brothers, Green Wolf, Black Wolf, and White Wolf, protectors of the Underworld, were commanded to take charge over us and protect us from this resident evil.

As Aiyanna continued to study the petroglyphs, she noticed Luke secretly accessing his cell phone to sneak a few pics before returning it to his pocket.

Backing away from the writings, Aiyanna scratched her head. "So, time is either *frozen*, or *floating*, depending on how it's translated. It's not altogether clear."

"Hmm. The difference could be significant," Luke suggested.

He turned to the shaman to pose a question. Aiyanna and Akecheta readied themselves for the translation.

"Can you please tell us whether there is a way out of this world? A way to return to our Earth World realm?"

The shaman pondered. He then revealed that while he possessed the power to come and go between the two worlds, which he had done on numerous occasions—and which perhaps helped to explain the robe and cedar staff—he wasn't sure that the path could be endured by those lacking "special knowledge" in the mystical arts. When Luke revealed the four sacred herbs of Ma-ona he had stashed away in his buckskin pouches, the shaman's eyes lit up.

"Perhaps it is possible," he said. "But the journey would be arduous and fraught with peril." He paused. "Do you plan to take... the other-worldly lost souls with you?"

Luke hesitated, then nodded. "Yes. If possible."

Shaman Howahkan turned to their native guide and uttered something. The guide backed away and motioned for the others to follow him back to the village. The three bowed and thanked the shaman for his help.

～

BACK IN THE VILLAGE, Luke was aware of a noticeable reduction in the level of activity as the people retreated from the lagoons, marshes, and inland fields and set about preparing their common meal of the day, what might be termed their eventide meal. Two short blasts of a conch shell from the village Day-Keeper announced the higher eve-tide. Regarding the passage of time, Luke recorded the following in his journal:

> The village "Day-Keeper" performs a vital function within the community and answers only to the shaman. It is his duty to track the tides and the passing days, making use of vertical bamboo posts implanted by the coast-line. Carved notches in the posts mark and identify the rise and fall of the tides. During the two annual flood seasons, special notched poles were employed. The Day-Keeper would announce the tides, or time of day, by trumpeting through a conch shell, obtained from a freshwater species of conch commonly found in these waters. A long blast would indicate first high tide, serving as a morning alarm clock for the people. The higher eve-tide would be signaled with two back-to-back blasts of shorter duration.
>
> The time period between eve-tide and first high tide is called the "quiet-time," equivalent to nighttime in the Earth World, a time for restful sleep and bodily rejuvenation. By convention, the half-day periods between the two high tides are divided into four equal time periods, or "quarter-tides." Aiyanna remarked that the number "four" is a sacred number among most Indigenous peoples, so she was not surprised by this convention. The time of day is designated by the ending quarter, such that "first-quarter-tide" would roughly translate as 9:00 a.m., "second-quarter-tide" as the noon hour, and so on.

The "three amigos," as Luke had by now dubbed Aiyanna, Akecheta, and himself, were asked to join Chief Hotah for dinner, which they gladly accepted. The meal was prepared over an open pit resembling a Hawaiian luau. Starting with a kind of whitefish wrapped in seaweed, accompanied by a mixture of wild rice and mushrooms, the chief then proudly served the main dish: a roasted meat of some kind, with a gamey but pleasing taste. When asked what it was, the chief proclaimed, "We only serve our honored guests the very best!"

Akecheta had trouble with the translation but finally turned to Luke and Aiyanna with a wince: "Roast dog!"

Luke almost choked as he swapped astonished looks with Aiyanna. Akecheta was fazed as well. Not wanting to dishonor their host, they decided the better part of discretion would be to swallow their pride—as well as the remainder of their portion of dog.

The dessert went down much easier: a sweetened corn and rice pudding garnished with a fig-like fruit. The sugar was derived from sugar beets. Both the beets and the figs were cultivated in the more fertile regions of their realm, where "the water falls from the dome"—confirming Luke's earlier assumptions about local weather systems—and were originally "imported" from the Earth World, compliments of an unnamed shaman from the distant past.

Following dinner, Shaman Howahkan joined them, and the talk turned to the recently arrived otherworldly lost souls. Akecheta and Aiyanna did their best to translate, but the process was slow and laborious and continued well into the evening. The shaman explained that these people spoke the same native tongue as Luke and Aiyanna and ranged in age from young adults to older men and women. They numbered approximately twenty. The first of these began to arrive "thirty-four flood seasons ago"—which by Luke's reckoning was seventeen years—which had given them sufficient time to acquire limited native language skills.

"The young girl, in particular, was able to adapt rather well," the shaman said.

Luke and Aiyanna's eyes brightened.

"The young girl?" Luke asked. "Can you describe her?"

From the shaman's description, it had to have been none other than his sister, Alice!

The shaman explained that initially this girl was taken under the wing of an older woman, who was the first to arrive two seasons prior. Luke surmised that woman to be Laura Emery, but he would need to confirm it.

"When can we meet these... lost souls?" Luke asked.

"At first high tide," the shaman answered. "After our quiet-time and an accustomed period of rest and sleep, we can take you to them. They live in a common area at the far edge of the village."

"And the young girl. We will get to meet her as well?" Luke asked.

The chief and shaman exchanged anxious looks.

"That will not be possible," the chief said. "For you see, she has been promised to the eldest son of the chief of our neighboring village to the east."

Luke straightened up. "Promised? What do you mean *promised?*"

The chief inhaled sharply. "A promise of matrimony, of course. To seal the bonds of alliance between our tribes."

Luke's head spun. *So, there are other villages in this world! Of course. Why wouldn't there be?* He then recalled the vastness of the vista presented on the first day of this journey.

Aiyanna took Luke's hand and pressed it between hers. Leaning toward him she whispered in his ear, "I now understand the meaning behind Alice's cries for help in my most recent dreams."

Chapter Fifty-Seven

REUNION OF LOST SOULS

The Underworld Realm. Day Three

For Luke it was a long lunar night—a not-so-quiet-time. Besides the difficulty of acclimating to the perpetual twilight and an elongated circadian rhythm, his head was filled with troubling visions of Alice being held captive as the pending bride and princess of the Underworld. On the one hand, there was immense relief knowing that she truly was alive as Uncle Lobo had said. But her rescue now seemed more remote than ever, as were their own chances of ever returning to their Earth World. It seemed that everything was now in the hands of Shaman Howahkan, who alone knew the way back. But would he prove to be a reliable ally?

After a brief midday meal, the three amigos were escorted to a rise on the edge of the village where they were led into one of the larger lodges, an oblong structure that appeared to serve as community meeting hall. A low rectangular stone slab, table-like in appearance, flanked on both sides by woven floor mats, ran down the center of the room. Taking their places at the far end of the slab, the three were asked to please be seated. Before long, people trickled in and took their seats at the table. Unmistakably Caucasian and not native to this realm, they were a ragtag bunch who looked like refugees from the apocalypse, dressed in an odd mixture of native apparel and what may have been left of their own worn-out clothes from another time and era. Most of the men remained unshaven, with mixed attention paid to conventional grooming practices. Luke had counted eighteen people in all—eleven men and seven women—when the last of them walked into the room, bringing the total number to nineteen. She appeared to be the oldest, in her early sixties, and was dressed entirely in native weave.

Up till now, no one had uttered a word. The others seemed to hold this woman in special regard, allowing her to be the first to speak. Standing at the far end of the table, she addressed the three new strangers among them. She spoke in modern English, with a distinct and familiar Wisconsin accent, addressing Luke and Aiyanna directly.

"My name is Laura Emery. Those you see before you have come from the world above. We are all present... except for one." She paused to gather her composure. "From the looks of the two of you, and your fresh attire, it appears that you are recent arrivals to this realm." She stared at Akecheta. "The Native American among you must have a different story to tell."

Luke stood and introduced himself and his two companions and how they came to be in this place. The others nodded and proceeded to introduce themselves and recount one by one their own similar traumatic passage through the cornfield portals. As they did, Luke opened his notebook to a page with a list of names, which he began checking off. These were the missing persons that Sam's computer model had linked to a crop circle event, but whose bodily remains were never identified or recovered by GPR scan. Of the twenty-six names listed, Luke was able to account for eighteen, including Laura and Alice. One name in particular struck him: Ed Hauptmann. He decided it would be best not to bring up the subject of Ed's niece, Emma, at this time.

But two of the men present had remained silent throughout the interrogation. They were not on Sam's list. When questioned, the younger man responded in French, "*Désolé, mais je ne parle pas anglais.*"

Aiyanna immediately responded in French.

"*Comment t'appelles-tu?*"

"Pierre LeBlanc," he replied.

Aiyanna learned that Pierre had come from the eighteenth century— 1763 to be exact—in a manner similar to what Akecheta had experienced.

The second man, Hans Hauptmann, speaking with a thick German accent, recounted a similar experience, saying he had fallen into a deep ravine in 1855 during a hunting expedition near Devil's Lake, Wisconsin. Laura confirmed that the German arrived around the same time as Ed Hauptmann, whereas the Frenchman's arrival was more recent. About five years earlier.

"It is all rather confusing," Laura said with a nervous laugh.

"Yes, from what we have learned from the shaman," Luke said, "time as we experience it continues in this place but is linked to all eras, past and present. A common timeline of sorts. Returning through a portal would take you back to your originating era and timeline, displaced by the time spent in this realm, of course.

"Do you think such a thing is possible?" Laura asked.

Luke noticed the troubled look on Aiyanna's face. "We certainly hope so," he said. "That is why we ventured here. To save... you and the others."

(He started to say, *To save my sister Alice*, but had to bite his tongue.)

He cleared his throat before continuing, addressing everyone at the table. "You see, we are scheduled to meet with Chief Hotah and the shaman later today to discuss plans for doing just that. They said that it may be possible. What we will need to know is, how many of you would be willing to undertake this difficult journey? It would not be without risk. Some of us may not even make it through."

They all took a moment to consider, looking at one another, seemingly trying to gauge the others' thoughts.

The man who had introduced himself as Ed Hauptmann was the first to speak. "Can you say what the chances of success would be?"

Luke calmly deliberated. "We will know better after we meet with the shaman. I just ask that you to consider it for now."

The youngest woman, Sarah, who appeared to be in her late teens, timidly asked, "What if we don't wish to go back? Do we have a choice?"

There was another moment's pause. From all outward appearances, the girl had totally adapted to the local native ways since her arrival just over five years prior, adopting the dress and elaborate braided hairstyles of the women. He would soon learn that she even spoke their native tongue quite well.

"Yes, well that is a personal decision each of you will have to make," Luke replied. "We can meet again in a day or two to have your decisions. We will need to give the chief an accurate head count so that the proper preparations can be made."

As the room cleared, Luke asked Laura to remain behind. Once they were alone with her, he began.

"First, I want you to know, Laura, that your husband, Jake, and your sons, Seth and Scott, are well. Although their lives, too, have been something of a struggle, starting with your sudden disappearance seventeen years ago."

Luke recounted his first meeting with Jake and Scott and the painful happenings involving Jake's second wife, Gloria, and their eldest son, Adam.

"They were all tragic affairs," he concluded. "But, on the brighter side, you now have a granddaughter. Adam's wife, Milly, gave birth five months ago, and they are now living with Jake and Scott."

Laura's face brightened. "My, that is something to celebrate."

"And an incentive for returning, wouldn't you say?" he added.

"Hmm." Laura nodded wistfully.

Luke paused, exchanging glances with Aiyanna before continuing.

"Laura, you mentioned someone who is not with you today. Can you please clarify?"

She sighed. "Yes, of course. Little Alice."

Luke brightened. "Ah, *little* Alice! Only, I don't imagine she is so little anymore. She was six years old when the cornfields swallowed her up sixteen years ago."

Laura was stunned. "You know about Alice?"

Luke leaned forward and said in a whisper, "Yes, Laura. You see, Alice is my sister."

"Oh my God!" she said, gasping quietly with her hand over her mouth. She took but a moment to put the pieces together. "So, that is what really brought you here. To save your sister."

Luke nodded. "Yes. And we have no intention of leaving this place without her. But now that we know you are all alive and well, we will do everything in our power to take you back with us. *All* of you. The *lost souls* of the Underworld!" he said with an ill attempt at humor. Leaning forward, he resumed his original line of questioning. "So, Laura. What can you tell us about Alice?"

She let out a deep sigh. "Well, I was the first to arrive from our time period. Alice arrived about one year later. I immediately took her under my wing and cared for her like she was my own. Such a sweet girl."

"I know. And I want to thank you for all you've done. Without you, she surely would have..." He gulped, swallowing his last words.

Aiyanna cleared her throat and picked up his train of thought. "And now we were informed that Alice has been promised in marriage to the son of a neighboring village chief. A village that lies to the east. What can you tell us about that?"

Laura explained that it all came about rather suddenly, about five tidal weeks earlier. She was not privy to the details, but it had something to do with "bonds of kinship and alliance" between the two tribes. It was said that the son of the other chief was smitten by Alice's beauty and chose her above all others.

"She now resides in that village under armed guard," Laura continued. "I know this because I accompanied her there. I am trusted and considered something of a surrogate mother to her and would be involved in the 'giving away' ceremony."

"And when is this... ceremony to occur?" Aiyanna asked. There was trepidation in her voice.

"Approximately three tidal weeks from now," Laura replied. "Before the next, or lesser, flood season."

Luke inhaled sharply between clenched teeth and squeezed Aiyanna's hand. "Then we must act quickly," he said. "Do you think we would be permitted to visit her?"

"Hmm. That might be possible. We would need Chief Hotah's permission, of course."

Luke nodded. A plan was beginning to hatch in his head.

"Laura, I must ask you to please keep my relationship with Alice between the four of us. The chief and the shaman must *never* know. We need their help and right now they seem willing, even eager, for our departure. There's no telling what they would do if they found out the real purpose for our being here."

Laura nodded. "Yes, of course. I understand."

LATER THAT DAY, Luke, Aiyanna, Akecheta, and Laura met in private with Chief Hotah and Shaman Howahkan to discuss a plan for returning to their Earth World through a *natural* exit portal. Laura, who had become quite fluent in their speech over the past seventeen years, was helpful in breaching the language barrier.

"After all," Luke said, "we can't go back the way we came."

The shaman smiled. "Certainly not! But the exit portal you seek is not easy to find. It is located in the Caverns of Antiquity, several days' journey from here across the Great Sea. The journey is fraught with danger and there is no guarantee of success. Such a trip will require careful planning and preparation."

"And how long would these preparations take?" Luke asked.

The shaman pondered this. "Depending on the number of people making the journey, perhaps twenty tidal days or more."

Luke swallowed hard. "Three weeks? Any chance of doing it sooner?

"Our boats are made for local fishing," the chief explained. "Only a few are built to withstand longer voyages at sea. If there are many people, more boats would need to be built. That will take time."

"And there is the period of fasting and prayer required to strengthen the spirit to endure such a journey," the shaman added.

"Yes, I can understand that," Aiyanna agreed reluctantly.

The shaman, too, seemed increasingly anxious over the timing, saying that it would be well if they could expedite their departure before the coming flood season. Although Luke suspected that he really wanted them gone before the wedding.

Laura spoke up. "What if we put our people to work building the boats? Perhaps this can speed things up a bit. Some of the men have already demonstrated their penchant for boat construction and seamanship."

The chief perked up. "Yes. I have noticed that ability in some of your men. But then there is the question of navigation. You will need our men to pilot the boats and to return the boats to our village once you are delivered."

The chief explained that their system of navigation utilized markers positioned along the shores. Where markers were not available, the quartz patterns in the overhead domed sky would be used. They reminded Luke of star constellations, only these patterns remained fixed, which made navigation a bit easier, like following a road map pasted on the ceiling. They were also told that to navigate over open waters or foggy conditions, they would use magical stones that pointed the way, "given to us by Ma-ona and Turtle in their divine wisdom." Aiyanna would later recognize these stones to be lodestone, a rare form of magnetite that occurred naturally as a permanent magnet. "The four cardinal directions, held sacred in all Native American traditions," Aiyanna later explained, "are thereby ascertainable even at these subterranean depths."

The shaman continued, "I will instruct the pilots on the course to follow. Your travels will take you in a generally westward direction. But once they deliver you to your distant landfall, there is still the ground journey through a labyrinth of caves to the final portal." He turned to Akecheta. "I leave that to you, my son. I will instruct you on the path to take, but it is not without its own perils."

Akecheta nodded. Luke could almost read his thoughts: *I know. I made the journey once. Spirits willing, I can do it again.*

Luke patted his thighs. "So, it is settled then. We will speak to the others and come up with the number of travelers and initiate a construction plan for the boats."

He silently signaled to Laura.

Laura spoke up. "Oh, yes. There is one more request, Chief. I was wanting to take Alice some things in preparation for the upcoming wedding ceremony."

The chief took a moment, exchanging nervous looks with the shaman, who finally nodded his approval.

"Certainly," the chief said. "When do you wish to go?"

"Uh, tomorrow... if possible."

Hesitating, the chief turned and barked commands to his attendant, who bowed and backed away out of the lodge.

"We will have a boat waiting for you at first high tide to take you to the eastern village," the chief said. "Overland travel is possible, but boat travel takes half the time. You should be there well before the first-quarter-tide."

Almost as an afterthought Laura added, "And if at all possible, I would like to take Aiyanna with me. Aiyanna knew Alice's family and would like to convey their best wishes for her." She paused. "You see, Alice often visits Aiyanna in her dreams and makes this request."

The chief raised an eyebrow, then turned to the shaman. After some back-and-forth banter, he voiced his approval.

"Thank you," Aiyanna offered in her best ancient dialect. "Speaking for Alice's family, we greatly appreciate it."

FOLLOWING THEIR EVE-TIDE MEAL, Luke and Aiyanna met back at their lodge to compare notes as they tried to come to better grips with the situation.

"I'm trying to figure out why some of the lost souls made it through the portal, and others did not," Luke said. "Of the twenty-six on Sam's list, we can only account for eighteen, including Alice and Laura."

"Hmm. Perhaps they lacked the proper protection," Aiyanna offered.

"By proper, you mean *magic*. Tobacco. Herbs. Guardian spirit."

Aiyanna smiled. "Without your White Wolf, you surely would have been devoured by the panther, n'est-ce pas?"

Luke chuckled. "Yes, well, I'd like to interview them further. Find out what their... *tobacco* habits were. What kind of spiritual lives they lived before arriving here. Perhaps they were into yoga or transcendental meditation or attended regular prayer meetings."

Aiyanna puckered her lips with a nod.

"And this time travel thing," Luke continued. "One could argue that for us moderns we were simply displaced to a special subterranean realm à la *Journey to the Center of the Earth*. Not time travel at all!"

Aiyanna lay back and stared up at the roof. "Well, I think that for us, and the other lost souls from our era, the notion of time travel is a moot point. We share a common modern-day timeline, so we come and go together, past or present." She turned, propping herself up on an elbow. "But Akecheta, Hans, and Pierre. They are the *real* time travelers here."

Luke pursed his lips. "So the question is, how did we all end up on the same timeline?"

Aiyanna considered this. "Well, as the Wall inscriptions suggest, this realm exists in a shared 'floating' time dimension that attracts visitors from different eras. Perhaps the nature of that attraction has to do with shared heritage and family lines. A kind of kinship quantum entanglement phenomenon."

Luke raised an eyebrow. "Quantum entanglement!"

"Yes," she replied. "Einstein initially dismissed the notion of quantum entanglement as 'spooky action at a distance.'" She laughed. "But he has since been proven wrong. I think that with so many lost souls from our era coming through our 'unholy portals,' we may have created an overwhelming attractive force to kindred travelers from other eras. Akecheta was obviously attracted to me."

"So, are you saying Pierre and Hans are distant relatives to one or more of our other modern-day lost souls?"

"Perhaps. After all, Ed and Hans do share a common surname and came through a portal at about the same time. Pierre may likewise share a common lineage with one of the other lost souls."

Luke contemplated that. "Like maybe Sarah. Didn't they both arrive at about the same time?"

LATER THAT EVENTIDE, Aiyanna was walking alone by the sea, contemplating the next day's journey, when she noticed young Sarah some distance away conversing and holding hands with a young man from the village. Oh my! she thought, now understanding a possible reason for the young girl's misgivings over leaving this place. The young man appeared to be doing most of the talking, with Sarah simply nodding or shaking her head from time to time in response to his words and gestures. Suddenly spying Aiyanna, they smiled and quietly walked off, disappearing down an adjoining trail.

Chapter Fifty-Eight

THE EASTERN VILLAGE

The Underworld Realm. Day Four

The next day, while Laura and Aiyanna set off on their day trip to the eastern village to meet with Alice, Luke and Akecheta began the task of boat building. Given the time constraints, it would prove a formidable challenge. With Sarah serving as his native language interpreter, Luke began by enlisting the help of experienced native boat builders and organizing their lost-soul members into teams charged with specific tasks. There were the reed gatherers and processers, bamboo harvesters, tar and resin gatherers for waterproofing, and finally the boat fabricators themselves.

Boat design would mirror the largest of their existing seagoing vessels, measuring approximately eighteen feet stem to stern, five feet wide at the midsection, with a simple open deck, much like a Viking ship without the sails, but resembling more an elongated basket than a boat in Luke's estimation. However, as long as it stayed afloat and was seaworthy, Luke figured that was good enough.

Luke was told that each boat could be expected to accommodate up to four lost-soul passengers with supplies and provisions, in addition to a two-man native crew. All able-bodied men would be expected to handle the oars on the outbound trip. The native crews would handle the return trip alone. Depending on how many people decided to make this trip, they might require up to six boats in all. That would mean three new boats in just three weeks' time to supplement the three available existing boats.

～

IT WAS EVENTIDE when Aiyanna and Laura arrived back from the eastern village with a mixed bag of news.

"The good news is we saw and spoke with Alice, and she appears to be in good health," Aiyanna said. "She was ecstatic when we told her that Luke is with us."

"Yes, and she could barely contain herself when we told her of our rescue plans," Laura added.

Aiyanna explained that Alice was being detained in what was termed the "wedding lodge" with two to three guards posted outside the door "for her protection" at all times. Strangely enough, though, she had yet to meet her intended groom. Perhaps it was just the custom. But when they asked some passing villagers about his whereabouts, they appeared confused by the question. One even said that the chief "had no living sons."

"That's odd," Luke said. "Maybe a mistranslation?"

"Well, perhaps," said Aiyanna. "But... I sensed otherwise."

That same eventide, the three amigos plus one—Aiyanna, Luke, Akecheta, and Laura—met with the other lost souls in the great meeting lodge to try to get a final count on the number of anticipated travelers. All but two individuals appeared willing to attempt the journey. One was Hans, the older German fellow from the nineteenth century. He said he had grown accustomed to his adopted village and that he was too old to endure the rigors of such a journey.

The other was young Sarah, who lowered her head and confessed that she was seeing a young man from the village and had developed a relationship.

"Was it the same young man I saw you with last eventide?" Aiyanna asked.

Sarah hesitated, then answered sheepishly, "Yes." She looked up. "He

347

really is quite a nice young man. His name is Odakota. It means 'friendly.'"

Aiyanna smiled. "I am sure he is, Sarah. But please consider the consequences. This may be your only opportunity to return to your native world... and to the family that loves you."

Sarah looked down again. "I don't think I will be missed," she said sadly. "You see, I was running away from home at the time and just chose the wrong cornfield to hide out in." She let out a humorless chuckle.

Laura mouthed the words *child abuse*.

"Well, if you change your mind, please let us know," Aiyanna said.

Sarah nodded.

Aiyanna had another thought. "Sarah, when you see your friend Odakota, can you please ask him what he knows about the chief's son in the neighboring village? Laura and I just returned from seeing Alice and were confused by the news we heard concerning her intended groom."

Luke added, "Yes, and we understand there is an overland trail to that village. Can you please ask your friend if he is familiar with such a trail?"

"Sure, I can do that," she replied.

After the meeting, the three amigos and Laura remained behind to work out the details of their rescue plan.

"I think our best shot is a clandestine overland rescue the night before our departure," Luke suggested. "Get Alice back here before they awake, then cast off before they realize she is missing."

"Yes. And I think I know just the duo who could pull that off," Aiyanna said with a furtive glance toward her fellow Bear clansman.

Luke smiled. But it was a halfhearted smile.

Laura picked up on it. "What's the problem, Luke?"

"Well, you know, our rescue scheme could be putting everyone's lives in jeopardy. I've had mixed feelings from the start about not telling the others so they can make an informed decision on whether or not to leave."

"But we can't risk the possibility of someone spilling the beans," Laura said. "I mean, I can't vouch for the integrity of my fellow lost souls. I think for now we need to keep our plan under wraps."

"Hmm. Okay, I guess. You know them better than we do," Luke said.

In the end they all agreed.

SEVERAL DAYS after their eventide meeting in the conference lodge, Sarah introduced Odakota to Aiyanna and Akecheta. With all the activity surrounding preparations, the three of them—Odakota, Aiyanna, and Akecheta—were able to sneak away unnoticed on a secret overland day trip to the eastern village. Odakota led the way. It took only three hours, not nearly as long as the chief had initially led them to believe. Once there, they remained hidden along a tree line outside the village as Aiyanna pointed to the "wedding hut" where Alice was being detained. Two guards were on duty at the time.

Odakota, however, was free to venture into the village and blend in unnoticed. A smooth talker and eavesdropper, he was able to obtain some vital and disturbing information. He discovered that while the chief did have a son, the boy was not yet a man. Such prepubescent marital arrangements were not considered unusual. More troubling, however, was his finding that the term "wedding" was code for a ceremony of a completely different sort involving a blood sacrifice of some kind. There was also talk about a "prophecy" inscribed on the Wall.

BACK IN THEIR own village they relayed these findings to Luke and Laura. Luke was beside himself. It all seemed to confirm his worst fears. He frantically insisted they double down on their efforts.

"But first," he said, "we must pay another visit to the Wall!"

Back at the Wall, Odakota scoured the petroglyphs for clues. Eventually, the young man was able to identify an obscure inscription located low and to the right. He did his best to decipher the meaning, with Sarah translating:

In the end times the blood of a young virgin bride recently arrived from another World shall usher in a new age of prosperity and growth.

"So, does that mean sacrificial blood?" Luke asked.

"Or perhaps menstrual blood, or the blood of childbirth?" Aiyanna added.

Sarah relayed the question to her young suitor and told them his reply.

"Odakota says it's not really clear. Could be either."

Luke rubbed his chin. "Hmm. That's not good."

As they returned to the village, Luke got to thinking. "You know, I had mixed feelings before about not informing the others of our rescue plans. But now, if we're talking about human sacrifice, then we are *really* putting everyone at risk!" He paused. "And I'm especially worried about Sarah and Hans being left behind. I hate to think what would happen to them once people learn we've made off with their sacrificial lamb."

"Yes, I was thinking the same thing," Aiyanna said. "I think we need to persuade them that it would be in their best interests to go. Perhaps you can talk to Hans. Laura and I will try to convince Sarah."

Luke agreed.

Chapter Fifty-Nine

THE RESCUE

The Underworld Realm. Final Days

Days turned into weeks as construction of their small flotilla continued at a breakneck pace. Luke quickly realized this was all taking a lot more effort than any of them had anticipated. The days immediately preceding their scheduled departure were spent in frenetic states of preparation: gathering provisions, putting the finishing touches on their boats, and performing the necessary fasting and spiritual rituals prescribed for such an undertaking. The three new boats would be completed on time—just barely. However, a demonstration of their seaworthiness for extended voyages was not a luxury that time would afford them. The native boat pilots as well as Akecheta would have to commit to memory the navigational instructions from Shaman Howahkan. But Luke insisted on translating them to written instructions, which he recorded in his journal. He even attempted a crude map of the intended route—"with apologies to Google Maps," he quipped.

Two days before their scheduled departure, Aiyanna received a surprise visit from Sarah, who informed her that she had had a change of heart.

"I hope it's not too late for me to change my mind," she said with a tremor in her voice.

Aiyanna was overjoyed. She took Sarah in her arms and gave her a big hug.

"By no means is it too late! I was hoping you would come around. Luke and I were so worried that with Alice gone, they would grab you as a last-minute substitute bride. Oh my God! That would be so terrible!"

Sarah wiped the tears from her eyes. "Yes, that's what Odakota told me as well."

Aiyanna stood back and questioned her further. "So, what about you and Odakota?"

"Well, he is planning to replace one of the pilots and join us on the voyage. When we arrive at the portal, we plan to go through together. Hopefully, we will both end up in the same century," she said with a nervous laugh.

Aiyanna sighed. "I hope you are right, Sarah. You see, that's where my knowledge of this whole thing breaks down." She then thought about the shaman. "But if the shaman can do it, then perhaps Odakota can too."

ON D-DAY MINUS ONE, Hans also had a change of heart and committed to making the voyage. Luke had felt compelled to inform him of the stakes involved and their plans to rescue his sister, which finally convinced him that it would be the wiser thing to do.

"Ja, I may be an old actor, but I can still play the hero part!" he said with a guttural chuckle.

The travelers finalized their preparations by participating in a sweat lodge ritual hosted by Akecheta and Shaman Howahkan. Two kivas were made available to accommodate their number. One for the men, and one for the women. A fire was prepared in the center of each kiva and rocks placed on the glowing embers. When all was ready, sage water was sprinkled on the heated rocks. The sprinkling continued, the rocks sizzled, filling the kiva with clouds of steam. As the people began to sweat, the host sang and offered tobacco and prayers of thanksgiving and supplication to the spirits, appealing principally to Turtle—the deity having dominion over the Underworld—and the Black, Green, and White Wolves, protectors of this realm.

Following the ritual, a great feast was prepared and gifts exchanged between Chief Hotah and the travelers. Each traveler was given a crystal pendant to confer an added measure of protection on their upcoming voyage and to ensure safe passage through the portal. Luke presented the chief with his climbers' helmet, and Akecheta offered one of the flutes from his war bundle. In exchange, they were each presented with an obsidian-bladed knife, "sharper than any steel blade," Luke noted.

∾

THE FEAST LASTED WELL into the eve-tide quarters. However, sometime before the fifth-quarter-tide, Aiyanna and Akecheta found an opportunity to excuse themselves, ostensibly "to make last-minute preparations for the next day's journey." Meeting up outside Laura's lodge, the two of them slipped away, Akecheta with his war bundle slung over his shoulder.

Just beyond the village limits they paused to recover a straw mannequin wrapped in a blanket and shawl, which Aiyanna had prepared and placed there the day before, concealed among the cattails and bulrushes bordering the marsh. Then, picking up the trail that would take them to the eastern village, the two set off, with Aiyanna leading the way.

They reached their destination unhindered in about three hours' time, just ahead of the sixth-quarter-tide, or midnight hour. As anticipated, not a soul was stirring as the sleeping villagers took full advantage of their quiet-time. But Aiyanna and Akecheta took no chances. Remaining hidden among the marsh grasses, they wended their way to Alice's incarceration, or "wedding," hut. When they arrived, they were expecting to see guards posted, but there were none.

"That's odd," whispered Aiyanna. "Where are the guards?"

Akecheta put up his hand, signaling her to remain behind while he carefully crept toward the hut. She watched with bated breath as he climbed the short ladder to the hut's door and disappeared inside. A moment later he reemerged and headed back quickly to Aiyanna's position.

"She is not there," he said.

Aiyanna's heart raced as she considered the possibilities. Had she been moved to a different hut? Or had the unthinkable already happened? She cleared her head and focused. An idea came to her.

"You must be familiar with the powers of waruka'na," she said to Akecheta.

The warrior turned. "Yes, I am familiar with this shamanistic practice."

Reaching into a pouch in her upper vest pocket, she produced a wad of tobacco. "Do you have your smoking pipe?"

Smiling, Akecheta removed the pipe from his war bundle. "Are you able to perform such a ritual?" he asked.

Aiyanna took a worried breath. "I hope so. I saw my Uncle Lobo, himself a shaman, perform it once and later asked him to instruct me on its use."

She gathered some nearby brush and prepared a small fire, using a matchstick she pulled from a small waterproof box tucked away in a pants pocket.

"Quicker than flint," she said with a smile.

Akecheta seemed impressed.

She then divided the tobacco, packing a small portion into the pipe and tossing the remainder on the fire. As the smoke from the fire wafted upward, she held out her arms and began to chant in Hocąk, praying to the spirits and looking up toward the quartz-speckled sky dome. Akecheta lit the pipe, took several puffs, and passed it to her.

Seated on the ground with legs folded, Aiyanna went into a trance, chanting all the while. Several minutes passed before she spoke.

"I see a hut, smaller than the last. But there is no ladder. The hut is mounted directly on the ground, a kind of rock plateau. Nearby is an altar, hewn from granite. There is a sign over the altar." Her lips mumbled the words on the sign before continuing. "I see three armed guards. Two are posted by the entrance to the hut. And one stands watch over the altar."

When Aiyanna came out of her trance, she slumped over, exhausted by the experience. Akecheta placed a hand on her shoulder. She opened her eyes and sat up slowly.

"Alice is being held in a retaining lodge in preparation for tomorrow's ceremony," she whispered. "I feel she may have been drugged to induce sleep."

Akecheta nodded. "Yes. The words you mumbled in your trance were also... disturbing." He swallowed hard. "They speak of a ceremony that combines a wedding... and a human sacrifice!"

Aiyanna took a quick breath, then looked up and to the right. "Over there," she said, pointing. "Just beyond that far rock outcropping. That is where they are keeping her."

After putting out the fire, she picked up the mannequin. With Akecheta leading, they carefully made their way through the tall marsh grass toward a distant rise near the canyon wall. Concealed behind a large granite rock formation, they sidled along the wall until Akecheta signaled her to stop. He crouched and pointed.

"There it is. The hut and altar from your visions."

Aiyanna kneeled down close behind. "So, what do we do now?"

"Leave it to me. I will signal you when all is ready."

Akecheta unwrapped his war bundle and removed one of the remaining flutes. Placing it to his lips, he began to play. It was a haunting, plaintive sound that echoed softly off the cavern walls toward the three distant armed figures. Looking about, they exchanged some words, apparently intrigued by the sound. But to Aiyanna's amazement, they remained in place. The two men guarding the hut seated themselves on the ground, legs crossed, while the third guard leaned lazily against the rock altar, letting his weapon fall to the ground. They seemed mesmerized by the sound, as though they themselves had been drugged.

Akecheta picked up a small rock and tossed it in their direction. There was no reaction from the guards.

"Go now!" he said. "Take the straw figure and do as planned!"

Aiyanna picked up the mannequin and stealthily made her way toward the hut. The door was latched on the outside with a single leather strap wrapped around two mating poles, which made it impossible to unlatch from the inside.

Once inside, she breathed a sigh of relief when she saw Alice wrapped in a blanket asleep on a straw mattress. Aiyanna quietly approached and tried to gently rouse her from sleep. Alice groaned. It would take more persuasion.

"Wake up, Alice! You must wake up!" she whispered in Alice's ear.

Alice opened her eyes.

"Aiyanna," she said weakly. "Is this a dream?"

"No, it is not a dream, Alice. We have come to rescue you as promised. You must get up!"

At this point, one of the guards stirred and Aiyanna could hear him approaching. She crouched beside the doorway as he opened the door and peeked inside.

The guard said something to Alice.

A groggy Alice replied in his native tongue.

The guard mumbled something then closed the door, apparently satisfied that all was well. Returning to his post he joined his fellow guard seated on the ground under the spell of Akecheta's flute.

Aiyanna finally managed to awaken Alice and had her stand up and swap blankets with the mannequin. She then laid the wrapped mannequin on the straw mattress in a sleeping position, careful to conceal the body and head entirely. As she led Alice toward the door, Alice stopped abruptly.

"Wait! Stop!" she said.

Returning to her straw mat, she reached down and picked up a small leather pouch.

"I must not forget this," she said. "Luke will be asking for it."

Aiyanna didn't quite understand but went along with it. "Okay, Alice. But we must go. Now!" she said with an increased sense of urgency.

As she went to open the door, she found that it was now latched from the outside. The guard, even in his stupor, apparently knew enough to relatch the door.

Aiyanna's heart raced as she tried to unlatch the strap from the inside with her buck knife. But the bamboo spacings were too narrow even for the blade to penetrate. Her anxiety reached a fevered pitch as she heard footsteps just outside the door. She raised her buck knife in a ready pose. With a sudden motion, the door sprang open. She lunged with the knife.

"Shh!" the lone figure responded as he blocked the advancing blade.

It took her a moment to realize who it was.

"Akecheta! You scared me half to death!"

"Come!" he said. "Quickly! We must go."

On their way out, Akecheta explained that, as an added precaution, he'd drugged the guards' drinking water. "They should have a good sleep now," he said with a grin.

Being sure to relatch the hut door, the three quickly made their escape along the canyon wall and down into the marshes toward the trail that would lead them back to their village.

Chapter Sixty

EXODUS

The Underworld Realm. Day Twenty-Six

Luke stirred as he drifted in and out of hypnagogic states of half-sleep. When slumber at last overcame him, it was not a restful sleep but one fraught with disturbing and fleeting images taking him backward and forward in time, an amalgam of states of mind bordering on the terrifying.

Suddenly he is a child again, enduring the pain of loss and his father's rejection. Then, in dark, deep water, he is holding his breath until his lungs would burst, fighting his way to the lighted surface. As he breaks through, he finds himself standing by the Wall with an Ancient One who, holding a lodestone from a suspended string, incongruously repeats the words of Horace Greeley: "Go West, young man!" Now, falling through space, vertigo overtakes him as he slips into a deep, confining space, a crevice, pressing him on all sides. All at once, there is the refreshing, saving image of a young girl, her hands reaching out. *Luke, it is me! Your sister, Alice! Wake up!*

Luke opened his eyes. The stark bamboo walls stared back.

A familiar voice whispered to him from nearby. "Luke, I have someone I want you to meet."

It was Aiyanna's voice. The ragged images and remnants of half-sleep were dispelled. He turned over to see Aiyanna standing inside the entrance to the hut. Another, shorter figure also stood there to her right, silhouetted against the dim light.

Luke sat up. Still groggy, he wiped the sleep from his eyes.

"Who... who is that with you, Aiyanna?"

"Luke, it is me. Alice!"

The pieces quickly came together. The midnight rescue! It worked!

"Oh my God! Alice, is it really you?"

Luke staggered to his feet and approached his sister. Placing his hands on her shoulders at arm's length, he said, "Let me see you." He studied her up and down for a moment, then gave her a big hug. "My, how you've grown!"

She giggled, that same giggle he remembered from the day she went missing.

"And you, too, Luke. You have certainly turned into a handsome young man!"

He laughed. "Not the pudgy little dude you remembered, eh?"

She smiled, then held out a small leather pouch, crinkled with age. "I think you and the guys were looking for this."

Luke couldn't believe his eyes. "Freckles will be so happy."

"What about Chuck?" she asked.

Luke saddened as he told her of Chuck's passing as a young Marine.

"So much has happened these past sixteen years," he said. "But Mom will be *so* over the moon to see you!" After another big hug, he stood there studying her, memories racing through his head.

Aiyanna cleared her throat.

Luke regained his sense of presence. "Uh, yes. But first we must find our way out of this place!"

At that moment, Laura entered the hut with bowls of food. This was the same hut Laura had shared with Alice these past sixteen years and now shared with Luke and Aiyanna.

"The first-tide conch blast hasn't yet sounded," she announced, "but our people are already beginning to stir in anticipation of today's exodus."

Luke gathered his thoughts as he took the bowl of porridge Laura offered him.

"Laura, have all the people meet in the conference hut once they've finished eating. We need to review our boat assignments and final instructions. Make sure everyone has their crystal pendants. The shaman said they are vital for ensuring safe passage through the portal. And please instruct the women to wear their hooded blankets and face scarves." Luke then spoke softly to his sister. "Alice, when we leave our compound and head to the boats, you must keep your head down, face covered, and stay to the center of the moving crowd. No one, except for us and Sarah, must know that you are back in the village. Understand?"

"Yes. Of course," Alice said.

"Now, just wait here while we meet with the others in the conference lodge. Aiyanna will come get you when the time is right. Okay?"

She nodded. Luke gave her a kiss on the forehead.

With everyone gathered in the conference lodge, boat assignments were made to distribute the thirteen men and nine women "officially" making this voyage evenly among the six boats, allowing for at least two men per boat to assist at the oars.

"Akecheta, Aiyanna, and I will be in the lead boat," Luke said, "with Laura, Sara, Hans, and Robert bringing up the rear in boat six."

What Luke didn't mention, of course, was that Alice would be in the lead boat along with himself, Aiyanna, and Akecheta, bringing the "unofficial" total count to twenty-three. Sarah's beau, Odakota, and a trusted native friend would be piloting their lead boat. Odakota had already negotiated this position with the other pilots. As lead pilot, he would be the bearer of the magical lodestone.

Finally, Luke repeated the instructions concerning the hooded blankets and crystal pendants. "When we leave this lodge for the boats, I want everyone walking together. No one is to make eye contact with anyone from the village. Especially not the chief and the shaman!" *God forbid someone from the village should recognize Alice!* Looking around the table, he concluded his remarks. "Are there any questions?"

There were no questions.

As the first trumpeting blast from the Day-Keeper's conch shell signaled the first high tide of the day, Akecheta entered the lodge to announce that the boats were ready and loaded with provisions and the native pilots were at their posts. It was time to leave.

IN THE EASTERN VILLAGE, the period preceding the first high tide brought the changing of the guard. The relief guards laughed as they approached the sleeping guards at their posts. The potion had the desired effect, as it took some effort to revive them. One of the replacement guards removed the leather strap from the door post latch and checked inside.

"We don't need to wake her now," he said to his companion as he looked inside at the covered bodily form on the mattress. "Let her sleep."

PERCHED on a nearby veranda overlooking the lagoon that served as the village harbor, Chief Hotah and his shaman looked on as the shoreline became a beehive of activity of lost souls boarding their assigned boats and making final preparations for departure. One figure in particular caught the chief's attention. A young woman, not wearing a crystal pendant. He ordered his attendant to bring her to him.

She approached the veranda with her head lowered.

"Look up at me!" the chief commanded. "And remove your hood and scarf."

The woman hesitated but eventually did as she was told.

The chief leaned forward for a closer look.

"I know you," he said.

"Yes. My name is... Sarah," she said.

The chief's eyes narrowed. "Sarah, why are you not wearing your crystal pendant?"

"I am sorry. But I... uh, I seem to have misplaced it," she answered nervously.

"You mustn't be so careless," he said. He spoke to his attendant. "Give Sarah your pendant."

Sarah took the pendant and placed it around her neck.

"Thank you, Chief," she said with a low bow. "I shall not be so negligent with this one."

The chief smiled. "Good! Now go in peace and rejoin your fellow travelers."

Sarah backed away and quickly returned to the others preparing to embark.

~

THERE WAS a spring to her step as the young woman returned to the others. Sarah's ruse had worked! She knew the chief would be diligently scanning and checking the travelers for any possible trouble. The fact was, she had given her original pendant to Alice, slipping it into her hand as they traveled en masse from their compound to the lagoon harbor. As a distraction, she had deliberately passed close by the chief's position hoping he would notice the missing pendant.

~

WITH EVERYONE now settled in and on board, the chief and shaman made one final tobacco offering, chanting and praying to the spirits and gods for a safe journey. The men then took to their oars and pushed off.

The chief watched as the boats proceeded in a V formation from the lagoon into the broader open sea, with Luke and Aiyanna's number one boat leading the way. Odakota raised his magical lodestone, tethered and suspended on a string, high into the air, allowing it to freely rotate and align itself to magnetic north-south. Pointing westward, he indicated to the others the path they would follow.

The chief breathed a sigh of relief, glad now that they were gone, removing any threat of meddling with their carefully laid plans for a virgin bride sacrifice. He and the shaman exchanged approving nods.

~

IN THE EASTERN VILLAGE, it was first-quarter-tide when one of the guards on duty entered Alice's hut to rouse her for this important day. When she did not respond, the guard approached her straw bed and discovered the ruse. His draw dropped.

"Quickly! Sound the alarm!" he cried out to his companion standing guard outside. "She is gone!"

~

WHEN CHIEF WAKIZA, the village chief, was informed of the missing "bride," he went into a rage.

"Who is responsible for this!" he bellowed. "Bring me the guards on duty!"

The six guards covering the two shifts were brought before the chief and the medicine man, together with the straw mannequin and blanket.

"Whatever happened here," the chief said as he inspected the evidence, "it is obvious the girl did not act alone." His eyes shot daggers at the guards, who by now were on their knees trembling. "She was aided in her escape!"

Chief Wakiza had no patience or tolerance for failure, especially for something of this magnitude. He had the six men draw lots. The two losers were summarily executed, their heads crushed like melons between the chief's own war club and the sacrificial stone altar.

The chief ordered a thorough search of the village and surrounding area while the medicine man invoked the powers of waruka'na in an attempt to ascertain the girl's location.

"I see a young woman wrapped in a blanket, huddled in the bowels of a large fishing boat at sea, far from shore and any familiar landmark," the medicine man related from the depths of his vision. "There are six boats," he continued. "In one, I see the young woman. Accompanying her are two native pilots, and three people not of this world. They travel toward the west over the Great Sea."

The chief took a deep breath and clutched his war club. "I will have my vengeance!" he vowed with a roar.

He immediately assembled a war party—twenty-four of his finest warriors—and set out in hot pursuit. Although Alice and her rescuers had a good half-day's head start, he was certain the speed of his warrior crafts could overtake them. His westward course would take him past the village of Chief Hotah, less than a quarter-tide away. There he learned of the departure of the otherworldly lost souls.

Chief Hotah was gobsmacked and livid. "I trusted them!" he shouted. "I had no idea of their deception and plans to rescue the young woman from your village!"

Skeptical at first, in the end Chief Wakiza had no reason not to believe him.

"Actually," Hotah explained, "the shaman and I *encouraged* them to leave, fearful of their reaction once they learned of the sacrificial fate of one of their own."

Shaman Howahkan provided Wakiza a detailed description of the navigational directions he had provided to cross the western sea and journey through the labyrinth of the Caverns of Antiquity toward the earthly exit portal. Chief Wakiza thanked him and immediately set out with his war party to resume his pursuit, more determined than ever.

CHIEF WAKIZA'S medicine man remained behind in the eastern village. There was one more thing he needed to do, something he resorted to in only the direst of circumstances. Placing himself into a trance, he chanted and danced himself into a frenzy. Calling upon the dark powers and spirits of the Underworld, he summoned the Great Serpent—the Underwater Panther—and its panther minions to seek out the flotilla, destroy her accomplices, and bring back the young woman unharmed.

THE FLOTILLA of lost souls continued on course across the western sea. They had been told it would be a three-day journey, including stops for rest and food. Luke agreed with Akecheta, who had insisted that they make every effort to push on, stopping only when absolutely necessary. He knew all too well they would be pursued immediately once their ruse was uncovered. So it was that they were able to make good progress that first day. One distant shoreline or the other always remained in sight, and Luke was surprised by the number of villages they passed along the way. This Underworld realm was much larger than he had realized.

It was past eventide when they made their first landfall for a much-needed rest stop and meal. The native pilots remained set off and to themselves while the lost souls gathered together around a common campfire. It was only then that the others in their party realized that Alice was among them. They were astonished to learn that her "wedding" was actually a cover for a sacrificial ceremony. Reactions were mixed. Happy that she was saved, many nonetheless protested that they should have been informed beforehand.

"You jeopardized our lives to save your sister!" Ed Hauptmann protested. He was the one who initially expressed concern over knowing the risks before making a decision to go.

"Well, we can't turn back now," said Nancy, the woman from the fifth boat. "We need to push on!"

"Hang together, or surely we'll hang separately," said one of her fellow boatmates. His name was Alex, a former American history professor well acquainted with the perils of open rebellion. Allen, their third boatmate, nodded in agreement.

In the end, they all agreed it was best to push on. Akecheta insisted that they not linger at this site any longer than absolutely necessary, and so after less than two quarter-tides of rest—or about five hours by Luke's wristwatch—they set out again on the open sea.

THE EMBERS of the eventide campfires were still glowing when Chief Wakiza's war party reached the refugees' eventide campsite. The chief smiled, realizing he was closing in on them.

"Quickly!" he shouted to his men, as he climbed back into his reed canoe. "We are not far behind them now!"

IT WAS close to first-quarter-tide of the next day when Akecheta, with the eyes of a hawk, noticed a faint disturbance on the waters of the distant trailing horizon. Ever since they'd left the village, he had remained vigilant for pursuers, knowing full well that the eastern village chief would not rest until they were all found and slain and Alice was recovered. They were both warriors, so he knew how the chief thought. Now, there in the distance, visible only to someone accustomed to viewing such things, he saw the approaching canoes. He whispered to Aiyanna, who perked up and looked astern. She touched Luke lightly on his leg and pointed, so as not to arouse the attention of the native pilots in the bow of their boat.

"We must double our efforts," Aiyanna said softly. "We are being pursued."

Luke turned and looked. "Yes. Well, I think this is the time we start praying—in earnest."

LUKE RECALLED his mother's words: *"I will pray for her and ask our congregation to pray. I think that is all we can really do."* He quietly recited the Lord's Prayer and the twenty-third psalm. It all came back to him from the deeply embedded reserves of childhood memory.

It wasn't long after that when another development occurred, more immediately disturbing and threatening than the first. Echoing across the water, there came a loud, screeching hiss. Luke recognized the sound immediately: the penetrating cry of an underwater panther about to strike!

The waters around one of the trailing boats began to stir as the creature's wavy, serpent tail broke through the surface in multiple locations. Swirling around the boat, the beast created a whirlpool that set the boat spinning. Slowly at first, then with increasing speed and intensity, boat number five, with its five screaming occupants, was sent into a death spiral. With an agonizing crunch, the reed boat began to break up, disintegrating into bits and pieces that mixed with the churning foam of the once placid waters. The two native pilots howled as they were tossed into the water, while the three passengers—two men and a woman—tried frantically to hang on. All at once, the sea swelled as the beast's enormous catlike head, eyes glaring red, breached the surface and rose to thundering heights. Reaching out with its talons, it grabbed the woman, drew her in for closer inspection, then discarded her like a torn rag doll, broken and lifeless. With a bloodcurdling howl, it came crashing down on the remnants of the boat and its hapless victims. Grabbing one of the men between its jaws, it dove below the surface of the sea to the far depths. A moment later it rose up again, reached for the two native pilots, and took them to their watery graves as well. The remaining man, the boat's sole survivor, managed to find refuge among debris that had been thrown clear of the main wreckage. But he had obviously not escaped injury.

Stunned and confused, those in the other boats looked on helplessly while Akecheta and the native pilots each picked up a bamboo harpoon and braced themselves for an attack. There, in the not-too-distant waters, were the protruding tails of several serpents seeming to gather for a coordinated second attack. It was impossible to determine their exact number, but surely the next assault would be overwhelming. The native men began to chant prayers of supplication, tossing offerings of tobacco and other herbs into the waters. Luke and Aiyanna were praying also, to God or whatever spirit would lend an ear.

Suddenly, a mist formed over the water. In less than a minute, the refugee flotilla was enveloped in a dense fog that grew thicker by the second, so much so that those in one boat could not see those in the adjacent boats, even clouding their own to the point of concealing stem from stern. The native pilots began signaling one another using animal sounds so as not to attract the attention of the Great Serpents, striving to maintain their distance from one another while following Odakota's lead. It seemed to work. The sounds of the serpents began to fade.

FROM OUT OF the gray void came a faint and plaintive cry for help as Laura's boat—boat number six—bumped into something with a dull thud. Hans leaned over the side and grabbed a body. It was the man who had been thrown from the destroyed vessel. Hans pulled the man on board and wrapped him in a blanket. He was still alive but obviously in shock, having suffered a serious but nonmortal wound to one leg. Laura recognized the man as Alex, the history professor. Sarah took charge, giving him water and preparing a place on the crowded deck for him to lie down.

~

As they pressed on through the fog, the men found themselves straining at the oars, which had become draped in great wads of seaweed, reducing their progress to a sluggish crawl.

"Freshwater kelp of some kind," a frustrated Luke remarked.

They struggled as best they could through the pernicious sea of grass until finally, almost as quickly as it began, the seaweed lessened its grip, and the path forward became clear and free-moving once again. By now, much to everyone's added relief, the banshee howls of the Great Serpents had faded entirely as the boats continued silent and unimpeded through the cover of dense fog.

By Luke's reckoning, it was late afternoon—or three-quarter-tide—when the fog began to lift. As it did, he noticed something strange. The waters to the far left and right of them had taken on a noticeably blue-green tint of seaweed lying right below the surface, while the water straight ahead was clear and free of kelp. From all appearances, the forward path through this Sargasso-like sea had, somewhat miraculously, been cleared for them! But as he looked behind, the path just traveled slowly closed in again. Luke shared knowing smiles with Aiyanna, Akecheta, and Alice. Even the native pilots smiled and nodded.

"It looks like our prayers have been answered," Luke said softly, for fear of jinxing the blessing.

Aiyanna said what Luke was thinking.

"Like the parting of the Red Sea!"

They all nodded, each one certain that the prayers they had prayed—to their God, gods, or spirits—had done the trick. Luke thought of his mom again, and his boyhood memory of her singing in the choir, "Amazing Grace," her favorite hymn—and his as well.

He asked that they all raise their oars and take a moment to say a prayer for those who were lost: Nancy, Allen, and the two native pilots. The woman, Nancy, he recalled from the previous day's campfire.

"We must honor Nancy's words," he said. "'We can't turn back now. We need to push on!'"

By now the kelp had totally dissipated in an ever-widening sea, and they were far from any shore. They decided it would be best to continue on through the quiet-time, with the men rowing in shifts, one native pilot remaining on duty for each shift to navigate, while the others rested, ate, or slept. Some of the women also took turns at the oars to keep the boats moving. Progress would be slower, but it was better than sitting like dead ducks as they feared the chief's men could appear at any time.

IT WASN'T long after the Great Serpent attack when Chief Wakiza and his warriors came upon the splintered wreckage of that ill-fated craft. He gloated over its destruction and vowed the same for all remaining refugee boats. But as he and his men entered the dense fog, they realized their path would not be as quick and easy as planned. And when they encountered the sea kelp, their progress slowed to a snail's pace. The men's oars became thick with draping seaweed, turning each stroke into a struggle. The cleared path laid out for the refugee travelers had indeed closed up for their pursuers, further reducing their progress. The chief roared his displeasure with clenched fists raised in anger to the gods.

Chapter Sixty-One

DELIVERANCE

The Underworld Realm. Day Twenty-Eight

It was roughly second-quarter-tide of the following day when the lead pilot announced landfall. Aiyanna shielded her eyes for a better look. The approaching shoreline was strewn with jagged rock and gigantic pillars of quartz and limestone, creating narrow channels and treacherous wave action that required careful navigation. Proceeding single file through the channels, the five surviving boats safely made their way to the pebble-strewn shoreline beyond. After beaching their trusty crafts and clambering ashore, the people celebrated their arrival with high fives and body stretches and began unloading what was left of their provisions. Their wounded male companion, Alex, was laid on a blanket and continued to be cared for by Sarah, who was quickly joined by Odakota.

That's when Aiyanna looked up and noticed the still and silent figure of an old man seated high on a rock promontory overlooking their position. He had long, flowing white hair and a pale complexion. A young Native American boy, looking to be about ten years old, was seated by his side.

Soon everyone followed her gaze. Akecheta seemed particularly struck by the old man's appearance and that of his young companion.

The old man whispered something to the boy, who nodded and announced in Hocąk, "You have one among you in need of healing. I will bring him medicine to make him well. You must all rest now, before you begin the next and final leg of your journey."

Aiyanna and Akecheta clearly understood the boy's words. Aiyanna translated into English for the others.

The people were dumbfounded. "Who is this medicine man?" they mumbled to one another. "How and what does he know about our journey?"

The old man climbed down from the rock, guided by the young boy.

Through the boy, the man explained that, like themselves, both he and the boy were from the Earth World, but from a different age. They had been sent to aid the people in their flight from Underworld bondage and human sacrifice to rejoin their own people in their own time.

"Your pursuers have been delayed, but they persist and are but a half-day's journey away," the old man said. "From the village shaman, they know of the path you are to take through the labyrinth of caves to the Earth World portal." The man pointed toward a wide cave entrance in the rock to the right from which a stream flowed into the sea. "That is the path they expect you to take. If you do, they will seek you out and destroy you, if the Great Serpents don't find you first!"

By this time all the people had gathered around the medicine man to hear the words he and the boy spoke. They looked at one another, then to their leaders, Luke, Aiyanna, and Akecheta, for guidance.

Aiyanna addressed the boy. "So, what would your master have us do?"

The boy spoke for the old man.

"There is another path. It is the path that brought the two of us to this place. It is more treacherous, perhaps, than the path you were to follow. But your pursuers will not know of it and will not track you." The old man pointed to a steep trail above him that meandered up the side of the mountain and disappeared over a high crest. "If you take that path, you will continue upward for the better part of this eventide until you reach the mouth of another cave. Entering that cave, you will continue your ascent through cavernous pathways, some narrow, some wide, that interconnect with larger chambers. Knowing which chamber path to follow is the key, as many will terminate in blind ends, or precipitous bottomless pits, crevices from which there is no return. Some chambers harbor beasts of unfathomable terror, minions of the Great Serpent. But if you persevere and follow my lead, you will arrive by day's end in a great chamber—the Chamber of the Earthly Dead—where the 'Song of Death' wails and the dead of your world reside. If you endure the 'Song of Death' and make it beyond, you will reach the final exit portal you seek."

He paused before concluding, "Darkness largely prevails in this realm, so you will need a torch to light your way. For myself"—the old man laughed—"I have no such need. Like the bat, my ears can *hear* the way, and the boy serves as my eyes."

There was silence as the people considered his words. The outspoken Ed Hauptmann was the first to respond.

"Delightful! So, we are to follow Batman here into the Batcave with his boy Robin! How do we know he is telling the truth? It could be a ruse!"

"Perhaps he is really the evil shaman is disguise!" said another.

Akecheta appeared to sense the turmoil as he took Aiyanna aside.

"Aiyanna, I know of this man through Ho-Chunk legend. A great storyteller of my clan once told us of the blind elder accompanied by a young boy who exorcised the 'Song of Death' from the Eagle Cave. He is a great healer, a wise man who speaks the truth! He speaks neither Hocąk nor the ancient native dialect of this Underworld realm, and therefore requires the interpretive assistance of his young companion."

Aiyanna relayed his words to the others.

Following a short span of silence, Luke stood, assuming an authoritative stance. "Okay. Those who wish to follow the old path, you are free to do so." He took the pages from his notebook containing the detailed instructions and held them up for all to see. "For anyone wishing to travel that path, here are the directions. You are free to take them. But for myself—and I think I speak for Aiyanna and Akecheta as well—I will follow this man's advice and take the new path."

Finally, after some grumbling, everyone fell in line.

"But only if the old man leads us there himself!" Ed Hauptmann boldly demanded.

Aiyanna spoke to the boy. After a brief exchange with the medicine man, he replied. Aiyanna smiled and turned to Ed.

"It was always his intention to do so," she said.

Further assurance was provided when Alex, having been treated by the medicine man, showed immediate signs of improvement, such that by eventide he was up and about almost as if nothing had happened.

As they shared their eventide meal, Aiyanna took the old man and the boy aside and quizzed them further.

"When you spoke of the 'great chamber' and reaching the portal, what did you mean when you said, 'if you make it past'?"

"The 'Song of Death' can steal the mind," the old man said. "But you need only focus your thoughts to keep from going mad."

"I see" was all she said.

The old man sensed her concern and smiled. "But you needn't worry. I will take the 'Song of Death' and, if necessary, carry it with me into my own time so it will bring no harm to you and your people."

Perhaps earplugs would also be in order, she thought as she devised a backup strategy.

THAT EVENTIDE, after a good rest and full bellies, the people prepared themselves for departure. They didn't want to risk any further delays, and the caverns would be no brighter were they to wait till the next day. Odakota teamed up with Akecheta in preparing as many bamboo torches as they could fashion, cannibalizing one of the boats for its reed, bamboo, and flammable tar material. Looking about, Odakota saw Luke distributing what he learned were "glow sticks" from his backpack to the team, gesticulating instructions for their proper use. Aiyanna, meanwhile, set about making earplugs fashioned from wax and cotton balls from her first aid kit. When she ran out of cotton balls, she resorted to the insulation from her hunting vest.

Bidding farewell to their faithful boat pilots, the refugee band headed single file up the winding mountain trail with the medicine man and boy leading the way. The men took what harpoons they could carry, although their ability to wield them effectively in the close confines of cavern space was limited. One of the last to leave, Odakota turned to his trusted pilot friend and exchanged some parting words, then handed him the magical lodestone before joining Sarah and Akecheta, the last to leave.

"What did you tell him?" Sarah asked.

"To tell my parents and our pursuers that I died a warrior's death at sea, falling victim to the Underwater Panther."

The mountain ascent proceeded without incident. Even Alex, the injured history professor, was able to negotiate the path with some help from Odakota and Sarah. In about four hours' time the advance party reached a level clearing at the mouth of the cave and waited for the others to catch up. Once the group assembled, the medicine man instructed them to enter the cave and continue on to the first open chamber, where they would reassemble and wait for further instructions. Luke and Aiyanna led the way, with the others following in quick succession.

～

As the others made their way into the cave, Akecheta stood on a rocky ledge to enjoy a final view of the Great Sea and Underworld realm through which they had journeyed. It was a spectacular vista, stretching as far as the eye could see: jagged marble and granite cliffs rising up on all sides of a vast sea, their faces adorned with silver braided streams of cascading waterfalls. It was at once rugged and beautifully majestic. Subdued lighting from the quartz-studded sky dome evinced a surreal and mystical quality unlike anything that existed in his native Earth World realm.

A final glance at the sea revealed a distant smudge on the water: a small flotilla of boats heading in their direction. As expected, Chief Wakiza and his warriors had finally managed to penetrate the kelp forest in their relentless pursuit. But hopefully, the medicine man's ruse and their change of course would succeed in throwing their pursuers off track.

～

Gathering in the first chamber, the ragged band paused to rest and plan their next moves, which promised to be more arduous and perilous than anything they had encountered so far. Luke took the eighty-foot length of climbing rope from his knapsack and strung it out like a charm bracelet to keep everyone connected and on the same path, trying to maintain a four-foot spacing between each person.

Initially, the caverns reminded Luke of his first day's encounter with this Underworld realm, with quartz crystals lighting the way. But here there was no stream, only an occasional thin coating of water trickling down over the rocks. He realized they would have to rely on the water they'd brought with them in snake-leather pouches to stay hydrated. Continuing on, the path turned increasingly rugged, narrow, and steep, cloaked in damp darkness. At each chamber stop, they gathered to await the medicine man's next set of instructions. They now had to rely on the glow sticks and torches to light their way. Luke soon lost track of the number of chamber stops and even began to question the wisdom of the medicine man. Luke checked his watch. Over six hours had passed since they first entered the cave.

Upon entering the next chamber—by far the largest one encountered up till now—the medicine man announced they were nearing the end of their journey. Beyond this place, he said, they would face but one more challenge: the "Song of Death" and the great Chamber of the Earthly Dead.

Suddenly, from out of the darkness came a familiar but disquieting sound signaling a more immediate and pressing danger.

"I sure don't like the sound of that!" Ed said, nervously pacing with glow stick in hand.

"Underwater panthers," Luke whispered.

Within this warren of interconnecting chambers and echoing rock formations, it was impossible to tell from which direction—or directions—the beasts were coming. Like screaming banshees, the wail of the panthers grew louder—and closer!

Two dark lateral passageways led off from the main chamber, from which the sounds now seemed to emanate. Focusing on the passage to the right, Luke froze in his tracks. Two glowing red dots glared back at him.

"There!" he cried. "In the darkness."

Before the others could respond, a dark form crept from the shadows and slithered up the chamber wall. Akecheta stretched out his torch to throw more light on the subject. High overhead the creature crawled across the craggy ceiling surface, its red eyes aglow, stealthily navigating a forest of stalactites until it came directly over Alice's position. Like a spring trap, its front talons reached down and snatched up the young woman with a shriek. At the same time, a second creature pounced unseen from the dark passage on the left and quickly had Sarah in its clutches.

"Alice, no!" Luke shouted.

Seemingly content with their two prize catches, the beasts bolted for the exits. But there they were met with the snarling growls of three angry wolves who had suddenly appeared out of nowhere, blocking their way! The White and Green Wolves confronted Alice's captor, while the Black Wolf faced off with Sarah's beast. The panthers let out bloodcurdling shrieks as they confronted their adversaries. This gave Akecheta, Odakota, and Luke enough time to organize their own counterattacks from behind.

Luke took a flare from his knapsack, attached it to the end of a harpoon, and lit it. Rushing forward, he thrust the flame into the first creature's face, aiming for the eyes, as the two wolves pounced on the beast, going for its throat. The beast let out a shrill, agonizing cry as the flare found its mark. A skewered flaming eye remained on the spearhead as Luke withdrew the harpoon from a now empty, oozing red socket. To Luke, the wolves appeared to loom much larger and fiercer than he had remembered. Perhaps it was an illusion resulting from the close confines of this space. Or perhaps the spirit wolves assumed whatever proportions were necessary to accomplish a given task.

At the same time, Akecheta and Odakota attacked the other, smaller beast with their harpoons from behind while the Black Wolf made a frontal assault. In the course of battle, the creatures were forced to release the young women to bring both sets of claws to bear on their attackers. Alice and Sarah scrambled for safety, taking temporary refuge in a rock cleft on the far side of the chamber, where they huddled, shuddering in terror. Suddenly, with a powerful sweep of its serpent tail, the second beast sent Odakota flying against the chamber wall, knocking him unconscious—or worse. Akecheta continued the fight as he mounted the back of the beast, wielding his obsidian dagger with trained precision and effectiveness.

Laura was huddled with the others on the far side of the chamber, safe for the moment. Looking up, she saw Aiyanna conferring with the medicine man. Through his boy interpreter he directed her to a small cleft in the wall. She nodded, then quickly joined Laura and the others.

"What did he say?" Laura asked.

"He said we must take that passage," she said, pointing. "It will lead us to the final great chamber. The Chamber of the Earthly Dead. There we will be safe from the panthers and need only endure the 'Song of Death' but for a short time."

Aiyanna took a pair of earplugs from a waist pouch and stuffed them in her ears.

"But just in case," she continued, handing Laura the pouch, "take these and distribute them to the others. Go quickly now! And wait for us on the other side."

"What about you?" Laura asked.

Aiyanna looked over her shoulder. "I must save the girls." Turning back to Laura, she said, "Now go! Before it's too late!"

Laura did as instructed. One by one, she handed out the earplugs and directed the band of lost souls into the tunnel. Laura took a deep breath as she was the last to go. It was a tight squeeze as she scrambled on her hands and knees through the dark, narrow passage. Even the earplugs could not completely deaden the sound that greeted her. It was the sound of wailing and great lamentation. The "Song of Death"!

The seemingly endless passage terminated at last as Laura tumbled onto the floor of a dank, dark open space. Rising to her feet, she drew a glow stick from her knapsack and lit it. Greeting her were the astonished faces of the other lost souls, bathed in the green, ghoulish artificial light of the glow stick. They instinctively joined her in a great communal hug as she broke open more glow sticks. What they saw took their breath away.

Back in the main chamber, the two men were nearing total exhaustion as their face-off with the underwater panthers continued. The first panther, the stronger of the two, tossed Luke and the two wolves aside as it appeared to spy Alice crouched against the wall. It went for her!

Suddenly, from out of the shadows sprang Aiyanna. Brandishing a harpoon in one hand and a buck knife in the other, she interposed herself between the beast and Alice. With a warrior's cry, she lunged at the beast, catching it off-balance. The startled panther stumbled and fell back and was immediately set upon by the two wolves that had regained their footing.

At this point, the medicine man raised his arms and began singing the "Song of Death," stealing its refrain from the adjoining chamber, where the main party was now safe and secure. The two panthers simultaneously stopped and abruptly turned. The "Song of Death" rose in pitch and intensity as it resonated within the beasts and the close confines of the chamber. The panthers howled in distress. The lesser panther fled screaming toward an exit passage and disappeared into the darkness to escape the song's powerful grip. The stronger panther, however, crawled slowly and determinedly toward the medicine man, all the while shrieking and hissing in pain. But the song's intensity only increased the closer it came. Akecheta, Luke, and Aiyanna cupped their ears to deaden the sound. Odakota continued to lie motionless. With a rising crescendo and final burst of the song, the beast rose to its full height, let out an agonizing screech, and exploded into a million fragments of dust and bone, absorbing the full fury of the "Song of Death."

The force of the blast brought down a shower of rock and dust upon the men. But the "Song of Death" and the underwater panthers were no more. Drowsy and worn, but with only minor injuries, Akecheta and Luke slowly rose to their feet, helped up by Aiyanna.

"My, you are quite the warrior," Luke said.

"I couldn't let you guys have *all* the fun," she said with a smirk.

Alice and Sarah, still trembling, emerged from the shadows and ran to join them. Then, spying the motionless and seemingly lifeless body of Odakota, Sarah cried out and rushed to his side. The others joined her as they tried to revive the young warrior, but to no avail.

"Please, step aside!" the young boy commanded. Startled, they looked up to see the medicine man and his boy standing over them. They had no choice but to obey.

The medicine man knelt down beside the young warrior and began to pray. Taking herbs and earth medicines from a pouch, he laid them on the young man's chest and continued chanting. Suddenly, there was a great gasp and a jerky movement as Odakota showed signs of life. Shakily, he regained consciousness and opened his eyes, looking up.

"Sarah!" he said in a faint whisper.

She erupted in tears of joy. "I thought I lost you!" she cried.

A tearful Luke clung to his sister and Aiyanna. "I'm beginning to grow weary of this place," he said with understated resignation. "I think it's time we leave and join the others."

Aiyanna grinned, then backed away and pointed. "Follow me! I know the way."

When Aiyanna emerged from the tunnel into the green glow of the final great chamber, she was greeted with cheers and a warm hug from Laura. Looking up, she was astounded at what she saw.

Unlike the other chambers they had passed through, which were raw and natural, this space had obviously been fashioned by human hands to serve as a communal burial chamber. With a high vaulted ceiling, its walls were pockmarked with recessed niches hewn into the rock containing the relics, skulls, and bone fragments of countless human remains. At the far end of the room was a huge stone throne carved into the wall. Lying before it facedown in a large semicircle, as if worshipping the throne, were hundreds of whole human skeletal remains.

One by one, Luke and the remaining travelers emerged from the passage to join the others. The medicine man and the boy were the last to come through. Taking a few minutes to gather their thoughts, they continued to study their surroundings. Aiyanna noted that although the "Song of Death" had been transferred to the underwater panther, the room remained acoustically active, resonating sonorous and deep with every spoken word. It appeared to have been designed that way. "To send messages into the afterlife," the medicine man explained.

Alex, the history professor, was especially impressed. "This place is amazing!" he said. Addressing Aiyanna directly, he continued to expound.

"It reminds me of the Hypogeum of Saflieni in Malta. A Neolithic subterranean burial vault specially constructed to resonate at certain baritone frequencies. 'Super-Acoustics,' they call it. Used by ancients to alter the consciousness. I'd like to come back here someday, under more favorable circumstances of course, to study this place further."

But, of course, based on what the medicine man had told them about "one-way portals," Aiyanna figured that would not likely be possible.

Akecheta turned to Luke and spoke in broken English, words he had managed to acquire over the past four weeks. "You are good man, Luke. True warrior." He paused a moment, then held out a flute he'd taken from his war bundle. "Please, take gift to remember me," he said. "And take good care of Aiyanna!" he added with a smile and an approving nod toward Aiyanna.

Luke took the flute and gave the Bear clan warrior a firm hug. "Thank you, my friend. I will never forget you and all you have done for us."

Akecheta then turned to Aiyanna and embraced her. Speaking in Hocąk, he said, "I will see you in your dreams, young Aiyanna, warrior princess. Always remember. Listen to your heart!"

Aiyanna wiped the tears from her eyes. "You make me proud, Great-Uncle, to be a Ho-Chunk and a Bear clansman!"

Luke then turned to Ed Hauptmann, who was standing nearby. "Ed, can you please hold out your hands for me?"

Ed obliged.

"I see you're not wearing your wedding ring," Luke said.

Ed gave a twisted smile. "Yes. I lost it when I first came through the portal, however long ago that was. I lost track."

"That was ten years ago, Ed," Luke said. "Listen, when we get to the other side, back in our world, there is something I need to share with you about your family. And I would rather it come from me and not the news media."

Ed nodded. "Sure, Luke."

The medicine man then spoke and made an announcement through his young companion, with Aiyanna translating. "It is now time for you to go," he said. "Each of you must return to your own time and place in the Creator's Earth World. I will show you the way."

The medicine man led them to a far corner of the chamber and removed a rock that had concealed a small opening in the wall.

"Follow this narrow tunnel on your belly. It is the portal that will take you to your world. Once you exit, there is no turning back. There you will find yourself in a larger space where you may stand and walk. Continue down this passage, and it will lead you to the mouth of a cave that opens to the light of day of your world."

The people lined up, now eager to go. Hans and Pierre were the first in line.

"*Auf wiedersehen, meine guten freunde!*" Hans said as he entered the tunnel.

He was followed by Pierre. "*Au revoir, mes amis! Bonne chance!*"

The others followed, with Luke and Akecheta the last to go.

BORN AGAIN! That's how Luke felt when he emerged from the mouth of the cave and stepped into the twenty-first century and the natural light of his world.

Just minutes before, he had crawled through the narrow portal and onto the cave floor. Looking back, he was surprised to see that the opening, like a self-sealing one-way door, had closed and ceased to exist, just as the medicine man predicted.

"Amazing!" he whispered.

Ahead of him he heard the crunch of fading footsteps of the others who had preceded him through the portal. When he reached the mouth of the cave, Aiyanna and the other twenty-first-century survivors were there to greet him. Counting Luke and Aiyanna, they numbered eighteen in all. The eyes of many—notably Laura, Alice, and Sarah—remained fixed on the cloudless cerulean sky above. Luke looked up. Indeed, it was a glorious color he had almost forgotten existed.

But there was one additional non-modern-day survivor among them, bringing their total number to nineteen: a young man from another world whose love for a certain young woman defied, perhaps, the very laws of nature and the preternatural. Odakota and Sarah, united in love eternal! They had squeezed through the portal together, embracing one another and never losing touch or hope as they emerged intact, tumbling like newborns onto the floor of the cave. Perhaps that was the key. A melding of body and soul. To Luke, it seemed an anomaly but one he was forced to accept and even willing to ascribe to the miraculous. Either that, or perhaps it was thanks to the combined action of their crystal necklaces.

"So where are we?" Luke wondered aloud.

From where they stood atop the high bluffs overlooking a bend in a great river, the scene before them was both idyllic and mystifying. Hiking along the bluffs, they came to where another smaller river joined the first. A town appeared below them where the rivers joined. Descending the bluffs, they approached the town and its inhabitants. A signpost read WELCOME TO GOTHAM!

The ragtag refugee band soon attracted the attention of the local citizens. Luke approached an older woman getting out of her car.

"Excuse me, ma'am. Can you please tell me what day this is?"

The woman stepped back with a start and looked him over. "Why, it's Thursday, the twenty-fourth of September."

"Thank you, ma'am." He paused. "And the year? What year is it?"

She laughed. "Why, it's 2015!" She drew closer, squinting in bewilderment. "Listen, young man. Are you okay? You all look so... interesting, 'n so."

Chapter Sixty-Two

A BRAND-NEW DAY

Thursday, September 24, 2015

Detective Dan Meyers was jubilant. Cruising along Route 14 out of Madison toward Gotham with red lights flashing, he was bent on a mission. His only thoughts were of Luke, Alice, and Aiyanna. *I can't believe it! They're alive! And the others too.* Yes, those many others who had gone missing these past seventeen years. Those *lost souls*, as Luke had referred to them in his text message. Laura Emery as well. Dan had to chuckle at the very thought of it. Old man Emery would be vindicated after all.

Earlier that morning in the Sheboygan County Sheriff's Office, Dan was on his third cup of coffee when he received a text message from Luke. He figured it was a prank. Someone had stolen Luke's phone. But then came the live phone call from Inspector Clive Morgan of the Gotham Police Department. This was no prank. It was the real deal. The whole world had somehow turned upside down. *Alice through the looking glass!*

After the call, he turned to his deputy and shouted out, "They're alive, Sam! Can you believe it?"

Sam looked befuddled. "Who's alive, Dan?"

Dan laughed. "Luke! Aiyanna! Alice! The whole lot of them!"

Sam's jaw dropped. He was speechless.

Dan clapped him on the back. "C'mon, partner. We've got some rescue work to do!"

It took time to absorb the full impact of the news, but when Dan eventually announced it through the office intercom, there were rounds of cheers and applause throughout the complex. It suddenly became real.

When Dan said he was leaving for Gotham, Sam asked if he could go along.

Dan paused. "No, this is something I need to do alone," he said, laying a reassuring hand on Sam's shoulder. "What I need you to do, Sam, is stay here and arrange bus transport for the others. Okay?"

Sam nodded.

When Dan pulled up to the Gotham Police Station, reporters were already gathered outside. "How the hell did they find out?" Dan grumbled under his breath. Inspector Morgan met him at the door and apologized for the reception.

"Not a problem, Clive. Tell me, how are they?"

Clive chuckled. "Remarkably well, considering what they've been through. Here, see for yourself."

He led Dan into a conference room where all the lost souls were gathered. Dan's face lit up when he spied Luke and Aiyanna.

"Hey, Sport! You certainly gave us a scare, dontcha know!" he said, deliberately underplaying their encounter.

Luke grinned as the two approached each other. Dan gave him a firm hug and, choking up, whispered in his ear, "Sorry, Luke, for doubting you." For the first time in a long time he felt like crying. He then backed off and approached Aiyanna with head bowed. "Please accept my apologies, Aiyanna."

Pausing, she smiled and gave him a hug. "Oh, what the hell! Let bygones be bygones!"

Luke turned and introduced Dan to Alice. Dan took Alice's hand and smiled. "My, you certainly are the spitting image of your mother, young lady. And she is going to be *so* happy to see you."

Dan set about the mundane task of documenting the people who had been brought back. He explained they would be transported back to Sheboygan for further processing, including a medical exam and making arrangements for reuniting with families and loved ones. When it came

Laura's turn, Dan gave a twisted smile. "Welcome back, Laura. Looks like I owe Jake an apology as well."

With all the initial paperwork completed, Luke, Aiyanna, and Alice accompanied Dan to his police cruiser while the others waited for Sam's bus to take them back.

"We've got one stop to make before heading back to the office," Dan said.

CYNTHIA'S HEART was beating faster than normal today. Ever since she got the call from Dan Meyers this morning, she could barely contain herself. Pacing from one end of the house to the other, she tried to occupy herself by straightening things up, if only to make the time pass.

It was close to four in the afternoon when the sheriff's cruiser pulled into the driveway. Cynthia was standing on the back deck, wringing her hands in anticipation. Her knees nearly buckled when she caught the first glimpse of Luke getting out of the car. Then Aiyanna. And finally— could it be? She cupped her hands over her mouth and gasped at the first sight of Alice. Her little angel! Returning from the dead. But how could it be? She had prayed. Her entire congregation had prayed ever since Luke went missing. It would take a miracle, she thought. And now her prayers had been answered.

"Mama! Mama!" Alice cried out as she ran to her mother. Sobbing uncontrollably, Cynthia embraced her long-lost daughter. Alice was sobbing too. Then Cynthia backed away and held Alice at arm's length.

"Oh, my! How you have grown!" was all she could say.

Yet for Cynthia, this was a bittersweet moment, overcome by pangs of remorse and melancholy, thinking about those lost years that she would never get back. School years, senior prom, high school graduation. All lost. But then she thought about the future. Alice appeared well and strong. And beautiful. There were still plenty of happy memories to be had. A future wedding, perhaps. Future grandchildren. Yes! She cherished the thought.

"Mama! Luke and Aiyanna saved me, you know," Alice said, turning to her brother and her newfound friend. "They came to my rescue. I owe them my life!"

Cynthia turned to Luke and Aiyanna and embraced them together, kissing them each on the cheek and holding them tight.

"Oh, what you must have gone through," she said. "I don't think I ever want to know."

She turned to Dan. "Thank you, Detective. You have been a good friend to Luke and Aiyanna. Thank you so much."

Dan smiled sheepishly and nodded.

"You have a wonderful son, ma'am," he said. "And Aiyanna is... well, a staunch and true friend. And from what Luke was telling me, quite the warrior!"

Luke and Aiyanna smiled.

"Well, Dan, please do come inside once," Cynthia pleaded. "I've prepared some bars and lemonade and—"

Dan's tip of the hat interrupted her. "Thank you, ma'am, but I do need to be getting back." Pausing, he smacked his lips. "Oh, I almost forgot. There is one more thing."

Reaching into his pants pocket he produced a small plastic specimen bag and handed it to Cynthia.

"I thought you might want to add this to your artifacts collection."

She opened the pouch and unwrapped its contents.

"Why, this is a splendid specimen!" she said teary-eyed as she removed and studied the arrowhead. "Where did you get it?"

Dan glanced at Luke, then Alice. "Hmm. Let's just say, from sacred grounds."

Cynthia smiled. "Thank you, Dan. I shall cherish it always."

Dan smiled and turned to Luke and Aiyanna. "Listen, you two. Enjoy your reunion. I'll drop back in the morning to pick you up. We've still got your vehicles, remember?" he said with a chuckle. "And there's the formal debriefing and medical evaluation. You understand."

"Thanks, Dan," Luke said. "We appreciate it."

"You got it, Luke," Dan said as he backed away. He was whistling a little tune as he returned to his cruiser.

"That's a familiar tune," Cynthia remarked. "Isn't it from *Oklahoma!?*"

Luke grinned. "Yes. I think you're right, Mom."

EPILOGUE

For Luke and others directly affected by recent events, life eventually resumed a level of normalcy. Like a large rock tossed into a fast-moving stream, the immediate perturbations were severe, but the ripple effects soon faded and were lost entirely in the swirling currents of time, eventually becoming indistinguishable to a downstream observer. So it was that rational thought would take over, slowly transforming the memory of what happened into a simple fantasy absorbed by the humdrum and pressing exigencies of daily living.

But not all was forgotten. Luke's sister, Alice, went on tour promoting her book, *My Life Beneath the Maize*. The book received mixed reviews, as confusion and controversy continued to reign over what really happened. When Luke and Aiyanna and others tried to retrace their steps for the authorities, each one came up with a different location for the mouth of the cave from which they emerged. Those caves that did lead to extended passageways failed to give any evidence of a "portal" as described by the survivors, which didn't surprise Luke.

Each recovered missing person had their own story to tell, which over time mostly faded into the realm of family fable. Many had trouble coping with the immediate notoriety and the reassimilation into modern society and long-lost family relationships, exhibiting symptoms of PTSD.

One even attempted to take her own life, saying she now wished she had remained behind, as "it wasn't such a bad situation, being cared for and living underground."

But young Sarah and Odakota—who became "Odie" to his friends—adapted amazingly well, thanks to the support they received from Luke and Aiyanna and her family. In time, the Black Bears, Larry and Rachel, legally adopted Odie and accepted him into the Ho-Chunk tribe.

Of course, the tabloids and "ancient alien" theorists pounced on the story as proof positive of alien abductions and that alien life forms were ultimately responsible for driving the course of human history. Tabloids were plastered with headlines like "The Pied Piper of Plymouth Brings Back the Lost Children of Atlantis!" The History Channel even approached Luke about doing a series to rival *The Curse of Oak Island*, but ultimately settled on a single episode of *The UnXplained* hosted by William Shatner. The Ho-Chunk and other Indigenous peoples, on the other hand, largely shrugged it off and accepted Luke and Aiyanna's account of events at face value, having grown accustomed to the role of "alien" or "the other" in broader American culture.

But in the balance, life was good for the principal surviving heroes. The events cemented lifelong friendships with Dan and Sam, with Dan becoming best man at Luke and Aiyanna's wedding one year to the day following her disappearance. Sam was also a member of the wedding party. Aiyanna's sister, Adrianna, was maid of honor, with Alice and Sarah serving as bridesmaids. To accommodate all sides, they settled on two wedding ceremonies: a traditional Christian church wedding in Elkhart Lake and a Ho-Chunk ceremony in Black River Falls. The Ho-Chunk Casino in Madison closed down for a day to host the wedding reception. Alice caught the wedding bouquet, and Sam the garter. So it came as no surprise to many when they tied the knot four years later.

Besides saving Alice, one of the more satisfying outcomes in Luke's estimation was the joyful reunion between Jake Emery and his first wife, Laura, missing for seventeen years. They had a lot to catch up on. And their two surviving sons, Scott and Seth, were over the moon at having their mom back. They didn't try to understand it, but they did learn the particulars that sent her into the Underworld realm. Laura reported that after returning from her yoga class that fateful Saturday afternoon in

September of 1998, she decided to head up to Elkhart Lake to visit her sister. On a whim, she pulled off the side of the road by a cornfield to have a smoke and snag some ears of corn, just ahead of an approaching thunderstorm. The rest was history. The way Sam figured it, Laura was likely the first person to experience the life-altering effects of what Aiyanna had dubbed the symbiotic bioelectrical terrestrial event phenomenon not long after the first Santoma GMO corn was introduced to the area's farmers in the mid-1990s.

Luke and Jake had shared a special bond since their first emotional encounter that July day in 2015. Jake became "Uncle Jake" to Luke and Aiyanna, and he and Laura enjoyed special seats as guests of honor at their wedding reception, with Scott, Seth, and Adam's widow, Milly, also in attendance.

And what about Dr. Nathaniel Greene? It turns out that Nate was forced to resign his post at the university for nondisclosure of his business ties with the giant conglomerate and for receiving personal kickbacks from government grant money. "What goes around comes around," Dan Meyers was heard to say.

But a hidden silver lining did border that ugly cloud as Aiyanna, in collaboration with the Santoma Corporation, continued to investigate this symbiotic GMO-corn–giant mushroom phenomenon. While the research remained proprietary and the results were never published, Aiyanna's team proved successful in further modifying the corn's genetics to block this symbiotic relationship, effectively sealing that "unholy portal" into the Ho-Chunk Underworld for all time. It was not surprising, then, that after a year or two, the area's mini crop circle phenomenon mysteriously ceased, along with a significant decline in missing persons cases, a fact that did not go unnoticed or unappreciated by Dan and Sam and other local law enforcement officials.

Within a year of their marriage, Luke and Aiyanna purchased a five-acre country estate in the rolling hills country south of Wisconsin Dells, a place that harbored fond memories for the two of them. Aiyanna continued her research into the giant mushroom phenomenon and gained notoriety as a subject matter expert, publishing numerous articles and achieving tenure as a senior fellow and, eventually, full professor at the University of Wisconsin.

Luke, meanwhile, became a successful freelance writer working mainly out of their new home. The popular "Pied Piper" moniker stuck, and he eventually adopted it as something of a nom de plume. "I'm not proud," he was known to say. "When you can't beat 'em, join 'em!" Although he did drop the "Plymouth" reference, noting that while he appreciated the literary alliteration, he was not actually from the town of Plymouth.

For recreation, Luke and Aiyanna turned to mountain climbing and spelunking, exploring the heights and depths of nature's geological landscapes. They harbored secret hopes of one day locating the natural portal into the Underworld realm through which Aiyanna's Bear clan ancestor, Akecheta, stumbled so many years earlier in his rendezvous with interlocking destinies. Was it a fluke of nature? Preordained? Luke and Aiyanna spent countless enjoyable hours debating that point with her father and Uncle Lobo.

To ease the pain and help combat the effects of PTSD, Luke and Aiyanna established an online support group for the Underworld survivors. Once a year in late August they would host a cookout billed as "A Reunion of Lost Souls" for survivors and their families. And what was served at these annual events? Bratwurst, German potato salad, smoked brisket of bison, roasted butternut squash, and of course, fresh corn on the cob!

In time, membership in the support group expanded to include the families of those missing persons whose remains were eventually located and recovered with the help of Sam's unprecedented hybrid forensic computer model, for which both he and Dan received critical acclaim throughout the law enforcement community. "Truly, a *groundbreaking* development in forensics," a noted investigator was quoted as saying.

But even Dan had to admit that the entire experience was nothing short of a miracle. He summed it up best when he raised his glass to toast the new bride and groom in the grand ballroom of the Madison Casino on August 20, 2016: "A modern-day legend born of desperation and love."

THE END

AUTHOR'S NOTES

Fact or fiction? Do "giant mushrooms" actually exist? Amazingly, the answer is a qualified yes! As Anne Casselman puts forth in her article, "Strange but True: The Largest Organism on Earth Is a Fungus," the mycelium of certain varieties of mushrooms in the *Armillaria* genus—also called "honey mushrooms"—have been known to extend for miles over vast expanses of terrain. She notes that the first massive fungus, *A. bulbosa* or *gallica*, discovered in 1992 near the town of Crystal Falls, Michigan, was documented to cover 37 acres. Soon after, a specimen of *A. ostoyae* was discovered in Washington State covering 1,500 acres, or 2.5 square miles. But the prize for size goes to the 2003 discovery of a 2,392-acre *A. ostoyae* behemoth in Oregon! The king of mushrooms! Not only the largest living organism in the world, but likely the oldest as well. Of course, the Wisconsin variety that takes center stage in my story exceeds them all. Alas, it is but fiction. But who knows, perhaps it really does exist and only waits to be discovered!

Turning to GMO corn: Is "genetically modified organism" (GMO) technology as applied to farming—and more specifically commercial corn farming—a good thing or a bad thing? Well, it all depends on who you ask. Battle lines were drawn almost as soon as GMO agriculture was introduced in the mid-1990s. Based on an analysis of 6,000 studies reported by Dana Dovey in *Newsweek Online* (posted February 22, 2018), scientific consensus generally supports the judicious use of GMO technology for commercial corn production. However, many environmentalists continue their opposition, citing the threat of increased allergic reactions and the risk of inadvertent transfer of modified genes from one plant species to another—something called *gene flow*. I remain noncommittal in my treatment of the subject. Rather, I employ it as a convenient jumping-off point and rationale for my invented symbiotic relationship between GMO corn and giant mushrooms resulting in the creation of those "unholy portals" into the Underworld for poor "lost souls" unfortunate enough to wonder into the wrong cornfield at the wrong time.

So, why Wisconsin? Well, it might have something to do with the fact that my wife, Janet, hails from the Badger State—Sheboygan County to be precise. We were married in a small country church not far from the farming community of Howards Grove where she grew up—her first home, and what would become a second home away from home. Like the folks in my story, Janet and her family are direct descendants of the first wave of German immigrants to the region in the 1840s. So, as we made repeated trips over the years from the East Coast back to her homeland with our two growing sons, my fondness for cheeseheads, brats, and dairy farms only grew. When I wasn't rooting for the Eagles, I was pulling for the Packers!

Historical accounts of Sheboygan County were drawn principally from Gustave W. Buchen's *Historic Sheboygan County*. The quoted reference in chapter 22 ("Sons and Daughters of German Immigrants") to the "beer drinking, dancing, card playing, and Sunday amusements" customs of the first German immigrants to this region are taken directly from Buchen (p. 235). Likewise are the descriptions of the history and pristine beauty of Elkhart Lake, which I have had the pleasure of visiting numerous times over the years. The lake was initially surveyed by the government in 1835 by Nehemiah King, who dubbed it "Great Elkhart Lake." Located in the remote and largely inaccessible "northern Wisconsin" wilderness of early days, the lake remained a hidden treasure, visited only by the most venturesome by horseback or horse-drawn wagon. With the coming of the railroads, the lake quickly grew in popularity as a favorite vacation spot, with folks coming from as far away as Milwaukee, Chicago, and Saint Louis.

As my fondness for this beating dairy heartland of American grew, my admiration for the people most attached to the land—its Indigenous population—also blossomed into a deep respect for their culture and traditions. Reading the works of Paul Radin (*The Winnebago Tribe*) and David Lee Smith (*Folklore of the Winnebago Tribe*) and other online sources, my fascination and respect for the history, folklore, and oral traditions of the Wisconsin Winnebago (Ho-Chunk) and other woodland tribes of this region only deepened.

Winnebago, or "People of the Bad Waters," was the name given to these people by the Algonquin tribes that also settled this area and refers to the sometimes foul-smelling marshlands of the regions they settled. In 1994 the Wisconsin Winnebago drafted a new constitution, replacing the previous one established in 1963. Structured after the federal and state governments, the new constitution formally restored the tribe's traditional name, *Ho-Chunk Nation*, variously translated as "People of the Big Voice" or "Sacred Language." When French explorer Jean Nicolet landed at the Red Banks on the northern shores of Green Bay in 1634, he was reportedly greeted and entertained by upward of 5,000 Ho-Chunk warriors. Nicolet was the first European to make direct contact with Native peoples of Wisconsin. Historians estimate the total Ho-Chunk population at that time to be upward of 20,000.

My story might be considered a modern-day folktale. Drawing on the myths and legends of the Ho-Chunk, I have attempted to weave a tale that combines the myriad threads of ancient Native American culture with today's world while striving to maintain the highest degree of respect and regard for their origins and authenticity. I apologize if I failed in any way to do so or offended anyone in any manner of speaking.

One area deserves special attention: human sacrifice. While an essential element in the final chapters of the story, I am not suggesting that "human sacrifice" is in any way a part of Ho-Chunk culture, past or present. On the contrary, the story's Ho-Chunk protagonists (Akecheta and Aiyanna) express outrage at this practice and do everything in their power to prevent it. However, archeological evidence does support the existence of such practices among the pre-Columbian Cahokia culture of the central Mississippi River valley, as described by anthropologist Timothy R. Pauketat (*Cahokia: Ancient America's Great City on the Mississippi*). Andrew O'Hehir further writes ("The Sacrificial Virgins of the Mississippi"): "Cahokians performed human sacrifice, as part of some kind of… community-wide ceremony, on a… large scale… Simultaneous burials of as many as 53 young women (quite possibly selected for their beauty) have been uncovered beneath Cahokia's mounds."

A summary account of Ho-Chunk myths, legends, and beliefs included in this story follows:

Corn and Tobacco: The origins and importance of these two essential crops to Native American culture cannot be overstated and is beautifully captured in oral tradition ("Ho-Chunk Oral Tradition," *Milwaukee Public Museum*). Described in chapter 2 ("Akecheta"), it nonetheless bears repeating here. "It was no wonder, then, that corn and tobacco were believed to be the direct gifts of Mother Earth: one to sustain the body, the other to fortify and protect the spirit. It was said that from one breast of Mother Earth grew corn; from the other breast grew the tobacco plant."

Ice Giants: The origins and legends related to the Ice Giants depicted in chapter 2 ("Akecheta") are described by David Lee Smith (p. 10). According to oral tradition, these Ice Giants once roamed the land devouring whole villages. To restore balance to his creation, Ma-ona the Creator, also called Earthmaker, sent Rabbit and Turtle, two principal deities, down to Earth to destroy these two-legged giants, leaving only remnants in the far north country to provide a check on human overpopulation.

Eagle Cave Mystery: The legend of the Big Eagle Cave Mystery recounted by the ancient Bear clan storyteller in chapter 8 ("Rivers, Lakes, and Caves") was adapted from "Big Eagle Cave Mystery" (*The Encyclopedia of Hočąk (Winnebago) Mythology*).

Burial Rites: The description of the burial rites performed for the deceased warrior depicted in chapter 26 ("Bear Hunt") represents an amalgam of various story accounts given by Paul Radin (pp. 92–107) for the major Ho-Chunk clans, embellished by my own interpretations.

Bear Clan Origin Myth: The origin myths varied from clan to clan, with even multiple versions existing within the same clan. The origin myth recounted by Shaman Lobo in chapter 39 ("Shaman Lobo") contains the major elements of these myths, which are described in more detail by Paul Radin (p. 177). Water and the raven both play key roles in the creation myths. Water, particularly in the form of "white foam," is considered to be imbued with creative and curative powers. The Ho-Chunk word for raven is *Kaǧi*, which is the same word given for the Menomonie people, considered a brother tribe to the Ho-Chunk ("Bear Clan Origin Myths," *The Encyclopedia of Hočąk (Winnebago) Mythology*).

Wolf Clan Origin Myth: The legend of the four Wolf brothers—Gray Wolf, Green Wolf, Black Wolf, and White Wolf—plays a pivotal role in my story (ref. "Ho-Chunk Oral Tradition," *Milwaukee Public Museum*). As related by Shaman Charlie "Lobo" Graywolf toward the end of chapter 49, the four Wolf brothers were created in the beginning by the Earthmaker. Only one, Gray Wolf, remained in the Earth World, while the other three were sent to be protectors of the Underworld, destined to become the guardian animal spirits of my three traveling Underworld heroes—Akecheta (Black Wolf), Aiyanna (Green Wolf), and Luke (White Wolf).

The Underworld: As described by Paul Radin (p. 268) and David Lee Smith (p. 46 footnote), the Ho-Chunk view the cosmos as being composed of four layered worlds set one on top of the other. From top down they are Heaven, Sky, Earth (man's world), and the Underworld, each presided over by a separate deity. Turtle is generally thought to preside over the Underworld, although as Radin notes, "There seems to be some confusion as to who rules over the last (world), because it is also definitely stated that Traveler (a Water-spirit) is in control of it" (p. 268).

The Underworld is believed by the Ho-Chunk to be a vast water-filled realm that communicates to the Earth World above through caves, lakes, and other natural portals. This world is dominated by the Great Serpent, or Underwater Panther, and its minions which possess magical powers capable of interfering in the affairs of men in the Earth World above in various nefarious ways.

In my story, however, the Underworld, with its native human inhabitants, more closely resembles a lost civilization as might be envisioned by modern-day hollow-earth theorists; or *Agartha*, an ancient legendary kingdom said to be located in the Earth's core. I explain this deviation by inventing a new myth, that of the Ancient Ones rescued from annihilation by the Ice Giants of old by being led by Turtle, at the direction of Earthmaker, to a specially created region of the Underworld designed for human habitation. A place where time stands still, forever protecting these people from the ravages of the Ice Giants. Of course, the underwater panthers with their potent powers remained intact, on the prowl, ever waiting, ever threatening to ambush our modern-day heroes!

Finally, let me say, *Pinagigi!*

Thank you! For reading.

ACKNOWLEDGMENTS

First and foremost, I wish to thank my wife, Janet, whose passion for reading and words of encouragement spurred me on. And for those many visits over the years to her family and childhood home, affording me the opportunity to explore and appreciate the unique cultural experience that is Wisconsin. To my beta readers—Crystal Watanabe of Pikko's House; David R. Bowne, author and Ph.D. Environmental Sciences; my longtime associates and fellow engineers Richard Kral and Barry Juran, PE; and my good friend and South Jersey angler extraordinaire, Fred Klein,—for their candid and constructive feedback at various stages of the book's development. Kudos to Ivan Zanchetta (Bookcoversart.com) for a jaw-dropping cover design, and to Hal Taylor (haltaylorillustration.com) for the Wisconsin state and county map illustrations. And finally, let me thank my hardworking editors, Nikki Busch (nikkibuschediting.com) and Barbie Halaby (monocle-editing.com), without whose critiques and professional assistance the book would simply not have made it to the finish line. They are able to take a suit off the rack and turn it into a tailored Versace! *Ciao e grazie*!

ABOUT THE AUTHOR

Stephen Goldhahn, a process engineer by profession, received his master's degree in chemical engineering from the University of Maryland and spent the major portion of his professional career working and consulting for the food and biopharmaceutical manufacturing industries. Over the years he has enjoyed mixing it up with his creative side as a part-time musician, singer/songwriter, poet, and history buff. In the eighties he helped to establish an original rock band and, together with his brother, Ron, formed an independent record label to record and promote their music. His appetite for creative writing evolved from his songwriting experience. His debut novel, *Greenwich: The Final Project*, a historical sci-fi time-travel mystery, was well received and established him as a respected author. Now retired from the consulting business, Stephen plans to devote more time to writing and traveling with Janet, his wife of thirty-plus years. Together they call South Jersey their home and are the proud parents of two grown sons, Kevin and Michael.

Visit and follow Stephen Goldhahn on Facebook, Medium, Twitter, and Instagram, and at his author website: www.stephengoldhahn.com.

BIBLIOGRAPHY

Ancient Origins: Reconstructing the Origins of Humanity's Past. "The Legends and Archaeology of Devil's Lake: A Place of Ancient Power in Wisconsin." Posted by Jason and Sarah, May 10, 2019. https://www.ancient-origins.net/ancient-places-americas/devils-lake-0011896

Buchen, Gustave W. *Historic Sheboygan County*. Sheboygan County Historical Society and Sheboygan County Historical Research Center, 3rd printing, 2015.

Casselman, Anne. "Strange but True: The Largest Organism on Earth Is a Fungus." *Scientific American Online*, October 4, 2007. https://www.scientificamerican.com/article/strange-but-true-largest-organism-is-fungus/

Dovey, Dana. "GMO Corn Is Safe and Even Has Health Benefits, Analysis of 6,000 Studies Concludes." *Newsweek Online*, February 22, 2018. https://www.newsweek.com/gmo-ge-corn-farming-agriculture-816261

Encyclopedia Britannica Online. s.v. "Ho-Chunk People." Edited by Amy Tikkanen, accessed November 11, 2020. https://www.britannica.com/topic/Ho-Chunk

The Encyclopedia of Hočąk (Winnebago) Mythology. s.v. "Big Eagle Cave Mystery." Compiled by Richard L. Dieterle (copyright 2005). Accessed July 20, 2020. https://hotcakencyclopedia.com/ho.BigEagleCaveMystery.html

The Encyclopedia of Hočąk (Winnebago) Mythology. s.v. "Bear Clan Origin Myths." Compiled by Richard L. Dieterle (copyright 2005). Accessed July 20, 2020. https://hotcakencyclopedia.com/ho.BearClanOriginMyth.html

Extreme Science. "The Largest Living Organism: Fungus *Armillaria ostoyae*." Accessed November 6, 2020. http://www.extremescience.com/biggest-living-thing.htm

Loew, Patty. *The Native People of Wisconsin*. Madison, Wisconsin: Wisconsin Historical Society Press, 2015.

Milwaukee Public Museum Online. "Oral Tradition." Accessed June 6, 2022. https://www.mpm.edu/educators/wirp/great-lakes-traditional-culture/oral-tradition

Native Languages of the Americas (blog). "Ho-Chunk Indian Fact Sheet." Sponsored by Laura Redish and Orrin Lewis. Created in 1998, last updated in 2020, accessed November 9, 2020. http://www.bigorrin.org/hochunk_kids.htm

O'Hehir, Andrew. "The Sacrificial Virgins of the Mississippi." *Salon Online*, August 6, 2009. https://www.salon.com/2009/08/06/cahokia/

Pauketat, Timothy R. *Cahokia: Ancient America's Great City on the Mississippi*. New York: Penguin Books, 2010.

PowWows.com (blog). "25 Favorite Native American Recipes." Posted by Paul G., April 21, 2020. Accessed November 11, 2020. https://www.powwows.com/25-favorite-native-american-recipes/

Radin, Paul. *The Winnebago Tribe*. Lincoln and London: University of Nebraska Press, 1990.

Sheboygan County Wisconsin. "A History of Sheboygan County." Accessed November 7, 2020. https://www.sheboygancounty.com/government/about-the-county/history

BIBLIOGRAPHY

Smith, David Lee. *Folklore of the Winnebago Tribe*. Norman and London: University of Oklahoma Press, 1997.

Top 100 Baby Names Search. "Sioux Girl Names." http://www.top-100-baby-names-search.com/sioux-girl-names.html

Top 100 Baby Names Search. "Sioux Boy Names." http://www.top-100-baby-names-search.com/sioux-boy-names.html

Tribalpedia Native American Indians. s.v. "Winnebago Tribe." Accessed February 11, 2019. https://www.tribalpedia.com/us-tribes/s-z/winnebago-tribe/

US National Park Service Online. "Bison Bellows: Indigenous Hunting Practices." Updated November 6, 2017. https://www.nps.gov/articles/bison-bellows-3-31-16.htm

Wikipedia. s.v. "Genetically Modified Maize." Modified January 25, 2008.

Wikipedia. s.v. "Ho-Chunk." Accessed May 23, 2016. https://en.wikipedia.org/wiki/Ho-Chunk/

Wikipedia. s.v. "Ho-Chunk Mythology." Accessed May 23, 2016. https://en.wikipedia.org/wiki/Ho-Chunk_mythology/

Wikipedia. s.v. "Jean Nicolet." Edited October 19, 2020. https://en.wikipedia.org/wiki/Jean_Nicolet

Wisconsin Historical Society. "Black River Falls, Wisconsin—A Brief History." WHS Library-Archives Staff, 2009. https://www.wisconsinhistory.org/Records/Article/CS2460

Wisconsin's Wild Mushroom Guide for Beginners. Accessed November 11, 2020. https://sites.google.com/site/wisconsinswildmushrooms/Home/

ALSO BY STEPHEN GOLDHAHN

Greenwich: The Final Project

A Haddonfield, NJ biotech engineer sets out to investigate a mysterious mental illness that has beset the region since colonial times. It becomes a race with time to lift "the curse" that has rendered present day Greenwich, NJ a virtual ghost town.

"A great read! I loved this book for its unique combination of pre-American revolution history, biotechnology and time travel... The way the author handled time travel to the past made me almost believe it would be possible." — *Arlene J, 5-star Amazon review*

"*Greenwich*... is hands down one of the most riveting and well-crafted books I've read in quite a while...absolutely amazing for a debut novel!"— (5 stars) *Danielle Hudson, Senior Reviewer—Indie Book Reviewers*

"This book . . . has a unique way of combining well researched historical content, along with a serious and scientific plot line about genetics. The author displayed an intimate knowledge of South Jersey, both geographically and historically." — *Donald Piccoli, 5-star Amazon review*

"I truly was impressed with the quality of literary prose and overall professionalism, from the cover art, to the editing and the formatting." — (5 stars) *Candice Waller Senior Reviewer – Indie Book Reviewers*

"*Greenwich*... is a brilliantly and powerfully-written tale of epic proportions, both in scope and breadth of topics and even crosses genre lines in a way I've never seen... Highly recommend." — (5 stars) *Cara Patterson—Indie Book Reviewers*

". . . I was unable to put it down for very long and finished reading it in three days. I like historical novels as well as mysteries and science fiction. This book has a combination of all three." *Julie Fournier, 4-star Amazon review*

"Great novel. Lyrical and flowing narration, intense drama... Clean editing and an ending that brings it all back around full circle. Recommend read for Literary Historical Fiction and scifi/time-travel."— (4 stars) *Tony Alcott—Indie Book Reviewers*